THE AFTERLIVES

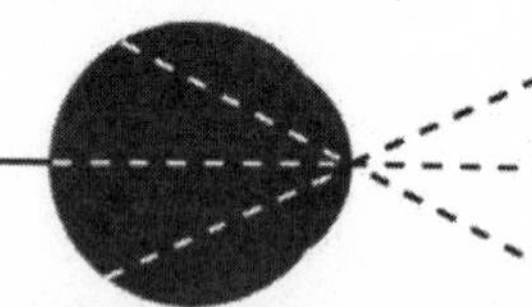

This Large Print Book carries the Seal of Approval of N.A.V.H.

THE AFTERLIVES

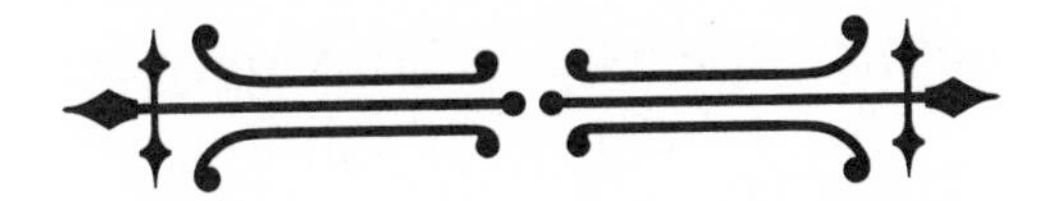

THOMAS PIERCE

CENTER POINT LARGE PRINT
THORNDIKE, MAINE

This Center Point Large Print edition
is published in the year 2018 by arrangement with
Riverhead Books, an imprint of Penguin Publishing Group,
a division of Penguin Random House LLC.

The text of this Large Print edition is unabridged.
In other aspects, this book may vary
from the original edition.
Printed in the United States of America
on permanent paper.
Set in 16-point Times New Roman type.

ISBN: 978-1-68324-809-5

Library of Congress Cataloging-in-Publication Data

Names: Pierce, Thomas, 1982- author
Title: The afterlives / Thomas Pierce.
Description: Center Point Large Print edition. | Thorndike, Maine :
Center Point Large Print, 2018.
Identifiers: LCCN 2018009468 | ISBN 9781683248095
(hardcover : alk. paper)
Subjects: LCSH: Spouses—Fiction. | Future life—Fiction. |
Time travel—Fiction. | Large type books. | BISAC: FICTION /
Family Life. | FICTION / Literary. | FICTION / Ghost. |
GSAFD: Ghost stories. | Love stories.
Classification: LCC PS3616.I3595 A38 2018b | DDC 813/.6—dc23
LC record available at https://lccn.loc.gov/2018009468

For my friend
Charles Thomas

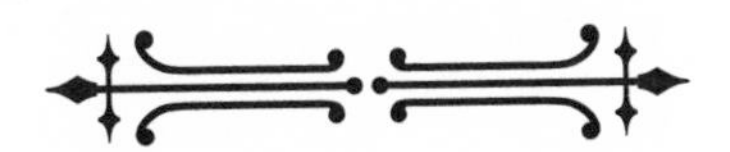

THE AFTERLIVES

The dog is on fire! She rips the cloth off the dining room table and chases him into the kitchen, but the dog slams into the cabinet, rattling all the china, and collapses on the floor at her feet, all his fur burned away. Her poor dog! How on earth did this happen? Her little dog is dead, and all she can do is scream for help.

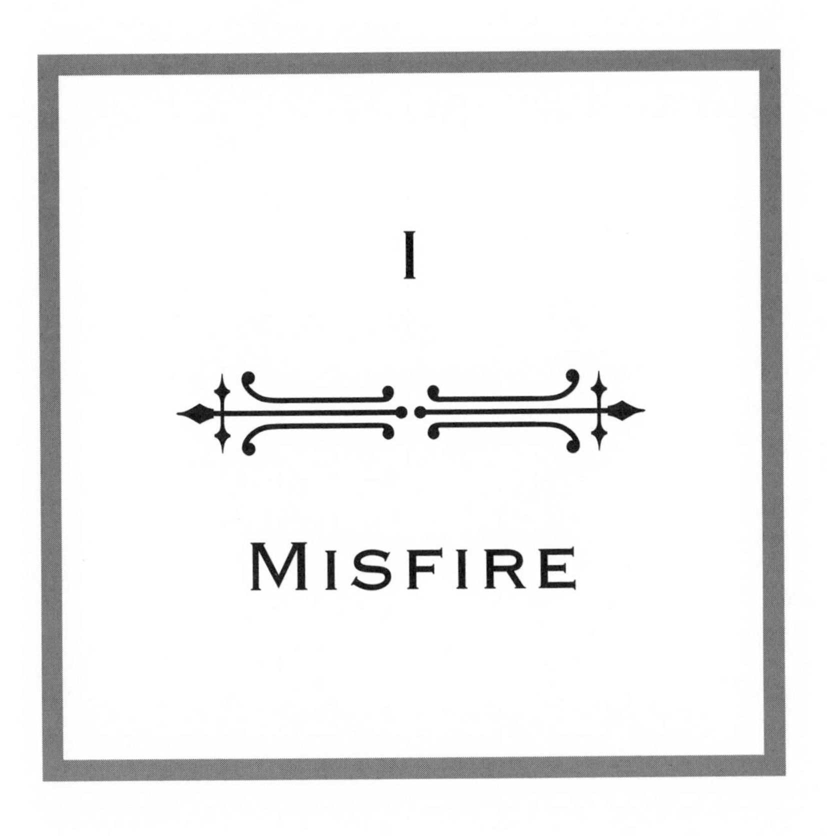

I

MISFIRE

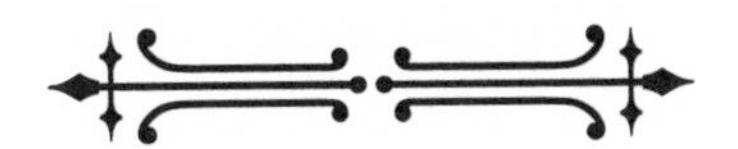

Exit heartbeat.
Exit breath.
Exit every mood, every memory.
Exit you.
To where?

First, their voices—the nurse's, the doctor's, my parents'.

"He looks so puffy," I could hear my mother saying. "Is it normal he looks so puffy?"

I was a rabbit pulled from the black hole of a magician's top hat. The doctor pointed to the television on the opposite wall and asked me if I knew what it was for. I thought he was joking. Next he asked me for my full name. This question frightened me more than it probably should have. I was Jim Byrd, wasn't I? Didn't he know I was Jim Byrd?

My chest was incredibly sore and bruised. Days would pass before I'd recall my collapse in the parking garage down the street from my office. A gash in my forehead had already been sutured. One of the nurses, a young girl with henna tattoos all over her hands and wrists, explained that the gentleman who'd discovered me at the base of the stairs leading up to P2 had administered CPR until the paramedics arrived with their defibrillators.

"If not for him," she said, "you'd probably still be dead."

"Dead?"

The nurse blushed. To have mentioned the fact of my death, I gathered, had been a slipup. She backtracked: Not an actual death, more like a figurative one, or, rather, a technical one. An almost-death.

Sudden cardiac arrest was the diagnosis. I had a long history of passing out, though until now I'd always understood these episodes to be a symptom of a simple fainting disorder. Childhood doctors had advised me to eat more to keep up my blood pressure. But new tests revealed my true condition, which amounted to a vast electrical problem in my body.

A misfire, my cardiologist called it.

"But was I really dead?"

"Clinically."

Dying, he clarified, was a process, not a single event. It was like a wave pulling back from the shore, the sand shifting color, dark to light, as the water leached out of it. Even where the sand appeared dry, sometimes you could dig down a few inches and find more water. You died, and then you died a little more, and then just a little bit more until you were all the way completely dead—or not, depending.

"For how long was I?" I asked.

"Well, that's difficult to say. Given that you seem to have suffered no brain damage, I'm guessing not more than five minutes. You're very lucky."

"I saw nothing," I said.

"I'm sorry?"

"While I was dead. I saw nothing. No lights, no tunnels, no angels. I was just gone. I don't remember anything."

The doctor arched his eyebrows but was silent.

"What does that indicate to you?" I asked.

"I wouldn't read too much into it."

"Read too much into it?"

"I wouldn't give it too much thought, is what I mean. Look on the bright side. You're back. You're only thirty-three. Still a young man. You have more life ahead of you, Mr. Byrd."

To help guarantee this, he recommended that I have a device installed in my chest that would regulate this electrical problem, and soon thereafter I became one of the earliest recipients of a HeartNet, a very advanced implantable defibrillator that looks a little bit like a small onion bag only with tighter mesh. The bag wraps tightly around the heart, squeezing it, fusing with it. Located at its top is a little shrunken head—a node, its brain. I'm told it's practically an artificial intelligence, that's how smart this technology is. If never powered down, HeartNet will keep my heart beating for as long as its battery allows. About two hundred years, apparently. Due to the longevity of its batteries, the device has actually created confusion in some cases. I understand that there've been instances where HeartNet has failed to recognize that a body has already given up on itself and so continued pumping blood, undeterred. Hospitals have been forced to store bodies in their morgues with still-beating hearts.

My HeartNet is in constant communication with its manufacturer in Sheldrick, California, and I have the ability to monitor the diagnostics it provides in real time on my phone. A few taps on the screen, and an image of my own heart appears there, pumping and quaking. Blood flow through the four chambers is mapped as a staticky blue and red, outtake and intake. Beats per minute, electrocardiographic charts, echocardiographs, blood pool scans. It's all there at my fingertips. If you select a certain option, the device will even alert you every time it saves your life—which is to say, every time your heart fails to beat properly of its own accord.

I experienced this for the first time about two weeks after the procedure. I wasn't running or lifting weights or having sex. I wasn't involved in any sort of strenuous activity whatsoever. I was simply sitting on the couch watching television. Receiving the alert—three delicate chimes, like a call to meditation in a Buddhist temple—I immediately shut off the TV and dressed.

I was wasting my life!

I desperately needed to be out of the house—but where to go? I wasn't sure. This was a Friday night, about nine o'clock, and I had nowhere to be. I walked up and down the road a few times, then came back home and read three pages of a book on the later Roman emperors before sitting down on the couch for more television.

For weeks after that I worried that I wasn't making the time count. I'd been given a second chance, and I needed to take advantage. One morning I got in my car and just started driving. West, naturally. Maybe I'd go all the way to the Pacific, I wasn't sure. I didn't have a plan. Crossing the North Carolina border and entering Tennessee, I felt alive, but by the time I reached Kentucky, the monotony of the drive had settled in, and I'd lost interest. I spent one night in a nice hotel in Louisville, toured the famous bat factory there, drank some whiskey, and then drove back east.

Not long after that I bought a plane ticket and flew to Ireland. I drank beers alone in a pub in Cork and listened to some decent music. Then I flew to Munich to see an old friend who'd settled there after graduate school, and one night I went home with one of his coworkers, a German girl who spoke very little English. Seeing my scar, she ran her fingers along it gently, a look of concern and pity on her face, and insisted, via hand signals and broken English, that she be on top lest I overexert myself. I tried to explain that the problem wasn't the plumbing but the electrical, but this only further confused matters. She showed me her toilet and held up her fingers: One or two?

A few days later I returned home—to Shula, North Carolina.

The White Hairs, we called them, the old geezers who'd flooded into Shula over the last twenty years and seized control of our local government and civic groups and boards. You sometimes got the feeling there'd been a convention—a gathering of all the nation's old people—and together they'd voted Shula as their new home. You couldn't really fault them for it. Shula was beautiful after all, quaint but busy, the Blue Ridge Mountains visible in most directions.

The White Hairs, really, had become the backbone of our town's economy. Businesses thrived downtown—the antique stores and folk-art galleries and sandwich shops. Most restaurants were successful as long as they offered early seating. Large gated communities had sprung up to accommodate them—clusters of condominiums and townhouses with shared shuffleboard courts and swimming pools. To address their many medical needs and conditions, we'd added a second hospital, not to mention the various rehab centers and private practices.

I'd had a front-row seat to many of these changes in my capacity as a commercial loan officer. My uncle, a soft-looking man with a hint of a British accent acquired after only two years of graduate school in London, was an executive with a national bank, and it was with his assistance that I'd finagled my way after college into a leadership development program designed to train promising new employees for careers in credit analysis and commercial lending.

I'd been grateful for his help but also surprised by it. My uncle and my father had never been particularly close. I can recall only two childhood visits to my uncle's home in Connecticut, a mansion with a horizon pool and a wine cellar. "All hat, no cattle" was how my father used to describe his brother, and I will admit that my uncle did put a premium on appearances. If he was bound soon for a vacation on a fancy coast, for instance, you better believe he'd find a way to worm that tidbit into the conversation. Still, when he'd offered me his help, I'd accepted it gratefully. What did I care if he was only intervening as a way of lording his good fortune and connections over my father? A leg up was a leg up. After completing the program I'd taken a job at a branch in my hometown.

Shula was not a particularly old city, though we celebrated its heritage and culture regularly with parades and photographic displays at the public library. A lake at the edge of town—now not much more than a neighborhood runoff pond at the center of a weedy meadow—had once been a popular tourist destination. There'd been dances in the pavilion there—parties, vacations. There'd been a small amusement park with roller coasters and merry-go-rounds in the adjacent field. People had been happy there once. You saw these people in photographs in their full-body bathing suits, their swim caps. Women with coiffured dogs in their laps; men with slick hair on water skis.

Their bright, untroubled faces, their voices rising up like so many clanging, noiseless bells—what had their lives been like? They were gone now, all of them, disappeared into the blue haze that surrounded the town.

Some mornings the fog was so thick and impenetrable you'd forget the rest of the world was out there. Other cities, other countries, other lives. The mountains—blue, soft, ethereal—were more like suggestions of geological features than actual ones. Always they lingered in the distance. You could never seem to reach them. They had no edge, no sure boundary or beginning. Science confirmed their ancientness. The landscape was wild but intensely familiar. We were living in the ruins of mega-continents, on rolling hills ground down by millions of years of erosion.

Crust. Thrusting sheets. Bedrock. I found it somewhat comforting to think of my limited time here on the ground in the context of that larger, deeper history.

It was on one such foggy morning—about six months after my trip to Germany—that I was in my office at the bank and made a discovery that, arguably, changed the course of my life. I was reviewing the loan application for a Tex-Mex restaurant called Su Casa Siempre. The loan was a relatively modest one. The restaurant wanted to expand its dining area to the second floor of the house it occupied. On my desk I had a spreadsheet of its operating expenses, and I was whizzing through row after row of expenditures—Air-Conditioning Repairs, Catering Supplies, etc.—when I came to one marked Extermination and noticed an unusual figure:

JANUARY	$79
FEBRUARY	$79
MARCH	$79
APRIL	$2079

Two thousand dollars in extermination costs? This April spike seemed to me an excessive figure—I was intrigued. Very likely it was a typo, but already I was imagining cockroaches dancing across the plates, breeding in the oven, spewing from the outlets. A harried line cook leaped into view swinging his spatula at rats the size of raccoons.

I called the restaurant owner, and when she didn't answer the phone, I had to leave a message: "Please call me at your earliest convenience," I said.

Out in the lobby I could hear the tellers laughing and chatting. The *fortune* tellers, they called themselves, because one of them had once brought a pack of tarot cards in to work and taped a card to each of their counters.

Fool, Magician, Death.

Jokes such as these in workplaces such as ours were not easily given up. We recycled them endlessly: to pass the time, to kill awkward silences, to feel like part of a team. Two of the Fortune Tellers were ladies in their late fifties—Susan and Diana were their names—both with short, fashionable dyed hair; tan, deep cleavage; and photos of their grandbabies on proud display, tacked to the cubicle partitions that separated them. The third teller was named Darryl, and he was roughly my age, a stoner with a silver stud in his ear who refused to tuck in his shirts despite company policy and who was never not swigging a five-hour energy drink.

Our lobby was like most bank lobbies: a room with red carpets, off-white walls, and deposit slip kiosks. I had only to take two or three steps outside my office door to participate in conversations with the tellers, which I rarely ever did. I got the feeling that they preferred to be left alone. They didn't like any interference from outsiders, the outsiders in this case being anyone on the other side of their counter. They were cliquey, is what it was.

I would often lean back in my chair and listen to their chatter. On that particular morning, Diana was telling the other two about a medical procedure—elective—that she was seriously considering. Apparently she had never much cared for the color of her eyes, which she described as "mud brown," and she was thinking she might try something called an eye-dye. For five thousand dollars, a doctor would inject her eyeballs with a specially designed virus—a *boutique* virus, whatever that was—which would alter her at the level of her DNA and, over a period of a few days, transform her muddy brown eyes into a watery blue.

Darryl was very excited about this idea. He said he had a cousin who'd done it, and did Diana want to talk to her about it? Diana said she absolutely did want to talk to Darryl's cousin about it. That reminded Darryl of something else he'd seen recently, a new brand of condom that turned green if it detected the presence of a sexually transmitted disease.

"Say what?" asked Susan, who was always happy to play the role of the fuddy-duddy. She didn't quite understand. How would this condom work exactly? You'd slip it on and it would do—what? Turn green if the other person had AIDS or herpes or whatever else?

Yes, Darryl confirmed, precisely, except this magical contraceptive would also reveal if *you* had those diseases. It tested both partners, simultaneously, through contact with any of the various secretions.

"Wait wait wait, hold up," Susan said. "Let's think about this for a minute. In order to secrete any fluids, there must first be penetration. There must first be the entry of the one organ into the other. The sexual act would need to commence, would it not, before the condom could tell you if one or both partners were diseased? Wouldn't the penis need to ejaculate at least a modicum of fluid first?"

This question went unanswered because Susan, the fuddy-duddy, had uttered the words "penetration," "penis," and "ejaculate" in rapid order, and now they were all giggling at the strange turn in their morning talk show. That's how their conversations seemed to me, like empty talk show banter. Sitting at my desk, I couldn't see them, and I often imagined them addressing a camera as they sat in tall chairs around a coffee table.

When I stepped out into the lobby half an hour later I found Darryl standing bowlegged with his hands shaped like pistols at his waist. A dueler's stance. He was staring hard at a kitten calendar on the far wall and seemed ready to draw and blast a hole through a feline head. Diana, hand over her mouth, was stifling a laugh, and Susan was thudding her palms together violently, fingers stiff and arched away from each other, her bracelets jangling on her tan wrists. Darryl drew his hand-pistol and fired at the wall.

"That's when the other guy dropped dead," he said. "Just crumpled down on the ground. It looked incredibly real."

"What's this?" I asked.

"Darryl went to Tombstone last week," Susan said. "While he was in Arizona visiting his sister."

"Oh," I said, "so you saw one of those gunfight reenactments at the O.K. Corral? That it?"

"Yes, sort of. But these weren't actors. They were holograms of the actual historical figures. Wyatt Earp, Doc Holliday, and all the others. I'm not sure how they accomplished it," Darryl said. "They might have cut Earp's face from a photograph and grafted it onto an actor's body. Looked amazing, not like those lame holograms you usually see. I have a picture of my sister trying to hug him. He looked real as you and me, I swear. All the little hairs on his mustache twitched in the breeze."

"Amazing," Susan said. "Just think if they'd had that sort of technology back when we were in school? Maybe I would have paid more attention in history class. Imagine sitting in class and watching Anne Boleyn getting her head chopped off at the front of the room."

Diana laughed. "Kids watching beheadings in public school. You're too much, Susan, honestly."

"Well, it would be historically accurate, and anyway, that was just the first scene that popped into my head." Susan was clearly embarrassed. "They'd watch other stuff, too."

"Like the Spanish Inquisition," Darryl said. "Confessors on the rack?"

"All the men moaning and dying on the field at Gettysburg?" I said.

"Viking raids," Diana said. "Rapes and murdered babies."

"Oh, stop it," Susan said, smiling a little. "Now you're just making fun."

Eye-dyes, holographic cowboys—in the months after my surgery, the world was making less and less sense to me, generally. Why did the dentist want to drill holes in my molars and fill the holes with a glass composite? What was the point of a labradoodle? Sometimes I got the feeling I'd been brought back to life on the wrong planet.

My phone rang, and I ducked back into my office to answer it. On the line was Ruth Glazer, the restaurant owner, returning my call. After a few quick pleasantries, I asked her if anything unusual had occurred in March or April of last year.

"Uh, unusual?" she asked. "Shoot straight with me, Jim. Is there a problem with my application?"

"Not a problem, I don't think. Just humor me."

The owner was quiet for a few seconds. "I'm humoring."

"The extermination expenses?"

"Hold on," Ruth Glazer said, papers ruffling. "All right, so, yeah, I'm looking at it. We spent just over two grand last April. That what's bothering you?"

"I wouldn't say it's bothering me," I said, though it was starting to now, a little.

"Listen, all restaurants have to deal with this stuff. Comes with the territory. I'm sorry, but isn't this sort of an odd concern?"

I didn't care for her tone. I was her loan officer. A representative of the bank. I could ask whatever questions I pleased as long as my questions pertained to the application, to the investment we would be making in the proposed venture, which in this case was a renovation to the restaurant's second floor, an addition that according to the architect's plans would accommodate twenty-four more dinner guests per seating.

"Hey," the owner said. "You still there?"

"I'm still here."

"So?"

"Two grand just seems like such a large amount for an extermination."

"It's not so much," she said.

"Not in the grand scheme, maybe," I said, not really knowing what I meant by it. The grand scheme of what? I thanked her for her time—and for choosing our bank—and then hung up the phone.

Su Casa Siempre was located in a pretty two-story house in a slightly grungy neighborhood on the periphery of Shula's so-called historic district. The town's character could vary from street to street, and here, on this block, you might have thought our town was in the middle of a mountain hipster renaissance. Fixed-gear bikes. A hot-yoga studio. A climbing gym. Not one but two microbreweries. A pizza place in an old gas station with intact but defunct pumps. It was the epicenter of the resistance to the White Hairs. That's not to say that the White Hairs didn't visit this part of town—because they did. They found it charming, like everything else. They recognized no territories, as such.

I'd never actually eaten at Su Casa Siempre, but I'd passed by it a hundred times and more. When I arrived, people were sitting at tables on the veranda that wrapped around the front of the house. Around back was a patio with dormant heat lamps and lights strung up along a fence that separated the patio from a gravel alley with a large green Dumpster.

The main dining room was packed when I ventured inside, every table filled with dinner guests. The hostess told me I'd have a thirty-minute wait unless I wanted to eat at the bar. She led me through the restaurant, and I sat down on a high metal stool. The bartender quickly delivered a menu and asked if I wanted something to drink. I pointed to the black erase board propped on the liquor shelf. *Fangaritas*, it said.

"One of those, please."

A few minutes later my drink arrived: a slushy red margarita in an embarrassingly large glass. I was sipping on it when I realized that I knew the woman sitting at the end of the bar. She was wearing a cottony purple dress with thin straps over her freckled shoulders. Her hair, straight and dark, swished softly across her face as she made fierce notes on the top sheet in a stack of papers. To the left of her papers was a frosty glass of white wine. Her name was Annie, and we'd dated briefly in high school, though we hadn't been in touch since those days. I watched her work for a few minutes before summoning enough courage to go over and tap her on the shoulder.

"No way!" she said, springing off her stood.

We hugged. She smelled exactly the way I remembered. Like spearmint.

Annie was the first girl who'd ever shown me much interest. I'd known her, tangentially at least, since kindergarten, but it was only in ninth-grade biology class that I began to notice certain things about her—the faint constellation of freckles around her eyes visible beneath her makeup, the thin perfect gap between her two front teeth, the spearmint-scented cloud that followed her wherever she went.

Always spearmint. The outer pocket of her backpack seemed to contain an endless supply of the green packaged gum. She unwrapped the foil from each stick with such precision, peeling back the paper and flattening the foil on her desk under her fingernail before bringing the stick to her parted lips. Once the gum was in her mouth, I was pleased to observe, she wouldn't allow herself the pleasure of chewing it until she had folded the foil into a tight silver accordion and placed that accordion in the back pocket of her biology notebook. This was a performance enacted sometimes three and four times in a single class. It was curiously erotic, despite the formaldehyde smell that hung in the room. How had this amazing girl escaped my attention for so long?

Annie was at the restaurant alone, finishing up a little work before going home for the evening, but she invited me to join her at the bar for a few minutes. I explained the nature of my visit, that this was in fact a covert investigation on behalf of my employer. Sort of. She thought that was funny.

She gave me a quick rundown of the last fourteen years in her life: a theater major at the College of Charleston, two not-so-great years selling medical equipment over the phone, five slightly better years working as a paralegal for an immigration law firm and then later as an assistant arts manager at a live theater in Charleston. She had a twelve-year-old daughter named Fisher, who Annie said was "one of the coolest girls on the planet." They'd just moved back to Shula in order to be nearer to her parents, and Annie had taken a job as an outreach coordinator and sometime director for Shula's live theater.

Through the grapevine I'd heard something about her having had a kid and also something about a marriage. Something about a dead husband, too. A drowning, maybe. Something tragic. A topic to avoid, surely.

I asked her if it was strange to be back in Shula again.

"A little. I missed the mountains. The little mirrors at the intersections on the curvy roads. The cool mornings. But everything's changed. There's a CVS where my favorite meat-and-three used to be. And have they renamed the streets? Or made new ones? I keep getting lost. I make a wrong turn and end up behind strip malls that didn't used to be there. I always seem to wind up at the backs of things, not the fronts. My parents think it's funny. It's not like Shula's a big town, you know? The GPS in my brain is screwy, I guess. So you never left, huh?"

"Just for college. Chapel Hill."

"Right, I knew that."

We were both quiet for a moment.

"Hey, I have an idea," she said. "Let's not pretend like we don't know anything about each other. Let's be honest and just admit that we've looked each other up, occasionally, over the years. What's the Internet for, if not prying into the lives of people we used to feel up."

"Okay, agreed."

"Good. So. My husband died."

"Yes, I was really sorry to hear about that. How long ago was it?"

"Seven years. Not quite eight." She grimaced. "And I was sorry to hear about your heart attack. How are you feeling, by the way?"

Not a heart attack, I corrected, but cardiac arrest. An important distinction. Heart attacks were what killed old fat men who'd been eating cheeseburgers and fried chicken all their lives. Cardiac arrest could kill anybody at any time—even strong, able-bodied men such as myself.

I got out my phone and tapped on the screen. My heart blossomed into digital view. I'm not sure why, but I found it soothing to be able to look at it whenever I pleased. Sometimes, when I had trouble falling asleep at night, I'd turn up the volume and listen to my heart beating. Bringing home a puppy for the first time, they say it's best to stick a ticking clock in the box because supposedly the sound reminds the dog of its mother's heart and brings it comfort. I was kind of like that puppy. As long as I could hear my heart, I was still alive. I was still here. This—the possibility that, at any moment, I would cease to be here—was what made it so difficult to fall asleep, I think.

I raised the volume so that Annie could hear my heartbeat over the noise of the restaurant. She seemed confused until I positioned the screen directly over my chest, creating a little window through my skin and rib cage.

"State of the art," she said. "Looks healthy to me."

"Yes, I'm all good now, though it was a nail-biter for about four or five minutes. Technically I was dead there for a bit."

She squeezed my arm and let go again. "That's so weird because . . ." She looked embarrassed. "Well, I've been checking out services at this new church in town. The Church of Search. You heard of it? I won't lie, it's a little weird. Nondenominational. Nominally Christian. It's based in LA, but they have satellite campuses all over. This one meets in the old Masonic Temple here in town. A friend of a friend recommended I try it. Each week you listen to a different featured speaker—astronauts and Walt Whitman scholars and theologians. Sort of like TED Talks but with a Jesus bent. Anyway, a couple of weeks ago, the speaker was a lady who died and then came back again. She called herself Miss Lazarus. She told us she met God and He's like a giant sun except instead of heat he radiates love. Nice, huh?"

"Very. I like that."

"So, did you visit a giant God-sun? Any good news for me from the other side? Did your dead grandparents come to collect you at the arrivals gate?"

"God, I wish. Unfortunately I am unable to confirm the existence of a heaven. I saw nothing at all."

"Nothing?"

I shook my head.

"Well, that's alarming."

"Isn't it?" I took a sip of my drink. "And thank you for saying so. Most people brush it off when I tell them. They tell me not to worry. My dad thinks it was good for me. A wake-up call. He's been an atheist since the sixth grade, when he read a book about the heat-death of the universe. As for my mother, I tell her about what happened and she starts throwing scripture at me. She says we all fall into some sort of deep sleep when we die, a thoughtless coma, and we only wake up again when Jesus returns to judge the living—"

"And the dead, sure." Annie nodded. "But does she actually believe that?"

"If my mother's pastor told her the only way into heaven was a strict diet of frog legs, she'd eat nothing but frog legs for the rest of her life."

Annie arched her eyebrow. "What about you?"

"Would I eat the frog legs?"

"Before your heart problem, what did you think would happen when you die?"

Growing up, I explained, I'd always been told (primarily by my mother) that one of two fates awaited us all: heaven or hell. Glitz or doom. Heaven was a sparkling, glistening place, populated with voluptuous, gender-neutral angels and boisterous choirs singing songs so sweet your ears wept tears of joy. As for hell, it was much as you'd expect: eternal torture at the hands of the devil. As an adult, my conception of each place had evolved significantly, of course. Maybe heaven was achieving unity with God. Maybe hell was being cut off from the rest of Mother Universe; it was eternal isolation and darkness. But to have gone through at least the first few stages of death and to have returned without any glimpse of what lies beyond had been, to put it mildly, belief-shattering.

"Well, maybe you just weren't dead long enough," Annie said. "You didn't go deep enough."

"Possibly. Yes. I don't know."

She took a sip of her white wine. "By the way, from now on, when people ask you about this, I think you should lie. Just tell them it was all unicorns and cotton candy on the other side. Consider it a kindness."

She smiled; a joke.

"I'm pretty sure that's how new religions get started."

"Well, the important thing is that you survived, you're doing better." She cupped her hand over mine on the bar. "I'm glad you're still with us, Jim."

I couldn't decide if she was flirting with me or expressing sympathy—or both. Was it appropriate for me to reciprocate? Her husband had been dead for seven years, which seemed to me like more than enough time for us to flirt, guilt-free. I could feel each of her fingers on mine. Her nails were painted red. Her touch was soft and cool. I felt as if some rare, magical hummingbird had alighted upon me, and even to glance at it might scare it away. I tried to remain calm, still. My heart was beating faster now, and because I'd left the HeartNet app open on my phone, we could both hear it accelerating. I might as well have flashed her an erection; that's how exposed I felt.

I snatched the phone off the bar, embarrassed, and she returned her hand to her lap under the bar. That was when I spotted the restaurant owner, Ruth Glazer, at the far end of the bar with a towel over her shoulder. She was a slim, red-haired woman. She grabbed a television remote from behind a tray of overturned shot glasses and, pointing it at one of the two flat-screens on the wall, changed the channel to a soccer game. I signaled over to her. We'd met once before, at the bank when she'd delivered a stack of documents, and she rushed toward me now with an outstretched hand.

"Jim! You should have told me you were coming. I could have sent over something special."

An impromptu visit, I explained.

"Let me at least show you upstairs while you're here. Show you what our plans are."

I looked at Annie. "Care to have a look upstairs?"

"Sure, why not."

Together we followed Ruth around the corner of the bar and down a narrow, carpeted hallway, at the end of which was a staircase—a tightly winding staircase of dark red wood, very pretty though in obvious need of repair.

"Use the rail, please," Ruth instructed, gripping the bannister like she expected the steps to buckle. We did as we were told. We reached the second floor, where there was a bathroom, two bedrooms, a linen closet, and old shag carpets on the floors. The smell of mouse urine mixed with the cooking smells rising up from the kitchen below us. Distantly we could still hear the chatter and clatter of dinner guests.

One of the bedrooms was full of giant crates and collapsed boxes. Ruth explained that they'd mostly used the space for storage until now. What she wanted to do was rip out most of the walls and open up the space for more tables.

"Very nice," I said, nodding.

"Takes a little imagination, doesn't it?" Annie said. "These sorts of projects?"

"Very much so," Ruth said proudly.

We were moving back to the stairs when I stopped the owner.

"I'm sorry," I said, "but I have to ask. This won't affect your loan, but why the two thousand dollars in extermination fees?"

"That again?" Ruth said, and rubbed the back of her neck.

"Did you have, like, a family of possums living up here? It's just such a strange, large amount."

She sucked in her lower lip and chewed on it in a way that suggested she was perturbed.

"Okay, I'm going to show you something, but I'd appreciate a little discretion once I do. It's not a secret, but it's not exactly something I want advertised either."

She took a few steps down the stairs, and I assumed we were on our way to the kitchen, where she would reveal a hole in the baseboard behind the stove, the entrance to a rat's nest, something terrible and stomach-churning, but she stopped us halfway down and pressed her back flat to the wall.

"Do like me," she said.

And so all of us stood side by side, butts against the wall as if we were making room for a person to pass with a large tray of food. We'd been standing that way for two or three minutes, silently, when I asked her, as pleasantly as possible, what the hell we were doing.

"You'll know it when it happens," she said.

"When what happens?" Annie asked.

"Just wait."

We waited.

"Just wait," she said. "It can take some time."

"How long?" I asked.

"Depends. You can't rush it."

Annie's stomach growled. "Sorry," she said.

We waited for a few more minutes and then Ruth said, "It never happens when you want it to. I have no control here, you have to understand. She's not a magic trick."

"She?" Annie asked.

Ruth nodded and invited us downstairs to her office for another demonstration. She said she had something else she could show us since this didn't seem to be working tonight. "Keep hold of the rail as we go down," she warned.

Her office was a small room off the kitchen. The flimsy white shelves on the wall over her desk were overloaded with papers and files. Under the desk sat a small pea-green safe and a stack of blank employment forms. She shut the door and sat down in a roller chair. We unstacked two dining chairs from behind her door and arranged ourselves near her computer, which she'd just turned on.

"I think I should just play you this without any introduction," she said, turning the computer speakers toward us, fiddling with the knobs.

What we heard when she pressed Play was a whooshing noise, sort of like a vacuum cleaner or television static.

"So what is this exactly?" I asked.

She smiled. "This, my friend, is the proof."

THE TALE OF THE DOG ON FIRE

The story Ruth told us that night in her office began, as such stories so often do, with the purchase of the house itself. A longtime restaurateur, she'd relocated to Shula from Austin in order to be nearer her girlfriend and had noticed that what our town lacked was a decent Tex-Mex option. The house on Graham Street was an obvious choice for its proximity to downtown and to a gravel parking lot across the road, not to mention the fact that with an upgrade to the kitchen and the demolition of a few walls downstairs, Ruth would easily be able to transform the space into a cozy and charming restaurant. It was only after Ruth had signed on the dotted line that the seller, via her real estate agent, warned Ruth about the staircase.

People were always falling on the stairs, the agent said.

Something odd about them.

Little accidents, strange incidents.

The damnedest thing.

Just be careful.

Ruth thought nothing of these warnings. So what if the stairs were a little dangerous? The house was old—uneven, forever settling—and anyway she didn't plan to use the second floor that much, except perhaps as storage.

The trouble began not long after Su Casa

Siempre opened its doors, when Ruth learned that her head chef was having an affair with one of the servers. The chef—a rather intense but talented woman—was married, unhappily, and the server was a real beefcake, not very smart but hardworking and quick-footed, one of the best waiters on staff. These little flings, Ruth explained to us, were not so unusual in the restaurant business, and so she never even considered intervening. As long as people performed their jobs, her policy was to never involve herself in their personal business.

But then one night the chef's husband showed up during a rush, demanding to see his wife. He'd discovered some incriminating texts on his wife's phone and was irate. Ruth tried to convince the poor guy to go home and wait there—not because she wanted to protect her chef, who apparently wasn't a very likable lady anyway, but because she didn't want the couple to make a scene in front of the diners. But the husband refused to leave until he saw his wife, and so Ruth, desperate to resolve this quickly, sent them both upstairs to one of the old bedrooms, asking them to please keep it down.

For about fifteen minutes the couple was up there screaming at each other, but then their voices dropped off suddenly, and all was eerily quiet. Ruth, who'd been hanging near the bottom of the stairs in case the fight escalated, rushed up and peeked into the bedroom. There she discovered the chef and her husband, pants around their ankles, up against the wall, fucking each other with such intensity that they didn't even notice the interruption. Ruth brought the door closed again and went downstairs to wait in her office.

That's where she was when the husband had his accident a few minutes later. Coming down the steps, he somehow tumbled forward and broke his wrist at the bottom. No one saw it happen. He swore that he hadn't just fallen, that someone had pushed him. They looked to the chef, who insisted that she'd still been upstairs, in the bathroom. Ruth wasn't sure who to believe. The chef had a notorious temper, and so it wasn't implausible that she'd given her husband a shove. But then again, only minutes before, the pair had been having sex, which suggested to Ruth that they'd resolved their differences, at least to some degree.

Anyway, someone wound up calling the cops—it was never quite clear who made the call—and, in the confusion, the cops were inclined to arrest the chef for assault and battery. It was a mess. To keep this from happening, Ruth had to make a statement, had to confess that she'd inadvertently witnessed the couple fornicating roughly against the wall. In the end, the police didn't arrest the chef, though she did leave the restaurant early for the night to be with her husband in the emergency room.

Not long after that Ruth fired her chef—for altogether different reasons, believe it or not—and hired a new one. Life continued. Business was good.

A couple of months later, a server was coming down the stairs after stowing away some boxes when she fell, too. She didn't break any bones, thankfully, but, like the chef's husband, she swore that something had pushed her, or at least knocked her. Ruth gave her a week off work and then hired a repairman to examine the staircase, to see if any boards were loose, etc. When the repairman reported that the stairs looked just fine, Ruth had him install an extra handrail along the wall as a safety precaution.

Then something even stranger happened, she said. Something that convinced her she needed to take more drastic action.

Another night, another server. A young guy. He was coming down the stairs, drying his hands with a towel, when he burst into tears. A volcano of wailing and crying. This poor guy couldn't control himself. The other servers dragged him into Ruth's office, out of sight, and had to physically restrain him. Once they managed to calm him down, however, the guy was unable to tell them what had triggered it. It was inexplicable. Ruth sent him home for the night.

A few weeks later a customer, looking for the bathroom, reported seeing a strange dark-haired man standing halfway up the stairs, a panicked look on his face, but when Ruth went to inspect, she saw nothing.

After that she began performing experiments. Sometimes, after closing, she'd sit at the bottom of the stairs and just wait. What she was waiting for, she wasn't entirely sure. She'd watch. She'd chat.

"Chat?" we asked her. "Really?"

Indeed, Ruth said. She'd sit on the stairs and whisper words into the darkness:

Hello?

Is anyone there?

I'm here if you want to talk.

Mostly she felt like a fool. There was nothing there. Of course there wasn't. People had fallen—and so what? A server had burst into tears, but people cried all the time, didn't they?

Then, one night, Ruth felt it.

Like a cool hand across her neck.

A wave of sadness.

A gently undulating wave of sadness.

A sadness that rippled through her.

But not all the way through her.

Really there were no words to describe it.

A strange feeling of life on top of other life.

Overlapping histories. Overlapping stories.

She was crying, she realized then. Whatever it

was, it had reduced her to tears. She hadn't cried in years, and yet—tears! This was serious stuff. She wasn't sure what to do about it. She retreated into her office, slammed the door. But it clung to her, this terrible feeling.

Clearly the stairs were haunted. She was going to have to wall them off entirely. She wasn't the sort of person who believed in ghosts, but whatever was happening, it was real. That same night she made a sign and hung it on the bottom post.

DANGEROUS! DON'T USE
THESE STAIRS UNLESS YOU MUST!

One afternoon—this was maybe a year later—a woman showed up and asked to speak with Ruth. She had a card. Her name was Sally Zinker and she was a professor at UNC. A physicist. She was legitimate, in other words. She'd seen the sign on the stairs and was curious to know why it was there. Ruth was reluctant to tell her. She didn't want word to spread. What if it hurt business? But then the woman—this scientist—smiled and explained she'd heard some stories. Her mother-in-law, who was very old, had known some people who lived in this house once, a long time ago, and so she was familiar with its history. There'd been a fire, the physicist explained. A death. The house had an unusual energy.

What the physicist wanted to do was run some

tests. Ruth had no problem with these tests as long as she was covert about it. Ruth was curious, too, after all. If this woman could explain what was happening with math or physics, great. Ruth wasn't one of those people who needed there to be mystery in the world, she said. Fuck mystery. Shine a light in all the dark places. Kill the dark. That was fine by her.

Sally Zinker showed up on the appointed evening with two giant duffel bags of gear. As instructed, Ruth locked her up inside the restaurant alone for the night, and when Ruth returned the next morning, the physicist looked tired but basically unfazed. She thanked Ruth and left and that was that. Weeks went by and Ruth began to wonder if she'd ever hear from the woman again. Maybe it had been some sort of weird practical joke. Maybe she'd dreamed Sally Zinker.

Eventually a package arrived in the mail, a manila envelope that contained a letter, a CD, and a stack of glossy 8x10 images. The pictures showed what looked like storm systems—swirled blobs of yellow, orange, and red. One image showed a blue splatter. Sally Zinker had circled the splatter with a marker. *Very odd,* she'd written beneath it, though she didn't say what the splatter was or what it might indicate. The attached letter, which was only a single paragraph, thanked Ruth for the opportunity and explained that the most interesting discovery, the most compelling, was the recording she'd burned onto the CD. A twelve-second clip of audio recorded at roughly 1:33 a.m. EST on the stairwell.

It was at this point in her tale that Ruth clicked the file on her computer once more.

"What am I supposed to be hearing?" I asked.

She cranked up the volume and restarted it.

This time a voice burped up from the noise, each syllable barely distinguishable from the noise that surrounded it. It had said something—but what? I was going to have to study it more carefully, listen two or even three more times.

Annie sat up a little straighter. "The dog's on fire? Is that what it said?"

With a blank, far-off expression, Ruth nodded.

She played it for us again.

"Now that time I heard something different," Annie said. "I heard *doll got flyer.* Or, *dole got higher.*"

"No, she's definitely saying the dog's on fire," Ruth said. "I won't even tell you how many times I've listened to this."

"So what happened to her dog?" I asked.

The owner shrugged. The three of us sat there quietly for a moment. At our feet, I imagined it: a flaming dog, tail wagging like nothing was wrong.

"Okay," I said, "but what about the two grand? What's this got to do with that?"

"Oh, well, for years I just kept people off the stairs altogether. I made sure I was the only one who went up there. No one else was allowed. I didn't want any lawsuits. But then I read a story in a magazine about a guy who claimed he could get rid of ghosts. This was more recently, just a couple of years ago. I hired him. He set up a cot at the foot of the stairs, and he slept there for a couple of hours on a Monday afternoon, while we were closed. Supposedly he had an ability to talk with ghosts in his dreams. But it didn't work for us. He wasn't able to extinguish the dog, as it were. I'd already paid him."

Annie asked to hear the clip again. Ruth clicked it, and it played through, all twelve seconds, but this time I didn't hear the voice.

"Dog supplier," Annie said. "She's saying *dog supplier*. Like a pet store is a dog supplier. It's probably just some radio commercial that the recorder picked up."

"No, it's real," Ruth said.

I tapped the computer screen with my index finger. I asked her if she could please send me a copy. If she could email me the file?

Annie gave me a sly look.

Ruth started a new email and dragged the sound file into it. "So there you have it, Mr. Byrd. The full story. I know it's kind of crazy, but I trust this won't keep you from approving the loan?"

I nodded and said of course this wouldn't stop me from approving the loan. I'd only been curious, after all, not suspicious. My phone vibrated in my pocket. It was only later, as Annie and I shared an enchilada platter and nachos, that I checked my mail to ensure I'd actually received the file. I placed my phone flat on the table so that Annie could see what I was doing and would know I wasn't just checking my mail in the middle of dinner. The file was there in my inbox as an attachment.

TheProof.mp3.

The scar on my chest is small and pink, across my upper left breast. Like the opening of a shirt pocket.

I used to sometimes take a marker and draw little pens and business cards sticking out the top. I did this as a goof, standing in front of the bathroom mirror before work, but eventually, looking at my chest with its pocket, it really was a kind of shirt I began to see.

A shirt that would eventually turn to tatters.

A shirt I would one day have to remove.

Annie saw my scar for the first time a week after our reunion in the restaurant. We were parked in front of her parents' house. She was in my lap, bra off, and my shirt was half unbuttoned.

She pulled away, I thought for a better view of my chest and the scar, but then asked if we should maybe relocate. I suggested my place, a twenty-minute drive, but she was nervous she'd fall asleep and didn't like the idea of not being home when Fisher woke up in the morning. Plus, there were her parents to consider. She hadn't prepared them for the possibility of her sleeping elsewhere for the evening, and now it was after midnight, well past their bedtime, and anyway, even if Annie *had* prepared them, staying out all night meant they'd have questions regarding her life decisions, a conversation she wished to avoid.

It seemed to me that she had given all this some thought before now, that possibly she'd already considered every option available to us and had concluded that sex simply wouldn't be possible for us tonight and was only trying to nudge me gently toward the same unfortunate realization. I still had my hand on her upper leg under her skirt, my fingertips at the fringes of her underwear, and my mind cycled, helplessly, again and again to the car: Why not *here*—with the seats back? Why not *now?*

Then Annie sighed and said it would have to be the house. She nodded across the lawn at her parents' two-story colonial. Perhaps sensing my uncertainty, she kissed me again and said I didn't need to worry, as long as we were quiet. We dressed. After I moved my car down the street, out of sight, she led me across the yard, through the garage, and into the dark kitchen, which smelled strongly of vinegar. The smell rose up from all the counters and tables, from every surface. My shoulder knocked a pot hanging from a rack over the island, and it clanged against another pan for half a second before Annie grabbed both and quieted them. I apologized. She poured us both tall cups of water, which struck me as a very sensible thing to do. I followed her up the stairs, past the door to her parents' bedroom, through which I could hear the noise of a sleep apnea machine. Fisher's door was next. Annie motioned for me to continue down the carpeted hallway to a second set of stairs. Just before going up, I turned back to see her sticking her head in the door of her daughter's room. Then she brought the door closed again, gently, and met me on the stairs. We ascended together to a renovated attic, Annie's childhood bedroom.

"Have you ever dated a mom?" she asked.

"Not really."

She smiled coolly. "Not really?"

"I haven't, no."

She removed her shirt. "Well, it's not always like this, I promise. Moving cars, sneaking around. It's so high school, isn't it?"

I took off my jacket and tossed it across a

chair near the bed. The room had low, sloped walls, small circular windows, and a private bath. I felt like we'd checked into a quaint bed-and-breakfast. Most of the artifacts of Annie's childhood, it seemed, had been removed and replaced with tasteful lamps and area rugs. Along a far wall was a large stack of cardboard boxes, labeled with markers. Annie set our waters down on the only nightstand and turned on two oscillating fans—one near the door and another at the foot of the bed—before removing the rest of her clothes and sliding into bed. I tugged off my shirt and pants but waited until I was under the covers to stretch the elastic band of my boxer-briefs over my erection.

The bed frame was a cheap metal contraption and scraped against the floor loudly as soon as we began to move against each other. She squeezed my arm and I went still for a moment, perhaps giving the bed an opportunity to cooperate.

"Okay," she said. "Sorry."

To avoid more noise, I tried to keep my movements slow and soft but thirty seconds later I forgot myself, and the bed belched so enormously against the floor that Annie slapped my back. We were both very quiet. Her eyes flicked left, toward the door, as she listened for any stirrings in the rest of the house. An odd whispery giggle escaped her then, and she cupped her hand over her own mouth.

"I'm so sorry," she said. "You probably think this is insane, don't you?"

"Maybe we shouldn't be in the bed?"

We migrated to a rug on the floor, her on top of me now, and finished there. Annie disappeared to the bathroom for a few minutes, and then I did the same. She didn't indicate that she wanted me to leave, so I slid back into bed again alongside her.

I woke up the next morning to find Annie sitting cross-legged on a yoga mat under the circular window. In her hands was my phone. Realizing I was awake, she blushed and offered it to me quickly.

"I'm not snooping. Your phone buzzed, and I thought it was mine, and then I clicked on it and . . ."

She showed me the screen. There my heart was beating, electric blue and red.

"I haven't looked at anything else, I swear," she said. "There are such things as boundaries, I do realize. I support boundaries. I have a friend, she goes through her husband's emails and his texts religiously. Like, every night. She doesn't even suspect he's having an affair. She says she just likes to know who he's talking to all day. She says it's a form of intimacy."

“Feel free to snoop. I’ve got nothing to hide.”

“Does watching your heart on here make you feel more or less mortal? Be honest.”

“A little bit of both.”

“I don’t think I could stand it. I think you should delete it.”

“Well, I sort of need the device.”

“Not the device, just *this,* the app.”

She stood, tossed my phone into my lap, and went into the bathroom. The shower kicked on. I sat up in bed, feeling the pleasant breeze of the fan on my face. I was naked under the sheets. Already I could hear noise downstairs: laughter, news radio, pans. The smell of coffee swirled into the room. I followed her into the bathroom naked, as if to prove to myself—and to her—that I wasn’t feeling modest, that I wasn’t afraid of her seeing me naked in the daytime, and closed the door behind me. She didn’t seem to mind my being there, so I sat down on the toilet lid. The bathroom was very small, nearly closet-sized, and I was maybe one foot from the shower.

“Let’s just say, hypothetically, that ghosts exist,” I said.

“Hypothetically.”

“Right, hypothetically. The voice in the recording—it’s real. Wouldn’t that indicate to you that we may not simply disappear when we die? That we are more than our bodies?”

She considered this for a moment. "I'm not sure. It depends on what ghosts are, exactly. Because what if ghosts are more like cicada shells? Husks left behind when a person dies. Like an echo. Or maybe ghosts are visitors from the future. Time travel might be involved." She laughed at herself. "I have no idea what I'm talking about, by the way. You do realize that, right?" She grabbed a springy white loofah hanging off the hot water nozzle and ran it quickly between her legs. The water glided down the glass in lazy sheets and splattered loudly at her feet.

Who was this incredible person? We'd only dated for three, maybe four months in high school. I don't think we'd been in love back then—or had we? I'd been too young to recognize it, if we had been. It seemed possible to me that we were now, but I was trying to be careful not to overinflate any feelings I had for her. I had a tendency to overinflate.

What I really didn't want was another Marlene situation. Marlene was the woman I'd been with for two years after college. We'd met at the wedding of a mutual friend. She was redheaded, freckled, and short, with large, flat breasts, a homebody but very extroverted and elegant when she needed to be, which was often since she was a director of marketing and advertising for Shula's Chamber of Commerce. I'd fallen hard for Marlene, so hard that by the end of our second month, we'd moved into an apartment together, cosigned a lease. Unfortunately I began to cool on the relationship about three days later, though it took me more than a year to figure that out and another six months to extricate myself, which, in the end, I'd done somewhat passive-aggressively by buying a foreclosed property at auction outside the city limits, a house that I knew Marlene would hate. The fallout had been messy and protracted. She still lived in Shula, and I saw her from time to time, though we hardly said much more to each other than hello. She was married now, to a contractor, with two sons.

Ever since Marlene I'd been wary to trust too fully in what I felt at the beginning of any new relationship. And yet here I was, moon-eyed, watching Annie shower, entertaining a crazy idea that maybe she should just give up her house hunt and come live with me instead in my foreclosure.

She wrapped a towel around her waist and stepped out of the shower onto the white mat, wiping her feet dry with little quick kicks. Then she shimmied the towel-wrap up snug under her armpits and opened her medicine cabinet. I relished each of these little maneuvers, much as I had her chewing gum wrapper routine all those years ago. I couldn't believe that I was here, that we'd slept together.

I left the bathroom to give her some space and to put on my clothes. The unpacked boxes were stacked along the wall between a dresser and the door. The top box was open. Peering inside, I saw photographs in identical black frames. I studied these photos as I buttoned my shirt. There, in one, I saw a younger, fleshier Annie, her hair long and braided over her bare shoulders. She was wearing a strapless bikini. Beside her was a man with thick blond hair and a muscular body. He had aviator sunglasses over his eyes, and his arm was wrapped around her waist. He made appearances in other photographs, too. In another they were seated on a patio with other couples, a flaming dessert at the center of the table, a birthday celebration maybe.

"Anthony," Annie said, standing behind me now in a T-shirt and shorts. Her face softened. "Be honest, does it freak you out I'm a widow?"

"I don't think so, no."

"I would understand if it did. You don't have to pretend like it's a nothing."

The bedroom door jiggled, and my eyes darted over to it.

"Mom?" a soft, slightly irritated voice said.

"Be down in a minute!" Annie called.

We didn't move again until we heard Fisher's footsteps on the stairs.

"I don't think you can come down for breakfast," Annie said to me. "I hope you understand.

I'll get them to go for a walk before we sit down to eat, and you can make your escape then."

She opened the door and then was gone.

I rarely had reason to visit Shula's public library, but when I was unable to dig up anything very interesting online about the history of the restaurant—or, rather, about the people who'd lived in the house it now occupied—I stopped by one evening after work. Inside, White Hairs were sitting in all but a few of the plush reading chairs distributed across the main floor. They lounged and chatted. With fashionable reading glasses over their noses, they devoured Scandinavian detective novels and flicked at their tablets. They were very technologically adept, these old-timers, unwilling to slip into obsolescence. I could feel them watching me as I stood at a computer terminal and tried to navigate the library's intranet.

Public records, newspaper articles, obituaries—I scoured them all for clues.

The house, I slowly pieced together, had originally been built in 1920, like many others in that neighborhood. In 1924, a man named Robert Lennox had bought it. Robert had been a prominent businessman in Shula. Numerous advertisements for his furniture store, Lennox & Sons, appeared in the *Shula Journal* between the years 1898 and 1929. I gathered that the store had been founded by Robert's father. The same year he bought the house, Robert had married a woman named Clara Hopstead, also of Shula, and, as far as I could tell, they'd lived there for eight years—until 1932, when it was partially destroyed. In a fire, cause unknown. Robert died in the fire, but apparently Clara survived. According to the library's records, her obituary appeared in the local newspaper in 1934, but for whatever reason that week's paper was missing from the archive.

One of the librarians, a slim man with greasy dark hair, was eating a salad in an aluminum tray at his desk. I approached, explained the missing newspaper, and asked how I might track down a copy elsewhere.

He munched. "Missing?"

"Yes, not there."

"Huh. Well, that's odd, isn't it? We don't loan them out, typically. Could be we never had it to begin with."

"Is there somewhere else I could look?"

"Oh," he said, putting down his fork. "Well, I doubt it. We're the only library in the country, I guarantee you, with old copies of the *Shula Journal*. Not exactly the *New York Times*, you know? If it's not here, it's nowhere. Sorry." He smiled. "Why, you doing some family history? A genealogy project, I'll bet."

"Not quite," I said.

"We have an archivist, part-time. She's here once or twice a week. I can put you in touch. She might be of some assistance."

"Thank you, please."

He scribbled down her name and email address. That night I wrote her to ask if she might be able to help me track down more information about the deaths of Robert and Clara Lennox.

"So there really was a fire," Annie said.

"Yes, but Clara didn't die in it. She lived another year or two."

"Meaning, she wouldn't be haunting the house and it wouldn't be her voice in the recording . . . ?"

I shrugged and took another bite of my cheeseburger. I had no idea of the rules of hauntings. We were driving around town on our lunch breaks, eating fast food as we checked out potential houses for Annie and her daughter. We entered a hilly suburb of very modest homes, squat midcentury two-bedrooms with just enough charm to not feel depressing. Around a curve we came to a For Sale sign, and Annie pulled into the driveway. No one appeared to be home, so we got out to have a look around. I walked up to the house, cupped my hands over my eyes, and peered through a front window into a dining room furnished with only a table and chairs.

“I don’t think anyone’s living here,” I said.

Annie nodded and unlatched a gate that led around to the back. The grass was a bit soggy, though it hadn’t rained in two or three days. A doghouse sat empty at the far corner of the yard. A frayed hammock sagged between two trees. Through the trees I could see a neighbor in his underwear collecting beer cans from his yard. Already I didn’t like the idea of Annie living here.

“We should probably go inside and make a recording, huh?” Annie said.

“Why?”

“So we can listen for any voices. I don’t want to share my house.”

“What would you do if you saw a ghost? A real one, I mean.”

Annie assumed a strange, slightly crouched pose, her hands in front of her face, as if warding away an evil spirit. With a deep, tremulous voice, she said, “I am harrowed with fear and wonder!”

“A play, right?”

“*Hamlet*, dummy. The king returns as an apparition in his battle armor, but he won’t say a word to anyone.” She raised her arms again, her eyes widening. “ ‘Stay!’ ” she yelled, taking two quick steps toward me. “ ‘Speak, speak.’ ” Her voice was pleading. She was looking into my eyes desperately. “ ‘I charge thee. Speak!’ ”

She bowed. *Scene.*

"Fear and wonder about sums it up for me these days," I said. "Last night I had this dream where I couldn't find any pencils for a test, but this morning I heard a report on the news about a man who walked into a movie theater, scooped out his eyeballs with a spoon, and threw them at the audience. Most people thought it was part of the movie. So you can understand if I get my nights and days confused sometimes. Nothing adds up. Sometimes I feel like maybe I've had a brain injury and didn't realize it."

"I think your brain is fine, Jim."

"Okay, but the other day, I was sitting at a red light when I realized I was nodding yes and no to sex questions posed by a radio DJ. Everything feels inverted, turned around. At this very moment, a thousand satellites are circling the earth, and the government can use them to zoom all the way down to our arm hairs if they're in the mood, and yet an entire airplane drops from the sky, and we can't ever locate it again. People pay hundreds of dollars for a blanket that tells you the temperatures under the covers and above. Viral eye-dyes. Condoms that glow green when they detect STDs. Pills that cure baldness but make you limp. Pills that make you stiff but make you lose your hair. So why not ghosts? is my question. Why not the voice of a dead woman on a CD that sounds like a broken vacuum cleaner?"

Annie was listening to me with a wry expression that indicated she disapproved of what I was saying but was, for the most part, amused.

"You're a bit of an oddball, huh?" she said finally.

She slid behind a row of hedges and stood up on her tiptoes, trying for a better view through a high window. I suggested we just call the realtor, but she demurred, asking instead that I give her a boost, which I did, my arms wrapped around her legs, the side of my face against her butt.

"What do you see?"

"Bedroom. Sort of small, though. Fisher wouldn't like it."

Annie slid back down through the hoop of my arms. We were very close together now, both of us quiet, uncertain. I kissed her, and her hands slid inside my suit jacket.

"Come over tonight," I said.

"I promised Fisher we'd get dinner."

"Bring her, too, then."

Annie's hands dropped away, and she took a step back.

"What?" I asked.

"Nothing."

"You don't want me to meet Fisher."

"It's not that I don't want you to meet her."

"What, then?"

The back door squeaked open, and we shoved our way out of the hedges. An older woman dressed in a long pink nightgown walked over to us with a very serious expression on her face.

"Sorry," I said. "We didn't think anyone was home."

The woman said nothing.

"We like your house," Annie added. "I'll call the realtor and make a proper appointment. Very sorry."

"There's just too much yard," the woman said. "Otherwise I'd never sell. I'd stay forever."

"Understandable," I said, already moving toward the gate.

Annie was two steps behind me.

"I raised two kids in this house," the woman said. "For sentimental reasons, it will be difficult to leave, but I must."

"I can imagine," Annie said. "Sorry again."

The gate popped shut behind us. We rushed back to the car and drove away. Both of us were quiet until we reached the end of the street, then Annie laughed. *"It will be difficult to leave, but I must,"* she said, drolly. "She was a ghost, right?"

I smiled. She drove me back to my office. Just before I got out of the car, she took my hand. "If you're interested, you could check out this church on Sunday, the one I was telling you about. The Church of Search. Fisher will be there with me."

"Is that what you want?"

"It's up to you. Either way is fine with me."

I nodded and told her I'd think about it.

We'd been to church together before, actually, many years earlier, as teenagers, when she'd dragged me to an overnight youth group lock-in. She'd been a hard-core Baptist back then, a borderline fundamentalist. After the doors had shut, we'd spread our sleeping bags out in the church gymnasium and played basketball until two a.m., at which point the group leaders rolled out a giant television and played us a movie called *Afterward, Pt. 2.* The film, I gathered, was the second installment in a series about the end of days. The main character was a female journalist who'd been an atheist until the events predicted—or at least hinted at—in the Book of Revelation began to actually happen: war, famine, disease. The production value was terrible, but its intended message was clear: the end times looked a lot like the world as it was today. *Repent,* the movie counseled, *while there's still time.*

We were watching this in our sleeping bags, and I was stretched out behind Annie, pressed to her back. In the darkness, it seemed unlikely anyone would notice. I remember breathing hard into her neck, my arm draped over her side, a position she'd encouraged, as we watched the female journalist in the movie do battle with the devil, who was disguised as a world leader advocating unity and peace.

Then the lights popped on, and we all slid

away from each other, blinking heavy in the brightness. The youth minister had us all circle up at the center of the gym. He sat on a stool in the center and talked to us about Paul's First Letter to the Corinthians, in which Paul said that he would become all things to all men in order to save them. If a man was weak, Paul would be weak. If a man was Jewish, Paul would be Jewish. If a man was a Gentile, Paul would be a Gentile. Whatever it took to bring that man to Christ . . .

"If a man was a pothead," some kid said, which got us all laughing.

"Hey, well, good point," the youth minister said, smiling big, and pretended to take a toke of an imaginary joint. "Some people would say that's exactly right. That if you really want to help a man—or woman—you need to walk in that dude's shoes for a little bit. Do y'all think that's true?"

Some of the kids nodded.

"Maybe so. Now, I don't think Paul is telling you to become an addict," the youth minister said, still smiling. "But I do think he's telling you to be smart when it comes to the business of saving souls. Jesus washed Mary Magdalene's feet, remember? Remember? He scrubbed them with his own two hands."

After the youth minister's talk, he'd asked if there were any newcomers present. Annie nudged me, and I raised my hand. I was one of five. The youth minister shook each of our hands. Then he said he wanted everyone to stand up, one by one, to tell the group when we'd been saved. I'd never been put on the spot like this. One girl said she'd been saved in the third grade at a Bible camp. Another girl said she came to know Jesus on the youth group ski trip last winter. "On a diamond slope," she added, and everyone smiled. Annie told the group she'd been saved in the third grade in youth group.

I was next. The gymnasium doors were locked. Everyone was watching me. The easiest thing to do, of course, would have been to make up something, but I couldn't do that. What would God do to the person who lied about being saved? I didn't want to test him. I took these things very seriously as a child. I felt like God was watching me all the time. Uncertain of what to say, I jumped up off the floor, ran to the bathroom, and threw up.

I did my homework on The Church of Search. The church had no discernible creed, no tenets, no specific set of beliefs, but it was clearly situated within the Protestant tradition of worship. Jesus and the New Testament were not the exclusive avenues of salvation, but they were referenced and alluded to more often than any other spiritual leader or text.

From what I could tell, the church was a net for skeptics and wannabe born-agains, for Jimmy Carters of the digital age, for people who wanted to *feel* God but didn't know how anymore, who worried their intellects and logic were getting in the way of a genuine spiritual experience, who liked Christianity generally but were ashamed of its history, for people who thought religion should make room for science and discovery. Predictably it had many critics. According to traditional religious folks, The Church of Search lacked the most crucial element of the churchgoing experience: pastoral care and leadership. To atheists, The Church of Search didn't go far enough in its deference to science and reason.

I showed up at Annie's church that Sunday unsure of what to think. Services were held in the old Masonic Temple near downtown, a white stone building with steps leading up to a single large door. I was greeted out front by a man with squiggles of red hair and a scowl on his face.

"No way that's Jimmy Byrd," he said, and seized my hand.

"Wes?"

"The one and only!"

Wesley Riggs. I hadn't seen him in years. I'd once been friends with his younger brother,

Michael, who lived in California now. Wes and I had never interacted much in high school as he'd been two years older than me. Vaguely I remembered him running for student body president, an election he'd lost. He had a dentist practice in Shula now, though we never really crossed paths. We ran in different circles, I suppose.

"Welcome," he said. "Welcome to The Church of Search. Your first time?"

I nodded.

"You're going to love it," he said. "Come on over here, come with me, I'll find you a good spot."

He led me through a small lobby and into a large wood-paneled room with dark red carpets that looked as though they hadn't been replaced in decades. Three empty wooden throne-like chairs sat on a low stage at the front of the room.

"Ignore all the Masonic stuff," Wes said. "They don't even meet here anymore. City owns the building, and we pay to use it on Sundays."

He directed me to a metal folding chair in the front row. I didn't really want to sit at the front of the room, but I thought it might be impolite to protest. He asked me if I had a phone, and when I held it up, he bumped his against mine.

"Now you've got the program, brother. This is a state-of-the-art church. My wife and I were attending services at a Church of Search in

Nashville, when we were living there, and once we moved back to Shula we really missed it and thought we'd start up a satellite here, too. I'm a founding member. On the board and everything. We're about to start, so I'll leave you be, but we should get some coffee after this. You free? There's a place across the street. We should catch up!"

He retreated to the back of the room. The other empty chairs quickly filled with congregants. I guessed there were maybe forty people here, but with only a few minutes to go before the service, Annie and her daughter were nowhere in sight.

I texted her: *At the Church. You?*

"Hi," said the woman sitting directly behind me. "I'm Sudeepa."

"Hello," I said.

She had a baby in her lap, and toddlers on either side of her in chairs. One of the kids, a boy with shiny dark hair, was picking his nose gleefully.

"Bet you've never been to a church with holograms before, have you?" she said.

"Holograms?"

She smiled. "Oh, you're in for a treat."

A man in the corner of the room began strumming a guitar. Vaguely I recognized the tune as "Bridge Over Troubled Water." I'd never been to a worship service like this one. I'd grown up in the Lutheran Church—a compromise struck by my Baptist mother and my mostly nonbelieving father—and we'd spent most Sundays inside a pretty gray-stone church near downtown. I'd been an acolyte there as a teenager, though I hadn't been back since leaving town for college. I'd always enjoyed its pomp and rituals, but I'd never felt moved in any real way by its prayers and creeds and hymns. What I remembered most from the services of my youth were chunky organ notes tumbling down from pipes behind the altar, the pipes embedded in the plaster like a sideways rib cage, the skin of the wall peeled back to reveal them. Staring up at that wall I'd often wondered if it was meant to put you in mind of Jesus' emaciated body on the cross.

The Church of Search had no organ. No pomp, either. After the first song ended, the lights dimmed, and the group recited a prayer of thanks off their phones. The screens glowed faintly blue in the near-darkness, illuminating chins and mouths. Then the lights returned and there was more music. I looked back but still didn't see Annie. Sudeepa smiled at me as if to reassure me.

The song ended, and everyone sat down in their chairs for five minutes of silence. Then a woman in jeans and pearls strolled to the front of the room, bracelets jangling on each wrist, and, with a lilting voice, read a Mary Oliver poem about the world being created new each morning. There were other readings—from the Gospel of Thomas, from the *Bhagavad-Gita*, from Carl Sandburg. The lights flickered, and the room hushed. I checked the program on my phone and saw that next up was today's featured speaker: Dr. Mary Kendrick, a biblical archaeologist. When I glanced back up, a woman was standing before me, just a few feet away, in front of the three wooden chairs. For a moment she stood very still, staring out beyond all of us, as if waiting for the go-ahead from an invisible director at the back of the room.

She looked at us then with a grin and introduced herself. Since I was in the front row, I was looking up at her face. She had tan skin and large, crater-like pores. On her upper lip was a fine dark fuzz. A microphone headset curled around her right ear. If you squinted right, you could see that something was off about her. She had a slightly grainy and pixelated aspect. She wasn't actually there. But where was she being projected from? I saw no machinery along the floor, the wall, or the ceiling—no mirrors or lights or little black boxes or futuristic glass pyramids. I couldn't figure it out, couldn't source it.

"Turn it up," someone shouted. "I can't hear!"

"Sorry," Wes said.

He stood up in the middle of the room and fiddled with a small back remote control. Dr. Kendrick expanded in all directions, until she was almost twelve feet tall. A giant. A mythic being. At the back of the room a small child began to wail.

“Wes, you created a monster,” a man yelled.

A few people laughed.

Wes clicked the remote again but instead of shrinking, the pastor ballooned up like a Macy’s Day parade float, a cartoon character. The ceiling decapitated her at the shoulders. Was her head above the roof, looking out across the town?

“Sorry, sorry,” Wes said, pushing more buttons.

The woman’s body disappeared, but her voice remained. She was in the middle of a story about having been detained once in Israel, the result of some confusion over the Jordanian stamps in her passport. Then, finally, she flickered back into view, life-size again, normal. People settled down to listen.

Dr. Kendrick paced as she spoke. She gestured. She’d been involved with a recent effort to excavate a first-century fishing boat from the Sea of Galilee, the second of its kind exposed in the last twenty years as the lake waters receded due to drought. Though she had no reason to believe this boat had ever been used by Jesus and his disciples, she had no reason to disbelieve it either. Radiocarbon dating suggested the boat would have been on the water during the years of Jesus’ ministry, as a matter of fact. It was at least conceivable that he’d been onboard.

A 3D image of the boat, like the legless husk of a dead bug, popped into view a foot from Dr.

Kendrick's face, floating there, turning slowly so that we could see it from all angles.

At the conclusion of her talk, she zapped away. A few people clapped. Others stood immediately to collapse chairs. The service, apparently, was over. I looked for Annie. She still wasn't here, but I saw that I had a text from her.

Fisher woke up sick. So sorry!!!! Will make it up to you.

I added my chair to the stack that was amassing on a long metal cart near the storeroom. Wes patted me on the back: Coffee now?

Across the road from the Masonic Temple was a café called BeanHead. Wes and I sat down across from each other at a greasy table near the front window. We talked about a sixty-four-mile bike ride he was planning, about a black bear that had recently been spotted Dumpster-diving behind the Best Buy, about a new kind of doorbell technology that could scan your fingerprint and announce your arrival with a theme song picked especially for you, about The Church of Search.

"Do you know Annie Creel?" I asked him. "She's the one who suggested I come today."

"Annie Creel, sure. Harriet—my wife—knows Annie better than me. They've been out to dinner a couple of times. Such a sad story, though. You know about her husband, I'm sure?"

I nodded. "A little."

"Drugs is what I heard."

"Drugs? I'm fairly certain he drowned."

"Not like the newspaper's going to say he drowned 'cause he was fucked up, you know? Anyway, I'm not casting stones here. My brother—you remember Mikey—he's deep into ayahuasca. He's got some kind of guide, calls herself Stone Fox, and he and his friends go over to her house on Sundays, wear white pajamas, and throw up in buckets as they hallucinate."

"Mikey does this? Really?"

Mikey had made a small fortune as a day trader and, last I heard, spent most of his time shuttling back and forth between San Francisco and Aspen.

"Scout's honor. He calls it his church." He smiled. "So—what'd you think of The Church of Search? I'm curious. We ditched the flat-screens last year and upgraded to holograms. Lots of other satellites are doing it. Didn't it feel like she was really right there with us?"

"Sort of," I said. "Nearly."

He sipped his coffee.

The couple at the table behind us, whom I recognized from that morning's service, were very politely discussing the end of the world. Their forks scraped against their plates as they outlined the various scenarios: climate change, biblical floods, alien invasion, nuclear disaster, overpopulation, the singularity, global pandemics. They seemed well versed in all the ways the human species might ultimately fizzle, their voices hushed but essentially un-frightened and resigned. They were very certain the end was near; the only real question, it seemed, the only thing worth debating, was the manner in which this fate might unfold.

Seated around another table, near the pastries display, was a group of sweaty men and women in spandex and shorts. They were slumped in their chairs, their legs stretched at odd angles, a maze of muscled thighs and calves. They were discussing endorphins, serotonins, exercise as a path to an ecstatic experience.

This was the new Sunday morning. Lattes and red-eyes. Runners' clubs. Metaphysics in the coffee shop. Each table, another sect, another order.

"Jim," Wes said, "how familiar are you with intelligent holograms?"

I shrugged. I had no idea what he was talking about.

"Smart holograms, they're sometimes called. Virtual assistants. Holographic artificial intelligences. One day, not too distant from now, holograms will be everywhere, man. When you walk down the street, half the people you see will be holograms. You'll have holographic hotties modeling the latest fashions outside clothing stores. They'll try to sell you things. Sandwich cards. Kombuchas. They'll find you a table at the restaurant. They'll check you into your hotel. The entire service industry will be upended by this, just you wait."

"That's a little depressing."

"How much do you know about the Council of San Francisco?"

"Nothing at all."

Very solemnly Wes explained that two years ago an ecumenical council of leading biblical scholars, priests, and preachers from various denominations, plus a team of advanced computer programmers and start-up billionaires, had convened in San Francisco in order to reach a consensus on what source material should be used in the creation of a digital Jesus consciousness. This group had gathered in a hotel conference room to debate what primary and secondary documents and research would need to be included to achieve a near artificial intelligence with a Jesus-based personality.

"The council never reached a clear consensus," Wes said. "But The Church of Search has been in talks with a company that's developing its own Jesus intelligence. ReJesus, they're calling it. He'll walk among us again. As a hologram."

I asked if they'd use a model or an actor to create their Jesus, and Wes shook his head. Forensics, he said. With skulls recovered from ancient tombs in East Jerusalem, they would map and design his features. Not just any skulls, of course, but the skulls of Jewish men in their early thirties. Galileans, specifically. ReJesus' face would be a composite of about a dozen different people who lived two thousand years ago, men who spent their days around Jerusalem, who toiled under Roman rule. Real people. The hologram would look like a man of Jesus' time. Dark-skinned, fit, lean.

"Please don't scare him off, Wes," said a voice at my back.

I twisted in my chair. It was Sudeepa, the woman who'd been sitting behind me earlier that morning at the church. She was standing there with a child in one arm and a large iced coffee drink in the other the color of cardboard.

"Wes's obsessed with this ReJesus idea," she told me. "He thinks it will solve all the world's problems or something. Did you enjoy the service this morning?"

I told her that I had.

"Well, you should come back again! Next week the speaker is a neuroscientist who thinks that God is talking to us all the time through magnetic waves."

"That guy's a quack," Wes said. "I don't know why they gave him a spot."

"Is he?" Sudeepa asked. "Shame. I thought it sounded interesting." She looked at me. "The problem is, with so many different talks, you never know what to expect. One Sunday you're listening to a pastor from Texas who's helping to settle immigrants from war-torn countries and the next week it's a lady who thought she saw the Buddha in her bathtub. You have to be a little discerning."

"Here's the thing," Wes said. "The real Jesus—he was a hologram."

"Oh, stop it," Sudeepa said.

"A projection from God. Here but also not quite here."

"But he *was* here, Wes. He walked the earth. As a living, breathing *man*."

"Not according to the Docetists!"

"The *who?*"

"Group of early Christians. They thought Jesus was a phantom."

"You can't put a phantom on a cross," Sudeepa said.

"Yes," Wes said airily, "well, that was the eventual consensus, that you need a body to really suffer, to really sacrifice."

I tried to imagine Annie in the mix of this conversation. Were these the sort of people she kept as friends? I felt as if I'd wandered into somebody else's dream. Everywhere I went, it was the same. Even a trip to the CVS could be overwhelming. Wandering the aisles, looking up at the walls of hair-care products, shampoos, conditioners, waxes, pomades, curl enhancers, curl removers, thickeners, thinners, I would become disoriented and confused. Woozy. What sort of a place was this? I could no longer even tell you, not without a great deal of concentration and focus, what a 1099 was for. Or a swizzle stick. Or a motherboard.

Wes cleared his throat. “Sudeepa, you’re missing the larger point. This won’t be some dead recording. This will be an actual lifelike Jesus representation. Truly interactive. He’ll walk among us again! And he’ll be able to answer all our most pressing questions about God!”

“But what’s the point of that, when you can just pick up a Bible like a normal person?” Sudeepa asked.

“You don’t understand. ReJesus will be able to extrapolate. You won’t just get the same stale mustard seed parable. You’ll get an entirely new and contemporary story that explains a similar or related idea. Do you get it? This is huge. It’s almost like the Second Coming.”

“Except not at all like that,” Sudeepa said, annoyed.

“We live in such amazing times, don’t we?” Wes asked. “In my prayers at night I thank God for putting me on Earth when he did. I say, *Dear God, thank you for putting me here, now, and not back when we were trying to kill each other with swords.* What if I’d been born on some farm in the Dark Ages? What did people have to look forward to back then? A new plow? A trip into town every three to four years? Marriage to a cousin? Those poor idiots died from exhaustion. They were bludgeoned to death. They were trampled under cart wheels."

"My great-great-uncle was killed by a mule kick to the head," I offered.

Wes nodded eagerly. "Mule kicks. Lightning bolts. Pneumonia after a cold rain."

"People still die that way," Sudeepa said, setting her drink on our table for a moment so that she could shift the child to her other arm. "You do know that, right?"

"Nine times out of ten modern medicine can save you today. It's a question of access. The number of drugs in development, in labs across the country, the world, it's incredible. If not for the FDA, we'd have twenty new cancer treatments available by breakfast tomorrow. People don't die anymore, they just fail to find the right cure. We're more fortunate than anyone who's come before us. Because we're so close to having all the answers. We're at the cusp of a new era. Our entire evolution has led us to this point."

"It led us to every point before this one, too," Sudeepa said, rightly. "Plus all the others that haven't come yet."

"Just around the corner is immortality. Every one of us, if we hang on long enough, will live forever."

"But what about terrorism?" Sudeepa asked. "School shootings? The droughts? The water wars? Genocides? You can't tell me, not with a straight face, that this is the best time to be alive in all of human history. Wes, what about the Weeza virus!"

"Which one is that?" I asked.

"Weeza's from tick bites," she said. "Melts your insides. A death sentence!"

"Which ticks are these?" I asked. "The little brown ones or the little black ones or the bigger black ones with the white spots?"

"The little black ones with the double-white spots, though you need a magnifying lens to distinguish two white spots from one," she said. "No bigger than a pinhead, these little ticks, but killers. Ten years ago there was no such thing as a Weeza virus. They say it started with the squirrels, but how did the squirrels come to have it and why wasn't it transmitted to us before now?"

"Weeza was always there," Wes said dismissively, "we just didn't realize it. Everything you fear—the viruses, the violence—we've always been living with it, in some form. What's changed is that today we're just more aware. It only seems like there's more to fear because we've been so successful at identifying all the various threats."

"Do you really think we'll really be immortal one day?" I asked. "You think we could live forever?"

"Absolutely. Our parents were the last generation that will know death. Anyone under forty, if they take care and avoid cholesterol and saturated fats, if they stay fit, if they keep off the roads as much as possible, they'll make it."

"I hope he hasn't turned you off our church," Sudeepa said to me with a smile. "We're not all a bunch of crazies, I promise you."

Outside my door I could hear the Fortune Tellers were debating whether yogurt was the product of bacteria or if it was the bacteria itself. All this because Susan had spilled her Yoplait. Their morning news show banter was without end, a nonstop source of all the world's dumbest news and cheap headline fodder.

I had an email back from the archivist. Other than what I'd already found, she'd managed to locate only a short funeral notice for Clara Lennox, which had appeared in the state newspaper. The notice said simply: *THE FUNERAL OF MRS. CLARA LENNOX will take place at the South Methodist Church in Shula on Saturday 4th.* That was it. I read the sentence again—and then a third time.

I played *TheProof.mp3* on my computer. This time I had more trouble locating the woman's voice in the noise. It seemed possible that the recording could change from one playback to the next. Then, I heard it, a single syllable, a far-off utterance. She was still in there.

If ghosts truly existed, then surely we were surrounded on all sides? By my calculations the earth contained roughly 197 million square miles of surface area (land and water), and according to various population studies, 108 billion humans had lived and died on the planet. That meant that for every square mile, there had been roughly 548 deaths in our not terribly long history as a species. Even if we assumed only twenty percent of those who'd died remained as a ghost, that still would have left more than a hundred ghosts per square mile, not to mention the fact that we don't live all over the world but in pockets, here and there. We don't generally live in Antarctica or the Gobi Desert or on the ocean, and accounting for this fact would only maximize the figure, would only increase the number of ghosts per square mile.

Anyway, I approved Su Casa Siempre's loan.

Not all White Hairs, of course, had white hair. They came in many forms and shapes, in various states of being and decay. White Hair wasn't a hair color; it was Medicare and Social

Security checks; it was a box you checked on government forms. My parents, who still lived in Shula and who were not quite sixty, didn't yet qualify. I'd been seeing more of them, especially my father, since my surgery. He came around the house about once a week, typically unannounced, to see how I was doing.

One evening I came home and his car was parked in the driveway. Inside I found him in the kitchen grinding coffee beans.

"You're out of filters," he said. "I'm using a paper towel."

Growing up, I'd often heard my father referred to as a handsome man, though I feel incapable of making such a determination myself. Large and muscled, he lifted free weights every morning in my old bedroom, which he'd converted into a gym and home office, though at this point in his life he was mostly bald with a thick white goatee on his face. He was the sort of person who thought it foolish to invest in anything other than commodities—silver, gold, the elements. He would drive two hours north just to look at the first snow of the winter, to make a single snowball by the side of the highway, and then turn right back for home. He could lift a propane tank and tell you exactly how many medium-high grilling hours it had left to burn.

I sat down at the breakfast table. He started the coffeemaker and joined me.

“So,” he said. “How’s the ticker?”

“Still ticking.”

“I’m on blood thinners now. Did your mother tell you? Dr. Tamsin started me on them. You remember Little Ronny Tamsin? You were in my class together.”

I remembered Little Ronny Tamsin with his buckteeth and his giant blue Gatorades. We’d been seatmates at the same circle of desks that year in my father’s trigonometry class.

He looked around my kitchen and then sighed. I sighed back at him. One day, I suspected, all of our conversations would be like this, a nonstop sigh fest. Everything that needed to be communicated would be through a Morse code of sighing.

I knew that he did not approve of this house, its general shabbiness. I had a maid come every other week, but no amount of cleaning ever seemed to help. The house was small, a shoe box at the county’s edge, a fixer-upper surrounded by scrappy woods, on the other side of which two pit bulls yapped incessantly, day and night. My original plan had been to spend only two years here, renovating it myself before flipping it, but seven years later here I was, living among the ruins and mouse droppings, all my projects half completed. Above us, where I’d exposed the beams in the kitchen ceiling, chunks of drywall still clung to the screw heads.

"So," he said. "I'm just back from a conference."

"The thing in Miami?"

He nodded excitedly. "It was very interesting. You should have come with me."

Now that he was retired, my father finally had the time to fully immerse himself in all the things that really interested him: unexplained disappearances, unsolved murders, government conspiracies. He told me then about a particular panel at the UFO conference that had addressed the theory that the moon was actually hollow and that it might in fact be a spaceship dragged into our orbit by extraterrestrials at some point in our ancient history. As he laid out the finer points of this theory, a theory that he found "doubtful but plausible," the coffeemaker gurgled and spat.

"Did you hear me?" he asked.

"Titanium. You were saying that the moon's surface is made of titanium, like a spaceship would be."

"More than just titanium. Other elements, too, but yes."

The coffeemaker beeped. He poured us both cups, and we went into the living room together. My father stretched out on the sofa, kicked off his leather shoes, and gazed around at my furnishings. The room, I'll admit, was sparsely appointed: the couch, the television, a low metal table designed to look like an artifact pillaged from a fallen empire.

My father, I'm guessing, was worried by what probably appeared to him as evidence of a monastic lifestyle. Every time he came over he seemed surprised at how little progress I'd made in making a home of the place. To him minimalism wasn't a design aesthetic but an unfortunate condition that indicated an economic or spiritual malaise. He was a collector and a keeper, a stacker of boxes: of antique woodworking tools, old half-filled notebooks, RC Cola bottles, old power-line glass insulators, newspapers, the arm sling he wore in the tenth grade after fracturing his wrist.

This, the injury to his wrist, was the "greatest tragedy of his life," as it had allegedly scuttled any hope he had of achieving much in the years to come. He'd been a pitcher for his high school baseball team, and, though I've always found his logic both reductive and pointless, he maintained that if not for breaking his wrist, his fastball, which was "notorious all over the state," would have earned him a college scholarship to somewhere other than the tiny Podunk Baptist school he wound up at in rural Georgia. If not for that injury, he insisted, he would have been a doctor and not a retired math teacher with a shitty retirement package. He'd have had a summer house at the beach and been driving a Beamer.

He would, in other words, have out-succeeded my uncle the banker. All this denied my father because of a dumb wrist fracture.

However, if not for that injury, I was sometimes tempted to counter, there would have been no me. After all, it was at the Podunk Baptist school that he'd met my mother. She hadn't grown up in Shula but in a small town in South Georgia. Her father, who died the year after I was born, had taught economics at the school, and so my mother had attended tuition-free. She claimed it never once occurred to her to go anywhere else.

They'd met at a dance. When my father arrived, he saw my mother across the room standing by the punch bowl with a flower in her hair. Love at first sight.

For years and years, the night was described to me in exactly those terms, as more of a postcard than an actual event, a bad Norman Rockwell painting maybe, though of course the truth was more complex. In retellings of the story, new, more puzzling and even contradictory details would often emerge. Such as that Mom was in fact engaged to another boy at the time. Such as that Dad had arrived at the dance with someone else, too. About these other people, I know nothing. They have their own stories, surely.

"Your mother prays for you every night," he said. "Did you know that?"

"That's not necessary," I said. "I'm doing just fine."

"If she wants to pray, let her pray."

"That's not what you used to say. You used to tell her it was pointless."

"Did I? If that's true, I regret it."

"So you believe it does work, then?"

"I believe I shouldn't believe one way or the other."

I told him about something I'd read recently, about an interesting study that had looked at the brains of people while they were praying and meditating, specifically, Tibetan monks. What the researchers noticed was that the parietal lobes, which are responsible for sucking in the information of our everyday life and making sense of the onslaught, were curiously inactive during prayer. When people were praying, in other words, when they experienced that wonderful feeling of oneness with the universe, the brain was no longer working quite so hard to construct a meaningful series of events from the slop of our nonstop experience. It was no longer constructing reality, you might even say. My father listened to this with a sanguine expression on his face, one socked foot scratching the other at the end of the couch. Was this what was wrong with me? Had the cardiac arrest damaged my parietal lobes? I didn't ask my father this, but it occurred to me then that my brain was failing to construct the appropriate reality from the onslaught.

"Once upon a time you were going to be a preacher," he said with a smile.

He was referring to an essay I'd written in the fifth grade for a contest, and so I didn't feel any need to comment.

"I get it," he said. "You and me, we're the same. Hyper-curious skeptics. An infuriating combination. I wish I could say you'll find your way, but I'm not so sure. Look at me. I've figured out nothing. I'm constitutionally incapable of faith. I've always envied people who just believe in something, no questions asked. I look at your mother and I think she's got it all figured out. Secret of the universe. It comes easy to her. Me, I wake up in cold sweats at night. I toss and turn. I don't want to die, but then again, I don't want to live forever, either. There's no winning, is there?"

"I tried out a new church. You'd probably like it. The Church of Search. There's no preacher, no core set of beliefs. It's more like a lecture series than anything else."

"Can you write that down for me? Where's this happen?"

I scribbled all the information onto a piece of paper and handed it to him.

"Thank you," he said, slipping it into his already swollen wallet. "Perfect."

We sat quietly for a few minutes.

"Tell me," he said, "are you seeing anybody, Jim? Your mother and I worry you might let this heart situation keep you from getting out there and meeting people. You can't be afraid to live."

"It's only been a few months. Besides, I'm out there. I was on a date recently, in fact."

His eyes lit up. "I'm very glad to hear it! What's her name?"

I didn't want to tell him the woman I'd been out with was in fact my eleventh-grade girlfriend, not to mention the fact that I wasn't really sure where things stood between us. Annie and I had only traded a few texts since she'd missed our church date. Currently she was down in Charleston with her dad, picking up the remainder of her stuff from storage.

"It's nothing serious," I said. "Nobody worth mentioning yet."

"I can't even remember what it's like to go on a first date. It's been so long since I did it. To be honest, I only ever really dated one other woman before your mother. Her name was Franny Kidd. Her father was my pediatrician. She was sixteen, and I was twenty, which means by today's standards I could have gone to jail, I guess."

"Only if you slept with her."

He blushed. "Well, she was such a sweet girl. She died years ago in an industrial trash compactor. Totally crushed to death. Terrible, isn't it? A freak accident. I couldn't even fantasize about her anymore after I read about that. When I think of her, I can only picture her with a crushed head."

I grimaced because, somehow, we had veered into a discussion of my father's failed sexual fantasies.

"I was a late bloomer," he said. "Very serious, very introverted. I didn't know how to talk to girls. I gawked too much. Said the wrong things. Somehow I managed with your mom, which was a miracle given what a knockout she was. Don't look at me like that, it's true, she really was. Still is, for that matter. Prettiest girl I'd ever seen in my life. I was afraid to bring her home. I thought my brother would steal her away. He could charm just about anyone. He was never without a girlfriend. Charm goes a long way, I've realized over the years. When it comes to success, charm often counts for more than intelligence, believe it or not."

He said this as if it were a gross injustice, and I gathered he was not so subtly insulting my uncle's intelligence, perhaps even prompting me to take a side, which I wouldn't do. This wasn't a conversation I was interested in having, not to mention the fact that my job as a loan officer, arguably, was one that required much more charm than intelligence. Sensing he wanted to keep talking about my uncle, I brought out my phone to derail him.

“I have something that might interest you,” I said. “A recording.”

I didn’t mention ghosts or hauntings. My only instructions to him were to listen carefully to the recording and tell me what, if anything, he could hear. I plugged in some headphones, put them in his ears, and then pressed Play.

“The dog’s on fire,” he said loudly, without any hesitation. Then, “Whose dog is on fire?”

I pulled the headphones from his ears. “You understood that?”

“Yes, what was it?”

I told my father everything—about the extermination anomaly, about my trip to the restaurant (leaving out Annie), about the stairwell, about the physicist who’d made the recording, about what I’d learned at the library—and as I did, a childish grin snuck onto his face. He sat up on the couch and suggested we eat dinner there. Tonight. Right now.

My intention in playing him the recording had been only to change the subject, to give us something to discuss other than ourselves, and I wasn’t certain I wanted to take him to the restaurant. But when he stood up to go, I knew that I wouldn’t be able to convince him otherwise. My father had long enjoyed a reputation at the middle school as something of a hallway brute, a teacher not to be trifled with, but in truth he was a supremely sensitive man, who when criticized would often fall into long, brooding silences. My mother and I had always been careful of these moods.

I remember a particular weekend—I had my driver's license, so I was at least sixteen—when we were on our way to an amusement park in Tennessee and my father, coming to a sudden traffic backup on the interstate, slammed on the brakes and swerved our Volvo wagon down off the side of the road to avoid a collision. He'd been driving very fast, too fast, and he had a tendency to make hard, painful stops. My mother, in the passenger seat, fearing the worst, had grabbed the Oh-Shit-Bar, as we called it, and screamed, "Sweet Jesus, no!" As we reentered traffic, fueled by the rush of adrenaline, she began to lash out, berating my father for the terrible driver he was, pleading with him to please let me, a teenager, take over driving for the rest of the trip. An insult to his manhood, I would imagine. Without any comment whatsoever, my father took the next exit and whipped us back onto the interstate in the opposite direction. Now we were eastbound, heading for home. "What are you doing?" my mother asked. "Just tell me, Bill, please, what are you doing?" He didn't say a word. I didn't either. I knew better than to get involved. Besides, the amusement park had been my mother's idea of a fun Saturday, and I'd never been all that keen on going anyway. When we reached our house, my father disappeared into the backyard to mow the grass, and we didn't hear from him again until the next morning, at breakfast, when he acted as if nothing had happened at all: Amusement park—*what* amusement park?

We sat at the bar and ordered enchilada sliders and Fangaritas. I could barely taste the tequila. The restaurant was not as crowded this time but still busy.

"The physicist," he said. "Sally Zinker. That name is so familiar. I feel like I've read something by her or *about* her. The books and Web forums, it's all a blur. I remember loose particulars, but never things like names and central points. A function of my age, I guess."

"Maybe she was the keynote speaker at the Paranormal Club for Bored Retirees last year?"

"Oh, you know the PCBR?" He smiled. "Yes, yes, very funny, Jim."

"Why do you go to all those conferences anyway? You say there's no God, yet you have no trouble believing in aliens. I don't get it."

"It's not that I *believe* in aliens. They don't need me to believe in them in order to exist. It's a question of probability, Jim. Given the number of stars, the number of planets, they're out there, trust me."

"But what about ghosts? What's the probability that they exist?"

" 'Ghost' is just a word we use to explain something we don't understand."

"Go on."

He smiled. I rarely encouraged him to talk about such things, and I knew that he was grateful for the opportunity. Bringing his hands onto the bar, he looked forward, and, with a goofily serious expression that zapped me right back to one of his trig classes, he ran through some of the various possibilities as he saw them:

What we called ghosts were perhaps glimmers from some other, overlapping dimension, one that we'd one day be able to observe with the proper instruments. Or, possibly, we had conjured the so-called ghosts ourselves, collectively; we were capable, in other words, of somehow externalizing our thoughts, projecting them into what he called a psychic space, and these projections could sometimes be felt or heard with our more traditional sense perceptions. An alternate but related explanation: Ghosts were fractions of personalities, little pieces that had splintered away from a consciousness as pockets of energy. Like little volcanic eruptions of the mind that left invisible lava trails.

I began to feel like he was going out of his way to avoid the most obvious explanation of all, that ghosts were the dead, that they were disincarnate souls. When I pointed this out to him, he admitted it was possible, sure.

"I just have a hard time believing in the everlasting soul, that's my problem," he said. "I guess that's what it boils down to." He laughed. "I was reading recently about a couple who created a pact with each other. Whoever died first, that person would try to relay a message from the other side. As a kind of proof."

"What sort of message?"

"A signal. A word or a phrase or an image."

"Would that be enough to convince you?"

He shrugged. We were quiet for a moment. Then I said, "It's funny but ever since I died, I've—"

He grabbed my arm. "You didn't really die, Jim."

"I did. I was clinically dead."

"That's just a phrase doctors use."

"Correct," I said, not really seeing his point.

"What I mean is, if you'd died, *really* died, then you'd be dead, permanently, you'd be in the ground right now." He ripped a corner off his napkin. "So you can't sit there and tell me you died. I reject the premise of what you're saying."

I'd intended to tell him that ever since I'd died I'd been obsessively reading the stories of those who claimed to have made contact with someone on the other side—in dreams, through visitations—but his interruption had dropped me into an instant foul mood. Perhaps sensing this, my father turned his attention to the television over the liquor shelf.

The bartender wandered over, and I asked if the owner was around tonight. A pained expression edged its way across the guy's knife-sharp face. Ruth Glazer, he reported, was currently in the hospital. She'd been coming down the stairs earlier that afternoon, fallen, and very likely broken her ankle.

"The Dog on Fire," I said.

"You know about the Dog?" he asked, serious-faced.

"Do you believe in it?" my father asked him.

"As a courtesy to all injured parties, I feel that I must say yes."

"So you've never experienced it firsthand, then?" I asked.

"Nope."

"But you know about the recording?" I asked.

"We're all aware of the recording," the bartender said mysteriously, and then hunched forward, shoulders almost meeting his pockmarked cheeks, eyebrows scrunched in thought. "Here's the thing. Personally, I don't think we should mess around with the supernatural stuff. My sister had this good friend growing up, and when they were both in high school the girl got cancer and died. It was terrible. My sister never really got over it. They were super close, and, to be honest, they were both kind of weird girls.

They didn't have any other friends besides each other, and after her friend died, my sister went full Goth, white makeup, black dyed hair, the whole deal. Anyway, a few years ago, my sister starts seeing this psychic, right? And the psychic claims that her dead best friend, cancer girl, is in the room with them and not only that but she wants my sister to know that there's some kind of malevolent spirit that's attached itself to her. To my sister, I mean. This evil spirit, supposedly, is responsible for everything bad that's happened to my sister over the last decade: the car accident, the drugs, the thing with the baby."

"The thing with the baby?" my father asked.

"That's awful," I said.

"Yeah," the bartender said. "It really is. I mean, my sister's doing all right now. She moved back home, and she's got these two cats. She loves the cats, and she's happy."

"Maybe the evil spirit cleanse really worked, then," my father said.

"We're going to rip out the stairs," the bartender said, ignoring him. "When the renovations happen the plan is to just get rid of the stairs and rebuild them from scratch."

I doubted this was going to solve the problem. Whatever was happening on the stairs, I didn't think it could be obliterated with any new construction projects. It didn't live in the wood and the nails, is what I mean.

We finished our drinks, and I led my father down the back hallway toward the bathrooms. We stopped just below the staircase and stared up through its central spiral, the helix of wood spindles. Now that I knew the history of the building, knew that actual people had lived and died here, I was a little less eager to climb up and stand with my back against the wall. I wanted to know if the ghost existed, certainly, but if she did, I didn't want to risk upsetting her.

My father lingered at the bottom for only a few moments before grabbing the handrail and ascending with heavy plods.

"Like this?" he asked, once he was halfway up with his back against the wall, the rail at his butt.

I nodded and joined him there. I imagined her—Clara Lennox—passing right through me, my rib cage, my lungs, my heart. My HeartNet could withstand many stresses, but I doubted it had been lab-tested against any spectral energies. Naturally, I didn't want my father to see how suddenly fearful I'd become, and so I took my place beside him without a word, my palms pressed firmly against the cool plaster.

"What now?" he asked.

"I think we just wait and hope for the best. Or the worst, maybe."

We'd been waiting there, silently, for only a few

minutes when my father grunted, audibly, and popped off the wall. "Did you—?" He stood there and grabbed his left forearm with his right, and for a moment I thought he might be having a heart attack. His expression was difficult to translate. He seemed confused but also concerned—as if he'd just remembered he'd forgotten to turn off the stove before leaving the house.

"Are you all right?" I asked.

My father, I realized, had tears in his eyes. Had I ever seen him cry before now? I tried to remember a time. At his mother's funeral, he hadn't cried. He hadn't cried when his favorite cat got an infection after a fight with another cat and died under his bed. I'd never seen him cry during a movie or from an injury. But here he was, crying on this stairwell. I wasn't embarrassed, but I wasn't proud either. I looked away and pretended not to notice.

Without a word, he began moving down the steps and then walked back down the hallway. I followed. He didn't stop at the bar but continued to the front of the restaurant, scooting past the hostess and moving outside onto the veranda. I was right behind him through the door. When I asked him what was wrong, he shrugged and turned away from me. "I don't know," he said. "I don't know. I don't know."

We were standing by a window, on the other side of which a family of six was eating dinner together at two tables that had been dragged together. I tried to touch my father's shoulder, but he moved away from me.

"Just give me a minute, please," he said.

I jammed my hands in my pockets and stepped back. I stood there quietly, just a few feet away, waiting for him to recover from whatever it was that had just occurred. The evening air was warm, and the frogs and cicadas were screeching from a bank of forlorn trees across the road.

"Sorry," he said finally. "I'll be fine."

"Are you sure?"

He nodded and breathed deeply in and out a few times. I noticed that he was massaging his left forearm. The skin there was red and inflamed, as if he'd been scalded by hot water. I reached for his arm, to inspect it better, but he twisted slightly at the hip, swinging the arm behind his torso. I asked him again what was wrong, and he said it was nothing.

"Your arm," I said. "It's red as hell. Let me see it."

He grimaced. "I squeezed it too hard, it's nothing."

"What happened? Was it the ghost?"

He asked if we could please talk about it in the car, but I ignored him and demanded an explanation.

He shrugged wildly. "I'm not even sure where to begin."

"Try."

He stepped toward me and put his hands on my shoulders. Staring directly into my face, he pulled me into an awkward half-hug, one I instinctively resisted. We Byrd men weren't known for being very affectionate with each other. I couldn't remember the last time my father had tried to hug me like this. When he let me go, my eyes fell to my feet.

"You really didn't see any of it?" he asked. "Honestly?"

"See what?"

He glanced at the window. The family eating dinner there was watching us, and though I pretended not to notice, my father stared right back at them until they looked elsewhere—back at their plates, at each other.

"Come on," my father said, and stepped down off the veranda.

I followed him. He was walking so fast that I would have needed to run to catch up with him. He hustled across the road and stopped only once he'd reached my Sentra in the lot. He stood by the passenger door with his hands resting on top of the car until I clicked the key fob. He was in the seat before I'd even reached my door.

We drove a few miles without talking. On the radio a man with a deep, sonorous voice was interviewing a woman about the recent extinction of a particular species of monkey.

Researchers had preserved its DNA in the event we ever wanted to reintroduce the animal to the earth. My father stared out the window, seemingly disinterested, his left arm across his legs, meaning the red mark was fully visible to me now. I snuck small glances at it as I drove. This wasn't an abstract splotch of red; it had a discernible shape; it was a handprint! A messy one, certainly, but a handprint all the same.

"It was so odd," he said. "I was standing there, my eyes, and I felt something grab hold of me. There was a little pop. Like a champagne cork. A change in pressure. I could hardly breathe. I was still on the stairs, but the stairs were different now. They kept going, in both directions, up and down, forever. Infinitely! I had the strangest sense that I'd always been on those stairs. Some part of me had. Since the beginning of time, maybe. I couldn't decide if this was bad or good. It just *was*."

His voice trailed away, lost under the sea of radio chatter. He'd interrupted the silence so abruptly that I hadn't wanted to distract him by reaching for the radio dial, which I did now.

"So," I said, "you didn't see a ghost, then?"

He turned to me. "I didn't *see* a ghost, no."

"But you felt it. I mean, your arm. What's going on with your arm?"

His eyes fell to his arm. He stared at it as if it didn't belong to him, as if it had just fallen through the sunroof and into his lap. He clearly had no explanation to offer me.

"And where was I during all this?" I asked.

"You were right there. Beside me. You were there the whole time."

"But I didn't see anything. How long did this last?"

"Two seconds? Two minutes? I honestly have no idea."

A ghost on the stairs had reached out for my father, had grabbed his arm, had pulled him into—what? Another dimension. A ghost world. Perhaps I'd blinked at the worst possible moment and missed it. I hadn't been paying attention. I got out my phone and held it over my father's arm for a quick photo but he whipped it away as he realized what I was doing.

When we reached my house, I thought maybe we'd continue our discussion over a glass of wine, but my father said he was heading home. From the front stoop I watched him turn his car around. He waved before pulling onto the gravel road at the end of my driveway. His headlights flickered on the other side of the trees.

The next time I saw Annie I was downtown for a haircut. The streets were packed with people, and for a moment I wondered if I'd forgotten about a festival. But no—a White Hair, jaywalking, had been mowed down by a utility truck and was dead on the road. This was a shopping district, a place to stroll and buy Himalayan salt lamps and watercolor paintings of mountain ranges, a place where nothing unpleasant or obscene was ever supposed to happen. By the time I arrived, the police had already thrown a sheet over the poor woman.

"She couldn't have seen it coming," one morose White Hair said.

"A real sweet lady. She sure didn't deserve this," said another. "Nobody does."

"Somebody should sue that kid, that driver."

"I was here. Were you? I saw the whole thing. He didn't stop at all before he turned right. This is on him."

"Think of her children. Her grandchildren."

A larger woman, who it seemed had nothing at all to do with the accident or the victim, was sitting on a bench and sobbing with a giant half-eaten cookie in her hand. They were shocked, these poor White Hairs, concerned, angry. Death, for them, having already lived so long, was something that occurred in hospice beds, behind closed doors, their bodies full of tubes, not on the street, not in plain view. That one of their own had been struck down prematurely in such a violent way had them on edge. Death could still be unpredictable. It didn't obey any rules, follow any guidelines.

I was on my way to the barber around the corner, but the traffic jam that had formed on the sidewalk was keeping me from getting there. Nobody seemed capable of leaving the scene. The police had taped off an area up ahead, and they were working to disperse the crowd. Their eagerness to move people along only further aroused people's curiosity. The woman's blood was visible on the street. The kid who'd run over the woman was standing by a cop car murmuring his story, a far-off expression on his face. He was maybe twenty years old, and he was wearing a blue short-sleeved collared shirt with the power company's insignia over the pocket. A few of the White Hairs were glaring at him. I heard him called "dumb kid," "idiot," even "motherfucker." They resented him for the death of this woman—and, possibly, for his youth.

Annie emerged from an art gallery across the street. Just a few steps behind her was a bird-boned preteen with straw-colored hair: Fisher, I was sure. The girl had a shopping bag around her wrist, and in her hand was a slim cell phone. When I approached, Annie smiled though she seemed surprised or maybe even embarrassed to see me. I was resolved to be as normal as possible.

"Hello, you," Annie said. "Fisher, this is Jim Byrd."

"Good afternoon, Mr. Byrd," the girl said. "A right fine afternoon we're having, isn't it?"

She said this like a plantation lady, like a character from *Gone with the Wind*. I wasn't sure what to make of this act. Annie gave her a wry look, then smiled. This was some sort of joke between them, I gathered. The way they kept glancing at each other, checking in, the geometry of their bodies, I could tell that they were not just mother and daughter but good friends, too; they were a true pair.

"It's my mom's birthday tomorrow," Annie said, "so we're out gift shopping. We've got nothing. Any suggestions?"

"Well, there's a cigar store around the corner," I said.

"Oh, she'd just love that. You know her so well."

"I wanted to get her a xylophone," Fisher said.

Annie rolled her eyes—not to me but to Fisher. "Grammy wouldn't know a xylophone from a djembe drum, Fisher."

"Plus xylophone *lessons,*" Fisher added.

Annie looked past me, toward the scene of the accident. "Good Lord, is that woman still on the street? What's taking them so long?"

The three of us stared across the road at the crowd, the flashing lights, the lump under the sheet, the blood. The driver, who looked ill, was still standing with the cops. Fisher said she wanted to go over and get a closer look.

"Honey, don't be so morbid," Annie said.

"I'm morbid? You're the one who moved us to the town where all the old people come to die," Fisher said.

I'd never thought of Shula in exactly those terms, but she had a point.

"Well, it's our hometown," was all I could think to say.

"We were born here," Annie chipped in. "It wasn't always like this. Anyway, I don't want to hang here on the sidewalk and gawk. Jim, we're going to lunch. You should join us if you can."

She glanced quickly at her daughter. *Roll with this, please,* her eyes seemed to say. I was inclined to forget my appointment and go with them, but I was uncertain if this was a real invitation. I wasn't sure what to do, what the right move was.

"I don't want to impose," I said.

"You wouldn't be. I promise."

The three of us started walking together, away from the accident. The crowd had thinned out by the end of the block. Fisher wanted a meatball sub, so we ducked into a sandwich shop and sat down at a table near the back. It was midafternoon, almost three, and there were a few White Hairs in the restaurant already ordering dinner. The waitress brought us menus, and Annie excused herself to the bathroom. Fisher sat across from me with her thin arms crossed. We were quiet for a few minutes. She seemed to be studying me.

"So," she said. "What was it like?"

"What was what like?"

"Dying." She leaned forward. "That's you, right? You're Mr. Lazarus, right?"

So, Annie had told her about me, about my heart condition. They'd even given me a nickname. I wanted to interpret this as a positive sign.

"Mom said it was just like a long nap. That true?"

"More or less. I don't remember much."

"Much—or anything at all?"

I didn't want to scare her. She was too young to not believe in anything.

"My friends and I . . ." Fisher began. "Back in Charleston, I mean. We used to do this thing where we'd make each other pass out. It was a game, sort of. You'd stand against a wall, breathe in really fast, cross your arms over your chest, and then everyone else would push really hard against you at the same time. Then, when you breathed out, you'd black out."

"This was a game?"

"It was so fun. You'd only pass out for like three seconds, but you'd feel like you'd been asleep for three days. So weird."

"What was the point of that?"

Fisher shrugged and squeezed some lemon in her water. "We were twelve, so . . ."

And now, only a year later, she was a totally different person? The mind of her twelve-year-old self unknowable, mysterious, inaccessible? I didn't ask her these questions, only nodded with a smile, because I wanted her to like me. She was a very smart girl, that much was clear to me.

She brought out her cell phone, tapped on the screen, and showed me a picture of an orangutan spearfishing. This picture was evidence, according to her, not only of a tool-making intelligence but of the existence of an orangutan soul. For comparison, she next showed me a movie still of Tom Hanks from the movie *Cast Away*, a picture in which he, bearded and emaciated, was holding a spear aloft in his hand. Look into their eyes, Fisher instructed—Tom Hanks's, the orangutan's—and then try to tell me one of them had a soul and the other didn't. I admitted that the orangutan, perched on his rock with a pensive but hopeful sparkle in his dark eyes, did seem rather soulful.

A victor's smile flashed onto Fisher's face.

Our food arrived in red baskets. Annie had been gone for almost ten minutes. When I glanced to the back of the deli, she was striding toward us. She sat down, reached into her rather large purse, and removed a small package of Wet-Naps. She gave one to Fisher and then offered one to me. This—the distribution of the Wet-Naps—was the most maternal gesture I'd yet seen from Annie. The three of us scrubbed our hands at the same time in silence and then set the naps aside on the table.

Annie sat up straight in her chair, which had the effect of increasing the distance between us. Her dress spilled out around her. Her dark hair was tied up in a messy bun, and she tightened a few loose strands across her forehead by tucking them behind her ear. I wanted to clear the air, to know where we stood, and the longer we sat here together, acting like we were just friends, the more miserable and dejected I began to feel. I'd completely lost track of the conversation, I realized then, and when I tuned in again, Fisher was animatedly describing a process by which a brain could be mapped with a computer.

"Well," Annie said, "I'm convinced. Of course orangutans have souls. I mean, why wouldn't they, right?"

She looked over at me, a sandwich half in her hands, and smiled. I tried to smile back, but I was having trouble even seeming pleasant. It occurred to me that Annie had invited me along to eat with them as a way of nudging us toward friendship. I was going to leave this lunch and our texting would stop. We'd run into each other from time to time, surely—in the grocery store, on the street—and we'd be nice and courteous to one another. We'd ask after the other's parents. I'd ask her how things were going at the theater and with Fisher's school, and she'd ask me about my heart and the bank, or maybe just about the bank, since my heart condition was such a personal matter and to mention it would surely conjure in her head an image of the scar on my chest, the scar over which she'd once placed her palm as we made love at the bottom of her bed. One day I'd hear, through a friend, that she'd met someone else and that it was serious and they were maybe getting married, and I'd meet someone else, too, eventually, and somehow, we'd all wind up at dinner together one night, the four of us, and I'd know that it—our friendship—had all started here, on this afternoon, with sandwiches.

At the end of our lunch we emptied our baskets into the trash can. Fisher was the first one through the door and onto the sidewalk. Annie grabbed my elbow to keep me from following her daughter out.

"Hey," she said. "What happened? Where were you?"

"When?"

"I waited by the bathroom for like ten minutes."

"I didn't realize you wanted me to—"

"I gave you the signal." She arched her eyebrows twice. "Didn't you notice?"

I was dumbfounded. The signal? We had a signal? I shook my head mournfully.

"I've barely heard from you since your trip to Charleston," I said. "I thought maybe . . ."

"I've just been busy, that's all." She peered around me, and I turned to see what she was looking at. On the other side of the glass, Fisher stood on the sidewalk, staring at her phone. When I looked back to Annie, she kissed me. Her lips landed a little to the left of my mouth, then slid into place, locking like shuttles in space. The kiss was quick but forceful.

She studied my face for a moment, her eyes narrowing. A smile fluttered, then disappeared. "I'm not sure you really understand what it is you're signing up for. My life isn't my own. This is a big deal."

The bell clanged against the door, and Fisher stepped back into the restaurant, phone in hand, an irritated look on her face. Why on earth were we just standing here like idiots? What was taking us so long? It was time to go.

We pushed our way through the door together, into the sunlight, and were walking down the sidewalk when my phone made a noise in my pocket: Three chimes.

Robert Boyd Lennox

Rarely does he linger at home. He prefers it here, in his furniture store. The good years. The years of plenty. Fatty meals. New suits. He's standing in the middle of the showroom, surrounded by customers. With a plastic but effective smile, Robert extols the virtues of a wingback chair to a big-boned woman with gin on her breath. The time isn't even ten a.m. The woman is teetering. She'll never buy this chair, not in a million years.

What could Clara be doing right now? He can smell her perfume on his shirt. Their two scents have mingled into a single scent. Orange peels in an ashtray, perhaps.

Now it's aftershave he smells—and sweat and wet wool. So many people pressed together, so many coats, so many muddy shoes sliding across the greasy floors of the streetcar. He's a little boy, barely ten, and he and his brother Wendell jingle the change in their pockets as they ride the car to the end of the line, to Shula Park. They shove their way through the Saturday-evening crowds. A twenty-minute wait for the merry-go-round. Robert sits on the monkey, and Wendell claims the elephant. The Wurlitzer organ blares in their ears as they travel.

Out on the lake the motorboats bounce across each other's wake. Everything is so bright! *Electric Park*, people have taken to calling this place. The Southern Power and Light Company supposedly used over eight thousand bulbs to create the spectacle. Wendell says he wants to move here when he grows up. He wants to live in a house right by the roller coaster so he'll get to ride it whenever he pleases. Such a stupid dream but Robert doesn't have the heart to tell him. Eventually even roller coasters would grow boring. Everything bores you eventually. Roller coasters. Girls. Furniture, definitely—

He's locking up the store for the night. Sales are down. Nobody can afford a new couch in times like these. He shuts off the lights in the showroom and goes back to the office. His migraines have returned. His jaw aches. His eyes are like bullet holes. The headaches follow him into his sleep at night. There's no escaping them. Last night Robert dreamed a hot mouth with needle-teeth.

He smokes half a cigarette, stubs it out in the ashtray, and quits the store for home.

In the middle of the road, he waits for a car to pass, his tweed cap pinned under his arm, his right toe at the edge of a large orange mud puddle. A sinkhole straight to hell, no doubt. It would gulp him down. It already has. Sell the house, the house Clara loves so much, or shut down the store—a decision he can't much longer avoid.

A summer day in Shula. Sweat behind his knees. Sweat across his neck. He goes home for lunch. When he yells up the stairs for Clara, she doesn't answer. He only has an hour before he's due back at the store, and Clara promised him she'd stay home so they could talk about last night. He regrets the way he yelled at her. He wants to apologize, so where the hell is she?

In the dining room, he finds his lunch waiting for him, the fork very neatly arranged on the napkin, a ham sandwich expertly prepared and placed on the plate, the ingredients stacked with finesse, the finely sliced cheeses, a wedge of lettuce, two rounds of tomato, and it's obvious to him that she took such care with his lunch only out of spite. Never before has she made him such a picturesque lunch—and anyway, who in the history of the world ever needed a fork for a sandwich?

Such a strange girl, Clara, always flitting about the house in search of something, always speaking to the dog with that inexplicable fake Cockney accent. Now, to top it all off, she's convinced herself the stairs are haunted. Sometimes, as she descends, she hears a voice.

The dog senses it, too, she says. Always the dog is lingering there on the steps, barking.

Is this the same girl he fawned over for so many years? The girl whose very touch used to make every single cell in his body vibrate with nervous joy? The girl who very nearly married his brother Wendell? The girl who tapped on the glass late one night at the furniture store, drenched in rain, to tell him that she'd marry him after all?

Clara, her dress clinging wetly to her skin, is tapping on the store glass. She's carrying no umbrella, and she's soaking wet. After unlocking the door, he brings her inside and sits her down in a chair. He doesn't care if the chair gets wet; he only wants her to be comfortable. In the office he finds a spare shirt and offers it to her as a towel. She thanks him and then gives him her answer. She's decided she would like to marry him—that is, if he's still interested. He grabs her hands and kisses each tiny white knuckle.

They drive straight over to her house, where they announce the big news to her family. Her parents, who were just about to climb into bed, are so elated they open a bottle of wine that they've been saving for years, pouring just a little bit into all those glasses. To our new son, Mr. Hopstead keeps shouting. To our new son!

Clara's parents already have three sons, plus Clara and her sister, May, all of whom sit in the kitchen, sipping wine and tossing a red rubber ball to each other, one sibling to the next. Robert can make no sense of their game, can detect no logic in it. They do not toss the ball to him. Whatever is happening, he is not a part of it. He hears the ball bounce against the floor behind him, but when he turns, it's already in the hands of Clara's oldest brother. It rattles the plates on the cabinet shelf when it strikes a door.

Wedding planning commences almost immediately, despite the hour, and at the end of the night Clara's mother insists that Robert sleep on the green Dutch sofa in the living room. She brings out two blankets and a pillow for him and makes sure he's settled before leaving him. For a long time he lies there in the darkness, listening to the house's peculiar noises, its creaks and pops. At the far corner of the ceiling is a brown spidery stain, split with cracks. The tub, he realizes. The crack is directly below the bathroom.

He's almost asleep when he hears footsteps on the stairs in the hall. Clara pads into the room noiselessly and slips under his blanket. Her hand over his mouth, they make love for the first time, and when it's over she kisses him on the forehead and disappears to her own bed, upstairs. Robert stares up at the ceiling again, at that spidery crack, at the bulge of the plaster, marveling at this sudden change of events. Three weeks ago Clara told him she couldn't possibly marry him—and now this.

The next morning he drinks the Hopsteads' weak coffee and returns to work, whistling as he enters the building. His father is so distracted—where are last week's orders?—that he doesn't notice his son's good mood or the fact that he hasn't changed shirts since yesterday. Robert considers calling his brother, he even picks up the phone to do so, but decides against it. He will write Wendell a letter instead, explaining what has transpired. But once he has the nib of the pen against the paper, he isn't sure what, really, he can say that will help his brother understand what has happened between him and Clara. In the showroom a customer is waiting, clapping his thighs impatiently. Robert drops the pen back into the drawer and slides it shut. The letter can wait. There's time for that. Wendell is thousands of miles away. Robert owes him nothing.

That sandwich again. Such a ridiculously perfect sandwich. If he wasn't so hungry, he'd toss the meal in the trash, just to show her how little he cares, how little he needs her, but unfortunately his stomach is growling and unfortunately he needs her and cares about her very much.

He's about to take his first bite when he hears the front door open and close. He stands—but then sits again. Yes, he will remain seated. No sense in seeming too eager. He will wait here at the table. Clara can come to *him*. But it's a deep, timorous voice that calls his name from the other room.

Walking into the parlor, it's Mr. Hopstead he sees. Clara's father is an honest man, hard-working, but he's also a borderline simpleton, incurious, with an inflexible sense of right and wrong that, irritatingly, has little to do with the way life is actually lived. If not for Clara, Robert wouldn't have much to do with a man like this.

Mr. Hopstead wants to have a conversation with Robert, he says, a little chat about last night's fight, but Robert shakes his head. He's not in the mood for a conversation such as that, not with Mr. Hopstead, and besides, he already knows what Mr. Hopstead will have to say, that Clara is a sensitive girl, that she offends easily, that what's required with her is a more delicate approach.

Robert asks Mr. Hopstead to please stay uninvolved. He has his hand on his father-in-law's back, and he's guiding him toward the door, but the man comes to a full stop, refusing to be moved. "Every man has his demons," Mr. Hopstead says, "and the trick is learning to keep them locked up inside yourself." With that, the man goes out through the door and stomps away down the steps into the cold.

• • •

His wedding night. He and Clara have married at last, and the reception at his parents' house has come to an end. The guests are slowly making their exit.

"Be good to her," Mr. Hopstead tells Robert, squeezing his hand before setting off into the cold night.

Of course Robert will be good to her! He loves her more than life itself!

The house is a mess, but Robert's mother says to leave it for the morning. Clara follows Robert up the stairs to his bedroom. He shuts the door quietly and, not wanting to seem too eager, waits a moment before turning to her. But she's looking out the window, working on her buttons. What's she thinking about? When he slides out of his suit jacket and folds it over the chair, he hears a few rice kernels tick against the hardwood. The floors out in the hall creak as his parents turn in for bed. A door shuts. Muffled voices. "I'm exhausted," he hears his father say.

Robert removes his tie and his socks and his shirt. Clara waits for him in the bed with what seems to him a somewhat sullen expression on her face. Buyer's remorse? They are in his room at his parents' house, and even though they're married now, with no need to worry about being discovered, Robert reminds her they should probably keep as quiet as possible. Under the sheet, her skin is soft and cool against his. He slides on top of her, and she has her hands on his shoulders, her mouth a tight line, a slight hint of a smile.

Afterward, as he tries to fall asleep, his stomach feels swollen, achy. Maybe he ate too much cake. Maybe he danced too much. He doesn't want to pass gas, not with Clara right there beside him. How do other couples manage these situations? What if she's still awake and she hears him?

He slips out of bed, his feet meeting the cold floor, and dashes into the hallway, where he very quietly passes gas outside his parents' door. The floor pops beneath his feet, and his father's face appears in the crack.

"Is something wrong?" he asks, stepping into the hall. "God, Robert, that smell!"

He tells his father good night and returns to bed. He still can't sleep. Will he ever be able to again? They'll need their own house. Eventually. Soon. They can't stay here forever, with his parents. They need to be on their own.

At the top of a small hill on a quiet street it waits for them: a two-story brick house, built in the Queen Anne style, with an extraordinarily large veranda, painted white, ornamented with reliefs and balustrades. The window eaves protrude like the puffed eyelids of a man who hasn't slept in days. A small garden in the front yard is protected by a low wrought-iron fence. Two blocks away, there's a small community park.

He asks Clara if she likes it.

She pulls him close and kisses his cheek. "It's beautiful."

The house on Graham Street was built four years ago when a hundred-acre parcel north of downtown was divided and sold off as lots for middle- and upper-class families. A brand-new suburb with its very own streetcar stop. Not too far from the furniture store so Robert will be able to walk to and from work.

He leads her inside for her next surprise. In the dining room, he reveals a beautiful oak table. In the sitting room (*Tada!*), a green Dutch sofa, identical to the one at her parents' house. The staircase is at the back of the house, next to the kitchen, and he leads her up to the bedroom and reveals their new bed. Down the hall, he informs her, are two more bedrooms. (*Just in case.*) She flings herself onto the bed, rolls over, giggles. Robert can't remember ever feeling this happy and hopeful, but at the outer fringes of this happiness it still lurks, that mouth-filled face, so many needle-teeth, broken, wet, waiting to grind at his ears.

No matter where he goes, the mouth finds him. Even on the merry-go-round in Shula Park with his brother, he senses it's near. Under the pond, it swims, waiting to swallow up the skiers.

Over eight thousand lightbulbs! Robert wonders whose job it is to replace the lights. What a job that would be, the keeper of the bulbs, screwing and unscrewing one after the next, all day long. Wendell calls over to him from the line in front of the roller coaster, and Robert runs over to join him. As they stand there, hands jammed into their pockets, the strangest thought pops into Robert's head—that he's done this before, stood in this very line with his younger brother, a thousand times. But no, that's not quite it. It's not that he's already done it; it's that he's *always* been doing it. He's never not been in this line.

He's never not been walking down this hallway either. Everywhere he goes, it's the same. That feeling of déjà vu.

Robert follows a nurse to his appointed room, an austere but comfortable space with two twin beds, a writing desk, a small hanging closet, and a single window. Robert doesn't intend to be here very long. Just a few days, he promised Clara before leaving for Atlanta. He drops his suitcase on the opposite bed and stares out the window, to the lawn, where two bald men are sitting in Adirondack chairs. A knock at the door: it's Robert's cousin, Hal Skinner, a psychiatrist. They shake hands, and Hal encourages him to sit down while they determine, together, a regimen that might get Robert back in working order again. Talk-therapy sessions, swims in the pond, and a few ceramics classes in the art house?

Clara comes into the bedroom with a dog in her arms.

"Who's is that?"

"Ours." She smiles.

Why on earth? he thinks.

Why now? he thinks.

The last thing they need.

What the hell is she thinking?

All their problems, and she's adopted a dog.

"His name is Houdini," she tells him delightfully, pressing her lips to his hairy nape.

The dog, halfway up the stairs, is barking again.

Clara is out for the morning. Robert quiets the dog and listens for a few minutes. He doesn't hear a voice. Of course not. Clara's always had such a powerful imagination. The house is only four years old, and the previous owners moved to Raleigh, so how could it be haunted?

Clara, her right hand tight over his mouth, gazes down at Robert for a few seconds and then shuts her eyes, head tilting backward. They're on the green Dutch sofa in the Hopstead living room. The crack in the ceiling bulges like a face. He reaches up for her. Her arms are goose-bumped. The house is cold. He throws his arms around her back, feels her spine.

So he's troubled, is that it? Melancholic? Is there a word for what he is? His cousin says not to worry over labels. Robert hates to be away from home, away from Clara, but he needs his rest.

A nurse compels him to spend an entire afternoon sitting in an Adirondack chair near the pond. The "innervating sunlight," she calls it. The sun strikes the left side of his face as he rolls another cigarette. The arm of his chair is smudged black. Down the grassy hill, at the edge of the pond, a man in a gray sweater is screaming at the geese. A nurse carrying a tray of teas rushes over to help this poor man. Robert closes his eyes and rotates his face so that the sunlight falls more evenly upon it.

"There you are," his cousin Dr. Skinner says, walking up from behind with his hands in the pockets of his white coat.

Robert lights his cigarette.

Despite the protestations of the nurse, the man at the pond will not stop screaming at the geese. The geese are villains. Are miscreants. Thieves. Demons. Robert and his cousin watch the nurse struggle to subdue the man, who won't shut up about the goose poop on his shoe.

"I think the geese might have robbed that man,"

Robert says. "Or murdered his parents, maybe. He really has it out for those geese."

"That's our Mr. Croft. Arrived here yesterday. He caught his wife with another man and stabbed the poor guy in the eye with a screwdriver."

Robert wonders if maybe the man shouldn't be in jail.

"Probably," Hal says. "But he's got money. Lots of it. I think he paid off the wife's lover to keep it quiet and then he checked himself in here. He says he's had some sort of breakdown."

Robert nods, disinterestedly.

"Well, I've come to send you home, Robert. It's time."

"That's your professional advice?"

"It is. Clara will be glad to have you. You can always return. Door's open. You know that."

"Six months from now, I won't be able to afford this place. Clara doesn't understand what's happening, Hal. I've shielded her from it, which in retrospect maybe wasn't the best idea. She lives in a dream world. In that house all day. With the dog. We're going to lose the house, Hal."

"Clara understands more than you think, Robert. You'll be fine. Even if you lose the house. Anyway you can't hide here forever hoping it will all blow over."

Robert stubs out his cigarette on the arm of the chair and flicks it away into the grass. The man at the edge of the pond is quiet now. The nurse is patting his back as if he's a baby in need of a burp.

"What you're going through, this isn't just about the store," Hal says. "You do understand that, I hope."

Driving by the store, he sees that they've already repainted over the name on the brick above the door. History will forget Lennox & Sons. Will forget the Lennoxes. Will forget them all. It was all for nothing, all that hard work, all the hand-wringing and desperation. He shouldn't have hung on for as long as he did. Better to know when you're beat. The showroom sits dark and empty. He wonders what his father would think of this development, if it would kill him all over again. A legacy destroyed, he can imagine his father saying.

His father: Such a controlling man. So irascible. Temperamental. Unadaptable.

But the desire to impress his father, that never goes away, not quite. He's nineteen years old. The ice truck arrives midday, and the delivery-man drops a large block of ice into the metal wash-bin in the middle of the showroom. In front of the dripping block, Robert sets up a GE oscillating loop-handle fan, which, as it happens, Lennox & Sons keeps in stock. Not only will it cool customers on this hot August day, but it might even help them sell a few fans. This demonstration was all Robert's idea. He's helping a customer when his father strides into the store from his neighborhood business association meeting. Passing through the showroom, his father doesn't even seem to notice the four people who have huddled around the fan, the four people who surely would have left the store already if not for this attraction.

When his father emerges from his office an hour later, a little bit of mustard at the corner of his mouth, he walks over to the half-melted ice block and then looks over at Robert, who's doing his best not to seem too pleased with himself.

"We'll have a hard time selling this fan if people see that it's already been used," his father says. "Now we'll have to discount it as a floor model."

"I thought it would keep people in the store if they weren't sweating through their clothes."

"It'll keep 'em, but it won't keep the sort we want."

He unplugs the fan from the wall and moves it aside.

"Get this bucket out of here before it starts leaking," his father says.

Houdini won't budge off the stairs again. Robert swats at him with a newspaper until the dog finally runs off in search of Clara, in search of scraps.

Robert will have to close the store. There's no getting out of it. It must be done.

"Don't be mad," Clara says, "but I think you should call your brother."

"You'd love that, wouldn't you?"

"Why would I love that?"

She reaches for his hand, but he moves it away.

"I'm not calling him."

"He might be able to help. It's like you said, about weathering the storm. Maybe he could help you weather it. It's his name on the building, too, after all."

Robert says, "Wendell doesn't give a damn about the business and he never has."

They're on the sofa in the sitting room. It's almost time for bed. He picks up the book he was reading but then puts it down on his lap again.

"Have you been talking to him? Be honest!"

"To Wendell? Please. I'm not answering that."

"So you have then!"

"I'm not answering because I don't like what it is you're implying."

He and Clara are on the green Dutch sofa—the other one, the one in her parents' house—and her knees are tight on either side of him. She closes her eyes, and her head rolls back. Up above, in the darkness, the ceiling bulges, hideously. The whole house will collapse one day. It's falling apart all around them. Is she marrying him to escape all this? Does it matter? She stifles his moan with her hand, kisses his forehead, and leaves him on the couch. The ceiling bulge darkens, spidering outward. It's found him again. The mouth, wetly, eats at the corners of the room.

The plaster, a cereal mash.

The timbers, cracked and splintering.

He's smoking yet another cigarette upstairs in his chair by the window. The dog, Houdini, is asleep in his lap. His suitcase is half-packed on the bed. The gauzy white window curtain, whirled about by the fan on the dresser, floats across Robert's left arm. He can see down to the street below where a man in a wide white hat is hurrying along with long rolled papers under his arm, construction drawings maybe. Not far behind him, two women walk arm-in-arm in dresses with puffed-out shoulders and large belts around their waists.

"Robert, please," Clara says, coming into the room. "Don't leave again."

She is wearing a loose floral dress with a wide white collar and large white buttons. He's never seen this dress, though it couldn't possibly be new. How would she have bought it? Her brown hair is cut short, chin-length, one side held back with a little white clip. She's been crying. The dog's eyes blink open and then close again.

She asks him if it's something that she said, if that's why he's leaving her again for Atlanta. She's pleading with him. She just wants to understand why this is happening.

"Money's in the hutch," he says. "Don't forget the bills this time."

She's crying now.

"If anyone asks," he continues, "my brother isn't well, and that's why I'm gone. I'm visiting Wendell in California."

He glances at the suitcase on the bed and explains, for what seems like the hundredth time, that he just needs rest. He rolls another cigarette. Clara moves behind the chair and begins to delicately massage his temples, but he grabs her wrists and drags her out from behind the chair to his side. Clara's face contorts, reddens. She twists free of him.

"Fine, go," she says. "But I won't be here when you get back. I swear to God I won't be here if you leave again!"

She disappears through the door. Distantly he hears her footsteps on the stairs. The smoke puffs up over his head, a small storm cloud that he considers thoughtfully. The dog, hot against his legs, yawns up at him. Stringed saliva between the teeth. Long white teeth flecked brown. The ribbed dark palate. That mouth, it always finds him, wherever he goes.

A creak on the stairs. The dog leaps from Robert's lap and runs out the door. Two seconds later he's barking. Robert goes into the hall. The dog is on the staircase again, his nose jammed against a wall, growling. What a peculiar creature. Robert yells at him to please shut up, but Houdini keeps at it, yapping at the wall.

"There's nothing there!"

Irritated, Robert goes back into his room and falls back into his chair. His head is throbbing again. His suitcase, on the bed, needs packing. It can wait. Everything can wait. The curtain, flitting in the breeze, continues its flirtation with the end of his cigarette.

II

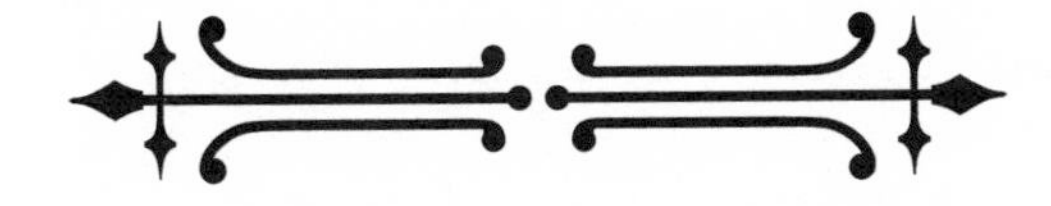

A Partial Existence

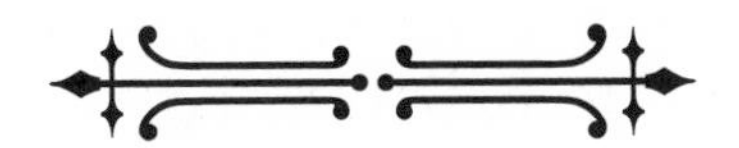

The most beautiful drive-up vista in the Blue Ridge Mountains is located just a few miles outside Shula on a mountain highway that overlooks our city. That's not just according to me but also to various vista-ranking websites and glossy magazines bankrolled by chambers of commerce. The overlook is a popular destination, especially in the fall when the leaves begin to change, and finding a parking space can be difficult.

On a whim, Annie and I bought a pint of orange juice and a cheap bottle of champagne at the BI-LO and drove up there one Saturday morning to mark the occasion of our one-year anniversary. Only as we were getting out of the car did we realize we'd forgotten to bring any glasses. I suggested we drive back down the highway to the gas station. Annie popped the champagne, took a swig from it, and then chased it with the OJ.

"Just as good," she said.

We passed the bottle and the orange juice back and forth between us as we took in the view. A group of White Hairs, standing near their cars with their camera-phones, looked at us disapprovingly. The men were wearing knee-length shorts and pastel golf shirts. The women were dressed in capris and hiking shorts, their hair dyes nearly as brilliant as the leaves: glossy browns, burnt siennas, cherry reds, platinum blonds.

"We're celebrating," I shouted over to them.

They pretended not to hear me.

"You don't care what they think, do you?" Annie asked me.

"I don't think we're supposed to be drinking up here."

Annie laughed. "You're joking, right? Oh my God, you're not." She hooked her arm in mine. "Honey, you've got to lighten up."

Annie and I had married only a few months after our reunion at the restaurant. There were those who said we were rushing things, but we didn't care. We wanted to be together. We needed to be. When I wasn't near her, I felt bisected, incomplete. Only now that we were together did I fully understand how lonely I'd been before her. A big black hole of loneliness nipped at my heels, and hers was the hand—long-fingered, soft—that kept me from wobbling back into it.

Rather than having a traditional ceremony—it was her second, after all—we'd said our vows in the sheriff's office at the courthouse. The only people in attendance, other than the sheriff, were

Fisher and our parents. To celebrate, Annie and I had flown to the Dominican Republic for a long weekend and stayed in a beach resort where they delivered breakfast on a tray each morning to our cabana.

I sold my ramshackle country house, and together we bought a two-story colonial within walking distance of her parents' place. The neighborhood was a relatively new one—two rows of homes on a southeast-facing hillside. Our yard was partly wooded, full of rhododendron and mountain laurel, the soil rocky and rooted. At the bottom of our driveway was a small stone koi pond, though by the end of our third month there, hawks had eaten all the fish and I hadn't bothered to restock it again.

We'd picked this particular neighborhood in case Fisher ever wanted to visit with her grandparents after school, though she hardly ever availed herself of the opportunity. She preferred the solitude of her own bedroom—her post-apocalyptic young adult novels, her crystal-growing kits, her new electric bass. We hadn't suggested the instrument to her because, really, what parent suggests the electric bass over the guitar or violin? I initially feared her choice indicated some deficit in her character: a self-confidence gap, an inferiority complex, but when we asked her why she'd picked it, she explained that her new best friend, a girl named C-Mac (whom Annie and I didn't care for) had already taken up the guitar and together they were going to form an all-girl band, an idea that seemed reasonable enough to me and so I bought her a Fender.

Annie had settled into her new job as the outreach coordinator—and sometime director—at Thrill Arts!, a small but determined theater in Shula. Six weeks out of the year her life revolved around rehearsals, and the rest of the time she incubated (her word) arts-based programs in homeless shelters, detention centers, and prisons. The first program she created was a playwriting workshop for mostly well-behaved inmates at the Department of Corrections forty-five minutes outside of town.

In many ways, she was ideally suited for such a job. Annie was in no way a diminutive or meek woman. Brassy, her mother called her, not always affectionately. At times, it was true, she could be loud and overbearing. Brutally honest, too. I once heard her tell a friend, over the phone, to dump a guy because the way he'd behaved after missing just about every Trivial Pursuit question strongly indicated to her that he was not only an idiot but also a sore loser. After staking out a position on something, Annie didn't tend to back down. But she was also thoughtful and patient and lived according to a very simple maxim—that she treat all people fairly and with compassion. And so it was that, twice a week, she'd drive out to the prison and help prisoners work through their problems by writing and table-reading one-acts.

The White Hairs were big supporters of the arts, generally, but when it came to theater, they mostly craved the typical fare—somewhat stale but eager productions of *Our Town*, *Rent*, *My Fair Lady*, and *Oklahoma!* (or any other play that ends with an exclamation point)—but Annie was committed to pushing back against that trend and staging more challenging and controversial works.

The first show she decided to direct she picked as a response to what was happening in the news. When the state legislature introduced an anti-abortion bill, Annie decided to stage a play called *Sky Writers*, which, despite its la-la title, is a gritty drama about a young girl's decision whether to have an abortion after being raped by her second cousin. Her life unfolds in both scenarios—the one in which she goes through with the abortion and the one in which she doesn't—each playing out in alternating scenes, and suffice it to say, the life in which she keeps the baby is far more difficult and degrading for all parties, baby included.

The politics of the play were fairly transparent, though its production set off far less controversy than Annie had hoped it might. Attendance was low, and the local paper didn't even pick up on the fact that she'd chosen the play as a direct provocation to the state legislature. Annie was disappointed. Short of taking to the stage and setting herself on fire, she wasn't sure what would agitate people enough to care about theater or politics. Her job, as she saw it, was to improve a world that didn't necessarily want to be improved.

The first year of our marriage was a happy and chaotic blur: new sheets, paint crews, bass lessons, shared calendars. There were meetings to attend, grocery store runs to make, emails to answer, emails to ignore. There was a trip to Atlanta for a friend's wedding, a day on a motorboat on the lake with friends, an afternoon at the hospital with my mother as she waited for a biopsy, a jaunt to the outlet mall to buy three new pairs of unpleated khakis in slightly different shades. There was bronchitis, then a stomach bug, an appointment with the doctor, a weekend of bedrest, a round of antibiotics, a round of probiotics, diminishment, replenishment. There was personal grooming to consider: nails to clip, teeth to brush, weight to lose, abs to define, new regimens, diets, pills with curious side effects, shampoos that promised thicker, more lustrous hair. There were firsts: Nutella banana waffles (Fisher's favorite), tractor pulls, cocktails with orange peel swirls, holographic whirling dervishes swirling through an old Masonic Temple repurposed as a church.

Business was the broom that helped sweep away any concerns or questions too grand or alarming. I buried myself in the everyday, in its many wonderful, stupid demands and distractions.

Annie and I were grateful to have found one another. We told each other this constantly. Reconnecting with Annie had given my life—that is to say, the *story* of my life—a pleasing symmetry. Life doesn't require or encourage such neatness, I realize, but we can only remember so much about ourselves and our stories.

We sat down on a large rock below the vista parking area to chat and sip. The champagne bottle, almost empty, was in a crook of the rock a few feet below us.

"What are you thinking about right now?" she asked me.

"I'm thinking how badly I need to pee."

"Just pee down there. Over the side."

"I can wait."

"I'm too drunk to drive," she said. "What about you?"

"Another twenty minutes, I should be fine."

"We didn't plan this out very well. We should have come in a taxi."

Someone cleared his throat above us, and we both turned to look up. A police officer was standing there, haloed in sunlight, his face so shadowed I couldn't distinguish any of his features.

"Hello," Annie said. "Can we help you?"

"You can't be drinking here," he said nasally.

Annie shook the orange juice at him. *"This?"*

The officer said nothing. I think he was sizing us up.

"We're not bothering anyone," Annie said.

"I could write you both tickets."

"For drinking orange juice?" Annie said.

I could see the top of the green champagne bottle below my feet—but could the officer? He asked us to please step up into the parking area, and once we did that, he requested our licenses. Annie groaned audibly.

"We haven't done anything wrong," she said.

The officer said nothing, only waited.

I pulled my license from my wallet and gave it to him. He clipped it to the top of his pad and wrote me a ticket on the spot. Annie didn't have her license with her, and for a moment the officer seemed uncertain of what he wanted to do. Then he let her off with a warning.

Twenty yards away, the White Hairs were pretending not to watch us as they fumbled with their binoculars and camera-phones. Probably they were the ones who'd called us in. Didn't they have anything better to do? After the officer was gone, we got into our car and sat there quietly for a few minutes. I started the car. I had the ticket in my hand. Annie grabbed it from me and dug around for a pen from the center console.

"It's paper," she said.

"Yes it is."

"First anniversaries are paper gifts." She smiled and drew a giant heart on the ticket. "I'm going to frame this and put it on my wall at work."

"Well, happy anniversary, I guess."

I merged the car onto the highway. I was fully sober now, and though our earlier giddiness was draining out of me, I was still in a fine mood. Annie was so proud of the ticket, and her enthusiasm was contagious.

Still, too much happiness could be dangerous. Because whenever I felt too happy, inevitably I would begin to wonder if the happiness was real. If any of this was real. I would begin to wonder if maybe I wasn't still sprawled in the parking garage, a gash in my forehead, my heart unable to sustain me, my thoughts, my very being. Instead of being resuscitated, I'd simply died. There'd been no surgery, no HeartNet, and everything that had happened to me since then had occurred in the space of a millisecond, my last, a fireworks finale of synapses. All that I'd shared with Annie, with my parents, with Fisher, all of it was a very odd though mostly pleasant dream—a heaven, perhaps—a farewell gift from my oxygen-starved brain, a movie of my own creation that was playing out before I tumbled away into oblivion.

The expansion to Su Casa Siempre had never happened. The restaurant had not renovated its second floor. Despite my having approved the loan, Ruth had dropped the project altogether. She wrote me an email, a few weeks later, to thank me for my efforts but offered little explanation for the change of heart, except to say that she was feeling overworked and ready for a change of pace.

The restaurant closed its doors soon thereafter, and the place sat empty for a number of months. I'd drive by on my way to work some mornings and wonder about the staircase, about the Lennoxes, about what had happened to my father. Then, one morning, a large white sign appeared in the front window:

THE BIZBY GROUP
BUILDING FOR LEASE

The Bizby Group was the parent company for Bizby Development and Bizby Property Management, both of which were helmed by Wilson Bizby. King White Hair, we called him, as his company was responsible for at least half of the gated retirement communities in Shula. They also owned and managed about a dozen commercial properties. I'd worked with Mr. Bizby on a number of projects over the years. He was a smart investor, a trustee on a dozen boards, a man accustomed to people's undivided attention and respect. The round, stylish glasses on his face were the frames of an eccentric architect, frames that served sartorially, it seemed to me, to offset the more traditional brass-buttoned blazers and pleated khakis he often wore. He spoke to people as if everything he said might somehow wind up in a *Wall Street Journal* profile of his genius and financial acumen. He'd once told me, at a lunch, that with enough money you could be a hundred times more effective than any dumbass saint. Dumbass saints, he said, were the ones handing out ice cream at the hospital.

"Call me crazy," he'd said, "but I'd rather build my own hospital and stick my name on it. If you want to do any good in this world, if you want to make any real difference, you've got to do some bad first. That's just how it works. Anyone with enough power and money to do long-lasting good has most definitely had some—shall we say—less meritorious dealings to get where he is. Or if he hasn't done them personally, somebody else has for him. It's as simple as that.

"When I die, I intend to leave my kids an incredible amount of money. They'll be able to do whatever they want. If they want to spend their whole lives working with cleft palate babies, then so be it, that's their right and they'll be able to do that because they'll have security. Or maybe they'll be developers, but developers with real vision and sway, and they'll improve Shula and make everyone's lives better. Or they'll start their own businesses and bring more jobs to town, which really is the best kind of good you can do. And if I've given them the opportunity to do all that good, then doesn't that reflect back on me? Haven't I, by extension, also done some good myself? Am I not investing a little equity of my own in those future good works?"

I'd understood his logic but also sensed that, fundamentally, he was wrong. There was no such thing as an equity stake in goodness, was there? He was an imposing man, born into his money, not the sort of person you wanted to argue with in a town as small as ours.

I ran into him at a meeting a few weeks after seeing his sign in the restaurant window and remarked to him that I'd noticed it. At first he didn't seem to understand which property I was referring to. Twice he asked me to repeat the address.

"The restaurant on Graham Street," he said finally. "That old, ugly house, sure. What about it?"

I couldn't really imagine mentioning a ghost to a man such as him, so all I said was, "That property has an interesting history."

"Yes, well, most of them do," he said dismissively.

Later that night, when I reported this encounter to Annie, she puffed her cheeks and jutted out her chin in imitation of Wilson Bizby. " 'Most of them do, Mr. Byrd, most of them do. Most of them do.' "

Bizby was on the board at Thrill Arts!, and Annie had butted heads with him near the beginning of her tenure when he'd tried (and failed) to mandate that all future productions first be approved by the board itself.

"That guy still hates me," she said now. "If I was a man and I'd stood up to him, he'd respect me. But I'm a woman so I open my mouth, and I'm automatically a bitch. He thinks I don't know my place. How dare I raise my tiny woman's voice to the great Wilson Bizby, you know?"

"His CFO is a woman."

"That means nothing, Jim."

She was right, of course, and I regretted mentioning it. I had no desire to defend Mr. Bizby—to her or to anyone else.

Annie was removing her makeup in the mirror over the dresser. She glanced back at me with a wry expression. "I hope he chokes on a chicken bone."

I nodded and continued stripping the socks from my feet.

"If you told him there was a ghost on the property," she said, "do you think he'd then be obligated—legally, I mean—to disclose that to any potential leasers?"

She was joking, mostly, but then again it did seem like a piece of information worthy of disclosure. After all, the ghost was sort of a liability.

Annie and I hadn't talked much about the house or the Lennoxes in the year since our wedding, though not because we'd lost interest. We'd simply been too distracted with each other, with the merger of our lives and families.

Annie's parents were not particularly warm or expressive people. Annie assured me that they were grateful to have me as a son-in-law, though I never would have known it. Conversations around their dinner table were safe, uninteresting, and uneventful. In the beginning I suspected this as a performance for my sake—*don't scare off the new guy*—but after a year I'd yet to hear anyone raise their voice or say anything of much consequence. It was only in the car, after our get-togethers, that Annie would decode the banter for me.

"Did you notice how mad Mom was at me?" she'd ask.

"She was mad?"

"Seething. She didn't make eye contact with me once the whole meal."

"I missed that. Why is she upset?"

"The way Fisher dresses." Annie rolled her eyes. "The way I *let* her dress."

"Does she dress provocatively?"

"According to Mom, she does."

Lee Anne Creel, Annie's mother, was a retired special education teacher, a very mannered Southern lady with drooping cheeks and dark red lipstick that crossed the border of her lips by a mile. Her idea of a fun afternoon was a trip to the Stein Mart for new jewelry and flower vases and giant shoe baskets. She practically worshipped Annie's older brother, Kurt, who lived in New York and hardly ever came home. Always Lee Anne was telling me about something profound Kurt had once said or something amazing he'd done or planned to do one day. Her love for Kurt, I came to see, had prevented her from developing a real relationship with Annie. Distracted by her son, Lee Anne didn't appreciate what Annie had to offer. The way she talked about Annie sometimes gave me the impression that she considered her daughter as a bit of a screwup, as a not-very-serious person. Presumably this had something to do with Annie having been pregnant at nineteen years old, though Annie's interest in the theater might have also contributed to this sentiment. This blindness toward Annie's good qualities predisposed me to not liking Lee Anne very much, though this wasn't a subject I ever would have tried to discuss openly with my mother-in-law. We lived in the South, after all.

Charlie Creel, on the other hand, was a very protective father—and very adoring, too. Abbott, he called Annie, as in Abbott and Costello. He owned three gas stations in town. He was a quiet man, who preferred the solitude of his recliner chair to any after-dinner conversation. The only books he'd ever read, or so he proudly claimed, were the Bible and a biography of Ben Hogan, the golfer. The two of us were friendly with each other, but I had no illusion that we'd ever truly be close.

As for my parents, Annie liked my father, generally, even though he'd given her a B-plus in trigonometry when what she'd really deserved was "at least an A-minus." This she'd once offered to him as a joke, not long after the wedding, but my father, misinterpreting the spirit of the remark, had failed to laugh or even shrug amicably and had instead offered a very solemn apology before explaining that, if given the choice, he would have done away with the alphabetical grading scale altogether and adopted a pass/fail system. Later Annie told me she found my father a tad too self-serious, a little goofy, but basically sweet-natured, which I realized even then described me about as well as him.

Annie's relationship with my mother, however, was more strained. In fact, ever since learning that my mother had once, about a decade earlier, protested an abortion clinic, Annie had gone out of her way to avoid unnecessary contact. When I pointed out that (a) Annie's parents were Baptist and also opposed to abortion at any stage of fetal development and that (b) protesting clinics was the sort of thing Annie herself might have done as a teenager, she countered that (a) her parents were religious, granted, but not in such a gross, in-your-face way and that (b) she'd never once protested a clinic, for the record, and even if she had, the comparison would be invalid since my mother had been in her forties at the time and therefore old enough to know better. You could blame a middle-aged woman but not a teenager, in other words, for having extreme views on God.

Navigating the maze of religious and political thought in the South, especially in a mountain town full of locals, transplanted retirees, and a small enclave of hipsters, was a challenge for us all. The only reliable way of remaining inoffensive and on good terms with most people was to never discuss such topics at all. No politics or religion at the dinner table—or anywhere else, for that matter.

Regardless, I understood Annie's reasons for not wanting to make nice with my mother, and I never complained, as long as they remained cordial. I might have even inadvertently encouraged the divide between them with the jokes I often told at my mother's expense. All my anecdotes about her added up to a somewhat absurd composite. The stories we tell about people (and ourselves, for that matter) only suggest them, only offer a hazy outline. In telling Annie only that about my mother that was strangest, darkest, and funniest, I feared I might have given her if not a wrong impression then at least an incomplete one. My mother could be narrow-minded and combative, absolutely, and her religious beliefs, rooted as they were in shame and fear, sometimes veered into *700 Club* levels of xenophobia, prejudice, and blind self-righteousness. But my mother, it should be noted, was also capable of profound sweetness and generosity. She'd give you her left leg if she thought it would help you run better, was how my father used to put it.

Fortunately my mother seemed to approve of my marriage to Annie, though I wasn't sure if that was because she liked Annie personally or because she was just happy to see me settled down, and in our hometown, no less. More than anything she wanted grandkids.

"You're young," she'd say. "There's still plenty of time!"

What I hadn't told my mother—because it wasn't any of her business—was the fact that Annie was set against having any more children.

I'd known this going into the marriage; Annie hadn't sprung this on me after the fact. She said she'd done the baby thing once and that was enough for her; it had nothing to do with me. She loved me, and she was sure any babies we produced would be lovely, beautiful specimens, but the fact of the matter was she was no longer interested in changing diapers at two a.m. and pumping milk four times a day for a year.

I understood this about her, I'd resigned myself to it in order that we might be together, though admittedly I did hope she might soften on the issue with time. Regardless, I was resolved to not let this become a wedge between us. This had been one of the agreed-upon conditions of our marriage, and I couldn't be mad at her for something about which she'd been honest.

My mother didn't know to resent Annie for the lack of grandkids, and I intended to keep it that way. If she had any complaints about Annie whatsoever, they were related to The Church of Search, to the fact that Annie had introduced me to it, and that I, in turn, had introduced my father.

For fifteen years my parents had been members at a Lutheran church, but when my father had stopping going, Mom had jumped back over to the Baptist church. She didn't attend services at the big one in town—where Annie's parents were members—but at a small country church about twenty miles up the highway, which she'd picked because it reminded her of her childhood in Georgia. The pastor at this church—a gently bigoted man with a small head of matted gray hair—had specifically spoken out against groups such as The Church of Search from his pulpit, and my mother had a habit of adopting his concerns and fears wholesale.

"Church without a pastor isn't a church," she told me one night. "It's a nuthouse."

You needed a leader, she said. A shepherd. Otherwise you were just wandering through the wilderness. This was a crazy world full of crazy ideas. You could get lost out there.

We were sitting in my living room, drinking white wine, and I could hear Annie upstairs, moving furniture around with Fisher.

"You and your dad," my mother said, "you encourage each other. I don't like it. You should see all these books he has. He reads nonstop. Ugh. And all these books about ghosts, Jim!"

"Dad's fine. You don't need to worry about him."

"Promise me you won't mess around with that stuff. You know how I feel about it. It's wrong. Ghosts are not to be trifled with. The Bible is very clear on that."

"I'm not so sure it is, explicitly, but I take your point."

"Deuteronomy. Don't sacrifice your children.

Don't consult with sorcerers or oracles or anyone else who casts spells or talks to ghosts."

"Do people still read Deuteronomy? I thought we'd agreed not to pay attention to that one anymore."

"It's just like it was with Wanda," she said, ignoring me.

"Ah yes, Wanda Trudeau," I said, nodding.

"Yes, Wanda Trudeau, exactly, yes," my mother said. "That poor girl."

Wanda had been a friend of my mother's in high school, and though I'd never met her, Wanda's lifestyle (my mother's word) had long served as a cautionary tale for any sort of excess. She'd been too wild, too strange, too promiscuous, too adventurous, too drunk, too *too.* Anytime I broke the rules, my mother would revive the old refrain: *Well, you know what happened to Wanda Trudeau, don't you? She wound up in a nuthouse eating pudding three meals a day!*

"Wanda fell deep into the occult," my mother said. "Ghosts and demons and Aleister Crowley. We found a dead bird once, and she smeared its guts all over the sidewalk with a stick, said she was trying to read the entrails. Jim, can you believe it?"

"Augury, I think that's called. Romans practiced augury."

"I don't care about any Romans, it was wrong,

and it was gross. All it took was one call to her parents, and that put a stop to that."

"Wait a minute," I said. "You called her parents?"

My mother, perhaps realizing she'd said too much, was quiet for a moment. "Well, what else was I supposed to do, Jim? Tell me that! What else?"

She was flustered and embarrassed now.

"Mom," I said uncertainly, "maybe you've told me this before, but how, *exactly,* did Wanda Trudeau wind up in the nuthouse?"

"I don't remember," my mother snapped. "Drugs, I think."

I crossed my legs and sat back in my chair. She took a long, sad sip of her wine. She rarely ever drank alcohol, and already her neck and chest were streaked red. Probably she was going to ask me to drive her home soon. She scooted to the edge of the couch and placed her wineglass on a coaster.

"Listen," she said. "You can belittle me all you want but—"

"That's not what I'm doing—"

"You can belittle me all you want, Jim, but I'm trying to help you. I love you, and I don't want to see you lose your way. Ever since you"—she nudged at the corner of her eye with the knuckle of her index finger, dramatically—"ever since your heart, you haven't been the same. You've been through a lot. More than most people your age. But I think there's something you haven't considered yet. What if everything that happened to you was a blessing in disguise? What if it was a test?"

"A test?"

A look of angry impatience flashed onto her face. She had a way of getting upset when you failed to immediately intuit what she was trying to say. "Yes," she said, "a test of your faith."

"Okay." I uncrossed my legs. "Perhaps. But I would think that a test of faith would first require me to have some."

"Please, you've got faith in spades. We all do. You've just put yours in all the wrong things, and that sets you up for a letdown. You go to a crazy church that fills your head up with fluff and what you need is a rock to stand on. There's only one rock that will hold you up, and it isn't ghosts or para-whatever—and guess what? It isn't Annie, either." She leaned closer to me. "Don't look at me like that, Jim, like I'm the bad guy. I'm telling you this to protect you. Hey, I remember what it's like, at the beginning, when it's all flowers and lingerie. You're in love with her, and she's in love with you, and you think nothing could ever go wrong between you. Well, let me tell you, she will disappoint you. We're nothing but disappointments, all of us, in the end. I'm not saying your marriage won't last. But she can't save you. And it's not her job to."

"I don't expect her to save me."

"You do, and you don't even realize it."

I yawned and set aside my wineglass. I had to be up early for work, I reminded her.

"You're mad at me."

"Not mad, just tired," I said, not quite honestly.

She stood up. "Fine, we can leave it there for now. I'll need a ride home, if you don't mind. You know what this wine does to my head."

I drove her home, as requested. I walked her to the front door and, once she was inside, started back for my car. I was almost there when the door swung open again. My father was standing there in his socks and shorts, a crumpled magazine under his arm, his head a dark spot in the foyer lights that gushed from the house. He raised his hand to his forehead and offered a sloppy salute. I saluted back and drove home.

Unlike Annie and me, my father rarely missed a service at The Church of Search. A thinking man's church, he called it. Long on possibilities, short on conclusions. One Sunday he called our house an hour before the service to make sure we were all planning on being there that morning. As a matter of fact, we'd intended to skip. Annie was fighting off a cold that had kept her up all night sniffling, and I had bought two small trees the day before that needed to go in the ground. We were going to take it easy, relax.

"You're going to regret it if you're not there for this morning's talk, I'm serious."

"We're a slow-moving train, Dad."

The truth was that I'd grown a little bored with The Church of Search, with the endless parade of speakers on topics so varied I was never quite sure how to integrate them into any sort of coherent understanding of the world. The previous Sunday we'd listened to a Hollywood producer describe a series of dreams in which an angel had instructed him to make a Jesus biopic, and while his story had been an interesting one and raised certain questions about divine revelation in modern times, it certainly hadn't been instructive to me in any obvious sense. Something highly unusual had happened to this man, definitely, but what difference did that make to my life?

"What's so special about this morning?" I asked.

"I wanted to keep it a surprise, but fine." He sighed. "Zinker."

"Zinker?"

"Sally Zinker. Ring any bells? Dr. Sally Zinker?"

The name was familiar, but I'd only been awake for about fifteen minutes at this point, and I'd yet to make the coffee. In fact, as we talked, I was standing in front of the coffee machine with the little black scoop, staring down absentmindedly into the bag of dark beans.

"Sally Zinker is the physicist who recorded the Dog on Fire," my father said.

"Right, I remember now, yes. Sally Zinker, right."

I hadn't listened to the recording in a long time—not since before the wedding, in fact.

"How did you know Sally Zinker will be here today?"

"Wes gets the schedule in advance."

"Wes Riggs?"

"We've been meeting up for coffee some mornings after the service. He's a smart guy. A little nutty maybe—but smart. He's convinced we're living in a computer simulation. Nothing I can say will persuade him otherwise. Given how far we've come with computers in just the last thirty years, he says there's only one in a million chance that we're not in a simulation right now."

"How long has this been going on?"

"Well, if we're in a computer, my understanding is we've never known anything different."

"No, not that—the coffee dates."

"Our discussions? I don't know, two months maybe. Anyway, go wake up your family and meet me at the church."

Off the phone I went upstairs to rouse Annie. She rolled over, buried her face in her pillow, and groaned. We'd agreed the night before to sleep late. She'd been putting in especially long hours that week at the theater, not to mention her cold. The floor by her side of the bed was littered with tissues, a miniature battlefield of mangled white parachutes.

"Dad just called," I said. "The presenter this morning is the lady who recorded the ghost at the restaurant."

She opened her eyes and looked at me. "Really? The ghost-hunter lady?"

I nodded.

"Give me twenty minutes," she said, and sat up drowsily, throwing the blanket off her body. She wandered into the bathroom for a shower. I could hear her blowing snot in the hot water as I gathered my clothes. I went down the hall, to Fisher's room, and promised her ten dollars if she could be ready in thirty minutes. We'd never told her about the ghost on the stairs, and the name Zinker would mean nothing to her.

"Make it fifteen," she said.

"Fine, deal."

I dressed in dark slacks and a blue button-down shirt, put on the coffee, and waited downstairs with the newspaper. By the time they both came down, we were already running ten minutes late. I got us there as fast as I could—about ten minutes—and parked down the street. Together we climbed the stone steps of the old Masonic

Temple, passed through its anteroom, and entered the main hall just as a song was ending. I could see my father in a folding chair about three rows from the front. He was sitting alongside Wes and Wes's wife, Harriet. The church wasn't very crowded. There were only twenty or so people there, and we had no trouble finding seats at the back.

Not long after we'd settled in, the church's logo—a warbling blue sphere the size of a basketball—popped into view at the front of the room and hovered about three feet off the ground. A blue light, sparking like a firecracker, radiated outward in all directions. Below the sphere letters appeared, three-dimensional, white and Plasticine, almost doughy: *The Church of Search*. When that fizzled away, the logo was replaced by a small paragraph of text that tilted slightly back. The text explained that the talk we were about to watch had been recorded four years earlier and had been lightly edited. This was not so unusual. Every so often, the church would send us a rerun from its archive, which stretched back six years.

The text disappeared, and the speakers crackled for a moment. A woman materialized at the front of the room. She was dressed conservatively, in loose tan pants and a white collared shirt, and I guessed she was maybe sixty years old. She was wearing very little makeup, though her lips—two thin parallel lines—were dark red. She had coarse brown hair that swept across her forehead and concealed her ears. She stared out at us, saying nothing, for what felt like an inordinately long time. Her eyes were a chilly blue, and very probing, but her lids were a soft bramble of sleepiness. She had the intensity of a trial lawyer and the insouciance of a model.

"Good morning," she said, her voice a little husky. "My name is Sally Zinker."

I checked the service program on my phone.

DR. SALLY ZINKER—"A Partial Existence"
Professor of Physics, UNC–Chapel Hill
Author of *The Reunion Machine*

She began with a brief description of her background—a hardscrabble childhood in Arkansas, her education, her work as an experimental physicist at UNC—but then she pivoted, stepping to the left and crossing her arms tightly. She stared out at us with a look of nervous excitement, as if what she had to say next might change our lives.

Her arms dropped to her sides, and she stepped toward us once more, moving so close to the front row that she nearly merged with it. The people sitting there leaned back in their chairs and craned their necks to see her better.

What she wanted to do now, she said, was tell us a story.

With that, she clapped her hands.

THE TALE OF TWO HANDS CLAPPED

Two hands clapped and made a noise. Both hands rejoiced. The noise was such that the clap had seemingly proved, once and for all, the existence of either hand. Flesh had met flesh. Skin, skin. Cells, cells. The slap had even stung a bit. The two hands were very happy with the outcome of their clapping experiment. They congratulated each other with more and more rigorous clapping and even a little bit of waving and thumbs-ups.

Hurrah! the Right Hand shouted. We're here! We really do exist!

We're here, said the Left, though a little doubtfully, because what had they confirmed, really, when you thought about it? They had existed at the exact moment of the clap, that much seemed certain, but fifteen seconds had passed since then, and now they had reached this new moment, and so how could they be sure they hadn't, since then, slipped into a more theoretical state of hand-ness? When Left Hand posed this question to Right Hand, Right Hand was stumped.

Left Hand suggested to his friend that the only

reliable way to confirm their continued existence, from moment to moment, was to keep clapping, indefinitely, and Right Hand reluctantly agreed that this was the case, that they were going to have to clap until the end of time if they wanted any sort of real assurance.

Sally clapped—hard.

She was a physicist, she reminded us, and she had devoted her life to unraveling the mystery of a subatomic particle called the daisy. Daisies were so small they were nearly unobservable, not to mention they were constantly flickering in and out of existence. One moment they were here and the next—poof, gone. What this meant was that the universe never fully existed. At least, not all at once. These little particles, the daisies, they were blinking on and off, on and off, like little lights, and this was happening all the time.

So, what did this mean?

Well, it meant that ours was only a partial existence.

A nonstop slide, back and forth, between being and nonbeing.

We were here—but also not here.

In fact, at any given moment, the universe only ninety-three percent existed.

You only ninety-three percent existed.

She clapped again.

Sally had never believed in God or heaven and, as was au courant in the scientific community, she'd written off most religious conceptions of an afterlife as wishful thinking. But then something happened. Something terrible. She lost a person very close to her. The love of her life, in fact. A gentle and kind and brilliant man. The beautiful brain that had produced this beautiful person, this brain was rotting in the ground, it was decomposing. This person she loved had been destroyed, and, desperate for any sort of information that might prove otherwise, she began to read widely on the topic of death. Theologians, survivors of near-death experiences, studies on consciousness—you name it, she read it.

More than anything she wanted to find something that might change her mind. She wanted to believe that the universe was not just a happy (or not so happy, depending) mistake, that we weren't just little bits of life clinging to a rock in the middle of a mostly dead galaxy. She wasn't looking for God necessarily. She was just searching for an indication that life did not end with the physical body, that consciousness might, in some form, survive the body's death.

Thus began her second career as a paranormal investigator.

She smiled.

Now, something she wanted to get straight before she proceeded: She didn't like the term "ghosts." Say the word "ghost" and people thought of Casper, Ichabod Crane, Patrick Swayze. She had no interest in ghosts per se—only in what she called "unusual phenomena."

She began by visiting supposedly haunted locations: The stretch of beach where an ethereal runner in gray sweats had been witnessed on numerous occasions sprinting up and down the sand. The apartment with the toilet lid that raised itself whenever you weren't looking. The creepy home where numerous people had claimed to hear voices behind the wallpaper. What differentiated Sally's investigations at these various sites from all the others that had ever been conducted was this:

She had in her possession an instrument that had never been used to study such phenomena. The instrument was something she had designed herself in her experiments with the daisy particles. The measurements provided by this instrument were too imprecise for use in a proper, publishable experiment, but they were useful if you wanted to, for instance, compare the activity of the daisies in one area relative to another. What if, Sally wondered, she were to use this device to study the daisies at these supposedly haunted locations? What might that reveal?

Well, at some of these sites, believe it or not, the daisies were in fact behaving abnormally. In some instances, more than forty percent of the daisies in a given field were flashing away into immateriality all at once. This was very odd. She'd never observed anything like it, in fact, in all her years of research.

A daisy hole, she dubbed this phenomenon.

A little puncture in materiality.

A thinning-out.

The universe as a pair of old pants, a bald patch on the knee.

Now: Had the daisy hole created the so-called ghosts, or had the ghosts created the daisy hole? Well, that was a chicken-or-egg question. Unanswerable at present. Regardless, what seemed certain to Sally was that the apparitions and mysterious voices that had been observed and in some cases recorded at these various sites were in some way linked to the phenomenon of the daisy hole. What we called ghosts, quite possibly, had a subatomic explanation or relationship.

These findings indicated to Sally a level of interplay between the material and immaterial worlds, an interplay that threatened so many of our most basic assumptions about reality. For too long, she said, science had built its case upon dumb matter alone, had trusted too implicitly in the idea that matter determined our existence and not the other way around. It was time, Sally said, to doubt everything. It was time to ask more questions.

What if consciousness, for example, did not dwell exclusively in the squishy mud of our brains? What if what we had observed of it was only the upper limbs of a tree that had roots deep in the immaterial? If this were the case, then consciousness really *could* persist after death.

Perhaps we had the ability, upon death, to vacate the body through the escape hatch of its daisy particles. The dead were not truly dead, in this case, though neither were they floating around on clouds with harps. They were loosed from materiality and therefore from time and space; they had returned to a dimension of pure thought and intention, a dimension that, according to Sally's experiments, was not entirely off-limits to us. After all, we weren't all here, remember? Did we recall how at any given moment we were only ninety-three percent existent?

One day, she said, in the not-so-distant future, we were going to better understand this process. We were going to figure out a way to harness the power of the daisy particles as they slid in and out of the physical world, and we were going to use them to open a stable line of communication with the immaterial world.

One day, in other words, we would be able to converse with the dead. We would be able to reach them. We'd wasted so much time waiting for them to visit us when really it was us who should be visiting *them*.

Thank you, she said. Thank you for having me here this morning.

She clapped again.

Except this time her right and left hands passed cleanly through each other and made no sound at all.

A few people in the audience audibly sucked in their breath. Annie looked over at me incredulously. Seconds passed, I'm ashamed to say, before I remembered that Sally was a hologram, that whatever this was, it was a production technique, a trick of editing. She fluttered her fingers at us with a smile and then disappeared.

After church my father invited me on a hike. He had, for a number of years, been a member of a hunt club that owned some two hundred acres of land outside of town, and once upon a time we'd routinely walked the trails in the nearby state park together. I hadn't been out there with him in a long time. He had developed painful heel spurs that made walking long distances uncomfortable, but he informed me that he'd recently found some padded inserts for his boots that might help and he was ready to give it a try.

To reach the trailhead, we drove right by the hunt club's lodge, a glorified mobile home that sat about fifty yards off a gravel road. I'd been in there as a kid with my father a handful of times. Even now I can smell the trash out back, see its messy countertops stained with coffee rings and littered with dried crusts of food. I can remember, with precision, the wall of photographs of dead bucks and does on beds of crunchy brown leaves, bloody and wet, their twisted necks and dark eyes. This display had always put me in mind of the Polaroids you see pinned to evidence boards on detective shows.

I'd never shot a deer—I was no hunter—and I think my father had always felt let down by my disinterest. I think he fancied himself the sort of person who'd be able to survive in the woods forever with nothing but a knife, and probably he could have. He could get a fire going with a flint in under three minutes, and every time we'd ever gone camping he'd insisted we use leaves instead of toilet paper. He used to make me spray down with a foul-smelling liquid that he claimed was a natural mosquito and tick repellent, a putrid concoction whose chief ingredient, I discovered years later, was deer piss.

Deer season had just opened. It was mid-October, but already the cold had settled into the mountains. The week before Shula had even had a few inches of snow, though it had melted by the following afternoon. I wore a thermal shirt under my field jacket, though I was soon sweating and had to carry the jacket under my arm. The sun was dim through the treetops and clouds, an overcast day. I glanced at my watch: Annie was at the theater by now, and Fisher was with her grandparents for the afternoon.

My father sucked snot from his nose and hocked a loogie with a high glistening arc. The snot landed somewhere off in the leaves. After we'd been walking for a few minutes, we fell into a discussion about Sally Zinker.

"One of the more interesting talks I've seen, that's for sure," he said. "I'd read about daisy particles before but never about anything like that."

"To be honest, I'm not sure I totally understood everything she was saying. Annie and I were talking about it on the way home. The universe only ninety-three percent exists? Such a specific number."

"Well, it's math, Jim."

"Correct me if I'm wrong, but if we partly exist, that means we partly *don't* exist, which means we're all, already, a little bit dead?"

He smiled. "There does seem to be some fluidity to it."

We followed a switchback in the trail. We were going downhill, into a narrow valley between two mountains. The woods were colder here—and quiet. We reached the bottom, where the trail elbowed up again, and hopped across a small trickling stream.

"She didn't mention the restaurant," I said. "I guess I really didn't expect her to, but I was hoping she might. Do you think she found a daisy hole there, too?"

"That would make a certain sense. Given what we experienced there."

"What *you* experienced," I corrected. "So do you think you passed through a daisy hole?"

"I'm not sure." My father stopped for a moment and, steadying himself against a tree, brought up his left foot. He stuck his finger in his boot and messed with the insert at his heel. "Whatever happened to me on the stairs, it was such a brief glimpse."

"A glimpse of what, though?"

"The beyond? All that's not this? I don't know if there's a good word for it, really. But it was incredibly real." He smiled. "It was a gift. I used to be so certain we were just this"—he tugged at the skin on his arm—"but now? There's just so much we don't understand about ourselves. We aren't who we think we are. We aren't even *where* we think we are. I know that now. I've felt it."

Why had this happened to him—and not me? I was incredibly jealous. I'd been there, too, and yet the hand of *whatever it was* had reached out for my father and ignored me altogether. Compared with him, I was a pathetic sightless mole wriggling my way through the dark, wet soil, oblivious to the wonders that lived above the surface. We mole-people, we soul-less moles, we'd been born in the mud, and we'd die there, too, vegetated, dreamless.

A gunshot echoed, not too far off, and something ripped through the nearby trees. We both froze and listened. My ears burned from the cold. We were about a half mile from the parking lot.

"We should probably be wearing orange," my father said.

"That sounded pretty close."

He stepped into the brush and pointed to a pine tree. About six feet up its trunk was a long splintery gash where a bullet had grazed it.

"That could have killed us," I said, feeling more and more indignant. "This is a state park! What the hell are they doing all the way over here?"

"They probably got turned around. That happens sometimes." He cupped his hands around his mouth and shouted, "You're in a state park! Stop shooting!"

No one shouted back. Whoever it was, probably they were embarrassed or scared. My father adjusted his boot insert again and started walking. He'd stayed so calm. It was infuriating. What if one of us had been shot through the head? Through the belly? If we'd been standing about five feet to the right, I'd have been bleeding out across the leaves, my father stooped over me, saying his goodbyes, telling me to hold on, telling me I was going to be fine.

For the longest time after my heart had misfired, I'd felt as if a tremendous curtain had been pulled away from the end of my life, and I'd done my best to feel liberated rather than frightened by the knowledge of the nothingness that awaited me. If there was nothing, then no one was watching me or judging me or keeping track of my numerous sins, scribbling down my every terrible thought in a grand, cosmic logbook. I was free.

But I had never really settled into that perspective. After all, what about all the others, the ones who'd nearly died, like me, but who had returned to report the inexorable happiness of God's white, bright love? Some part of me feared that my experience wasn't the rule but the exception. The oblivion I'd met, possibly, had flowed directly from the life I'd led up to that point. What if, fundamentally, I simply wasn't a good enough person to deserve an afterlife? What if some people have no soul and I was one of them? What if I had seen no afterlife because I didn't have the will or ability to believe in one? These were the questions that kept me awake some nights. I didn't want to die again. I didn't want to disappear! The world was at my back, pushing me toward it, shoving me over the edge of the grandest canyon, the darkest hole, down into that nonexistence.

"Are you okay, Jim?" my father asked.

I was having trouble breathing; my head spun; limbs tingled; deep in my chest a gawky bird was trying to escape my rib cage. I leaned forward until my hands were on the ground and stretched out across the trail. My father doubled back and knelt down beside me. Maybe I really had been shot and hadn't even realized it.

"Is it your heart?" he asked me, unable to hide his panic. "Jim, what should I do?"

"I'm fine," I managed to wheeze. "I'm fine. I'm fine."

"You're shaking."

Was I? I felt disconnected from my body. My head, swollen, was a hot-air balloon lifting free from my neck. I was dying! In the fucking woods! Like an animal! An animal-animal, I mean. My HeartNet had failed to do its job. Maybe I'd wandered too far off-track, too far from the towers, the satellites, *whatever,* and the device had lost contact with its maker in Sheldrick, California. I thought of Annie, pictured her face. If I focused on her image, would she be able to sense me as I departed the earth? Could I rouse the fine hairs on her neck and make her feel this last burst of love?

A few minutes later I managed to catch my breath. My father had his beefy hands on my chest and seemed ready to perform compressions.

"I'm okay," I said. "You don't need to worry."

He fell back onto his butt, and I dragged myself up into a sitting position.

"I haven't eaten much today," I said—to him, to myself. "It's just my blood sugar. I was just light-headed."

"Are you sure?"

I slid my phone out of my pocket and consulted my HeartNet app. No misfires. My heart was operating normally. I showed this to my father, but he didn't seem convinced by it.

He spat into the grass, and a little saliva dribbled down through his beard hairs. He wiped it away with his arm. Then he offered me a candy bar from his pocket, and we halved it. We sat there eating in silence, the caramel whiskering down our chins. Once I felt strong enough, I stood up and we resumed our hike. We reached the parking lot about twenty minutes later. In the car I turned on the heat.

"You really scared me back there," he said.

"Sorry about that."

"Has it happened before?"

"I told you, I was just hungry."

We started driving. When we passed the hunt club lodge, two blue trucks were parked in front of it, and I wondered if these were the men who'd shot at us.

By the time I reached home, I was scratching like hell. Something was crawling on my back, on my arms, on my legs, tiny tickles, only I couldn't find the culprit. I stripped down in the bathroom and turned this way and that in the mirror. I couldn't see anything on my skin. I called for Annie. She came upstairs in an apron and laughed when she saw me craning my neck for a better view of my back.

"I need some help," I said.

She knelt down and examined me more closely, her fingers across my skin.

"Tiny, itty bitty ticks," she said, mildly distressed. "God, how'd this happen? This isn't even tick season, is it? Aren't they usually dead by now? There's way too many to count."

When I asked her if these were the little black ones with two white spots or the little black ones with one big spot she said they were too small to tell. With the tweezers she plucked them loose from my skin, one by one. Every so often she ran the tweezers under the faucet. This went on for an hour. I was impressed by her diligence. I stood there naked, squinting at my arms, twisting my flesh around my bones for a better view. Down in the hairs, I could see them, like specks of dirt. I scraped them away with my fingernails.

"Careful," Annie said. "You don't want to leave the mouths."

Finally I got into the shower and washed with hot water and soap, scrubbing hard.

"Do you think they're in my hair, too?" I asked her.

She was sitting on the toilet, watching me. She shrugged. "I hope not."

For her sake, that night I slept on the couch. I didn't want to set these little suckers loose in our bedsheets. In the morning Annie was standing over me with a cup of coffee, smiling sweetly. "It's called a tick bomb," she said. "I looked it up. You walked right through a tick bomb."

Is there anything more lovely than a beautiful woman's hair held aloft as it passes through a shirt hole in reverse? Stomach, breasts, neck, chin, nose, eyes, hair sliding out last of all as a lustrous tumble back down across the shoulders?

Often we'd have to wait until Fisher was out. For school, for band practice. We'd meet at home during our lunch breaks and avail ourselves of the entire house. Sunlight streaming through the windows, we'd undress in the living room, our bodies fully revealed, the little stray hairs, the freckles, an unevenly clipped toenail (mine), some mild cellulitis along the upper arms (hers), the smell of her lavender deodorant, my aftershave. Sex in the daytime is somehow both more intimate and transactional.

Underneath me, her mouth smooshed hard against my shoulder, her wet breath vibrated my skin. She'd scratch at my back. I'd tug at her hair. We pushed at each other, pressed, groped, clawed, slapped, twisted, tweaked. Red finger-shaped marks formed around my neck. My saliva glistened on her chest. Gentle acts of violence. Violent acts of gentleness. On floors, counters, couches. We'd make love—and then linger with each other for as long as possible. There were two-hour lunches. Three-hour. We'd tell each other things. Confess. Unburden. One afternoon, as Annie stretched out beside me on the guest bed, she let me know that I was not the first person she'd slept with since Anthony's death. I told her that was hardly surprising since he'd been dead for seven years when we met.

"There were two others," she said.

I shrugged and said that wasn't really a shocking number. In fact, though I didn't say this, two in seven years seemed a little low to me.

"Well, what would be a shocking number?" she asked.

"Oh, I don't know," I said, wanting to be careful. "Ten or twelve?"

"It was three, actually. I'm not sure why I lied."

I wasn't either. "Who was the third? Who did you leave off?"

"Nobody in particular."

I suspected this wasn't the case. I imagined three faces, one with a game show's red X through it. "If you had to lose one, who'd it be?" I asked. "Who wouldn't make the cut? Don't say me."

She smiled, baggily, and touched my arm. “Not you.”

“Who, then?” I asked uncertainly.

“If I tell you, you’ll think less of me.”

“Impossible,” I said.

She scooted to the end of the bed and sat between my open legs to face me, her hands on my knees. She didn’t have on any underwear, but she was still wearing her bra, which in our rush we’d neglected to remove.

“It happened right after Anthony died,” she said, already blushing. “I was packing up the house in Charleston, and one of his friends came over to help me get some of the heavy stuff down the stairs. I honestly can’t remember who initiated it, but I felt terrible, even as it was happening. He was Anthony’s *best* friend.”

She covered her face with her hands and peeked at me through her fingers. “You’re judging me,” she said.

“Not at all. You were grieving. People act strangely when they’re sad.”

“I could have stopped it though.” She seemed disgusted with herself. “I haven’t talked to him since. I think we both felt too guilty to face each other after that.”

I wasn’t sure what to say—or what she wanted me to say. Did she need to be comforted? Consoled?

“I’ve never told that to anyone,” she said.

I leaned forward to place my hands on her outer thighs. She had confessed to me this sad thing and nobody else. Nobody else in the entire world. This felt incredibly significant to me. “I don’t think any less of you,” I said, hoping this would communicate all I was feeling in that moment, that I desired all of her—her weaknesses, her failures, her shames. I wanted to know everything. I removed her bra, stretched her out, kneaded at her back, her butt, with my knuckles and palms. I slid my fingers into the cracks of her armpits, sucked on her earlobes, lay down on top of her, tongued her shoulder blades.

We made love a second time. We fell asleep. I missed a meeting. Made a call. Apologized. Blamed a stomach bug, a bad lunch. Rushed back to the bank. Ignored the odd gaze of the Fortune Tellers as I beelined for my office.

I didn’t care. I was in love, and nothing else mattered to me. Sitting in my office chair, Annie two miles away at the theater, I swear I could feel the hum of every single atom that connected us across that distance.

I was downtown to meet with a prospective client for lunch one afternoon and afterward stopped by a used bookstore. Small carts outside the door were loaded with discounted paperbacks. The man who owned the shop was a White Hair, an older gentleman with a large head and square shoulders and dark eyes. He had the look of a man who read military histories on his lunch break. He was behind the register eating an apple when I walked in, and I nodded to him as I passed. The bookstore itself was very small and cramped, the floors as gunky as old mousetraps.

I wandered the labyrinth of teetering bookcases until eventually I was standing in the science section, at least a third of which was devoted to plant guides and bird books. The books were arranged by author, and the Z's were way down on the lowest shelf. I crouched down and turned my head sideways. I couldn't believe it, there it was, a slim hardback book, *The Reunion Machine* by Sally Zinker.

That I'd found it here in this decrepit used bookshop seemed significant to me, perhaps even fated. The title appeared in bold yellow letters on the front cover, like headlights through a highway fog. Beneath the title, it said, *A Physicist Breaks Down the Barriers Between the Living and the Dead.*

I flipped through it quickly. In her author photo, Sally appeared to be a few years younger than she had as a hologram. Her face was tilted slightly so that she was peering down at the camera, and her arms were crossed in such a way that, in a musical perhaps, would have suggested toughness.

I turned the book over to examine the jacket copy. *What if,* it asked, *there is no such thing as past, present, and future? What if everything is happening all at once? What if the material world sprang from a single thought? What if, upon our death, the shackles of time are broken and we are released to wander through our lives? What if there was a way to outmaneuver time and space and communicate with those who've died?*

When I slid the book across the counter, we opened it for the price and then started reading the jacket copy.

"Huh," he said. "You interested in this sort of stuff?"

I shrugged.

"I've got a friend who swears he used to get messages from one of his high school teachers, a lady who taught him French. They were real close. We used to call her his girlfriend. Anyway, she died, in a plane crash, and for a few months after that, my friend would wake up some nights speaking French. The message was always the same, he said. Your book. Your book. *Ton livre. Ton livre.* Finally, one day he got to thinking, and he opened up his old French textbook—and guess what?"

"What?"

"You won't believe it, but she'd written him a recommendation letter for college, and it was in the book. Right there in the book!"

"That's amazing."

He nodded. "It is, it is. It was sort of a shame though because my friend had already sent out his applications. Still, amazing, yes."

I paid the guy $6.50.

I didn't have a chance to read the book for a few more days, when I took it with me on a work trip to Atlanta. I read the first few chapters on the plane and then another fifty pages while eating dinner alone after my meetings. I called my father on my walk back to the hotel and told him what I'd been reading.

"That's fantastic," he said. "You'll have to let me borrow it when you're done."

His voice was in my ear thanks to an earbud, and it was easy to imagine he was walking right alongside me.

"Listen," I said. "I've been thinking. You proposed to me once that we should make some sort of pact, that whoever dies first should try to get a message to the other person."

"I said we should do this?"

"It would be something very simple. An image or, like, a sentence."

"Such as?"

"I don't know. Just something easy to remember but specific enough that it couldn't be random."

"The proof is in the pudding," he said.

"I'm sorry?"

"That could be our message. Proof is in the pudding. Easy to remember, right?"

"How about, *I'm still here?*"

"A little creepy, don't you think? Maybe a song. 'Puttin' on the Ritz.'"

"If you're blue, and you don't know where to go—" I sang.

"Why don't you go where fashion sits. Exactly."

"Let's give this message some more thought. We'll figure it out."

"Whatever it is, how will we transmit?"

"A dream. A crystal ball. Highway billboard. A giant skywriting airplane. Whatever it takes, doesn't matter."

"Okay, let's do it. Let's give it a try."

I read a few more chapters before going to bed that night—and then skimmed to the end on the plane the next day. Annie picked me up at the airport and was waiting for me outside Arrivals when I came through the sliding doors. She gave me a long kiss after I dropped my bag into the back seat of the car. Once we were on the highway she hit the gas hard, and we surged forward through traffic. We were doing ninety, at least.

She's always been this way in a car. She drives as if the place we're going might no longer exist if we don't reach it in time. If someone cuts her off or slams on the brakes unexpectedly, Annie doesn't flinch. She doesn't yell or get upset or express any sort of frustration. Cool, collected, precise—she could have been a NASCAR driver. Her entire body seems to work in perfect communion with the car. Where her foot contacts the pedal I think of the Sistine Chapel, the invisible spark traveling between the almost-touching fingers of God and Adam.

All this to say, we were home from the airport in record time, and our rush to the house—my raising the key before we'd even reached the door, her dropping my bag at the foot of the stairs, the unbuttoning of blouses and shirts as I followed her into the living room—all of it seemed like an extension of the drive itself: precise, coordinated, efficient. We'd both memorized the operating manual, we knew the conditions of the road, we'd plugged the destination into the GPS of our bodies.

Afterward I stayed right where I was, not letting her go. We were on the floor, and I was on top of her. Her legs, which had been lashed around my back, were resting on the ground. She kissed the top of my head and patted my shoulder, indicating she was ready for me to roll over, but I didn't want to budge, not yet. I didn't want her to release me. I was very glad to be home. She tapped my back again.

"We don't have much longer," she said.

Fisher was at her friend's house. Another band practice.

I rolled off her and reached for my bag. I brought out Sally Zinker's book and handed it to her.

"You bought her book?"

"It's about ten years old."

Amused, Annie read some of the chapter titles aloud: *Grief Makes Ghost Hunters of Us All. A Failure of Space and Time. The Ghost Particle. A Partial Existence. The Daisy Dead. The Future Dead. A Reunion Machine.*

"So what's the reunion machine?"

I smiled. "Get this—it's a device that would allow you to talk with the dead. It's got something to do with the daisy particles, with taking control of the particle's on/off switch."

"Wait, is it something she's already built or—?"

"Unclear. Either she's built it and she's being cagey about it, or she's simply suggesting such a machine could, hypothetically, be built, at some point, someday."

"So you've read this whole book already?"

"Most of it, yeah."

"How does the reunion machine work exactly? I mean, is it like a telephone?"

"She's a little vague on the mechanics of it."

I'd wondered the same thing. The chapter about the machine contained no schematics or diagrams or illustrations, and so imagining it was a challenge. A telephone, a pane of glass through which one could observe the spirit world, a special bodysuit that somehow projected you into the great beyond—anything seemed possible. Annie flipped back to the beginning, to the introduction.

"What about the Dog on Fire? Is that anywhere in here?"

"She doesn't talk about the Lennoxes, no, but she does write a little bit about a restaurant with a winding staircase, which I'm sure must be Su Casa Siempre. It's one of about a dozen sites where she detected a daisy hole."

The back door squeaked open, and Annie and I jumped up off the floor fast. She stepped into her skirt. I couldn't seem to get my belt to buckle right. We were both shirtless when Fisher and her friend C-Mac strode into the living room together, their instruments in black gig bags. Seeing us, C-Mac giggled and turned red. I told them I'd just arrived home.

"No shit," Fisher said.

"Fisher," Annie said. "Language."

"We're going downstairs to practice," Fisher said, irritated with all of us, with the world.

When they were gone, Annie and I continued dressing.

"Don't worry about her," she said, buttoning her blouse. "She's just in a new dumb phase."

And I thought: Who isn't?

We worried about Fisher's friendship with C-Mac. There was no democracy in this friendship of theirs. Annie had overheard C-Mac telling Fisher with the noxious flair of a cruise director what their plans were for the weekend. I'd walked into the house one afternoon and discovered C-Mac bending Fisher's body into strange yoga contortions that she said might help Fisher with her posture. Her posture's fine, I said. You don't know what you're talking about, C-Mac snapped. If any of this bothered Fisher, she never admitted it. She always seemed pleased to have C-Mac's attention, no matter how domineering and abrasive her friend could be.

The girl lived in a very modern home—it reminded me of a glass worm as painted by a cubist—on the west side of town. The roof was a giant solar panel. The driveway was a solar panel, too, apparently. Their three cars were all sleek and electric. Most of the time the girls practiced over there, and since Fisher was still two years away from her driver's license, we were constantly carting her back and forth.

I picked her up there one afternoon and we

were almost home when she started giggling. I asked her what was so funny, and she showed me her phone screen.

"Past life app," she said. "You answer a bunch of questions and it tells you about all your past lives. I was a Viking warrior, a devotee of the god Loki. My ship was called the *Dragon's Blood*, and we sailed to France and conquered Paris. I didn't survive the battle, sadly. A spear caught me right in the gut." She patted her stomach wistfully. "The last thing I remember thinking, as I lay there sprawled across the stones, blood gushing out of me, was how much I was going to miss all my pillaging and raping. I was very good at it."

"I doubt that."

"I burned your village down, actually. You were a peasant farmer back then, and I killed all your sheep and your children and I had sex with your wife."

"That's not funny. It's actually a little disturbing. I was asking you a serious question."

"And I'm giving you a serious answer, sort of. The app is stupid, but reincarnation is where it's at, Jim. It makes total sense. You've been a slave, a master, an idiot, a genius. Actually, it's even weirder than that because there's no such thing as you and me, not really. Us being individual souls, it's all an illusion. All of us are little leaves on the same house plant. God's got a major-major case of split personality. He's like this crazy sci-fi writer, and he's writing seven billion stories at once in his head."

I thought: But if I'm only a character in a story, then will I still exist after the story ends? After all, characters are only constructs, clusters of attributes and personality, a roulette, hypotrochoidal images produced when one circle rolls inside another, larger one. One could argue the character lives only as long as the reader remembers him, but I couldn't tell if Fisher's analogy allowed for any actual readers. God alone produced and consumed these stories. He fed upon his own fantasies.

"If I'm God's fantasy, I feel sorry for God," I said.

She smiled. "You're, like, point-zero-zero-zero-zero-zero-zero-zero-zero-zero-zero-one percent of God's fantasy. Remember, he's writing Gandhi and George Clooney and Amelia Earhart, too."

"Where'd you learn all this stuff?" I asked her. "Are they teaching this stuff in schools now? Do you take religion in middle school?"

She waved her phone at me, the font of all knowledge.

"But past lives really would explain so much," she said. "Like, C-Mac's convinced her dad had something terrible happen to him last time around."

"Why do you say that?"

"I don't know. I mean, he's just such a mad guy, you know?"

"Mad how?"

She shrugged. "Just mad."

Later that night, when Annie and I pressed for more details, a fuller picture emerged. The man had a serious temper. He yelled sometimes. He'd called C-Mac a bitch once. He'd kicked a cooler across the yard when he thought Fisher and C-Mac had ripped the pool liner (which they hadn't, she said). While they'd been practicing earlier that week, he'd stomped into the garage, flung a hammer at the wall, and screamed at them to shut the fuck up. As she tossed off these stories, Fisher seemed more amused than bothered by this behavior, which only made us worry more. Didn't she know adults weren't supposed to throw hammers and yell obscenities at children?

C-Mac's father, Dr. Mac, was a surgeon in town. We'd had few interactions up to this point, and I'd never witnessed any outbursts. He'd come over one Saturday morning and sat in the kitchen with me for an hour as the girls played down in the basement, which I'd cleared out to make room for their rehearsals. Fisher had put down rugs across the concrete floor, tacked tapestries to the walls, and bought lamps at the Goodwill. The bass shuddered up through our feet and legs like a million staticky insects crawling across our bones. I offered Dr. Mac a cup of coffee, and he blew ripples across the black surface for a few minutes before finally taking a small sip. He winced and placed the mug on the coaster. I asked him if he wanted any milk.

"Do you know where coffee comes from?" he asked.

"All over?"

"Yes, but do you know where it comes from on the plant itself? The coffee bean isn't really a bean at all. We just call it that because it resembles one. The coffee bean is in fact the pit of a dark purple cherry. The pits are removed and dried out and then roasted, et cetera. But the cherry flesh, it gets thrown out, which is a real shame because it could be put to good use. You can use the cherry flesh to make flour. Actual, usable flour. Coffee flour. Did you know that?"

I shook my head.

"We waste so much. You can judge a civilization by its trash, and we are the biggest wasters in the history of the planet."

I tried not to glance over at our trash can, which I'm sure was overflowing.

"It's best never to buy anything new," he continued. "It's a demand problem, not supply. If we stopped buying things, they'd stop making them. It's as simple as that. Thinking about all the junk people buy, it just makes me so sad. Our culture is sick, that's the problem. It's a cultural illness. We fill the hole in our hearts with curtain rods and phones. We're killing this world. Don't you ever wish we'd never settled these mountains? That we'd left them wild? Wouldn't it be great if the Shawnee still lived here in the Blue Ridge and not us?"

"I thought it was the Cherokee."

"That was later," he said, very academically. "First it was the Shawnee. 'Shula' is a Shawnee word. Or is rooted in one, I mean. *Shu-lah-weh*, or something like that. Means buzzard. People of the buzzard. They offered up their dead to the buzzards and vultures and only after the bones had been picked clean did they bury them."

"Nothing wasted."

"Exactly. The planet would be much better off if the Shawnee had won and not the British, believe me."

"More buzzard-people, less people-people."

He nodded.

"Be the buzzard," I said. "Waste not. Pick the bones clean."

"Claudine's guitar, for instance. I bought it used off a guy in Asheville. Supposedly he bought it from the guitarist from that band Horse Logic."

I told him I wasn't familiar with that particular band.

"I'll bring over one of their CDs next time," he said.

Next time. Fisher being in a band, I realized

then, meant that I was in a band now, too, a band of parents. And this guy, whom I hardly knew, in his V-necked merino sweater and jeans, was *my* guitarist. I was *his* bassist. We'd be sitting in each other's kitchens for years to come talking about coffee pits and anti-consumerism and Lord knows what else. I didn't disagree with him about consumption and waste—not really—but then again, I didn't especially like being lectured in my own kitchen. My primary impression of the man was that he was a know-it-all, not to mention a tad sanctimonious. He was very calm, very quiet. I had trouble imagining him yelling at the girls.

Still, I drove over to his house for a chat. Dr. Mac invited me in for a glass of wine. They'd just finished dinner and his wife—a malpractice attorney, if it can be believed—was loading dishes into the washer. The two of us sat down together in the living room with our red wine.

"You look like something is troubling you," he said.

"Yes, unfortunately," I said, and as coolly as possible explained that it had come to my attention that he, Dr. Mac, had something of a bad temper and that I would prefer if, going forward, he could please abstain from any future conniption fits when in the presence of my stepdaughter, Fisher. About halfway through my little speech, which I'd rehearsed on the way there, the man's jaw clenched tight and his face reddened, and I wondered if I was about to personally experience one of his tantrums. But when I finished talking, he sat there quietly for a moment, seething, regarding me with what seemed like total disdain. I waited for him to pounce. I realized then that his wife, Terry, was standing behind the couch, that she'd come in from the kitchen and had probably overheard most of what I'd said. I turned to acknowledge her.

"Well, first of all, I don't know where you're getting your information from," Dr. Mac said.

"So you're saying it's not true?"

"This is my house," he said, his voice loud but squinched. "*My* house."

"No denying that," I said.

Something quaked in my chest. A deep-down tremor that radiated outward from my heart. Feeling dizzy, I set my wineglass down on the coffee table and, dumbly, tried to stand, my vision already purpling. It was the parking garage all over again. Was I dying? My phone hadn't chimed, though.

I woke up on the floor. I wasn't sure how much time had passed. Terry was standing over me.

"He okay?" came Dr. Mac's voice from somewhere behind me.

When Terry nodded that I was, Dr. Mac strode past me and out of the room. I could hear his footsteps receding. Terry went into the kitchen and poured me a glass of water. I sat up and took it from her. I'd slumped forward and fallen to the floor, she explained. I'd barely missed hitting my head on the coffee table. She asked me if I felt okay, and I told her I was fine.

"No one's ever passed out in my living room," she said. "That was a first."

"I have a fainting disorder. Not a big deal. Comes and goes. Had it all my life."

A few minutes later, I felt well enough to stand and say goodbye. Terry walked me to the door. She crossed her arms and gave me a funny look, her jaw shoved forward. "Well, it won't happen again, okay? No more tantrums, no more yelling. Trust me."

"Thank you," I said. "I appreciate it. Fisher doesn't know I'm here. She'd hate me for being here, but"—I shrugged amicably—"a parent's job, right?"

"You don't need to worry," she said.

In the car I whipped out my phone. My HeartNet had not detected or recorded any usual activity. No skipped beats. No restarts. Nothing.

Like always the doctor's waiting room was full of White Hairs. They sat quietly, hands in their laps, their many documents and medical histories arranged in folders. They fussed with insurance cards and forms. They breathed heavily. A man in a tight red shirt and suspenders coughed fiercely into his hands, then smeared his hands across his pants. A small Indian woman with giant reading glasses asked her husband, who was standing by her chair with his arms crossed, to please sit down and relax.

Because of my heart condition, I sometimes felt as if I'd been inducted into their ranks prematurely. Here I sat, an honorary White Hair.

Eventually I was shown to an exam room. I changed into a paper gown and sat on the table for an hour before Dr. Westervelt finally made an appearance. He was a short, balding man with a look on his face that suggested never-ending indigestion. When I described to him the quaking I'd felt, the dizziness, the loss of consciousness, he nodded solemnly. He ordered the usual tests and later that afternoon returned to the exam room to tell me my heart was doing just fine, as far as he and his million-dollar machines could tell.

Perhaps, he said, all the recent headlines about HeartNet had even made me a little paranoid? I told him I wasn't aware of any such headlines, and he arched his eyebrows at me and took a step back, toward the door, as if positioning himself for a speedy exit.

"Oh," he said. "I thought surely you would

have been keyed into all that. I didn't mean to alarm you, if I have. I only wanted to discuss it with you, in case it had been on your mind."

I buttoned my shirt while the doctor pulled up an article for me to read on his tablet.

"Ignore the headline," he said, handing it to me. "It's way too sensational."

Man's Heart Hacked to Death Remotely, it said.

"Good Lord," I said.

According to the article, a Chinese hacker—a teenager, mind you—had broken into the HeartNet network—and figured out a way to instruct one of its devices to explode the heart of a random man who lived in London. This poor British gentleman had been on his way to work when it happened, when the onion-bag tech had squeezed his heart until it stopped beating. The hacker was only sixteen years old, and he'd hacked into HeartNet-Net simply for the challenge of it, inadvertently exposing major weaknesses in the company's cyber security systems.

I was astounded. I had never really considered the implications of my device being wirelessly connected to the company's network. Why had I never thought about this until now? What I imagined then was a bony hand clutching my heart, a tight grip that would never let me go. Did I need to have my device removed and replaced with an old-fashioned pacemaker? Did I need to take action?

Dr. Westervelt shook his head. Certainly not, he said. He counseled me not to worry, not to stress. The chances of another hacker exploding my heart was something like 1 in 350,000. How he had arrived at such an exact number, I wouldn't think to ask until I was in the parking garage searching for my car. Perhaps he'd made up the statistic on the spot to calm me. It did, in fact, have a calming effect, initially. His surety could be so soothing.

As for my recent *episodes,* as he called them, he wondered about the possibility of anxiety attacks. They'd cracked me open after all, and it was normal to feel more vulnerable after such an operation. He suggested the name of a therapist in town.

"A hypnotherapist, actually," he said. "I'm a big believer in avoiding meds whenever possible. More often than not the side effects are just as bad as the original symptoms. Take a pill and feel relaxed but maybe now you can't maintain an erection, which leads to—"

"More anxiety."

He touched his nose. "And more pills. Try the hypnotherapist first. I'm writing her name down here. A very nice lady. She helped my son quit smoking."

Back at work that afternoon, I couldn't keep myself from digging up and reading more articles:

Wi-Fi Heart Goes Die-Fi.

Man's Heart Explodes, Chinese Teen Blamed.

Can a Hacker Re-Code Your Heart?

The headlines were endless, though as far as I could tell, there'd been only a single instance of an exploded heart.

Scanning through an online forum for people with HeartNets, I discovered there was talk of a class-action lawsuit against the company that manufactured the device. From what I could gather, there were two basic camps of HeartNet recipients: those who thought we needed to sue the company and keep our devices and those who thought we needed to sue the company and have our devices surgically removed, immediately, lest we meet a similar fate. People were afraid, obviously. They didn't want to die, especially not in this ridiculous manner, and they were reaching out to others in the same predicament, hoping to find some degree of solace in the knowledge that their worries were shared by almost a hundred thousand others.

I hadn't spent this much time before on the Web forum. I realized that some of the discussion threads were as old as the device itself. One of the more popular threads, I saw, was called *Anyone else obsessed with their heartbeats?* I clicked on it and discovered that I wasn't alone; there were hundreds of people just like me, who, at least for a time, had been preoccupied with the heartbeat function on their HeartNet app. One woman wrote that for almost an entire year she'd kept headphones plugged in her ears. Cooking dinner, working out, researching her dissertation—her heartbeat had been the metronomic soundtrack of her life.

Another man, a retiree in Florida, wrote that he'd listened to it for so long that he heard it all the time now, every un-amplified beat forever booming in his ears.

I mentioned none of this to Annie or Fisher when they got home that night. I didn't want to alarm them, or perhaps, more accurately, I didn't want them to know that *I* was alarmed. Ever since marrying Annie I'd stopped obsessively listening to my heartbeat. I no longer fell asleep to its quaky rhythms. It wasn't a habit that I would have expected her to approve of or understand. And with her around, I didn't need the comfort of my own beating heart.

She'd always done me the courtesy of not fussing over my condition, though by no means would I say she lacked empathy. We talked about my heart, certainly, from time to time, but she'd never once asked how I was feeling after a run or a hike or, thank God, during sex. Maybe after losing one husband, she simply didn't want to focus on her second husband's fragile health. But no, that's going too far; my health was not fragile. My HeartNet was doing its job, Dr.

Westervelt had said. I had no reason to fear the unlikely assault of a bored teenager on the other side of the globe.

The story of Anthony's death as told to me by Annie was a simple one: He'd been out kayaking on a river with some friends one afternoon and had drowned. I'd heard the whispers about him having been drunk or stoned at the time, of course, but I'd never felt comfortable pressing her for more details. What did it matter? I suppose I never would have learned much else about it if not for Annie's brother, Kurt.

Not long after the wedding, I'd flown up to New York to visit a friend and while there I'd had lunch with Kurt in a Cantonese restaurant in Chinatown. To reach the restaurant you rode an extremely long escalator to a fourth-floor ballroom where waiters in red jackets served you dim sum from squeaky carts as a woman screamed, pleasantly, in Cantonese over a PA system. What she was screaming, neither one of us had any idea, but it was an endless source of entertainment. The food was excellent, and the ballroom was incredibly large and grand, the size of a basketball court, red carpet floors, white cloths on all the tables, a giant chandelier at the center of the room. Riding the escalator up from the grimy streets below and discovering yourself in a place such as that—it was easy to think you'd entered a heaven sprung from the mind of David Lynch.

"Try this one—crazy fucking good," was Kurt's refrain as we ate. He'd ordered us far too much food. Kurt—tall, brown-maned Kurt, the pride of Annie's family, denizen of the Upper East Side—managed assets and liabilities in the international operations division for Bank of America.

He'd been living with the same woman, a vegan chef named Kitra, for the last eight years but had given his family no indication that he intended to marry her or produce any offspring. "Children are boring," I'd heard him say once. Annie and Kurt were not especially close, though it was easy to see the family resemblance, plus they had the same airy laugh and busy eyebrows, always moving and bending and contorting, an eyebrow code that I'd never been able to entirely crack. But other than that, they were very different people. Kurt despised the fact that he was from a town like Shula, and he visited as rarely as possible. He seemed to care about his sister but considered her a bit of a bumpkin—and by extension, me, too. Not that he'd ever said so explicitly. I detected his condescension primarily in the way he studied me when I talked—a look of amusement, I guess you could call it, the same expression one might wear when regarding an especially smart chimpanzee at the zoo.

Somehow, during this lunch, Kurt and I got onto the topic of Anthony, who was still something of a mystery to me. From pictures, I knew he'd been a slim but athletic man with shaggy blond hair, a closemouthed smile, and deep-set eyes. A troubled face, I'm tempted to say. His go-to expression in photos suggested a self-seriousness; the angle of his chin, cockiness. He and Annie had met during her first year at the College of Charleston, through their dealer, a white guy with dreadlocks who made deliveries all over downtown on a Schwinn.

I hadn't been entirely surprised to learn that Annie had smoked in college—she'd grown up in what I'd call a semi-repressive environment, after all, plus she'd fallen deep into the college theater scene, a world I can only assume is widely populated by weirdos and potheads—but I admit that I was sometimes intrigued at the thoroughness of Annie's transformation after high school: the incense, the wall tapestries, relics that now live in a plastic tub in our basement. During her freshman year at college she waitressed at a hippie pizza place on the weekends and lived in a small apartment with another girl, both of them theater majors, their shelves filled with the plays of Albee, Dürrenmatt, Stoppard, Brecht, and so forth, books that had not gone into a plastic tub but had instead found a shelf in her office at Thrill Arts!

She and Anthony had been on-again, off-again for about a year. She was nineteen when she got pregnant, and I gathered—this is me reading between the lines—that only for the quickest of seconds had she considered not keeping the baby. Anthony was a few years older and was able to graduate before Fisher arrived. They married, and she dropped back to part-time at school, while Anthony went to work for his father's construction company.

I often worried about the fact that Annie was a widow as opposed to a divorcée. She hadn't decided to end the marriage. When I thought of her relationship with Anthony, I sometimes imagined a knife trying to slice through something that couldn't be separated—water, perhaps. She and Anthony had only been together for a few years when he died, and it seemed possible to me that they'd never experienced any of the challenges or problems that can arise between two people who are in love. If all she had were good memories, then was it truly possible for her to move on?

But the past is the past, was my unconvincing refrain. We were Annie and Jim now, and I didn't want to pry—or, more accurately, I didn't want to give off the impression of being too interested in Anthony. Asking too many questions about him seemed to me undignified or weak or insensitive.

The result of this attitude, unfortunately, was that I knew so little about him and my imagination, if allowed, would work overtime to fill the void. The Anthony who took up residence in my head had a reedy voice, and what he had to say was always very chill and beach Zen. *You do what you need to do, babe,* I could hear him telling Annie. *Don't sweat it, I got this.* Or, *Let's just listen to the ocean. Let the ocean guide you. The ocean knows best.* The Anthony in my head was a hippie dream husband, a patient and thoughtful man, unbothered, unfussy, who didn't sweat the small stuff, who spoke in koans, who knew the pressure points in a woman's foot that could bring her to orgasm. This Anthony sang Annie to sleep at night while strumming a ukulele he'd found half buried in the sand.

I'm not sure who brought up Anthony at lunch. Kurt, I think, though I can't say this with absolute certainty because we'd had a few drinks and it's possible in my state I'd been bold enough to ask. As I recall, Kurt was telling me about the weekend Annie graduated from college, about a sunset cruise they'd all taken together, when he made an oblique reference to the fact that Anthony's body had never been recovered after he drowned. I hadn't heard this part of the story before.

"Yeah, you didn't know that?" he asked. "He and his buddies were out kayaking, and they stopped for lunch and got drunk and stoned, and by the time they started to paddle back toward the car, it was getting dark. They think maybe he passed out. Super fucking sad, but if he was already unconscious at least maybe he went peacefully. Annie was down there for days, watching the divers try to find him, but they never did. God, it was awful, man. I didn't think Annie would ever be the same again. I mean, things worked out all right, in the end, but it was bad there for a while."

This was all news to me. I'd never heard about the divers, about Annie having been down there at the river, about their failure to ever locate the body.

"I think it's pretty typical for them not to find it," Kurt continued. "Maybe he wound up in the ocean. Fish food. Everything gets recycled anyway." He smiled and took a big bite of a shrimp dumpling.

So, Anthony was not a body in a graveyard. He was ribs in a sea bed; a skull encrusted with barnacles, home for an eel; metacarpals in a shark's stomach; pubis buried in an underwater trash heap of plastic bags and soda liters.

That didn't stop Annie from taking Fisher to visit the gravesite, however.

A few weeks before Christmas we drove down

to Charleston so that Fisher could visit with her grandparents, and on our way into town, we stopped by the cemetery.

The weather was eerily warm, almost seventy degrees, even though it was early December, and both Annie and Fisher were wearing cardigans over loose dresses. They sat down in the grass together at the foot of the tombstone, a family reunion. Fisher had hardly known her father, and so I don't think she was capable of comparing me to him, but I was always very aware of my status as an impostor. That's how I thought of myself, especially in that first year.

As Annie and Fisher communed with my predecessor, I decided to go for a long walk and give them some time alone. Exploring the endless rows of mowed grass and buried bodies, I kept myself distracted by trying to find the most ancient marker there. The oldest I saw belonged to a man who had died in 1801. The stone was so worn down I had to trace the shapes with my fingers to decipher the date. I had no desire to be buried. Or cremated, for that matter. I didn't like to think about the fate of my body. I've read about people having their ashes compressed into stones that can then be fashioned into jewelry for those left behind. But to what occasion would one wear such an accessory? *Oh, this? You like it? It's my mother, actually.*

Where were Clara and Robert Lennox buried? I

wondered. For some reason, it had never occurred to me they might be buried somewhere in Shula.

Annie and Fisher were waiting for me by the car when I returned, ready to continue on to the next stop in the Anthony Warren memorial tour: his parents' house, a beautiful white house situated near a marsh on one of the islands. The plan was to drop off Fisher there for a few days while Annie and I stayed in a hotel in town. I hadn't met the Warrens yet. They were standing in the driveway when we arrived, both of them in untucked men's dress shirts and garden shoes.

"Give your Gramma a kiss," Annie told Fisher.

Gramma had a pleasant, wrinkled face, a light fuzz on her upper lip. She squeezed Fisher hard and then introduced herself to me as JoJo.

"And I'm Anthony," Anthony's father said.

I shook his hand, firmly, to communicate confidence, though being there, I felt anything but that. Already I suspected I'd made a gross miscalculation in volunteering to come along. They'd set up a game of croquet in the backyard, which I gathered was a tradition, and while the ladies played and chatted with iced teas, Anthony Sr. and I shucked corn on the back deck for a low-country boil. He was an athletic man with a small-featured face and close-together eyes. I could feel him studying me as I pulled loose the spidery string from the cob.

"I'm glad you've come," he said, as if trying to convince himself.

"Thank you."

"Annie seems happy, and that makes us happy."

I nodded. "I know this must be a little strange."

"Why do you say that?" he asked, eyes narrowing, hands gone still.

I wasn't sure what to say. "Well . . ."

"Not strange at all," he said. "We're delighted to meet you. Put a face to the name and all that."

We watched the girls play croquet. Fisher knocked a ball too hard with her mallet and it rolled down a small hill into a small frog pond. Annie and JoJo were chatting, though they were too far away for me to understand what they were saying to each other.

"She really misses Annie," he said, meaning JoJo. "We had two sons, but she always wanted a daughter, and she'd really come to think of Annie that way, as her own. They were very close until Annie left town."

He grabbed a plastic shopping bag from between his legs and began to fill it with the corn husks.

"But we're glad she's found some real stability, we really are. As I'm sure you've heard, my son was a passionate guy. He wasn't easy. His third-grade teacher, she nailed it on the head. 'This one's got spirit,' she told us. 'This one's going to be trouble.' People with big hearts, they don't always know where the boundaries are, they have a hard time squeezing themselves into a normal life. They feel too much, you know? Now, our other son, William, he's more like you, I think. He's a producer for CNN, in Atlanta, very dependable, very unflappable. He's smart, and he's prudent. I don't have to worry about him." He let the bag fall down to his feet. "But you know, it's strange, as a parent, I sort of miss the worrying. That must sound very odd, but Anthony, the way he was, it made me feel necessary. I had a role to play, if that makes sense. Will doesn't need me like Anthony did. I'm not saying Will's got the world figured out—he really doesn't, despite what he says—but at least he's focused."

It was clear to me then that he'd already made a decision about me, that he had pegged me as a stable if boring alternative to his dead son. I was, in other words, Annie's safety net. What Anthony and Annie had shared, he seemed to be saying, was big, was passionate, was boundless, was reckless, and what she'd found in me was something more comfortable and predictable. I was a *Will,* not an *Anthony,* whatever that meant, and behind this categorization lurked a not-so-gentle criticism of my entire personality, of my entire way of being. But he knew nothing about me, other than the scantest details—my job, age, the way I dressed (a button-down shirt and khaki pants on that particular afternoon)—and how did that qualify him to make such assumptions about the largeness or smallness of my spirit, about the labyrinth of my heart? We cannot presume to know such things about people.

I excused myself to the bathroom. Sliding open the door, I stepped into the living room, which was well decorated, beach chic, a plush off-white couch, a low glass coffee table, wicker television cabinet. The bathroom was at the end of a short carpeted hallway. Conch shells ringed the sink, and a fat red scented candle burned in a silver tray on top of the toilet tank, filling the small room with an almost manly pinecone smell. I peed, rinsed my hands, and was on the way back to the living room when I passed an open door on my left, a bedroom with green walls and two twin beds. On the dresser by the window were photos in silver frames and above that, two Boy Scout merit badge sashes were pinned to the wall. I didn't count badges, but the one on the right was almost full, top to bottom. Will's, I assumed. The sash on the left had maybe eight badges in all: Swimming, Leatherworking, Wilderness Survival, and so on.

I was walking back into the living room when a framed picture flung itself from an end table—it really did seem that way to me then, as a flinging—and landed at my feet. Is it possible I knocked the table with my hip as I entered the room? Absolutely. I've replayed the scene a dozen times in my head, but our memories are highly unreliable and of little use in trying to re-create and understand these unusual moments. We are prone to exaggerate, to inflate, to deflate. We see only what seems significant in retrospect. And so I really can't say with any degree of certainty how the picture came to be on the floor, but what's undeniable is that it did come to be there.

Picking it up, I realized with dread that I was holding a picture of Anthony and Annie's wedding day and not only that but the glass had cracked. Just to be clear, the glass had not cracked evenly down the middle, severing Anthony from his bride as they fed each other white wedding cake. It was not so dramatic as that. This was a spiderweb crack across the bottom of the photo. The shape and length of the crack symbolized nothing, as far as I could tell. Still, how was I going to explain it to everyone? I considered just setting the frame back on the table. If anyone noticed, I could play dumb. But they'd know that I'd been in the house—for going on ten minutes now—and they would suspect me. I knew this because *I* would have suspected me. I couldn't just pretend it hadn't happened, and that meant I'd have to come clean.

Finally, I went outside onto the deck with the

photo in my hands, steeling myself for whatever came next. Mr. Warren had joined his wife and the girls out on the lawn. When I slid the door shut, they all turned to face me.

"What's that?" Fisher asked, the first to notice I was holding something.

"You won't believe this, but—" I said, already losing confidence, wishing I'd thought more carefully about what exactly to say. "Look, you have to understand this was a total accident, and I realize how terrible this is going to seem."

"What is it, Jim?" Annie asked.

"I was coming through the living room and knocked the table and a photo fell. I didn't even see what the photo was until I picked it up. I had no idea what it was."

Mrs. Warren—JoJo—stepped up onto the deck and took the frame from me. "Oh," she said.

"What?" Mr. Warren asked.

She showed the others.

"I'm very, very sorry," I said.

"Jim, it's fine," she said.

"It was an accident," Annie said. "No big deal."

"It's just glass," Anthony Warren Sr. said, taking the frame from his wife. "The photo's fine. You can't break *that.*"

"Right," I said, feeling relieved but also, suddenly, irritated. Everything Anthony Sr. said to me seemed vaguely threatening. What did he mean that I couldn't *break* the photo? Did he want me to know that what Annie and Anthony had shared together, their wedding cake bliss, I'd never be able to touch that or replace it? I had the strange impulse to grab the photo from him and rip it into a hundred pieces. To light the pieces on fire.

The rest of our afternoon with them is a blur, obscured by the steam of their low-country boil, all that shrimp and corn and potatoes at the center of the table. I was too preoccupied with the wedding photo incident to pay careful attention to the conversation. I remember Fisher calling shrimp the cockroach of the sea. I remember JoJo asking Annie if she still liked peanut butter cookies. I remember the contented smile that splashed across the woman's face when Annie said that she did, as if this knowledge implied not just a familiarity, unbroken, but a kind of possession.

Annie and I stayed at the Omni in downtown Charleston for the next two nights and on Sunday morning we picked up Fisher from her grandparents and headed back north to Shula. We were halfway home when the Suburban just ahead of us swerved wildly to avoid a police officer who was standing perilously close to the edge of the highway with a radar gun in his hand. The Suburban sideswiped the car in the adjacent lane and then careened back in the other direction and rolled down off an embankment along the side of the road. This happened so quickly that I hardly reacted at all. I had no time to brake or accelerate or scream. I looked over at Annie, who was reading a magazine, and back at Fisher, who was in the back seat on her phone. When I told them what had just happened, they didn't believe me at first. Neither one of them had seen a thing. I described the cop to them, his aviator sunglasses, his shaved head, the glint of his badge, his dark brown broom of a mustache. A movie cop, in other words. A total cliché. The absence of a police car was suspicious, Fisher said, because what was the point of checking speeds if you couldn't then pursue, and I admitted that was a fair point. I even began to doubt myself a little. Maybe I'd dreamed it up. Maybe it hadn't really happened.

But then, a few miles later, we spotted another cop on the side of the road.

I slowed a little so that we could observe him together. This second cop was identical to the first. An exact copy. His muscles bulged in his shirt. He pointed his radar gun directly at us, as if in admonishment, and his head turned ever so slightly as we passed.

He was a hologram.

All at once, it seemed, they were among us, these laser beam cousins of ours, air suffused with color and light and personality. We marveled at them, their movements, their particularity, their seeming vitality. They thrummed with life. We couldn't always tell the difference between us and them, not at first. A trained eye was required, especially from a distance. Walking through one seemed discourteous, and so we sidestepped, mumbled apologies unthinkingly, as if they cared.

Sometimes our curiosity would overwhelm us. Incapable of embarrassment, the children were usually the first to make the approach, to step inside a body, to wave their arms about, to laugh and giggle. We adults tried to be less conspicuous. We'd pretend not to notice what we were doing, surfing our palms into the light, swiping, testing.

But where were the mirrors, the projectors, the lamps, the plates? We searched in vain for the equipment or machinery responsible for delivering them here. The technology had advanced to such a point that the holograms were no longer tied to any obvious hardware or surface. Projector drones, reflective resins that could be painted on any surface—different companies, we learned, had developed different techniques. Reports even began to surface about a particular type of hologram that bypassed the physical world entirely and interacted directly with our brains. That is to say, somehow, this company was altering our perception of reality without us even realizing it, making us see and hear things that weren't really there, though these reports were all unverified, not to mention the fact that I'm not sure images produced in this fashion, technically, would even have qualified as holograms.

Grammers, I began to hear them called. A catch-all term for the walking and talking mirages.

Always, I was thinking about daisy particles, of a universe that only partly exists. Could one thing truly exist more than another? Were there gradients of existence?

They were immigrants from another dimension. Visitors. Passers-thru. Salesmen, too. Corporate shills. Ad campaign faces. Champions of causes and charities. Purveyors of fine linens and French fries. Hawkers of form-fitting mattresses and intelligent thermostats. Sometimes they were recognizable, even famous. Tom Bradys now stood outside every Subway in America, suave, confident, doing their best to lure you inside for a delicious foot-long turkey and provolone on wheat. Jim Carreys with giant scraggly beards loitered in urgent-care parking lots and tried to convince you not to vaccinate your children. Was that Salma Hayek modeling diamond bracelets in the window of your local jewelry store?

The dead were exhumed, reanimated, returned to us. Prince performed a sold-out show at the theater in downtown Shula, and I overheard a guy ask his date, earnestly, why Prince hadn't put out any records in so long. Not long after that I was on my way to a meeting with the city planning commissioner when I witnessed Robin Williams leap onto a park bench and tell a series of jokes in which he somehow segued, in rapid order, from Mahatma Gandhi's sex life to Bugs Bunny's carrot obsession to the last words of Jesus on the cross. We could see the dark hair over his forearms, a wrinkle in his T-shirt, the sparkle of sweat across his brow. I'd never seen Robin Williams in anything but his movies, and this impromptu routine was a revelation, no matter how macabre. About fifty people had gathered around him by the time he took a bow and thanked everyone for listening. He then directed our attention to a nearby booth for Amnesty International and asked us all to make whatever donations we could to such a worthy cause.

The White Hairs didn't care for the holograms, generally. I think they were confused by them, especially the more interactive and intelligent ones—the algorithmically advanced super-Grammers and so forth. A Grammer shoe clerk in the department store would offer assistance, and the White Hair, not realizing what they were talking to, would become upset when the clerk could only make suggestions and offer compliments and not actually deliver the right sizes. "I want to talk to your manager," the disgruntled old-timer would say. "Bring me your manager. Do you hear me? Where's the manager?" The Shula City Council, long dominated by White Hairs, narrowly passed a new law to keep the holograms off public property, which hardly mattered. They proliferated anyway. They followed us through the aisles of the grocery store, asking if we knew about the two-for-one special on canned chickpeas. They were parking lot attendants, waving us toward empty spaces. They were receptionists behind the front desk at the dentist's office, pointing to forms.

A woman appeared at the entrance of our bank one morning. I hadn't seen her enter. She was blond-haired and busty, dressed in a dark skirt and blazer, and rather than approach the counters she stayed standing just inside the doors with a pleasant smile on her face. She looked as if she might be waiting for someone to arrive, but after a half hour, Darryl poked his head in my office to ask if we needed to be concerned. He was thoroughly creeped out by this woman, enough so that he didn't feel comfortable bothering her. I volunteered to speak with her myself. As I approached, she turned and welcomed me to the bank. Then she asked me how she might be of service.

"Service?" I asked.

"What sort of transaction are you here to make this morning? A deposit, perhaps? I can help you find the deposit slips."

"I work here, actually. That's my office over there."

"Wonderful, I love meeting coworkers."

I waited for her to continue, but she didn't. She only smiled at me happily. Which is to say, eerily.

"Forgive me," I said. "But you're a hologram, right? You're a Grammer?"

She nodded. "But please, call me Diana."

The Fortune Tellers were watching me from across the lobby, unable to hear this conversation. To give them a shock, I waved my hand through the Grammer's face, as if to slap her. The hologram didn't react at all.

"Where are you being projected from?" I asked her.

She smiled. "I'm sorry?"

"I don't understand how it is you're here right now. Where's the projector?"

"If you like to report a problem with my service, please email *diana-at-holo-help-dot—*"

"I don't need to report a problem, but thank you."

I wandered back over to the Fortune Tellers. When I told Diana that she and the hologram shared a name, she laughed but then, very quickly, turned morose. She didn't want to share a name with—with that *thing*. She didn't understand: Of all the names in the world, why Diana? Couldn't we call it Helen or Audrey or any other name instead? Certainly the hologram didn't have a preference? Certainly it didn't think of itself as Diana when no one was talking to it?

When I called our corporate offices to complain on all our behalf, I was told that Diana was the name assigned to her by her manufacturer. We now had Dianas in over 312 of our branches at that very moment. There was no way to change the name, in other words. We were stuck with her, with this lady by the door, this lady who never changed her clothes or her hair or her smile, whom we could hear reminding every single customer about our new e-checking accounts with overdraft protection, who presumably stood there not only all day but all night, too, alone in the darkness, emotionless as the cleaning crew vacuumed at her feet.

We could become holograms ourselves now, too, if we pleased. Holographic recording shops started popping up all over the country—*HoloYou*, *The Slammin' Grammin*, and all the rest. Places where you could pay by the hour for the chance to record your story and be immortalized as a hologram. One day, the idea went, your great-great-grandchildren would be able to sit side-by-side with your hologram.

Our bank gave a loan to one such business, called *Hologramophone*, which set up shop in an old redbrick building close to downtown on Ivar Street, a building that, as it happened, had once been a furniture store called *Lennox & Sons*. Initially I thought this an amazing coincidence, to have stumbled upon a second building in as many years with a connection to the Lennox family, but then again, all the old buildings in Shula were constantly being either demolished or repurposed.

A few days before *Hologramophone* officially opened its doors, I took my father with me for a quick tour. The walls were still wet with paint. Construction debris and dust still littered the distressed concrete floors. Behind the front desk, on an austere white wall, loomed a large stenciled drawing of Thomas Edison and a phonogram, the rudimentary recording device he'd invented.

A tech—a young guy with long dark sideburns—led us past the lobby and down a long hallway of recording booths in which customers would be able to record a private message. For a spouse, for children, descendants, for the public, for posterity. They'd even have the option to time capsule it by checking a little box on a form: *Make this message available to ______ in five years, ten years, a thousand years.* In the future, people would be able to scroll through a list of names organized by topic or decade, select yours, and then beam you into their kitchens to learn about your life while they prepared dinner. Historians would decorate their talks and presentations with a chorus of primary-source holograms.

A new way to be remembered, the company claimed. A new way to connect. To preserve and be preserved.

The tech asked if we—my father or I—wanted to try it, and my father volunteered. He went into a booth, stepped on the two footprint decals on the floor, and, as directed, faced a milky white floor-to-ceiling panel. A tumorous red light flashed from within the wall, indicating that he was now being recorded. The door whizzed shut. Like a door from a spaceship. The tech smiled at me: Pretty cool, huh? My father emerged a few minutes later, laughing at himself.

"I had no idea what to say."

"Typically we'll advise people to write something down first," the tech said, nodding.

We returned to the lobby. The space had been gutted half a dozen times since it had been a furniture store, but Robert Lennox had stood here once, he'd stood in this exact spot among the settees and wardrobes. He was a real person, I reminded myself. Not a character in a ghost story. He'd really lived and really died. The furniture store had gone out of business a few years before the fire, but I'd never been able to find any records of his employment after that. He and Clara had never had any children. The facts of their lives, as I knew them, offered only a cold outline, a rough sketch.

I did know, however, that they'd been buried alongside one another not too far from the old furniture store—in a cemetery of the South Methodist Church. Though I wasn't exactly sure what I expected us to find there, other than their names on the tombstones, I asked my father if he wanted to go with me to find their graves after we'd left the hologram shop. We drove together in my car.

The cemetery was a small grassy square enclosed by a low stone wall. On Clara's tombstone was a small bouquet of flowers.

"What do you make of that?" I asked.

"She's been dead for almost a hundred years. I doubt she's got any relatives left."

"Maybe it's a service someone provides for all the old graves. A flower guild or something."

My father grabbed a flower and held it to his nose for a sniff, then returned it to the grave. I thought of their bodies down deep in the coffins, long since decomposed, their perfectly laid out bones. Devoted Wife, Clara's marker said. She was thirty when she died, four years younger than me. I shut my eyes for a moment and quietly let the Lennoxes know that we were here, that we wished them well and they therefore didn't need to bother us or mess with our heads. Not that I really thought they could hear me. It was an old habit, what I was doing, one that had sprung up from a dumb childhood belief that ghosts hanging around cemeteries had the power to enter my head and read my thoughts.

"You've read about Zinker's idea for a Reunion Machine," I said.

He nodded.

"You think it's possible?"

"Possible? Of course. What isn't these days? But I'm not convinced that's what we need, a world where the living can talk to the dead whenever they want. Life is confusing enough as it is."

"You think it would create confusion? I'd think it would clear a few things up. If you knew for a fact that we go on existing after we die?"

"Well, even with a machine like that, you'd never know it for a fact."

"Says the man who got pulled into some sort of ghost vortex on a staircase."

He smiled sheepishly. "I admit it was a profound experience. But it hardly answered any of my questions. I have a confession to make. I went back there recently—to the restaurant. I was driving by and saw a guy doing some maintenance work and convinced him to let me inside. I must have stood on those stairs for a half hour. Nothing."

"Nothing?"

He shrugged. "The farther I get from it, the less I know what to make of what happened to me the night we were there together. Maybe I'd had too much coffee, and my heart skipped a beat.

"But the mark on your arm. The handprint . . ."

"Everything has an explanation. What I mean is, there's nothing we're not willing to come up with an explanation for. Anything miraculous or amazing that happens to us in life, our brains are trained to pick it apart. To be skeptical. To create doubt. Think of the Pythia—the Oracle at Delphi—and her visions. People back then believed she could see past, present, and future. She could slide back and forth in time. She could speak to the gods."

"We should all be so lucky."

"Yes, but did you catch that scientist a couple of weeks ago at The Church? I forget her name. She studied the temple and she thinks that the oracle was probably hallucinating thanks to some vapors that escape through fractures in the rocks. She was breathing these fumes all day. The priestess was high, like, ninety percent of the time! So, it would be very easy to dismiss what she had to say as a product of those fumes, right? Admit it: Your brain wants you to. Our brains are very pleased with themselves when they can discount something incredible. When they can return the world to normal. You hear a voice on a tape, and somebody tells you it's a ghost. OK, what do you do next? You start thinking of all the reasons why it isn't, why it couldn't be. I'm not saying we shouldn't try to find logical, rational explanations for things. Because we should! I've spent my whole life doing that. But at a certain point, you either trust that there's more than meets the eye—or you don't."

We both looked at Clara's tombstone again.

"Like these flowers," he said. "Who put them here? For Clara Lennox. That's what I want to know. That's what my brain is trying to explain to me right now."

A lawn mower revved to life. A groundskeeper, a man with wild gray hair, was cutting the grass along the sidewalk in front of the church. He waved his gloved hand at us, and I nodded. We were on our way toward the wrought-iron gate through which we'd entered the cemetery, when he killed the lawn mower's engine and called over to us. He wanted to know if we needed any help.

"Sure," my father said.

"Nobody's been buried here since the sixties," the man reported as he walked up to us.

"Yes, it looks very old," I said.

"Y'all don't go to church here, do you?" he asked.

I explained we were just out for a walk, we were only exploring.

"If you're looking for Mary Pam, I can show you exactly where she's buried," he said.

"Who's Mary Pam?"

"Oh, she was a writer, back in the twenties. She wrote a book called *The Carnival Children*. I've never read it, but I'm told it's about lesbians. She's the one most people come to see. She's always got fresh flowers on her grave. I gather she's something of an icon. But she's not the only famous person buried here. We've also got Eustace Wilton. He wrote religious music and was a hero in the War Between the States. And there's Wendell Lennox, he was a big-time screenwriter."

My father and I exchanged glances.

"Lennox?" I asked.

"Don't ask me what movies he made. I couldn't tell you. I'm no film buff. This was back in the forties and fifties. I don't really go in for old movies. I figure anything worth watching gets remade anyway." He smiled. "Boy, times like these I wish I had a pamphlet I could offer you. For years I've been telling anybody who'll listen—every cemetery needs a pamphlet! It would tell you a little bit about all the people buried there. Wouldn't that be something? It would lead you on a little tour."

"There's a grave over there, another Lennox,"

my father said. "Clara Lennox. There are some flowers on her stone. Is there any chance you know who left them there?"

The man rubbed his chin. "I doubt I could say. I'm only out here a few hours a week."

"It's no problem. I was just curious."

I thanked the man for the information, and my father and I walked to my car. I drove him back to the hologram shop, where he was parked.

"See you Sunday," he said and slapped my knee before getting out.

He slapped my knee, he got out of the car and told me he'd see me Sunday, but did I say anything to him in reply?

Most of the time, my memories of my father are a jumble, one moment sliding into the next. When I think about him, he is saluting me from the doorstep. He is pulling out the chair for my mother at a seafood restaurant on the occasion of her fiftieth birthday; he is cracking his knuckles on a cold morning in a deer stand; he is jangling the loose change in his pockets; he is singing along to a song on the radio; he is asleep on the couch with a book on his lap; he is in a classroom drawing a parabola on the white board; he is massaging my mother's neck to help her migraine; he is sliding his hand back and forth across his bald head; he is laughing at himself for ordering a latte instead of an old-fashioned plain black coffee.

He is seated beside me in the car after a trip to the graveyard, a speck of dirt in his goatee, his hand digging around in his pockets for his car keys. It's always the car keys I think about, the way he leaned toward me to fish them free from his right pocket, his heavy breath, but for whatever reason, I can't recall if I said anything to him before he set off for his car. I try not to torture myself.

Anyway, that day was among our last together. I missed church that Sunday, but we did get coffee that same week, and then later I was over at the house to help my mother with something, I forget what, and he popped downstairs to say hello. In truth, he lived another three months after our trip to the hologram shop and the graveyard, and I must have seen him half a dozen times, but it's always that trip to Clara's grave that hangs in my head as our final moment together.

A few weeks after he died—from a stroke—I worked up the courage to return to *Hologramophone* and inquire about his recording. My father hadn't signed any paperwork as his session had been something of a demonstration, but I was grateful to learn that the tech had saved it anyway. I was given a small black cube, about the size of a ring box, and then shown into a small private lounge with a long gray couch and orange ottomans, very modern and slick. The cube had only two silver buttons: Play and Stop. When I clicked Play he immediately warbled into existence just a few feet away from me, a genie conjured from the lamp. He stood above me, as tall as he'd been in life. His shirt was bunched oddly at one shoulder, and his belt buckle was twisted slightly to the left of his navel. He looked down, at his shoes, which touched the ground, then up again, over my head.

"So I'm not really sure what I'm supposed to do," he said and then was quiet for a few moments, a very serious expression on his face. He hardly moved at all. I thought maybe that it was a technical glitch, that he'd frozen, until the muscles in his throat flexed as he swallowed. All at once he began to dance, an odd little jig, his arms gyrating at his sides as his feet shuffled and tapped and swept. This went on for almost twenty seconds before he stopped, abruptly, and smiled at his feet.

"Well," he said, "that's it, I guess."

May Hopstead Gadd

May is wearing a bright yellow dress for the occasion of her sister's wedding. She holds up a small mirror so that Clara can fix her hair. Clara is the more beautiful sister, so slim and elegant, but May, only twelve, already suspects she is the smarter one. On the shelf, above Clara's head, she spies a book called *Religious Ecstasies* and fights the urge to grab it. She asks her sister if she's sure she wants to do this, if she really wants to marry Robert.

May has never understood the appeal of the Lennox brothers. Wendell was handsome, certainly, but he was the vainest boy May has ever met, and she was grateful when he ran off to la-la land and left Clara in the lurch. As for Robert, he isn't attractive at all. His clothes appear to conceal nothing but knobs and joints, and his brow protrudes so far it keeps the sunlight from his eyes. Not only that, but he's positively mopey. Brooding! May can't imagine ever planting her lips upon a man such as that, no matter what's in his bank account. Surely it's the money that Clara's interested in. Because if not the money, then what? Maybe Clara should have followed Wendell out West, after all, and tried her luck in California.

• • •

Wendell's picture is in the newspaper. He's died. May hasn't seen him in more than fifty years, and there he is, white-haired, corpulent. She's sitting at her usual table at Myers, the diner she eats at before work on Friday mornings. The waiter brings her the wrong omelet. He apologizes and promises to return promptly with the right one. Spinach, onions, and sausage—how hard is that to get right? She tips the creamer into her coffee, watches it swirl down into the blackness. She's eating alone, as she does most days. For the last thirty years, she's reported every morning at 7:30 a.m. to City Hall, where she works for the planning commission. It's not a glamorous job, but it's a good one. She can't imagine retiring.

The headline: *Wendell Lennox—Blacklisted Screenwriter, Father of "The Skeleton Man"—Dies*. The article is a litany of his many films, most of which May has never bothered to watch. No mention of his brother, Robert, however. No mention of Clara. Not that May really expected to find their names here—but still. A life reduced to its papery accomplishments. About his upbringing, the article mentions only that Wendell hailed from North Carolina and that he was the son of a furniture maker. Not furniture *maker,* May thinks. A furniture *salesman*.

• • •

The first time she talks to him Wendell is smoking in the Hopsteads' small backyard between the laundry on the line, which still hasn't been collected. May, on the other side of the fence, climbs up and peers down at her sister's beau. The splintery wood digs into her forearms.

"So you like my sister?" she asks.

"What's not to like?"

He passes her his cigarette, and, putting it between her lips, she inhales with a quick suck. She coughs it all out.

"You'll get the hang of it," he says, laughing.

She flicks the cigarette down at him and it hits him squarely in the chest. Unfazed, he plucks it back up from the grass and takes another drag. Far off she hears the family dog barking. She drops down off the fence and runs after him.

She's always loved dogs. In college, she rides a train home from Baltimore with a cocker spaniel in a hatbox. She hasn't seen Clara in almost a year, but according to their mother, Robert is even worse than he used to be, especially now that the store is having trouble. These are hard times, their situation pitiable, but then again, whose situation isn't these days? No one's without trouble. One must make do, mustn't one? If only Clara hadn't rushed from one brother to the next, maybe someone else would have come along, someone more decent, better-looking, and not so gloomy. To think of Clara trapped in a house all day with a man like Robert, it's almost too much to bear.

That's why she's taking Clara the dog. Houdini was the runt of the litter and, as is true of most runts, the smartest of the bunch. (May has always thought of herself as the Hopstead runt.) Despite it being a flagrant violation of school rules, May has kept him in her room for the last few months, hiding him in her coat whenever she takes him outside to pee.

When her train arrives at the station, May carries the dog out front to where her father is waiting. Together they hop onto a streetcar with a stop not far from Clara's house. Her father says he'll wait for her across the street. "You won't come inside?" she asks. "I'd rather not," is all he says.

May knocks twice and when no one answers, she lets herself in the front door, calling Clara's name as she wanders through the parlor and the dining room. Next she shouts up the stairs and when no one replies, she goes up to the second floor, where, at the top of the stairs, she hears voices. The bedroom door is ajar, and through it she sees her sister standing behind a wingback chair. Robert is sitting there, smoking a cigarette, his eyes closed, and Clara is delicately massaging his temples. Seeing May in the hallway, Clara's eyes widen—whether with excitement or embarrassment, May can't tell. Clara leans down, kisses Robert on the forehead, and then hurries out into the hall, bringing the door shut behind her. Her finger to her lips, she quietly escorts May back downstairs into the parlor, where she puts on a record at low volume. She explains that Robert is having one of his headaches—a migraine, in fact—and now would not be a good time to disturb him.

But what's this! Houdini topples over the hatbox and plods toward Clara. She scoops him up in her arms, elated. She can't believe how adorable he is, so small and wriggly. They let him loose on the floor, and he sniffs his way toward the base of the stairs, where he urinates, cutely, at the edge of the rug. The sisters spring up into action, dabbing away the puddle with a cloth. It's clear to May that Clara loves the little dog and that she wants to keep Houdini here, and so May is somewhat mortified when Clara wonders aloud if Robert will let her keep him. *Let* her?

"You're a grown woman," May says to her sister. "And if you want a dog, you'll have a dog. It's as simple as that."

Clara smiles but doesn't seem convinced. Not for the first time, May feels slightly disgusted by her sister's weak will. If she were as beautiful as Clara, May thinks, she'd rule the world one day.

They sit down together on the floor at the base

of the winding stairs, the soles of their shoes touching, creating a diamond-shaped pen for Houdini. As he runs back and forth between their legs, they talk about the sudden change of weather (so much colder than it was last week) and about what May might do when she graduates next year (her dream: to find a place in the architecture school at Harvard).

"If anyone can do it," Clara says, "it's you."

What May can't understand is why they had to bury Clara alongside Robert.

"You never stop being husband and wife," her father says, pathetically.

"But after what he did." She doesn't bother hiding her irritation and disappointment.

"We don't know what he did or didn't do," he says. "And we'll never know."

May's father, swinging his arms hard, walks ahead to join his wife at the front of their procession back to the house from the church cemetery. May threads her arm through Frank's, pressing her cheek to his shoulder for a moment, his wool suit sleeve swishing across her face roughly but pleasantly. One day, she thinks, it will be her and Frank in the graveyard together, side by side. They've been married now for only a year. They met through mutual friends and eloped a few months later at the courthouse, all of it very simple and straightforward, dotted lines signed, vows taken. The decision not to have a proper wedding had been hers. She could spare her parents at least that expense.

A few people from the funeral join the family at the house. None of the Lennoxes attended the funeral—not Wendell or his mother, who still lives across town. To May, this is a gross insult, but her parents don't seem especially upset by their absence. May thinks of her sister—the bandages, the smell, all those months in and out of the hospital. That she survived as long as she did with burns so severe was something of a miracle, though "miracle" hardly seems like the right word to May, considering that her sister's survival only prolonged her misery. Perhaps it's good she's finally dead. Now they can begin to put those terrible years behind them. The saga of Clara and the Lennoxes has come to an end, at last.

After the guests have left the house, May helps store away the food, and then she and Frank go for a quick walk around the block, even though it's very late, before going upstairs to bed. They are staying in her old bedroom, the one she shared with Clara when they were girls. Frank throws back the wool blanket, and they climb in together, his crotch against her rear end. Through the walls she can hear her father snoring. How is it he's sleeping so well on today of all days? She resents her father. Everything about him—

his good manners, his pride in something as simple as the family silverware, his ignorance, his poverty. This room is even shabbier than she remembers it. The wind whistles through the cracks around the windows, and the floors flex beneath her feet. Frank doesn't come from much money, but May suspects this house is a shock to him, its dilapidations, its leaks, its layers of impenetrable grime.

She lies awake for a very long time.

The darling bud of May, Frank calls her.

When she's with him, it's lightness she feels, as if his love is lifting her up, whisking her away. She's almost ready to let it keep her, enfold her—but not yet.

Frank is a decent man, a poet, a gentle soul. She kisses his stubbled cheek and wipes away the lipstick with her thumb, rubbing more life into his face. Until the war started, he taught literature at an all-boys school in Philadelphia and directed their small theater program. May didn't want him to enlist. She pleaded with him to stay home. The world needs more good high school teachers than soldiers.

When his train disappears around the curve, she heads back to the house and tries not to feel alone. She's cooking dinner when she hears the trap snap behind the stove. Peering back there she can see it, the little mouse, its head crushed, its tail across the grimy tile like a flaccid nail. With her hand in a long yellow scrub glove, she reaches deep behind the appliance, her face squished against its metal side, and grabs at the trap. Walking it outside to the garbage can, lonely against the garage, its lid hanging sideways like a bad hat, she begins to sob.

Another goodbye, years later: At the end of a too-short summer, May drives her son Lewis to the station and watches him board a bus to New York, a giant duffel bag over his shoulder. His shaggy brown hair almost reaches his collarless linen shirt. He is a smart boy, though perhaps too introverted and overly sensitive. A bit of a loner. That could be May's fault. She worries that she's doted on him too much, coddled him.

The boy moves to the back of the bus and waves to her from the window. She goes back home and makes herself dinner. Yet another house in which to discover her loneliness. The phone rings a few hours later. Lewis is calling from a pay phone near his apartment to tell her he's made it fine. She doesn't need to worry.

At the bottom of an envelope, stamped and creased: a small gray feather. She twirls it between her fingers and smiles.

How ridiculous: Frank has such an incredible photographic memory and he speaks decent

French, but what makes him most useful to the war effort is the fact that he played with homing pigeons as a boy. The army has made him a Pigeoneer with the Signal Corps. What a silly word, "Pigeoneer." He's attached to a division that's been waiting and training in England for the last six months. *We must keep our birds healthy and happy,* he writes, *lest they flap off and fall hopelessly in love with one of the native woodpigeons, who are notorious flirts.* Is he talking in code? Has he fallen in love with some British ninny? Surely not. She tucks the feather back into the envelope and drops the envelope in a desk drawer, but when she checks for it again, a few days later, the feather is gone. The envelope contains only his handwritten note.

"What's this?" her son asks, holding up a framed photo.

"What's what?" May asks.

She's ninety years old, and even with her glasses she can hardly see three feet ahead of her, let alone a small black-and-white picture at the opposite end of the room. They're in the process of packing up all her stuff. Lewis approaches with the photo. She takes it in her hands. It shows her and Frank the week they eloped. They are smiling at each other, and he has his arm over her shoulder. She's not sure what to say about the photo, but then Lewis points to something stuck behind the glass in the left bottom corner. Slick, flat, gray, small—

The feather! Cleaning out her desk drawers a few years after the war, the pigeon feather appears from under a notecard. Its ugly yellow shaft, the dark vane soft but broken, like a mouth missing teeth. She wonders if this pigeon might have been with Frank at Omaha Beach. She pops open a picture frame and traps the feather there behind the glass for safekeeping.

"Daughters," Frank says. "Three of them."

"You don't want sons?" she asks.

He smiles and caresses her back. He's just home from the high school, his briefcase at their feet. They go upstairs and make love, but no babies—daughters or sons—are produced on this particular afternoon.

Lewis helps her disembark from the plane. A motorized cart carries May from the gate to the baggage claim, people jumping out of its path, and then she's made to wait on a bench while her son gathers her many suitcases. After more than fifty years in Philly, May has agreed to move back to North Carolina, to Chapel Hill, where Lewis teaches environmental science at the university.

Over the last week he has been helping May

sort through her life, helping her decide what to keep, what to purge, a kindness except for the fact that Lewis's objective, clearly, was to toss as much as possible before bringing it all back to his house. He says he doesn't like the idea of his mother living alone anymore. He plans to set her up in a spare bedroom on the bottom floor of his house. It's got its own bathroom, he told her, so you'll have total privacy.

May suspects it's him who cares about privacy most. His house is not terribly large, and he's shared it for the last decade with his girlfriend, a woman almost half his age who also teaches at the university.

A blue Taurus pulls up alongside the curve outside, and Lewis's girlfriend waves at them from the front seat. She is a long stringy woman with curled hair pulled back tightly behind her head. She doesn't seem excited to be here or to see May.

She's never going to marry Lewis. She's too young. Eventually she'll leave him, and he'll be back to square one. Lewis claims he'll never marry, that he's not the type, and neither is Sally for that matter.

It's Clara's wedding day, and they're at the Lennox house for a small party. Mr. Lennox stands up and delivers a toast—something vague about loyalty being just as important as love—and after that there's music on the Victrola. Robert takes Clara's hands and leads her in an awkward, shoeless dance in the middle of the parlor. At the end of the song—"Dreamy Melody" by Art Landry and His Orchestra—Robert kisses Clara, and everyone claps and cheers.

"There'll be no time for dreamin' tonight!" someone yells, and a few people actually laugh.

May is jostled awake by the lift of the mattress, the creak of the floor, the squeak of the door hinges. She rolls over to find that her sister has left the room. May tiptoes after her into the darkness of the hallway. From the top of the stairs, she can hear voices in the living room. Going down a few steps and peeking under the rail, she sees them on the sofa. Robert is stretched out flat, his head on a pillow, shirtless, his bare feet flexed and protruding in either direction. Clara is on top of him, and she has one hand across his mouth. The other hand is flat on his chest. She's bobbing up and down like she's riding a series of rapid but soft ocean waves. Robert makes a low, aching noise, exhaling hard against her hand, and then Clara leans forward to kiss his forehead. May sneaks back up the stairs and darts into the bedroom, climbing under the blanket. When Clara returns a few minutes later, she lies down on top of the blanket and stares up at the ceiling with a faint smile on her face.

"Where'd you go?" May asks.

"I had a splinter," she says. "I'm okay now. Go back to sleep."

Now it's May rising from bed. She's an old woman, her feet under the covers, her throat dry. She walks down the hall with an empty water glass and hears voices in the kitchen. She lingers just outside the doorway to listen. Lewis and his girlfriend, Sally, are having a discussion at the table. It's almost midnight.

"Lewis," Sally says, "I'm proud of you for taking such good care of her, I am. You're a good person, and what you're doing for your mom is so good."

"You said 'good' three times," he says, "which leads me to believe it's not."

"Baby, I'm worried about you. You need to focus on yourself right now. Don't you think our first priority should be getting *you* well? I know you want to be good to her—"

"There's that *good* again."

"—but what about three months from now?" she asks. "Or six months?"

As May finally steps into the kitchen, she taps on the door frame, announcing her presence.

"Hey," Lewis says. "Sorry, did we wake you up?"

"What's going on with you, Lewis?" she asks.

"Tell her," Sally says.

"It's nothing, really," Lewis says.

"Just tell me," May says.

Lewis takes a long sip of his wine.

"He's sick, May," Sally says, her index finger moving to the corner of her eye. "He didn't want to tell you, which is ridiculous because sooner or later you'd have realized."

Lewis gets up from his chair and moves toward May. He tells her he's going to be fine. He didn't want to bother her with it because it's not important, because he's going to be fine, and so she doesn't need to worry.

The car honks its horn as it swooshes by, only a few inches from the front bumper of May's Buick. Lewis has let the car roll too far forward into the intersection. He's learning to drive.

"I'm okay," Lewis says. "I've got this. Don't worry."

This is his third time behind the wheel, his first on such busy streets. May is in the passenger seat, hands cupped over her knees, trying not to feel nervous as Lewis reverses the car a foot and then waits for a break in the traffic so that he can turn right. This is one of the most dangerous intersections in town. May should have known better than to bring him here. Three cars line up behind them, waiting their turn. To escape this, Lewis is going to have to gun it, but she doesn't want to tell him that. He's such an easily flustered boy.

“Now?” he asks.

But it’s too late. Another car swoops around the curve and is upon them. He slaps the steering wheel with his palm and gives her a nervous look. The driver in the car behind them, growing impatient, honks twice, and Lewis startles.

“I think you should just do it,” he says.

“Is that what you want?” May asks, feeling relieved, though she suspects this is not the best way to teach him. She needs to act confident and give him firm directions. But then again, maybe the best way for him to learn is by example? They fling open their doors and run around the car to swap seats.

“Like this,” she says, turning and accelerating.

“It’s like an instinct,” she says. “You’ll get it, eventually.”

Sally knocks on the door to May’s bedroom as she enters and sits down in the chair by the bed. May has never particularly liked this woman: her knee-high boots with the silver studs, like something you’d see on one of those motorcycle ladies; her peculiar sense of humor; her brusque manner; the way her hair is perpetually wet, as if she’s always just stepped out of the shower. May has never understood what her son sees in Sally.

“He doesn’t want you to know what’s going on,” she says. “But I think you should. Because this is not going to end well, May, and you need to be prepared. We need to meet this head-on. Together."

They are on the floor at the foot of the stairs, legs stretched and flat, the soles of their feet pressed together. Houdini wanders back and forth between them, licking at their shins. May will miss having the dog at school with her, but she knows she can't keep him there. Clara will take good care of him.

"But why is Robert so unhappy?" May asks.

On this, the topic of Robert's unhappiness, his general moodiness, Clara is so often evasive. She says only that her husband is under a tremendous amount of stress and that he's doing the best he can under the circumstances.

"But if he's *troubled* . . ." May says.

Clara draws back her feet, the diamond broken. There's a difference, she says, between *having* troubles and *being* troubled, and she hopes May can appreciate that.

"Well," May says, "Daddy has troubles, and I don't see him moping about with migraines all day."

Clara looks at her bewildered, and May fears she's said too much. She doesn't want to hurt Clara's feelings, only to help her remember that there is a world outside this house. Clara stands up from the floor and dusts off her hands. She starts to say something, then stops. She shakes her head back and forth, as if in disbelief. Seeing her sister do this, May begins to regret her visit. The little dog leaps at her legs, and she's tempted to snatch him back up in her arms and take him with her when she goes, all the way back to school. As long as he never barks, maybe she could keep him hidden. Better with her than in this miserable house. But then, as if reading May's mind, Clara comes over and lifts the cocker spaniel off the floor and clutches him close to her chest.

"Daddy's a good man," Clara says. "He really tries. But honestly, May, do you really think it's Daddy keeping you in school? Do you really think he's the one keeping us all afloat?"

Keeping them all afloat? Is Clara implying that it's Robert who's supporting them all? May can't imagine that's the case. If he's taking money from Robert, surely her father would have mentioned it to her. Surely she'd know about something like that! May wonders if that's why he preferred to wait outside on the street rather than come in the house with her.

She thinks of Robert up there in his chair, smoking his cigarettes, his headaches. Of course it's true; of course he's the rock upon which they all stand. May feels embarrassed that it didn't dawn on her earlier. She feels sick to her stomach. Because, is she supposed to feel thankful? Is she expected to go up there and rub his dumb temples too? She has no intention of thanking Robert for his help. She never asked for it! Her only option is to quit school. She'll have to quit and find some other way. But no, she can't do that, she can't quit. She has plans, and her plans are predicated on graduation. She's trapped. She's no different from Clara. All this time and without even knowing it, May has been living in this house, too.

Clara asks if May would like a cup of tea, but May says she needs to be going. She's already stayed too long. She only has one day in town, and she promised their parents she'd spend most of it with them. "Of course," Clara says, as they move toward the door.

They both go out onto the stoop and kiss each other on the cheek. Clara has the dog in her arms, and May tells him goodbye. Before rounding the corner to where her father waits, May glances back for a final view of her sister. Clara waves as the little dog licks and nips, wildly, at the soft underside of her chin.

Seventy years later and the house isn't even a house; it's a restaurant. Every so often Sally picks up May at the nursing home and gets her out for a few hours, and today they've traveled all the way to Shula, May's hometown.

"Let's stop here for lunch," May says.

"Are you sure?" Sally asks. "Tex-Mex? Chi-chi Mexican slop. Plates of melted cheese."

May insists, and so Sally finds parking along the street. They walk together up the sidewalk, pass through the metal gate, and climb the porch steps—May grabbing onto Sally's arm—to the front door, where a hostess in the foyer asks if they'd like to eat inside or out. May would like to be inside, and they follow a girl to a table in what was once a sitting room.

"My sister used to live in this house," she tells Sally. "Back in the twenties."

"*This* one?" Sally asks, looking around. "You're kidding. For real?"

May nods and tells her the story, briefly—of the Lennox family and Clara, her marriage, the little dog Houdini, the depression, the fire.

Their first appetizer, chicken tacos wrapped in iceberg lettuce, arrives on a small red plate.

"That's incredible," Sally says, looking around. "I'll bet the people who own this place have no idea what happened here. So how did the fire start?"

"We never figured that out for sure, but we all suspected Robert. He had issues. Clara lived another year or so, but she didn't like to talk about it. It was too painful. From what I could gather though, the fire started upstairs, and she went up after Robert hoping to help him."

Sally picks up a taco, arches her eyebrows, and says it must be so weird to be sitting in this place again eating food such as this. May agrees that it is, in fact, very odd to be back, though everything that happened here, it's so distant from her now. It's been almost seventy years since her sister died, after all. That's more than twice as long as Clara was alive.

"Funny thing about time though," Sally says. "We think we live our life along these little points. Little plotted dots. Life on graph paper. Event, event, event. But I think that's only how our brains make sense of the world. More likely—and I'm speaking as a physicist now—everything that has ever happened and ever will is all being expressed at once. A single event. You're here right now, May, eating lunch with me, but you're also there, in that other room, talking with your sister. There's no such thing as 'back then.' No history. No future. No present either, except in the rather limited sense that everything that exists is the present. Everything simply is."

"I guess so," May says.

"What I mean," Sally continues, "is that Lewis is both dead and not dead. So are you, for that matter. So am I. If any part of us continues after death, it's already continued. Do you follow? Life and afterlife, it's all the same thing, one being an expression of the other and vice versa. This isn't entirely conjecture, mind you. The physics supports me. Or at the very least, it doesn't prove me wrong. We're here but also not here, and the part of you that's not here could be, at this very moment, spending time with the part of Lewis that's also not here. Honestly, some days, that idea is the only thing keeping me sane."

After the meal, May needs to use the bathroom, and Sally comes over to take her arm. Together they weave through the tables, and a waiter directs them down the hall. They pass the entrance to the kitchen, full of commotion, and a few feet later they come to the bathroom. The door is locked, and so May and Sally wait with their backs against the wall. This bathroom is a more recent addition. All of these walls are new, too. May would hardly recognize the place at all if not for the stairway at the end of the hall, which used to be visible from the living room. Looking at it, she can remember sitting there, on the floor, with her sister, the little dog Houdini running back and forth between their legs.

She goes over to the stairs and puts her hand on the bannister. Sally follows behind her.

"I just want one quick look," May says, already ascending. "I'm sure they won't mind."

Sally says nothing, only takes May's other hand and helps her climb. At the top of the stairs, May peers into Clara's old bedroom, which is empty except for a few towers of unused dining chairs. Without a curtain on the window, sunlight falls hard against the floor.

"Does it look different?" Sally asks.

It does, but May isn't sure if the differences

are in her or in the house itself. Regardless, she doesn't want to be here anymore. She wishes she hadn't come at all. Why revisit the past? Grabbing hold of Sally's arm, they turn and begin their slow descent, May's left knee, that old troublemaker, throbbing with each step. Distantly she can hear the cooks shouting orders in the kitchen and all those diners chatting, their conversations swirled, and it's possible to imagine that time is just like Sally says it is, that everything is happening at once, that everyone she ever loved is both dead and not dead simultaneously—all those people, here, in this spot, in this house, all that history compressed into a single moment.

She's almost at the bottom when she feels a cool charge at her back, like a thousand eyelids fluttering across her skin at once. Only when Sally gives her arm a squeeze and asks if she's all right does May realize she's crying.

But anyway, why be here when she can go elsewhere, when she can be with—

Frank offers her some gum. They're on their way to an afternoon movie.

"Or how about we skip the movie and go home and take a nap?" she says.

He smiles. Fine by him. It's Saturday. They're together—and they can spend the time however they please.

III

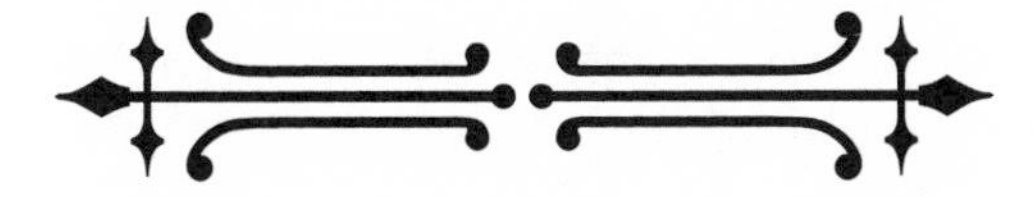

Grammers

We observed the common rites; we performed the tasks expected of us; we behaved appropriately, meaning we opened the doors to our loss, invited the world to share it with us for two—though no more than three—days.

I was over at my mother's house constantly in the months after the funeral, mowing the grass, repairing the chimney, which seemed to leak no matter how much I caulked the flashing, and dragging big limbs into the woods after storms. To help my mother inside, Annie and I took it upon ourselves to hire a cleaner, but that plan backfired. After the first clean, my mother came to me, irate, and reported that things were missing: a step stool, a milk glass pitcher, a cookie cutter.

"Who'd steal a cookie cutter?" I asked.

"We don't know who this woman is. She could be anybody."

"Her name is Celeste, and she comes highly recommended."

"This isn't what I wanted."

Eventually Annie and I managed to locate

each of the missing items: The stool was in the closet; the milk glass pitcher was on top of the fridge but out of sight. Searching for the cookie cutter in one of the kitchen drawers, I found all the condolence cards rubber-banded together, pink and blue, illustrated scenes of beaches and mountains, photographs of flowers and candles. I flipped through them quickly, read a few of the notes written by people I knew—distant relatives, friends of my mother I hadn't seen in years. A business card slid loose from the stack. A card for a psychic/spiritual counselor. On the back of the card, someone had written: *This lady's the real deal.* Whoever had sent this to my mother clearly didn't know her very well. I showed it to Annie.

"You think she could help us find the cookie cutter?"

"I think we should just buy her a new one."

"She'd notice. She'd say the old one cut cookies better. She'd say it was a gift from her great-grandmother. Irreplaceable. Or it was rusty and the rust made the cookies taste better."

Eventually we located the missing cookie cutter inside a mixing bowl, but when we showed my mother, she acted as if she'd known all along that it had been there and we'd been silly to waste so much time looking for it. She somehow managed to be both needy and ungrateful all at once—a terrible combination.

She called me at work after a giant storm. She required my immediate help. It was an emergency; the basement had flooded; the sump pump was broken. An hour later I was there, dutiful son that I was, standing in the dark, fetid water with my pant cuffs rolled up to my knees. Fisher was with me. She sat on the stairs playing with her phone. I was driving her to her bass lessons after this.

We'd been down in the basement for about twenty minutes when Fisher asked about the smell: What was it exactly? I told her I didn't know and I didn't want to know.

"This is so gross," she said.

Fisher stared at her phone for a few minutes and then asked if I was aware of a certain type of mold that grew in wet basements and crawlspaces, a mold that scientists had recently determined was capable, if inhaled, of migrating deep into the brain and altering its chemistry, of changing a personality, of erasing memories. Did I know there were people in the world whose brains had been infested in just such a way and who had been found wandering mindlessly in grocery stores or bathing naked in public fountains with no idea of who they were or what they were doing?

No, I said, I had not been aware of such a mold.

The floorboards above us creaked. Just then, the door at the top of the stairs busted open with a tremendous clatter, the knob striking the wall and knocking loose bits of cement, which crackled down along the wall.

"Any progress?" my mother said, coming down the steps.

She sat down beside Fisher, looking gloomy. Fisher leaned forward and handed me her phone. She'd located an online how-to video that she thought might speed things along.

I thanked her. "How-to videos for everything these days, huh?"

"How to cook crystal meth," she said. "How to dispose of dead bodies."

My mother grimaced but said nothing. I tapped the screen to start the video and propped up the phone on a nearby worktable. The man in the video was scrawny with scary neck tattoos—but helpful.

"Don't worry, we'll get her fixed up right in no time at all," he said.

"Your sump pump is a female," I said to my mother. "Bet you didn't know that, did you?"

She smiled. I rotated the PVC pipe, slightly, until it connected with the hole in the wall, through which it would spit the water outside the basement into the backyard. Leaning forward, I knocked the worktable upon which Fisher's phone was precariously balanced, and it tumbled and plunked down into the water. An eerie shriek—like the squeal of a deflating balloon—

escaped Fisher's mouth. She leaped forward to the edge of the stairs as I bent down to grope through the slime.

"Fuck fuck fuck," she said. "Jim, seriously, what the fuck?"

"I'm so sorry. My fault. I'm sorry."

"I had everything on that phone!"

"If it's busted, I'll get you a new one."

"I had sound files on there. Song ideas. I hadn't backed them up anywhere else. Oh my God, I can't believe this. I honestly can't believe this." She was pacing now, back and forth on the step, which was maybe two feet long. "Let me see your phone for a minute."

I wiped my hand across my pants and gave it to her, thinking maybe she could somehow use it to retrieve her own. A cell phone tractor beam, I don't know. I was panicked. She snatched mine from me and promptly threw it hard against the wall. It cracked against the concrete and then dropped down into the murky depths. I couldn't believe she'd done it. I hadn't thought her capable of such an act.

"Fisher!"

But she was already halfway up the steps. At the top she slammed the door shut.

My mother, who seemed to be coming out of a daze, asked what was happening with an irritating earnestness, and I yelled that I'd lost two fucking phones in this nasty fucking water was what was happening. She got very quiet then. I had pictures on that phone I hadn't backed up. Pictures of Annie. Of Fisher. Voice mails from my father! Searching with my hands, I was beginning to feel like every terrible shit ever taken in all of human history had squeezed up through the cracks of the foundation in my parents' basement; all that excrement was sludging around my ankles, digesting me. I was never going to get out of this basement. Maybe there really was mold down here. Why was I subjecting myself to this insanity? Not to mention Fisher and I were apparently enemies now, whatever fragile bond we'd had until now destroyed—or so it seemed to me then. And God, my father's voice mails. The one where he asked me if I'd meet him at BeanHead on Sunday for a chat. The one where he told me what time he'd be by in the morning to drop off a book. All of them gone, just like that.

Somewhere, far off, my mother's voice: "Why are you acting like this?"

I had the sudden urge to grab her by the shoulders and fling her down into the mucky water, to stomp on her chest with my foot, but this ugly urge quickly sinkholed down through my body and hollowed me out like a shotgun barrel.

My head was spinning, and suddenly I couldn't catch my breath. My lungs refused to accept the air. They were squeezed shut, unwilling to do their duty. I stepped forward, toward the worktable, but slipped down into the muck. I fell down onto my knees and caught myself with both hands. I crawled over to the steps and dragged myself onto them.

"Your heart!" my mother screamed, and started up the stairs. "Oh my God!"

"Wait," I wheezed. "Wait."

But she was already gone. I closed my eyes and tried to empty my head. When my mother returned a few minutes later, cordless phone in hand, I was already beginning to recover but still wasn't quite myself.

"The ambulance is on the way," she said. "Are you okay? What's happening?"

"It's not my heart," I said. "I'm fine. Cancel the ambulance. Call them back."

"You looked like you were dying!"

"Well, I'm not. Not today anyway."

"Are you sure?"

"I'm sure, yes, I'm sure."

She seemed unconvinced. I moved back toward the sump pump and stuck my hands in the water. I was covered in a silky dark, foul-smelling grime. After locating both phones, I apologized for having lost my cool. She didn't say anything.

I stripped down at the top of the stairs, and my mother brought me a towel, which I wrapped around my waist. Fisher was in the living room on the couch. When I walked in, she wouldn't look me in the eyes, and I could tell that she'd been crying.

"I'm sorry," she said. "I don't even—" She sighed. "I'm so sorry. I don't know what I was thinking. I just got so mad. I have stuff on that phone that I wanted to save, and now it's gone. I didn't back it up. I'm such an idiot. I'm sorry. Please don't tell Mom. Please don't tell her, okay?"

I put up my hand: Enough.

"I understand," I said. "I get it."

She looked up hopefully. "So you won't tell her?"

I wouldn't tell, I said. It was between us.

My mother brought us both iced sweet teas.

"Where are your clothes?" Fisher asked me.

My mother rushed upstairs to bring me one of my father's shirts and a pair of pants, which were far too large for me. A few minutes later the ambulance arrived.

The hypnotherapist brought me a glass of water and some roasted almonds in a little yellow bowl shaped like a flat elephant. I was sitting on a small sofa in her office. She worked out of a suite in a partitioned house close to downtown. The other businesses in the house, according to the sign out front, included an acupuncturist, a healing touch practitioner, and a marriage counselor.

Her name was Lisa Vaselli. She was a wide-bottomed woman with a kind, doughy face. She explained the process of hypnotherapy to me. She had a note from Dr. Westervelt and so she was well versed in my medical history. Still, she had questions for me. She asked me how much caffeine I consumed on a daily basis. She asked me if I sometimes woke up short of breath. She asked me if my stomach was ever tied up in knots. If I fidgeted. If I routinely experienced restlessness. Boredom. Did my throat feel lumpy sometimes? Could I swallow? Did I have trouble concentrating or focusing?

"No," I said. "None of that. It's more general. Everything I see, it feels so foreign to me. Not altogether foreign, mind you. Just vaguely foreign. Vaguely unsettling, too. Unreal. Or no, that's not quite it. It's an abundance of real. Layers of reality, stacked upon each other, that cancel each other out. Like the holograms, I guess."

"Ah, the Grammers, yes."

"Don't you ever feel like they're part of a separate world that has somehow overlapped with ours? In their world, they're the real ones, and we're the holograms. The two universes are slowly merging. They might become more and more real as time goes on, meaning, possibly, we might become less."

"It's funny," she said.

"What is?"

"Oh, well, I was having a lovely conversation with the scheduler yesterday at the dentist's office. We'd been talking for maybe five minutes before I realized she was a Grammer."

"Are you familiar with daisy theory? It's this idea in physics that not everything exists equally or uniformly. For instance, there's a chance you could exist a little bit more than me. Or me more than you."

"Daisy theory? No, I'm not familiar with that one."

I drank some of my water, swished it around in my mouth, let it collide pleasantly with my cheeks and tongue.

"So," she said, "you're feeling unsettled then. And Dr. Westervelt says your father died recently?"

I nodded.

"What were the circumstances? Was it sudden or . . . ?"

Over the last few months, the story of my father's death had become something I could recite, when necessary, with as little emotion as possible. A simple sequence of events. A montage. Almost like a poem for its brevity and reliance on a few crucial images. The bathroom floor. The pasted toothbrush. The body sprawled, half-naked. Tooth chipped on the edge of the sink. A stroke.

Bathroom, toothbrush, body, broken tooth, stroke.

Bath. Brush. Body. Tooth. Stroke.

Bath. Brush. Body. Tooth. Stroke.

"But," I told her, "this predates all that. It's been going on for a while. I lose my breath and feel dizzy. I've passed out in people's houses. It's embarrassing." I had my legs crossed and my right foot, I realized, was shaking. "I died once. Cardiac arrest. Does Dr. Westervelt's note mention that?"

"It does, yes. That must have been terribly traumatic."

"I think about it all the time. I was here and then I wasn't. It was like taking a dreamless nap. God didn't show himself to me. No feelings of ecstasy. No paradise. And I do not find this idea peaceful. Some do. There are message boards for people like me, and some people who see nothing, like me, they feel relieved. They say, *Well, at least I won't know to miss my life*. I find zero comfort in that. Because right now, I can feel myself sliding toward it. I feel like we're all marching toward the edge of a cliff. It's beautiful, sure, from a distance, but once your feet are at the edge, it's just a giant freaking hole."

"I understand. As has been said before, all anxiety is an expression of the ur-anxiety."

"Death."

She nodded sagely. "You're not alone. We all struggle with it, to varying degrees."

"What do you think happens when we die? If you don't mind me asking. What's your position on the afterlife?"

She leaned forward. "Jim, have you considered the possibility that you simply don't *remember* what happened to you while you were dead? Maybe you visited heaven and saw amazing things but you've blocked it out. You don't remember your dreams every night, do you? And yet we're told we dream every single night."

I thought about this for a moment. Why would I have forgotten something so significant? I couldn't fathom it.

"These attacks," she said, "they sound to me like echoes of your cardiac arrest. Your body, for whatever reason, might be reenacting its near-death. What I'd like to do is help you find a way to stay relaxed in these situations. To get control of your anxiety."

She opened the top drawer in a little table by her chair and removed a small black fob not much bigger than a matchbook. She squeezed it, and it began to emit a small clicking noise. Like a Ping-Pong ball being paddled back and forth across a table. She told me to make myself comfortable. I sat back with my head against the couch and listened to the noise. She asked me to count to twenty. With each number, she instructed, I was to imagine taking another step toward the ocean.

By the time I reached twenty, I was standing in the water. The waves slid warmly around my feet. Dimly I was aware that Lisa Vaselli, the woman with the wide bottom and the bag of almonds in her filing cabinet, was out there, nearby, and that she was the one telling me to experience the water as warm, that she was the one determining this sacred, blissful reality. What I mean is, I wasn't entirely on the beach. I was aware of also being on the couch. At her request, I sat down in the sand, cross-legged, and began a series of simple breathing exercises.

Then, suddenly, I was yanked back into my body. I fluttered open my eyes. Lisa was hunched forward in her chair, looking at me with a look of concern, her brow furrowed, face pale. She asked me if I was okay.

"Yes, fine, why?"

"You were just telling me that you were trapped on a set of stairs."

"I was?"

"You said you were on some stairs, and you couldn't get off them."

I didn't understand. I only remembered the beach with the warm water.

"Who is Dr. Zinker?" she asked me.

I didn't say anything. How did she know that name?

"You were calling out for someone named Dr.

Zinker. Does that mean anything to you? You seemed very distressed, very upset."

At that moment I didn't feel distressed at all. I actually felt somewhat relaxed.

"This doesn't mean hypnotherapy won't work for you," she said.

It hadn't occurred to me that it wouldn't.

"Sometimes, in hypnosis, we can fall into the deep end of the subconscious mind, and it can be a little overwhelming. We'll try again next time."

We talked for a few more minutes about some breathing exercises I might try at home before going to sleep at night and then I scheduled another appointment for the following month, which I didn't keep.

Since my father's death, I'd often thought about the message we'd proposed sending each other from beyond. The proof is in the pudding, he'd suggested. Or, "Puttin' on the Ritz." We'd never really settled on an exact message, but that didn't keep me from searching for one. After waking each morning, I'd lie in bed and try to recall what I could of my dreams. Out of a shower, I'd be sure to check the mirror and imagine words writing themselves across the steamy mirror. At a stoplight, I'd turn the radio to an out-of-tune station and listen to see if that loose noise might calcify into recognizable words. I confess I even bought a tape recorder, though I could never quite bring myself to leave it recording in the bathroom where he'd died.

To have undergone hypnosis and been lured, somehow, into a vision of a stairwell—a vision so similar to the one my father had described—what was I to make of that? I hadn't received any messages in this vision, none that I remembered anyway. If the hypnotherapist was correct, my own mind—my subconscious mind—had produced the staircase in the same fashion it crafted my dreams each night, from the slurry of my day-to-day experience, and if that was so, then nothing paranormal or truly strange had occurred. But no matter how I tried, I couldn't shake the feeling that my father had been trying to reach me while I'd been in the trance and that I needed to listen.

I'd been calling out for someone, the therapist had said.

For Sally Zinker, of all people.

Did my father want me to find the physicist? Was it through her machine that he would relay his message to me? It was a possibility, however unlikely, that I couldn't discount.

I found Zinker's book on Annie's nightstand and opened it for the first time since the funeral. In the chapter on the machine, I saw that Annie had underlined entire paragraphs:

A spectrum of specters, let's call it. While we tend to hover at the far end of the existence spectrum, perhaps these apparitions and phantoms lurk at its opposite end. They are here—but almost imperceptibly so. They have, through sheer force of will, reclaimed a sliver of materiality.

And then, on another page:

In as few as ten years, conversing with those who have departed the material plane could become as commonplace as face-lifts, and in this analogy lies an important point: To attempt these communications will be a physically demanding process, one that many will not elect to attempt. Why will the process be so arduous? Because the secret of its success will lie in not-so-subtle subatomic manipulations. Such a machine will have the power to talk to your dead loved ones, yes, but it will, necessarily, change you.

A few sentences later:

It would, as a matter of fact, make you cease to exist—temporarily.

I knew that Annie had been reading the book with interest—we talked about some of the ideas from time to time—but I was still surprised to find these notations.

I called Sally Zinker's department at UNC, but she was no longer on the faculty there. One of her former colleagues informed me that she had opted for an early retirement and moved back home to Arkansas. Where in Arkansas exactly, this colleague wasn't sure, as they were no longer in touch.

Sally had authored a few papers in her career, most of which concerned the daisy particle and most of which were behind a paywall online, but they'd all been written before the publication of her book and so I wasn't sure they'd be of much help to me anyway. I didn't want to understand the mechanisms of the daisy particle, after all. I didn't want a physics lesson.

When I wrote an email to Sally's university address, it bounced back immediately, though this was hardly a surprise since she no longer worked there. I read a couple of reviews of *The Reunion Machine*. One such review, by another physicist, said the book was an embarrassing misstep and had no real scientific foundation. He said it was a shame that someone like Dr. Zinker, who had contributed so much to our understanding of daisy theory, had tarnished her reputation with a bunch of New Age paranormal mumbo jumbo.

I searched *Sally Zinker + Arkansas*, but it turned up no address or phone number. Most searches of her name led me to various message boards dedicated to physics and/or paranormal research. She had a number of devotees, it seemed, though she had just as many detractors. On one website, I found a commenter who claimed to know her personally. He reported that following the publication of her book, Sally had stepped down from teaching and thrown herself fully into the project of using the daisy particle to talk with the dead. She'd set up her own lab in Little Rock, he said, and she was closer than ever to making contact with disincarnate spirits using a device of her own design. The comment was two years old, but I replied to it anyway and asked the commenter if he had any contact information for the physicist that he could share with me, on- or offline.

Sorry bro, he wrote soon thereafter. *Can't help you there.*

A few days later, Annie and I were out walking through the neighborhood after dinner. We huffed our way to the top of the hill where the road ended abruptly and gave way to dense mountain forest. Poplars, oaks, locusts. Fallen pine trees, moldering, were creeping with life. Mountain laurel and ferns sprouted up in the dark-soiled banks. All was lush, wet. It had been raining earlier.

Through the trees we could see an immense blue-gray rock, the size of two cars. Such an outcropping couldn't have gone unnoticed by the Shawnee. The Buzzard People—maybe they'd used this rock in some fashion. Maybe this was where they'd brought the bones for the birds to pick clean. It seemed plausible to me.

We were on our way back down the hill when I told Annie that I'd been trying to find Sally Zinker. I didn't mention my session with the hypnotherapist since doing so would have required that I explain my anxiety attacks. I didn't want her worrying about me.

"I've called UNC, and I've been digging around online, too," I said. "She's in Arkansas, but that's all I know so far."

"Well, don't even bother trying her publisher." She smiled coyly. "I tried finding her, too, a couple of months ago. Just before your father died. Her publisher said they couldn't give out information like that."

We were nearing the house now.

"Why were you looking for her?"

"Same reason as you, I'm sure," she said. "I mean, can you even imagine? Talking with the dead?"

I didn't say anything. She wanted to talk with the dead. Meaning, Anthony. Strangely, until now, it hadn't occurred to me that she might have been interested in Zinker's research for this specific reason. I imagined a package arriving in the mail: a small white futuristic telephone that would allow us to dial up anyone we wished, dead or alive. The idea was incredibly exciting—but also unnerving. Did I really want Annie having regular conversations with her dead husband? As if sensing my sudden unease, she looped her arm through mine as we went in through the back door.

Driving to work I noticed that the Bizby Group For Lease sign had been removed from the restaurant's window. Two white trucks were parked along the street, and a man in a sleeveless *WWE* T-shirt was on a tall ladder painting the balustrades. A few days after that a new sign appeared over the door. SparkBurger, it said. A fancy gourmet burger joint. The night they opened, Annie and I agreed to meet Wes and his new girlfriend there for dinner.

Wes was in the middle of a bad divorce. His wife had left him for another man. Another congregant at The Church of Search, actually. The affair had stirred up a minor controversy in the congregation because both Wes and Harriet were still attending services. Neither one of them had wanted to give it up. What was needed was some sort of church custody agreement, Annie joked.

Harriet's new guy was a sad-eyed, gray-haired gentleman who spoke with a slight lisp. He was incredibly wealthy, or so it was rumored, and had spent the last three years in near-isolation on a yacht in the Bermuda Triangle.

Annie was friends with Harriet, and it was

through that friendship that we'd received some interesting intel about this mysterious man, whose name was Cooper: He was divorced with no children; he and Harriet were already thinking about moving in together; he'd once won twenty grand off Michael Jordan in a poker game; he was into Tantric sex, like Sting, but he rarely lasted more than eight or nine minutes, though Harriet—and this part really creeped me out—had never seen any evidence of actual ejaculate, meaning, possibly, that Cooper was jizzing bursts of hot air inside her.

Oh, the things we know about people we barely know.

Annie hadn't wanted to eat dinner with Wes. She saw it as a mild betrayal of her friendship with Harriet to be social with the enemy—and they really had become that to each other, enemies. But Harriet was the one who'd cheated, I pointed out, and so why did we need to remain loyal to her? By cheating, hadn't she given up the right to an exclusive friendship with any of their formerly mutual friends? The injured party in this equation was Wes, surely, and I didn't think it was wrong to feel worse for him than for her. Annie scoffed at that because who was to say who wronged who first. The cheating, she said, was just the latest in what had surely been a long chain of mutual offenses. Wes hadn't cheated, perhaps, at least not in the sexual sense, but maybe he'd been distant, cool. Maybe he'd retreated in some crucial way.

Analyzing the dissolution of other marriages was a way, I suppose, of avoiding a similar fate. A preventative—like taking antacids before a big meal. If we could just understand what had happened to Wes and Harriet—or to any of the others—then surely we'd be able to sidestep any future troubles of our own. Always, it seemed, a lesson could be drawn: *Don't stop talking in the tough times,* or *An emotional connection to a person outside the marriage could be just as detrimental as a sexual one.* Annie and I had been married for almost two years at this point, and though I didn't feel our relationship was in any sort of distress, we did bicker more than we used to, and I'll admit that a few of the personality quirks that I'd found cute or endearing in the early days—her sulkiness when she didn't get her way, for instance, or her inability to hide her disdain and impatience for people, such as my mother, people who "didn't have a clue"—sometimes irked me enough to cut off a conversation and go for a short walk down the street. But I think generally we were still a happy couple. We fought, yes, but we always made up again.

Annie only agreed to the dinner with Wes on the condition that we make plans with Harriet and Cooper within the week. Fine, I'd said, fine, fine, whatever she wanted.

We arrived first. We hadn't been there together since our first date. The restaurant's decor was different. The walls had been chipped at, purposefully distressed, to reveal brickwork patches beneath the chalky plaster. Giant abstract paintings—like violent tie-dye—hung over each booth. Then Wes showed up, finally, with his new girlfriend. Annie and I were flabbergasted: his new girlfriend was none other than Sudeepa Hardy, from the church.

"I asked him not to tell you," Sudeepa said. "I was afraid you'd back out of dinner otherwise."

"I didn't even know you and your husband had . . ." Annie said.

"He actually moved out three months ago. We've been very discreet about it."

"Until now of course," Wes said, smiling. "This is actually the first time we've ever had dinner with another couple. You're our first! Aren't you honored?"

"Wes and I were both going through a rough time," Sudeepa said to Annie, as if trying to convince her that nothing truly indecent had occurred, that this made a certain rational sense.

"Yes, of course," Annie said. "It's good to have a shoulder—and all that."

"Harriet knows Sudeepa and I are seeing each other, by the way," Wes said, also to Annie. "This isn't some big secret you'll have to keep from her."

The waiter arrived. Annie buried her face in the menu and asked for a Diet Coke instead of white wine like the rest of us. Whenever Wes would compliment Sudeepa or look at her in a certain way—with longing, I suppose—Annie's foot would nudge mine under the table, and I'd feel her eyes on me. She'd never really liked Wes, even before the divorce. He could be a know-it-all, definitely. A tad smug.

We consulted our menus. The burgers were fancy and expensive. Organic, grass-fed, hugged daily. Goat cheese and sprouts. Roasted red peppers, basil pesto, and arugula.

"So," I said to Sudeepa after the waiter took our order, "how are the kids handling it?"

"They're fine, for the most part. My husband's actually renting the house across the street, and he comes over for breakfast every morning. We're trying to keep it as smooth as possible."

"That can't be easy," I said.

"We just have to respect each other's space."

By the time the burgers arrived five minutes later—small patties on whole wheat buns ringed with giant potato wedges—the conversation had begun to sputter. We each chewed quietly for a few minutes.

"Annie and I read a very interesting book recently," I said, hoping to rescue the night from disaster. "By a physicist named Sally Zinker. That name might ring a bell."

“Zinker,” Wes said, eyes narrowing. “She spoke at Search last year, right? She’s the one who thinks we can talk with the dead. The lady was a bit of a crank, no? Your dad and I talked about her a couple of times.” He smiled. “I tell you what, Jim, I sure miss talking with your dad. He had such a great mind. If it hadn’t been so sudden, I would have tried to make arrangements for him with that cryo-brain company out in Phoenix. They have to get to you fast though. Within fifteen to twenty minutes of death.”

“Cryo-brain?” I asked.

“They keep your brain in cold storage. Until the day comes when they can upload it to a computer and bring you back to life.”

“Store you on a hard drive and turn you into a hologram,” Annie said, goading him.

“One day, maybe, sure.”

Wes’s faith in technology’s power to save us was astounding to me, but then again, he was so full of hope and confidence about the future that a part of me really envied him. He didn’t need God or the afterlife, not when he had accelerators and scanners. Maybe he was right. Technology—the very thing that had chilled us to the mysteries of the universe—possibly was all that remained to unthaw us again. Our intuition had been so thoroughly squelched, our spiritual faith so deteriorated, that we somehow found it easier to believe the universe had started in a computer rather than a garden.

I excused myself from the table. I stopped by the bar where a woman in a tight black T-shirt was shoveling ice into cups. I tapped the bar to get her attention.

"This restaurant used to be something else," I said. "Any chance you know what happened to the previous owner?"

"No idea, dude."

I nodded. "Are there tables upstairs, too?"

"Upstairs?"

"Is there another dining area?"

"I think it's just storage or something up there, I don't know, I've never been."

"You've never been upstairs?"

"Nope."

I stepped into the back hallway. A guy was waiting outside the men's room, reading an article on his phone, so I slid past him and continued down the hall.

But there was a problem: Where the stairs had been was now a white wall, and at the center of the wall was a white closet-sized door. It was padlocked at the top. I jiggled the knob and shoved my shoulder against the door, lightly. No light shone under the door. I tried to peer through the crack but all was dark on the other side. They'd sealed it off completely.

When I turned, Annie was there.

"I thought I'd find you hiding back here. You can't leave me with those two, it's not fair. This is *your* dinner, you set it up."

"Look what they've done, they've sealed off the stairs."

As if to disprove me, she came over and jiggled the doorknob as I had. Then she looked up at the padlock in the top left corner.

"Did you know about Sudeepa and Wes? Be honest."

"I really didn't. It's not like Wes and I talk much."

She reached up and shook the padlock. "She looks better, doesn't she? Did you notice that?"

"Sudeepa?"

"She's lost some weight. Her hair's different, too." She knocked on the door. "Lost cause, I think."

We gave up on the stairs and returned to the table. Wes and Sudeepa were talking quietly with each other. Seeing us, they both sat up straighter, like teenagers who'd been caught making out.

A week or so after our dinner, I flew up to New York for a college friend's bachelor party. The organizer of this outing had us bar-hopping after each round of drinks, and so we wasted most of the evening walking and locating tables at each successive venue. I didn't get back to my hotel until almost three a.m. and slept horribly. Around dawn I woke up from a dream. The dream had been about my father, that much I knew, but I could remember very little else about it. We'd been at a table. In a room. Not a room I recognized. Just a room. With a window and a door. If he'd said anything to me, I couldn't remember now.

I drank a few glasses of water from the tap and fell back asleep. My phone vibrating on the nightstand was what woke me up again, close to noon. My skull felt scraped out, brittle as old Tupperware. I had a text from Annie: *Crazy Ben wrote a play about talking turds who fall in love just before getting flushed.*

Crazy Ben was one of the inmates at the prison where Annie ran her playwriting workshops. He was in jail for the attempted murder of his wife, and according to Annie the man was uglier than a cracked mop bucket. "I feel like it's attempted murder every time he looks at me," went Annie's joke. In a class of ten inmates, however, it was Crazy Ben who'd revealed himself as the most promising playwright. Week after week he'd astounded Annie with his elaborate and thoughtful premises, with his sharp dialogue and creativity. She was even thinking about staging a Crazy Ben play at Thrill Arts! as a way of raising money for the program.

Turds need love, too, I wrote back to her.

I jumped in the shower and then flipped on the television to watch the news while I dressed. *Is Your Heart Device Going to Kill You?* it said along the bottom of the screen. I turned up the volume. The silver-haired host was talking to a HeartNet representative with an aggravated tone. I quickly gathered that there'd been another heart hacking victim, a woman in Oklahoma who'd been found at the end of her driveway in her bathrobe. A hacker in Russia—identity unknown at present—had one-upped the Chinese teen by breaking through HeartNet-Net's now enhanced security and exploding a random heart on the other side of the world, again.

"There has to be some accountability," the anchor said.

"Certainly," the representative said. "And believe me, there will be accountability. We'll see to that."

"And who will be accountable to whom?"

"We will hold the guilty parties accountable! Obviously."

"Wait, I'm sorry, hold on, wait a minute, are you suggesting that your company isn't accountable for its own security?"

"I'm not really here to debate who is accountable for what, exactly, or who to whom. That's not why I'm here tonight. We are making a good faith effort to—"

"Okay, but tell me, what will you be doing for this poor woman's family?"

"The family, yes, thank you, God bless them. Our thoughts are with them right now. I assure you the family will be well compensated. We're in the middle of that now."

"Compensated how, exactly?"

"We're making that determination as we speak."

"You're determining how much this woman's life was worth, in other words."

"We want to take care of her family. We're trying to do the right thing, I assure you."

"And will there be other victims? What are you doing to make sure this doesn't happen to anyone else? What assurances can you offer all those people who have a HeartNet device in their chests right now, who are watching this and fearing for their lives?"

"Believe me, we're working around the clock on this issue. It's important to us that we fix this. It's very, very important to us."

I turned off the television and left the hotel. My flight home wasn't until later that evening, and at Annie's urging, I'd made lunch plans with her brother, Kurt. I walked all the way to Chinatown to meet him at his favorite Cantonese restaurant. He was already there when I arrived. Alongside him was his girlfriend, Kitra. I'd never met her before now. She was a pale waif, red-haired, and as far as I could tell, her entire lunch consisted of a single veggie dumpling. "You can control your appetite with your mind," she explained. "I've been doing it for so long I'm hardly ever hungry anymore. I have almost no appetite at all."

"It's true," Kurt said proudly. "You'd be amazed. She eats half a piece of toast every morning and then she rides her bike two miles to her restaurant."

"Plus my vitamins," she said.

"Yeah, she eats vitamins, too."

"I don't *eat* them," she said, grossed out, embarrassed. "I *swallow* them."

"So if I only swallow this dumpling," Kurt said, smiling big at me, "I guess I haven't eaten then, huh?"

"Don't be an asshole," she said, and turned to me. "He's such an asshole, isn't he?"

I shrugged, not wanting to get involved.

"Anyway," Kurt said, "Kitra and I got married. I called Annie this morning and told her the news."

"Oh," I said. "Congratulations."

"There wasn't any ceremony," Kitra said. "And we've decided not to wear rings."

"It's just a piece of paper, really," Kurt said.

"I don't even know why we bothered with it, to be honest," Kitra said.

Kurt ate another dumpling. He'd put on a

little weight since the last time I'd seen him. He was jowlier and his haircut, so short and spiky, accented the largeness of his head. Kitra rummaged around in her purse for her phone. She held it up to me and, without comment, showed me a picture of a horse.

"Yes, we bought a horse," Kurt said. "He's on a farm upstate. We've been up there a couple of times to see him."

"I didn't realize you rode," I said to Kitra.

"I don't. You couldn't pay me to ride a horse. Anyway, he's very old. He belonged to my friend, and they had to sell him because they were moving to the Philippines. The horse's name is Tobacco."

"Kitra was afraid they might put him down otherwise."

"I see," I said.

"I don't care much for the name Tobacco," Kitra said, "but it's too late to name him anything else, I think."

He motioned for the bill and then looked at me with a barely suppressed smile. "Annie tells me you're in the middle of an investigation. You two are on the hunt for some elusive scientist?"

"Well," I said, "*investigation* might be going too far. We read her book, and we're interested in getting in touch with her but she's a little tricky to track down."

"Oooh, I love a good mystery," Kitra said,

without emotion. "All I read are mysteries. If a book doesn't have a mystery to solve, I won't touch it."

I wasn't sure how much of a mystery this was. Probably Sally Zinker had just retired a little early and moved back home. Probably she just wanted to be left alone.

"But Annie says this lady's looking for a way to talk with the dead?" Kurt said. "That right?"

Typically Annie wasn't in the habit of sharing so much with her brother. I offered up a noncommittal nod.

"I'm sure it's Anthony that Annie wants to talk to," Kitra said. "God, that funeral. So, so terrible."

"You were there?" I asked.

"Kurt and I had only been together for—what?" She looked to him. "A couple of months?"

He nodded and stuffed another dumpling in his mouth.

"One of the saddest funerals I've ever been to," she said. "And I've been to quite a few, believe me. There must have been three hundred people."

"He was well liked," Kurt said. "A very popular guy. Lots of friends. Plus, his family's well connected down there."

"And poor Annie. She kept it together during the funeral at least."

"Yeah," Kurt said. "She really did. It was only after that that things got rough enough that Mom and Dad had to move down there for a while and help with Fisher. Rough days, for sure."

"But if she wants to talk with him," Kitra said, "why not just try a psychic?"

I must have made a face because Kitra's voice became very excited and fast. "I happen to have a very good friend who is psychically gifted. He's not like one of those people you see on television, for God's sake. He's legitimate. He put me in touch with my uncle Maury, as a matter of fact."

Her uncle Maury, Kurt explained, was the one who'd brought Kitra home from Tunisia after her mother died in the embassy attack, the man who'd raised her as his own. Embassy attack? Tunisia? Somehow I'd missed all this about Kitra and felt like I should have known it. I feigned familiarity with these events, saying something like, *Ah, right,* knowing I could get the full story from Annie when I was home again.

"He doesn't hold séances or anything like that," Kitra said. "What he does is sit down with you at a table with a pen and paper. He asks you to focus on the person you're trying to reach, and he closes his eyes and the pen writes what it will on the paper."

"It's called automatic writing," Kurt said.

"Well," I said, trying to be polite, "maybe we could talk to him then?"

Kitra got out her phone. A few seconds later my phone buzzed in my pocket.

"I sent you his contact," she said. "His name is Claude Wilkes-Weaver. He's a sculptor, too. We've got one of his pieces in our apartment."

"It's a nudie," Kurt said with a smile.

"A nude *figure,*" Kitra corrected.

"Giant boobs," Kurt added, demonstrating with his hands.

"A fertility goddess."

"Which is why it doesn't come anywhere near the bedroom," Kurt said, grinning.

The bill arrived. Ten minutes later we were downstairs on the sidewalk. I told them congratulations again and jumped into a cab. I still had about four hours before my flight.

Claude Wilkes-Weaver worked out of a studio in an old brick building near the expressway in Brooklyn. He buzzed me up when I mentioned Kitra's name over the intercom. The elevator was out of order, and so I had to climb four flights of stairs with my roller suitcase. By the time I reached his floor, I was completely out of breath. He opened the door before I could knock.

"*Entrez vous*," he said.

His hands were chalky with plaster. He was short with a skeletal face and deep-set eyes that flicked this way and that in their sockets. He was chewing gum and with each clinch of his jaw his face clicked and bounced, as if he had twice the ordinary number of ligaments beneath his skin. His studio was very small. In the far corner, under a steel-gridded window, was a single mattress. He had a long table against one wall that was full of sculpting tools. He led us over to a small table in his kitchen. Two chairs were at the table, arranged opposite one another but slightly askance. Claude motioned for me to sit down in one of the chairs. I couldn't remember the last time I'd felt so uncomfortable. When he asked me who or what I was looking for, I almost stood up to go.

"Listen, this doesn't have to be a big deal," he said. "In fact, it's really simple. I get out my paper and pen, and then we wait to see what happens. Sometimes it works, sometimes it doesn't. If it doesn't, it's half."

"Half?"

"Half price."

"Oh, Kitra didn't mention—"

"Thousand dollars."

"Just to—"

"That's right. But if that's too steep for you, tell me now. I'm in the middle of a project, and I'm meeting someone for dinner tonight."

"Does it usually work?"

He thought about this for a moment. "Seven times out of ten. Something like that. I don't keep a record."

“But if it doesn’t work, I still owe you five hundred?”

He nodded. I opened my wallet. I didn’t have that kind of cash. I hadn’t come prepared. Seeing this, he mentioned an ATM down the block I could use. Since I was Kitra’s friend, he said he trusted that I’d pay him afterward. We could proceed.

“So the dead speak through you?” I asked. “Or through your pen?”

“I have a guide. Her name is Angelique. She’s the one speaking with the dead and directing my pen.”

“And who is Angelique?”

“That’s not really important.”

“What is it the dead usually say?”

“They say whatever they want.”

“But—”

“The dead don’t know anything you don’t know,” he said, crossing his arms. “You shouldn’t expect to learn any grand secrets of the universe.”

He brought out a large sheet of paper, like something you’d wrap steaks in, almost as big as the tabletop itself, and then clicked his pen. Placing the nib of the pen near the top left corner of the paper, he closed his eyes and began to hum. A single low note. A droning noise. Then he trailed away into silence.

“I need you to hold the person in your mind,” he said. “You don’t need to say the name out loud, though you can if you wish. Focus is the main thing."

I closed my eyes and thought about my father. His face. His white goatee. His brawny arms. I pictured him as he'd once been, a hulk in the halls of the middle school. I saw him as he was at the end, sprawled on the bathroom floor, the towel around his waist, his tooth chipped. I saw him ahead of me on a hiking trail. I saw him on the stairs of the restaurant, his back to the wall, waiting, waiting.

I peeked open my eyes. Claude's pen was dancing slowly and lightly across the paper. It reminded me of the needle on a cardiograph machine. His eyes were squinched shut, and his head snapped forward as if he were dodging a bird that had just swooped down at him.

Claude's eyes popped open. He put the pen down on the table. The paper was a scribbled mess. Line after line of gibberish.

"Sheet music for the dead," he said.

I stood up and moved to his side of the table so that I could study it more closely. My father's message—was it there?

"Is this English?" I asked.

Claude picked up his pen again, studied the paper for a moment, and circled a series of numbers near the bottom of the page. I hadn't recognized them as numbers until he did this.

"An address or . . . a telephone number?" I asked.

"Looks like it," he said. "Yeah, maybe so. Ten digits."

"Has that ever happened before? Has Angelique ever given you a telephone number?"

He shook his head. "Don't think so. That's new. Usually it says something like, *With you.*"

He folded up the paper and handed it to me. He said it was mine to do with as I pleased—to decode or discard.

Now, as for the money.

"So, five hundred then?" I asked.

"Thousand," he said. "That's a message."

"Are we sure about that?" I asked.

"Very. Anything that isn't nonsense is a message."

I went downstairs and walked down the block to the ATM. Claude was waiting for me at the front entrance with my roller suitcase when I returned. When I gave him the cash, he counted it, nodded, and then slid the bills into his pocket.

I caught a cab to the airport. Sitting at my gate, an hour later, I unfolded the paper and stared at the sequence of numbers buried in the storm cloud of his scribbles. The first three numbers were 5-0-1. I looked them up on my phone.

The area code for Little Rock, Arkansas.

Was it possible that my father was helping me to find Sally Zinker, was pointing me toward her? I hadn't mentioned Sally Zinker or Little Rock to the psychic, and I highly doubted Kitra had contacted him after our lunch and told him anything about me. It was inexplicable.

My plane was boarding. I dialed the number as I gathered my things and got in line.

A robotic voice mail answered.

"Please state your name," it said, "your contact information, and who you're trying to reach."

"My name is Jim Byrd," I said, "and I'm wondering if this is the number for a physicist named Sally Zinker."

Three Wendell Lennox films arrived in the mail. I'd ordered them from a vendor in Minneapolis the same week my father died—the day after our trip to the graveyard, in fact—and my intention had been for us to watch them together. They'd been on back order; hence the shipping delay.

Wendell Lennox had his own Wikipedia page. Not only had he been a screenwriter, but he'd also been blacklisted. Well, not blacklisted actually, but *gray*-listed. He'd shared a name with a union organizer in Ohio who'd given a couple of quotes to the papers and who, consequently, had had to testify in front of the House Committee. Because of this name confusion, the studios had avoided Wendell's work for a couple of years. He'd moved to Mexico City for a while and stayed afloat selling B-movie horror scripts, one of which, *The Skeleton Man* (*El Hombre Esqueleto*), was a surprise hit and spawned a handful of sequels: *Revenge of the Skeleton Man*, *Son of Skeleton Man*, and so on. Despite his success in Mexico, Wendell's career in Hollywood never really recovered. It seemed he was mostly remembered today for the *Skeleton Man* movies, though he'd also written a number of dramas in the early forties—mostly concerning romantic entanglements, love triangles, and ill-fated affairs.

Most important of all, Wendell Lennox was Robert Lennox's brother. This was easy enough to determine, thanks to a genealogy chart published online by a distant relative. I'd even found an interview Wendell had given to a magazine, now defunct, in 1977, the same year he died. Briefly, in this piece, he referred to his childhood home in Shula, North Carolina.

"I was a good kid, mostly," he said. "I didn't get into much trouble. I was a little spacey. Very much in my head. My father owned a furniture store, and so I was there most days after school. He was a good man, very hardworking, and I think I got that from him. I'm a very hard worker. But I was obsessed with the movies, you know, and I left the very first chance I got and came out here to California. Selling sofas, I didn't have that in me. That wasn't what I wanted for my life."

No mention of the fire, no mention of his brother's death—what to make of that? Probably nothing. Unless prompted specifically to comment on it by an interviewer, I couldn't imagine anyone bringing up such a traumatic event for a magazine article.

The films that arrived in the mail weren't his Mexican horror films but a couple of the romantic dramas from the forties. I held up each case for Annie and asked her to pick. The DVD cases had no artwork, only white paper with the film titles printed in black.

The Woman on the Bridge, one was called.

Busy Beware.

A Ring for April.

She chose this last one. I dropped it in the player and then settled down on the couch beside her.

Fisher wandered into the room during the opening credits and, with a look of disgust, asked us if we were aware that somewhat recent advances in technology had made it possible to watch films in color and, gasp, 3D. Without a word Annie made room for Fisher on the couch.

"Thanks but no thanks," she said, going upstairs.

We settled in under a blanket. The movie was about two brothers who fall in love with the same dark-haired girl who comes into their father's jewelry store one afternoon. The girl seems to prefer the younger brother, the impetuous one, but her parents—practical, hard-up people—push her into the arms of the older one, who seems a safer bet because he plans to stay in town and take over his family's jewelry business one day. The younger brother, heartbroken, travels the world as an importer of fabrics, living for many years in Marrakesh as the paramour of an oil heiress, his life a bottomless buffet of sensual delights, none of which are able, ultimately, to help him forget the sting of that first rejection. It is only after he learns that the girl—who, as it happens, has been unhappy in her marriage all these years—has fallen over a garden wall and been impaled by a fence railing that he journeys home to see her again. Their reunion, sadly, is a brief one as the girl, April, will not survive her injury, but she presses her wedding ring into his hand, telling him to keep it as a symbol of her love for him.

The final scene was a tad maudlin, but it was hard to not feel moved by their last-minute declarations of love. It's never too late, was the message. A cliché, obviously, but one that might be true. When I looked up at Annie she was blinking away the tears.

" 'Three minutes with you is better than a lifetime without,' " I said, quoting the film.

" 'Let's make them count,' " she quoted back to me with a smile.

We wandered upstairs and got ready for bed. We kissed goodnight and flipped off the lights. In the darkness, I replayed Wendell's movie in my head. Were the brothers stand-ins for Wendell and Robert Lennox? It seemed entirely possible. And if they were, did that mean that the young girl in the jewelry shop was Clara? This was an interesting new angle to consider, the cinematic resonance of her death.

"I went to see a psychic," I said. "While I was in New York."

She snorted. "Really? I can't picture you with a psychic."

"Me either. But I did it."

"What happened?"

"Mostly I just felt like an idiot for being there."

She put her hand on my chest.

"What would you say to Anthony?" I asked. "If you could talk to him?"

"I don't know. I guess I'd want to make sure he was at peace."

My eyes still hadn't adjusted to the darkness. I reached out and ran my fingers across her face. Her eyes were closed.

"I want you to talk to him," I said. "I think you should."

"Good."

"I can't even imagine what that must have been like, when he died. Never do that to me, please. I couldn't bear it."

She didn't say anything for a moment.

"It doesn't bother you that I want to talk to him?" she asked.

"Should it?"

"Jim."

"Should it?"

Her hand was on my scar now. My chest pocket.

"No, it shouldn't bother you," she said.

"But you do still love him, right? I mean, how could you not?"

"I can hear your brain working right now. All the little gears, I can hear them turning. This isn't a competition, and I hope you don't think of it that way. I love Anthony and I love you, too. It's not one or the other, and one doesn't diminish the other. Love isn't a natural resource. You don't run out."

"An unnatural resource, then. I saw that crocheted somewhere once. A toilet seat doily, I think."

She breathed out a laugh. I didn't feel very reassured. I wasn't even sure she was right. In the audience of her heart a front-row seat was forever reserved for a person who was never going to arrive. As I saw it, all those seats belonged to me and Fisher now.

I got out of bed and went over to the closet. I pulled the little black cube from my sock drawer and brought it back to bed. Annie, eyeing it suspiciously, asked me what it was. I'd never shown it to her before now, and so I explained my trip to the hologram recording shop. When I placed the cube in her hand, she felt its weight and turned it over a few times before pressing Play. My father lurched into view at the foot of the bed, towering over us. He looked just as he had the first time I'd watched this—and the second and third and fourth time, too. His bunched-up shirt sleeve. His twisted belt buckle. The little curled white hairs in his goatee. His long, serious stare. He didn't glow or shine. He appeared as any person might in the semi-darkness—dim, wreathed in shadows. When he began to dance, Annie sat up in bed, putting more space between her and it.

"Well, that's it, I guess," my father said, like always, and disappeared.

Annie was very quiet for a moment.

"So was that being projected from the cube, or . . . ?"

"I'm actually not sure how it works. I can't figure it out."

She sighed. "Please don't ever make one of these. If you die before me, I do not want to find one of these in a sock drawer or a safe-deposit box."

"Okay."

"Promise me you won't. You haven't already, have you?"

"I haven't," I said. "And yes, I promise. But why?"

"Sit up here in the dark by myself, miserable, and watch you do a little happy dance over and over again? No thank you."

"I wouldn't have to dance. I could try and say something meaningful."

"Even worse."

I stowed the cube away in my sock drawer again and climbed into bed again beside her, my chest a few inches from her back.

"It's bad enough without holograms, trust me," she said. "I used to get these little flashes. The chair in the living room, the blue one with the flower print, he used to sit in that chair and read Bill Bryson. I say that like he was always reading Bill Bryson. He wasn't. Actually that may have only happened once, but when I used to look at the chair, I'd see him sitting there just like that. There and then gone. Very fast."

"You talked about getting rid of that chair last year."

She was quiet for a moment. "There's a little red stain on the right arm."

"The splotch, yes."

"Red wine. From Anthony. I have a very distinct memory of him spilling that wine. I was so mad. I'd just had the chair reupholstered. He thought it was funny. I could have killed him." She sighed. "It's not like he's haunting that chair.

It's more like I am. I'm haunting him *into* it. Does that even make sense?"

I wriggled closer toward her in the darkness so that our legs touched.

"There's an old Irish proverb," I said. "The barrier between heaven and earth is thinnest after someone close to you dies."

"This is still very new, very fresh."

It took me a moment to realize she meant my father and not Anthony.

"If he hadn't died—Anthony, I mean—I wouldn't have you."

She was quiet.

"I probably shouldn't admit that," I said, "but I do think it sometimes. It makes it difficult for me to really mourn him."

"I don't expect you to mourn him. You didn't know him."

"It's strange but a small part of me was sort of relieved when Mom called about Dad. I had this very brief moment where I thought, *Okay, so now at least we know how it ends for him, how it happens.* That was comforting. It was always hanging out there, this inevitable, terrible thing, and then once it was real, it was like I could finally start dealing with it. A stroke on the bathroom floor. That was always how the story was going to end, only none of us knew it yet."

"Anthony was always going to drown in a river."

"One day it will be you—or me. Probably me

first. My heart—odds are that's the end of my story."

She flipped over to face me. "It's not something I like to think about. Besides, you have your thingy." She patted my chest.

I folded my head toward her neck. My lips met her clavicle. I kissed her throat. Slowly we shimmied out of our underwear and began to make love quietly. It was noiseless, dreamy sex, hot-skinned, very languid and slow, otherworldly. Later, I woke up, and our bodies were still pressed together, one of her legs underneath me. She was awake, I realized then. I'd probably only been dozing for a few minutes. I let her go, and she slipped away to the bathroom. I heard the sink run. The hum of her electric toothbrush. The squeaky slap of the medicine cabinet door. I don't remember her coming back to bed before I drifted off again.

I was leaving the bank when I saw Wilson Bizby, King of the White Hairs, getting out of his Lexus across the street. I went over to him and shook his hand.

"SparkBurger," I said. "We ate there a couple of weeks ago. Not bad at all."

"Good, good, I'm glad to hear it."

"I did some business with the previous owner

of that house, actually. She was going to add more dining space upstairs, and the bank was prepared to give a loan. But then she backed out at the last minute. I never found out why."

"I wouldn't know."

"Of course, no. Listen, I won't keep you, I'm sure you're busy, but I have a question for you. This is going to sound strange, I realize, but the other night I saw that you'd blocked off the stairway at the back of the house and I was wondering why."

Wilson's face went ashen, blank. I hadn't thought him capable of such an expression. He seemed genuinely troubled.

"They're old, falling apart. Just a liability, that's all."

"I love old houses. I've always been interested in the history of—"

"Yes, old houses. Lots of history."

I wasn't sure what else to say. I didn't want Wilson Bizby, of all people, to think me a flake.

"The truth," I said, "is that something unusual happened to me on those stairs a couple of years ago."

Wilson's eyes narrowed. "What happened? Tell me."

Briefly I told him about the recording—the *Proof*—and then about my father's experience.

"Hold on, you've got an actual recording?" he asked. "Of a voice?"

When I confirmed this, Wilson's head sagged low against his chest for a moment. Then he looked up and asked me if I had another moment to spare. He wanted to tell me something, only he didn't want to talk about it on the street. I invited him back into the bank, into my office.

The Fortune Tellers were finishing up for the day when we went inside the building. Darryl had recently proposed to his girlfriend, and soon he would be leaving Shula for DC. Diana and Susan were incredibly upset about his impending departure. Their morning talk show was coming to an end. They'd been acting sullen for weeks. All my years of working with them, I had failed to notice something crucial about the nature of their triumvirate. Susan and Diana weren't just friends with Darryl. They were infatuated with him, though I think he, like me, had always mistaken their infatuation as a sort of doting motherliness. Quite possibly, I realized now, Susan and Diana didn't even really like each other. Quite possibly, their clique was no clique at all but an unspoken competition for the affection of a handsome, charismatic guy with a silver stud in his ear. All of this had only become clear to me in the last few days as Darryl prepared to leave his two fellow tellers behind.

I led Wilson quickly past them and into my office, bringing the door closed behind us.

"So," I said, sitting down.

"I've told no one about this," he said. "Can I count on you to keep this private?"

I nodded. "Of course, yes."

"I'm serious, Jim. I'm only telling you because you might be the only person who won't think I'm completely nuts."

"I understand. And no, I won't think you're nuts, whatever it is you have to tell me, trust me."

Wilson folded his hands, interlocking his fingers, and glanced out the window. He appeared to be summoning the will to tell his story. At length, he began.

The Tale of King White Hair

About a month after acquiring the property, Mr. Bizby was touring the restaurant with one of his contractors, a very dependable guy he'd relied on for years. The house needed some work: The plumbing was shoddy, the walls lacked proper insulation, and the foundation needed new concrete piers. All very typical repairs for a house that old. Nothing that worried him very much. The home inspection had turned up most of these problems, and Mr. Bizby had anticipated doing some renovations before leasing the house.

Eventually they made their way upstairs, where the contractor suggested that Mr. Bizby rip out all the non-load-bearing walls, replace the windows, and add an additional set of stairs so that The Bizby Group could rent out the second floor as a separate apartment.

Fine, Bizby told him, that was fine, great. As long as the house didn't collapse, etc.

Then the contractor's phone rang. He had to take a call. From an inspector about another project. Off he went down the stairs, through the house, and out onto the veranda, leaving Wilson alone on the second floor.

He took a piss in the toilet. Killed a spider on the windowsill. He didn't remember what else, but he was up there for just a few minutes before going down the stairs himself. He was halfway to the bottom when he saw her. A woman. A beautiful woman. She had brown hair, very fair skin, a little button nose. She came rushing by him going in the other direction. He looked up from his feet and there she was, this gorgeous blur of a woman. She seemed so incredibly sad. And upset. Distraught! That was the word he was looking for.

This happened in the space of about two seconds. Three at most.

At this point in his story, Mr. Bizby paused for a moment. He leaned forward, looked me in the eye. Before he continued, I needed to understand something important. About love. About relationships.

Mr. Bizby had been married twice. His first

wife had been a decent woman, though she could be very withholding, emotionally, and after their third child was born, the love had chilled a bit. They were still friends but not much else. He didn't touch her; she didn't touch him. Their lives were routinized. They each had roles to play, jobs to do, and for a long time this worked very well. He wasn't sure who cheated first. It didn't really matter. Eventually they were both sleeping with other people. This wasn't something they discussed openly with each other, but they both knew it was happening. They also both understood implicitly that these affairs had to occur within certain parameters. Never with mutual friends, for instance. Never in the house. This went on for a couple of years, until one day Mr. Bizby broke one of the rules and threw their lives into disarray.

His wife owned one of the little boutiques downtown—still did, actually—and one summer she hired an assistant manager named Talia. The first time he saw Talia—well.

What I needed to understand was this: In our lives we only ever meet two or three people who really get us, people to whom we are truly connected, not just by love but by something more ineffable. This person might be one of your parents. It might even be your optometrist. Whoever it is, you will feel—at a soul level perhaps—a deep and complex joy just being in his or her presence. If this person also happens to be someone you wish to sleep with, it's sort of a blessing and a curse. A blessing because, for a while at least, the sex and this other thing, whatever you want to call it, will be perfectly aligned, and the connection will be unlike anything you've ever experienced, just total bliss. But it's a curse, too, because eventually, no matter what, one of you will want to sleep with someone else and that will start to ruin this other, purer, lighter thing. In most cases, mixing the two is not wise. One connection is so clean and warm and the other just leaves wet stains all over the sheets. So, it's better when the person who really understands us is just a friend or a sibling—and not a lover.

Did I understand what he was saying?

(Sort of I did. I was thinking of Annie, of course. If such connections did exist, as he was describing them, Annie and I had that, certainly.)

Anyway, Mr. Bizby had this connection with Talia. She was younger than him, sure, and beautiful, but that had nothing to do with it. She could have been a decade older for all he cared. Age was beside the point; the *point* was the *connection*. The affair began within a matter of weeks and very quickly it became clear to him that seeing her only once or twice a week was not going to be enough. He needed to be with her all the time, always. So he asked his wife for a divorce, endured the inevitable scandal and chaos that ensued, and married Talia soon thereafter. They were together for twelve years in all before she died from cancer. They weren't perfect years, not by any means. They had their problems, their issues. Just because you belonged with someone didn't mean you were perfectly compatible. Compatibility was not a guarantee. That was important for me to understand. He knew what this sort of connection felt like, he said. He had experience with it. He'd *lived* it. He knew that it could be instantaneous, inexplicable, even difficult. He knew that it could happen in a single breath and that it could forever alter the course of your life, at least if you were the sort of person who stayed true to yourself.

Anyway, the point of all this, he said, was that he'd felt exactly this way when he'd passed the woman on the stairs. As soon as he'd seen her, he'd been overcome. After his second wife had died, he'd given up on ever feeling that way again and yet. And yet! Here was this woman on the stairs. One look from her and he ached. Physically. Spiritually!

So, she'd passed him, this incredible woman, and it was only when he turned that he'd realized she was already gone, that possibly she'd never even been there to begin with. Did I understand how devastating this was? His true love had appeared to him and disappeared in a single instant.

After that he started routinely visiting the stairs. Once and twice a week at first. Then three and four times. He'd sit on the steps, waiting for her to return. He'd stand. Walk. Run. He'd close his eyes and try to picture her again. He was desperate to summon her. One more look was all he needed. One more moment, however brief, if only to confirm that she was real, that he wasn't crazy. To feel so connected to a person who maybe didn't exist, the impossibility of it, it was heartbreaking—and strange. He couldn't sleep at night for thinking about her, remembering her sad, lovely face. But no matter how much time he spent on the stairs, she refused to reappear.

He hired a guy. An adjunct historian, a little rumpled fellow who knew his way around an archive. This gentleman put together a dossier on the history of the house and its occupants. Birth dates, death dates, marriage licenses. A police report on the fire. Write-ups about Robert and his furniture store. About Robert's brother, Wendell, and his days in Hollywood. About Clara Lennox, too. Poor Clara Lennox, who'd suffered terrible burns in the fire and who'd spent her final years living in a hospital in Raleigh.

Did I want to see a picture?

Of course I did.

From his wallet, Bizby removed a small black-and-white photo. He handed it to me. The photo showed a young couple: A very small and prim woman with dark hair was seated in a wicker chair with her hands in her lap, and behind her stood a man with a large bulbous forehead and deep-set eyes. He had one hand on the chair and the other in his pocket. She had a dreamy, faraway look. Their postures were very correct.

"It's her," he said. "Clara Lennox. The woman on the stairs. The moment I saw the photo, I knew it was true and I wasn't insane. That was the good news. The bad news was, I'd never be with her. Not in this lifetime anyway."

"The flowers," I said. "That was you. You put flowers on her grave."

He blushed and confirmed this with a nod.

It was getting to be very late now. The custodians had arrived to clean the bank, and a vacuum roared to life in the lobby.

"I need you to make me a copy of that recording," he said. "Please. Can you do that for me? I need to hear her voice."

"If you'll allow me to scan this photo?"

"Yes, of course."

I promised to email him the clip later that evening from home, which I did.

Looking at the photo, Annie was struck by the couple's seeming youth. They were like babies, she said. Clara, in particular, didn't look much older than twenty, and as for Robert, his head was shaped like a giant guitar pick, the way his ample forehead tapered down to such a small, pointy chin. She zoomed in on his face, lingering on the pixelated eyes, and decided that yes, he was the sort of person who would set a dog on fire. She swiped over and down to Clara's face again.

"She seems so fragile, doesn't she? Like a little doll creature. Beautiful though. Where'd you get this photo from—the library?"

After swearing her to secrecy, I told her Wilson Bizby's tale, which she found both romantic and pitiful.

"In love with a ghost," she said, shaking her head. "I never thought I'd feel bad for someone like Wilson Bizby, but I do." She twirled her hair in her fingers. "Do you think it's true—what he said about these connections?" She smiled. "Did you know as soon as you saw me that—"

"Yes."

"Really?" She considered this, then smiled.

"You didn't feel the same?"

"I guess I've just never thought about it in those terms. I think love's a little messier than that, personally. Don't get me wrong. I thought you were cute. A little dopey but cute."

She looked down at the picture again. "I don't want to see this again, okay? Keep it away from me." She was still looking at it, zooming in on their finer features: noses, eyes, skin. "It's too creepy. Even if I ask to see it, don't let me. I don't like having their faces in my head."

"Understandable."

"Those stairs. What's up with those stairs? A never-ending source of weirdness. It has to be a daisy hole, right?"

"You'd have to ask Sally Zinker."

"Yes," she said, handing me back my phone. "The elusive Sally Zinker. Wherefore art thou, Dr. Zinker?"

Sometimes I doubted Sally Zinker even existed. She was a character in a movie or an elaborate video game. She was an advertising campaign. She was a conspiracy theory website given skin and bones.

Flipping through her book one night I fell down into a sleep, a half-sleep, light and gauzy. I was aware that I was in my own bed, but the room felt altered somehow. When I reached out—for the pillows, the blankets—my hands passed right through them. I wasn't really there. I'd slipped away somehow. I was a ghost. I was a hologram. Or maybe I was here and everything else was a hologram. I couldn't figure it out. Again and again I reached out to the world—and again and again it refused to receive me, to touch me back, to confirm me. I began to panic, to scream, and it was then that I sat up in bed, fully awake, both my arms swiping wildly at the bedspread.

Annie was in bed beside me, a red pen in her mouth, her plays spread everywhere. She gave me a strange look.

“I’m fine,” I said. “Sorry. I just dozed off.”

“Your phone just made a sound,” she said. “It chimed.”

She kissed my arm, moved her papers to the floor, and flipped off her light. I went over to the dresser and grabbed the phone. I’d received an alert from HeartNet; the device had just saved my life. I couldn’t believe it. Had this coincided with my dream? Had I nearly slipped into a nonexistence?

“Who was it?” Annie asked.

“Low battery,” I said.

I climbed back into bed, trying not to freak out. A few minutes later Annie was asleep, and I was alone. I wriggled my toes under the sheets, watching the blanket move at the bottom of the bed. I rolled toward Annie, breathed in her hair, her skin, wondering how much longer I’d have nostrils, a nose, a brain, an olfactory sense, a thought such as this: I could live in a cloud of my wife’s hair and be happy. I didn’t want to disappear. I didn’t want to die! She slept on peacefully, her warm rump turned toward me, the blanket halfway up her leg, a burn mark on the sheet from the dryer. Everything felt significant, fleeting.

I wanted to appreciate every aspect of this moment, to preserve it, to live in it forever. Annie's light wheezing breath, the dance of the curtain across the AC vent in the floor, the clock's red flashing colon that held the hours from collapsing into the minutes. I was in agony. I was crying. Sobbing, actually, face pressed to the pillow, the heat of my face rebounding off the fabric. If I wasn't careful, I was going to wake Annie, and so I slipped out of bed, grabbed my cell off the dresser, and went downstairs to the living room. I didn't turn on any lights. The room was very still. Being down here, alone, surrounded by such stillness, made my tears feel that much more conspicuous and strange, and I managed to stop crying.

With a tap-tap-tap on my cell phone, I opened my HeartNet app. My heart leaped onto the screen. Blue and red static swished through the four chambers. I turned up the volume to better hear it beating. It was like a basketball dribbled in an otherwise empty gymnasium, reverberative, distant. The image of my heart on the screen was the brightest thing in the room, its blue light spilling across my palm and upper arm.

But I felt just as uneasy and unsettled. I was going to die. Any second I was going to die. It was going to happen now—now, now, now. A hacker on the other side of the world would explode my heart. Or the particles in my body would blink away at once. I'd be gone. Like my father, like everyone else. Whatever it was, I wouldn't even know it had happened. I wouldn't know to mourn my own loss. Everything I'd ever been would slip away. I'd lose Annie. Because there was no other side, was there? Because the only side was this one?

I shut off the HeartNet app and, despite the hour, called Sally Zinker's number again.

Please state your name, the robotic voice said, *your contact information, and who you're trying to reach.*

I gave my name and my number and said, "I want to reach my father. Or God. Or anyone, for that matter. I just want to know if this is it, if I'm going to disappear when I die."

I hung up and did a few of my breathing exercises. I was about to go upstairs again when the phone rang. An unknown number flashed. I answered after just one ring.

"Jim Byrd?" a woman asked.

"Sally Zinker?"

"Yes, yes . . . Are you there?"

"I'm here, still here. This is incredible. You won't believe how I got this number."

"Mr. Byrd, I don't have much time to chat, so let's get right to it. You're calling because you think I've built a machine that allows for communication with the dead. Am I right?"

"That's right, yes. So does that mean you haven't built it or—?"

"Here's the thing—I will neither confirm nor deny the existence of such a machine. Not over the phone. But I will say that if you are interested in discussing this topic further, you are welcome to come and see me here in Little Rock."

"I—"

"Hold on, there's a catch. Don't speak too soon. The deal is, I am in the middle of a study, and in order to complete this study I need more participants. So if you come, if I am to meet with you and talk about my work, you'd have to agree to participate in my study."

"Okay, but what sort of study is it, exactly?"

"I assume you are familiar with my research?"

"I've read your book, if that's what you mean."

"Let's just say my study is in keeping with my book."

"Does the study involve your reunion machine?"

"As I said, I will neither—"

"Confirm nor deny. I get it. I understand. I just want to be clear on what I'm agreeing to if I come out there. My wife would also be with me."

"Your wife, fine. She's invited, too. You can both come and see me. Same deal for her."

"Is it dangerous, whatever it is you'd be subjecting us to?"

"Hmm. I don't know how to answer that. For legal reasons, I mean."

"I got your number through a psychic. He wrote it down for me with the help of a spirit guide. Also, I have a recording that you made a long time ago. It's from a restaurant in the town where I live. The Dog on Fire—do you remember it?"

"Yes, of course. The Dog on Fire. She was one of the first cases I investigated. The *very* first, actually. I had a friend, an acquaintance, who was very familiar with that house, and we were on the stairs together one afternoon when she felt something. A presence, I guess you could call it. She was a much older woman, almost a hundred years old, in fact. She burst into tears. Scared me to death. I'd never seen anything like it. Anyway, I was absolutely intrigued. It was really what got me thinking about ghosts in the context of daisy theory. How funny you have that recording! A small world, is it not? Anyway, Mr. Byrd, as I said, I don't have much time to talk. I have a lot of other calls to return. Come to Little Rock—or don't. It's your decision."

"Oh, we'll come. We'll be there."

"Wonderful. That's wonderful news. I don't think you'll regret it, either one of you. Tell me, do you have a pen handy? Because you'll need to write this next part down."

Wendell Andrew Lennox

Double-chinned, over-doused with cologne—Wendell sits at a stoplight in his '98 Olds, cherry red with Tri-Tone leather interior. He's wearing a straw fedora to keep his bald head from burning and peeling.

He's on his way to Bucky Nesbitt's funeral. It was Bucky who stuck by him in the bad years, who took him to Mexico City and helped him sell black market scripts—*Hell Boys*, *No Home on the Range*, *Skeleton Man*, and all the other cowboy-horror schlock Wendell churned out on his Corolla, blasted on rum. Bucky was like a father to Wendell, and now the poor man is dead. He will be missed!

Tonight there will be a party, and people will tell the most wonderful Bucky stories. Everyone's got a Bucky story. The time Bucky threw up egg salad on Gary Cooper. The time Bucky, martini glass in hand, stepped right off a pontoon boat as it was skidding across the Great Salt Lake. If a well-lived life is measured by its crazy stories, then Bucky wins, hands down.

As far as Wendell can see, the avenue is lined with long, tan buildings—ugly, headache-inducing, no panache at all. Christmas lights dangle from the palm trees. The air is still, windless. He slaps his palm against the side of the car. Bucky was sick for almost a year. When did everyone get so old? Since when was it time to die?

One day, when Wendell gets sick, who will hold the water glass to his lips? Who will change his shitty sheets? Who will be there with him to squeeze his hand? He's never been married, never had kids. The closest he ever came to any of that was with Clara.

A letter arrives at his apartment all the way from Shula, North Carolina. He's been away from home for almost two years. He misses it more than he expected, but he can't go back there, not until he's made something of himself. He sprawls out across his bed to read the letter, expecting the usual news from his mother, but this one, he sees now, is from his brother. Robert has married Clara!

On the afternoon he meets Clara for the first time, Wendell and his brother have been out making furniture deliveries all day. They are still young boys, seventeen and nineteen, respectively—black-haired, bowlegged, unmistakably siblings. Robert is thick-necked with a large nose, his eyes deep-set beneath his brow. Wendell is the handsomer of the two, the more personable, but he is also easily distracted and a little lazy. He knows this about himself. They are arguing about the order of their deliveries, about the most efficient route. Wendell is the one who knocks on the door, and Mr. Hopstead answers, a ruddy-faced man with an upturned nose and a toothy smile.

"Yes," he says, "it will go right through here and into the living room, there against the wall."

The brothers measure the door and then strategize. They remove the door from its hinges and prop it up against the stoop railing.

Sofa hoisted, Wendell enters the house first, hands behind him, the sofa barely squeezing through the door frame. As he moves toward the living room he sees that a young girl is watching him from the kitchen with a cool, amused look on her face. Who is this! He forgets where he's going for a moment. The sofa leg nicks the wall, and Robert yells at him to watch where he's going. Seeing the girl, Robert turns red and wishes he hadn't raised his voice. The brothers pivot and guide the sofa into place against the wall. The girl—Clara—is observing them both with her arms crossed. Wendell winks at her, and she smiles.

Meanwhile, Robert fusses with the papers for Mr. Hopstead to sign.

Clara sticks out her tongue at a mannequin in a store window while Wendell preens in front of the glass. This is the future as he sees it today, on the occasion of his eighteenth birthday: he and Clara together forever, strolling and window-gazing their way through life.

Wendell wakes up with a hangover in his canopy bed. Another birthday, his thirty-eighth. The neighboring pillowcase is smeared with concealer and lipstick. Last night he brought home Valerie Green, the starlet, the fantasy of every man in America, and he fucked her twice. She's left him a note on the bureau across the room. *You're the best,* is all it says. He should feel like he's on top of the world, shouldn't he? Why doesn't he?

Leaves fling themselves from their branches and land on the ground just ahead of them, as if desperate for the chance to be stepped on by her. When a dog twists loose from his owner's grip and comes barreling toward them, Clara drops to one knee to pet him. She seizes the dog by its mane, her fingers deep in its brown fur, as it heaves its dripping tongue at her face. She loves animals, all animals, cats, squirrels, slugs, but especially dogs. She's still a girl—only fifteen, in fact—her brown hair parted down the middle, not quite stylishly, her green eyes so large and curious.

Wendell watches her with something like awe

and fear. Every particle in his body feels overly charged, ready to burst. He doesn't have a ring. The idea of a ring is only occurring to him now as the question leaps from his lips. She springs up from the ground to hug him and kiss his cheek. Did he miss her answer—or is this it, this burst of affection? The dog galumphs back to its owner, and Clara slides her small hand into Wendell's outer pocket as they finish their stroll through the park, in the direction of downtown.

Unsure what else to do, he buys them movie tickets at the Grand, and they sit near the back, in those plush seats, sacrosanct in the darkness, the silvery lights. She allows him to kiss the nape of her neck. After the movie he leads her two blocks over to his father's store and unlocks the back door. They lie down together on a sofa in the middle of the showroom. Lights off, he unbuttons her blouse and gets his hands on her breasts for the first time, but after a few minutes, she slides away with a nervous smile. She won't sleep with him, she says, not until they're officially married, which is fine with Wendell, really, because he's never been with a girl anyway. Probably there are girls sleeping with boys somewhere in America, but this is how it's done here in Shula, with girls like Clara.

He's holed up in a hotel room in Mexico City. The fans are on full blast, but he's sweated through his white linen shirt. He strips down, takes a swig of rum, and goes back to typing. He's past deadline for a script that will pay next to nothing but at least it's work. He should be grateful.

Bucky said he was going out for cigarettes, but he's been gone for hours. If only Wendell can finish this script, tonight he and Bucky will go out and celebrate with a trip to the whorehouse. The movie is called *The Skeleton Man*, and it's about a seventeenth-century conquistador who's raised from the dead with a mysterious elixir and who falls in unrequited love with the gravedigger's daughter. Wendell has reached the penultimate scene, the one in which the gravedigger's daughter, Maria, must lure the terrifying Skeleton Man back into the graveyard.

The door busts open and there's Bucky, already drunk as hell.

"*Hola, muchacho*," Bucky says, cigarette dangling from his mouth, a wild, pernicious look in his eye.

Why oh why did he ever agree to follow Bucky to Mexico?

Because the studios stopped calling. Because they wouldn't work with him anymore.

Wendell is in his manager's office, staring out the window at a piece of paper being nudged up and down the street by the breeze. Nobody's buying—but why? His manager, behind the desk, smiles nervously. “Either you’re in a dry spell, or your name’s mud.”

But that doesn’t make any sense! Wendell has never been a communist; he’s never been to any meetings; his scripts are entirely apolitical; he hasn’t been called to testify. His name can’t be mud if he hasn’t stepped in any!

“Just give it some time,” his manager says. “It’ll all work out. I’m sure of it.”

“Somebody’s named me for no good reason,” Wendell says. “It’s the only explanation.”

But nobody named him. This he learns years later when a reporter who’s researching the McCarthy era comes to visit Wendell’s condo in Miami to talk about those days. They sit together on the balcony, smoking cigarettes and looking down at the pool, where the geriatric ladies in swim caps are doing their daily aerobics. The water weights. The laughter. The back fat. Wendell leans forward in his wheelchair and grabs the balcony rail. His health is poor. He’s diabetic and despite his protective shoes somehow he managed to injure his left foot last year. The doctors removed the leg up to his knee. The loss of mobility has only exacerbated the weight problem. Even before the surgery, he was over two hundred pounds, and now—

Now he’s a fat fuck. A fat fuck in a wheelchair staring down at a bunch of old biddies who probably wouldn't even give him the time of day.

The reporter tells him that believe it or not Wendell was never actually named.

"I've had a look at all the documents, and I can tell you what happened if you really want to know."

Wendell says he does.

Unfortunately, it was all a big mix-up. There was another Wendell Lennox, a union organizer in Ohio, and this other Wendell gave a couple of quotes once to a newspaper there and then had to sit in front of the committee. The studios saw the name, thought it was Wendell Lennox the scriptwriter, and that was that. He was damaged goods. It had nothing to do with anything Wendell had ever written or done. Just plain bad luck.

On the set of *The Skeleton Man*, Wendell is loading up his plate at the catering table when he bumps into Maria Jurado, a black-haired beauty with a devilish smile. Maria is playing the heroine, the gravedigger's daughter, also named Maria, with whom the Skeleton Man falls dangerously in love. He convinces her to eat dinner with him that night, and they spend most of the meal gossiping and laughing about the rest of the cast. Then she asks him for any advice he might have about her career. She's so young, intoxicatingly young.

Wendell can imagine loving this woman, caring for her. He'd buy her—what? A villa. They'd live outside Mexico City and make babies together. She'd be his muse. He'd write scripts for her. None of this horror schlock. Real parts. He'd write an art film. Something surreal and strange. In the Buñuel mode. Maybe, with his help, with her name on the right films, Maria could even build up enough cachet to make the jump to Hollywood. All of this is flitting through his brain as they sip their wine, but at the end of the night, when he invites her back to his hotel room, she kisses him on the cheek, no trace of desire or lust at all in those lovely lips. There is something familial in the way she kisses him goodnight. This is the way a daughter kisses her father on his deathbed, he thinks. Wendell is almost fifty. He's close to bald, and since coming to Mexico last year, he has, admittedly, put on a little weight. He feels past his prime.

The next day, on set, he watches Maria—as Maria—lure the Skeleton Man back into the graveyard, where she will trap him in his coffin. The monster will spend the rest of eternity in that coffin. It occurs to Wendell that he approached the script all wrong. A better version might have sympathized more closely with the poor Skeleton Man, the former conquistador who—it should be noted—did not ask to be reanimated by the mysterious elixir accidentally spilled upon his grave. He didn't ask for any of this. If he could help it, he wouldn't be such a lusty corpse. The woman he desires does not desire him because he is hideous and ancient. As if that's not bad enough, presumably, once resealed in his coffin, he will not be able to rest again. The script does not mention this explicitly but logic suggests it's so. Now that he has been awakened by the elixir, it would seem the Skeleton Man's fate is to lie there, fully conscious, moldering, unloved, forever.

He was loved once. Truly loved. In his own time, surely he was.

At Clara's house for dinner with her family, Wendell goes out back to take a piss in the yard. Before venturing inside again, to the chaos of the home-cooked meal, of Clara's big-muscled older brothers, their sweaty-browed stares, he stands behind the billowing sheets on the laundry line and lights a cigarette. He hears a noise on the other side of the fence. A scraping sound. A small head appears at the top. It's Clara's kid sister, May. She's ten years old, a pipsqueak with light freckles across her cheeks and nose. He offers her a drag off his cigarette, and she coughs it all up, hilariously, and then runs off down the street. Wendell goes back inside, eventually. Clara's been looking all over for him. She kisses him quickly, in the hallway, so that her parents won't see.

• • •

But he doesn't marry her. He moves away. She marries Robert. There's a fire, and Robert dies and Clara survives, but barely. She suffers! She's disfigured and wastes away in a hospital, and Wendell never goes to her—but why? He's a coward, he supposes. Besides, what would he even say? He sends a card. Some flowers. Nobody forced her to marry Robert. That was her decision! He sends her more flowers. He hates himself. One day the phone rings: Clara has died. He doesn't attend the funeral; he sends more flowers, another card, this one to her family. *Thinking of you,* he writes.

Eventually—many years later—he visits the house on Graham Street. Though in need of repair, it is larger and lovelier than he expected it would be. Wendell knocks on the door. A woman with dark curly hair answers, and he explains that he used to know someone who lived here, a long time ago, and if she wouldn't mind, if it's not too inconvenient, could he look around for a few minutes? She seems uncertain but nods. Soon he's sitting on this woman's couch, fanning himself with his fedora, as the woman goes into the kitchen to fix him an iced water.

He is in New York with some regularity, but Shula is outside his usual orbit. It's been at least thirty years since he walked the old neighborhoods where he used to deliver couches and chairs for his father. Nobody here recognizes him anymore. No one knows to be impressed. If only he could wear a uniform, the way military generals do, with little bars and insignias and stars indicating and enumerating all his many accomplishments, the screenplays, the conquests, the adventures abroad, but as it is, he is anonymous, just another old fart in search of his past.

This is the first time he's ever visited this house—he's avoided it until now—though he's certain it must have looked much different back when Robert and Clara lived here. The television set in the corner, that's new obviously, and so is the green rug and those red curtains across the window. He stands up from the couch to examine the walls for signs of damage, but the restoration was done many years ago, and he sees no evidence of the fire.

The woman returns with his iced water. Her jean shorts sag in the back. She's got a small butt, scrawny pale legs, a craggy face. She's wearing sandals, and her toes are so stubby—little pink sausages bright red at the tips. Wendell doesn't even bother to flirt, not because he finds her unattractive but because he fears she wouldn't reciprocate, because she wouldn't want to entertain the possibility of him.

• • •

Wendell flicks his cigarette against the bedsheet that's hanging on the laundry line in Clara's backyard. It leaves a small black spot against the white but doesn't burn. Distantly he can hear May calling out for the dog. When he goes inside, Clara kisses him, quickly. Mr. Hopstead, coming around the corner, almost catches them. He drags Wendell into the parlor for a little chat. Agitated, antsy, Mr. Hopstead stands by the fireplace with his hands behind his back, swaying foot to foot.

The Hopsteads don't have much money. They rent this house, and the nicest thing they own is the sofa they bought on installments from the Lennoxes' store. Mr. Hopstead came to Shula as a teenager, fleeing his family's farm, and for many years he worked as a motorman on the streetcars. Now he works at the textile mill, though in what capacity, Wendell does not know.

Mr. Hopstead laughs uneasily and then claps Wendell on the shoulder and says he'll just come out with it. He's figured out about the engagement. He knows Wendell intends to marry Clara, and, contrary to what Wendell might think, he supports the idea.

"Granted, Clara is still very young," he says. "But this doesn't have to happen tomorrow, does it?"

Wendell says it doesn't.

The Lennoxes, Mr. Hopstead says, are good

and respectable people, and he would be proud to count Wendell as a son-in-law.

Feeling suddenly uneasy, Wendell manages to shake Mr. Hopstead's outstretched hand, but then, once they have returned to the kitchen and Clara smiles at him, he realizes that she orchestrated this, that she told her father everything in the hope that it would move things along more quickly. With so many people in the kitchen, Wendell can't ask her why she did this without consulting him first. He hates how damned happy she seems to be. This kitchen reeks of cooking gas and her brothers' farts. How do they stand it? He can hardly breathe in here, all this commotion, the heat still rising up off the stove. He's sweating through his shirt. Clara takes his hand, squeezes it, smiles at him again, pulls him into the hall.

"Did you talk to Daddy? Daddy said he was going to talk to you. Did he? What did Daddy say? Tell me everything."

In the house on Graham Street, Wendell sips his iced water, gazing up, trying to imagine what Clara's life might have been like here. She and Robert were married for a full decade. Surely some of those years were good ones. Possibly this could have been his life if he hadn't left town. Maybe he and Clara could have had children together—little beautiful Clara lookalikes. He could have taken over his father's store. Perhaps, working together, he and his brother could have saved the business. That Robert kept open its doors as long as he did was a real feat—but still, Wendell might have been able to help think of some off-the-wall solutions. Certainly, if he'd stayed and married her, Clara would be alive today. There wouldn't have been any fire. He could have protected her from that fate, at least.

Wendell can't help feeling somewhat culpable for what happened to Clara. He never took it very seriously, their engagement. He was too young then to know that infatuations, however strongly felt, have their expiration dates. But if it was an infatuation, then why does he long for her now? He'd cut off both arms right now if it would bring her back. They never even made love! Is that why he wants her so badly? If only he'd slept with her, just once, maybe she wouldn't continue to hold such power over him. He should have married her and taken her with him to California!

Wendell and Clara—teenagers—emerge from a movie at the Grand, blinking in the brightness of the lobby lights. Clara's neck is streaked red where he's been kissing and sucking at her skin. God, that skin of hers. She takes his hand, and they shove through the doors, into the night, in the direction of his father's store, where a sofa awaits them in the darkness of the showroom.

"What did Daddy say?" Clara asks. "Tell me everything. Isn't this so exciting?"

"I thought we'd agreed we'd keep it a secret for now," Wendell says irritably.

She looks up at him, wounded, about to say something, but then her oldest brother steps into the hallway, looking for his shoes. He finds them at the bottom of the stairs and sits down on the second step to jam his feet inside clumsily. He knows that Wendell and Clara are waiting for him to leave before resuming their conversation, and so he takes an especially long time to tie his laces, looping large, with extra flourishes.

"If you're going to kiss her, just do it already," he barks. "Don't mind me!"

He's standing at the bottom of the stairs, gazing up, picturing her at the top with a little dog under her arm. He should have come back to see her after the fire. He should have visited her in the hospital.

"So you knew someone who lived here?" the woman asks, hand on her hip.

"My brother, actually. Half a century ago."

"He must have been one of the first to live here," the woman says. "The house was built in 1918. My husband and I are doing our best to restore it to its original condition. When we bought it, it was three different apartments. We basically had to gut it. What did it look like last time you were here?"

"It's my first time here, actually."

"Oh."

He cups his hand over the post as he turns away from the stairs—but what's that? A dancing light at the periphery of his vision. A flash of blue and yellow and red, not against the wall, but midair. Like light through a prism. It's already gone. A trick of the sunlight on a mirror perhaps. Or—of course! His water glass. He twists it in his hand, trying to reproduce the flash against any of the walls.

"What are you doing?" the owner says.

Or is his wristwatch responsible? A glint of the metal, maybe.

"The light, on the stairs," she says, "It's funny there, isn't it?"

"What's doing it?"

"We don't know. We can't figure it out. It's not just the light either. My daughter, she hears things sometimes. Voices. She says it's like a telephone wrapped in a blanket under one of the steps. She had a sleepover with a bunch of girls. They stayed up all night just listening and messing around with a Ouija board."

"Any luck?"

She shakes her head. "No. One of them said she heard a dog barking. But, well, teenage girls, right?"

Wendell smiles and returns the glass to her. He's no longer sure why he's come here.

She's been dead for two years when he visits her grave for the first and only time in his life. He leaves a few flowers on her tombstone. He's in town for no other reason but this. Is she watching him from up above? That same afternoon, feeling no solace, he takes the bus to New York and gets a room at the St. Regis Hotel. Upon request, room service brings him a typewriter, an Underwood, which Wendell sets up on a fat dictionary at the end of the bed. He has decided to write a script about two brothers who fall in love with the same girl after she enters their father's furniture store one afternoon—or no, not furniture store. The boys' father will own a *jewelry* store, and the girl will choose the older, more stable brother. The younger one, hurt and sad, will run off to Hollywood and become a writer—or no, maybe not a writer. The younger brother could be a traveler instead, a wanderer, a rover, a lost soul. He'll travel the world in search of absolution. As a spy. No, not a spy. He should be something more believable than that. He'll import things. Fabrics, maybe.

Wendell takes a short nap and then calls downstairs to the kitchen for a turkey sandwich and some cookies. He unzips his pants, thinking of Clara, but now that he's been to her grave, he can't seem to disentangle the image of the girl who lives in his memory—soft-skinned, young, warm, in a light blue dress, latched onto his arm—from the idea of her corpse. Her death has robbed him of a reliable fantasy, too. Imagining her sunken features, her shriveled, worm-eaten innards, he opens his eyes, feeling disgusted with himself for even wanting to fantasize about her. He can't shake the feeling that in conjuring up her memory for his own gratification he has committed an unforgivable offense. He would apologize—but to whom should he apologize? To God? To her? He sits down at the end of his bed and begins writing again.

In bed with the letter from Robert again. That damn letter. Marrying Clara! Wendell wonders how long this has been going on. He doesn't want to know. He hasn't been in touch with Clara for over a year. The night before he left town he took her on a walk downtown and reassured her they'd be able to stay together. Once he was more established out there and had the means, he'd send for her. He'd sell a few scripts and find them a proper place to live. All of it was very exciting, very romantic, but then nothing ever happened. Neither one of them broke it off, not officially, though it's true that their letter-writing became less and less feverish. Her parents were having some financial trouble, something she'd never elaborate on, there was that, plus she didn't seem too interested in his progress selling scripts. She didn't even really like films. He supposes they simply grew apart. Whatever they had, it fizzled. Eventually he started seeing other women, and the idea of actually bringing her out West seemed increasingly far-fetched.

Still, he's shocked about this latest news, Clara marrying Robert. To hell with them!

He doesn't write them immediately, intending to give it some thought, but one month passes and then another and soon his inability to formulate a decent response becomes its own response and solidifies into an attitude that he convinces himself is justified. He enjoys thinking of their marriage as an act of betrayal.

The day after he leaves her behind in Shula, his train hisses to a stop just outside Chicago. A few minutes later a fat conductor ambles down the aisle with an explanation for the delay. A car accident on the line a mile ahead. Lean, handsome, hopeful—Wendell eats peanuts in his window seat, bits of fibrous shell falling all over his shirt and lap. He's eager to be out West as soon as possible, but he has no appointments there. No one is expecting him.

A woman with a green hat over her long blond hair taps him on the shoulder and asks if she might sit beside him. Her other seatmate, she explains, just won't stop talking. Wendell surreptitiously dusts the shell bits from his chest and makes room for her. By the time the train is moving again, a few hours later, Wendell is quite certain he's in love with this woman. She has the most beautiful eyes, and when she giggles, she puts her little hand over her mouth. When she asks Wendell if he has a girlfriend, he smiles and says he does not.

Wendell hands the owner his glass and peers up the steps one last time. This light—if only it was her. He tries to imagine her descending toward him. If he focused hard enough, could he will Clara back into existence? Could he bring her back from the dead with an elixir concocted from sweat, tears, bits of her hair, and his own heart's blood?

In his head, a typewriter is clacking noisily, the soundtrack for his every conscious dream: Enter Clara, rounding the staircase, her blood cool but not cold, a placid look on her face.

You jerk, she'd say with a smile.

Or better yet: *You sure know how to keep a girl waiting, don't you?*

Or even better: *I never stopped loving you but I stopped liking you a long time ago.*

Oh, how the audience would fawn over her!

But this isn't a script, this isn't a scene, this is real life, and Clara will not enter. Clara is gone forever. Wendell thanks the owner for letting him look around and leaves the house forever.

He revs his '98 Olds, waiting for the light to change. His old pal Bucky Nesbitt is dead, and he needs a good Bucky story, one that will help people understand what a total character he was. He can't believe Bucky's dead. Since when were all his friends dying off? We're dinosaurs, Bucky said once. He'll never have another friend like Bucky. What he needs is a story that will knock their socks off. Everyone will expect him to have one.

The time Bucky threw a fork at the trombone player when he and Wendell were in New Orleans for a shoot. The time Bucky stood up in the middle of a particularly boring premiere to belt out the national anthem. The time Bucky dragged him to a street party in Mexico City, turned around, his face gaunt but happy, and said, "Brother, we aren't ever going home, are we?"

IV

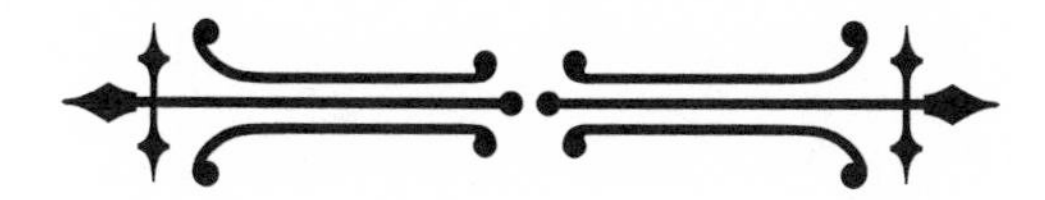

The Reunion Machine

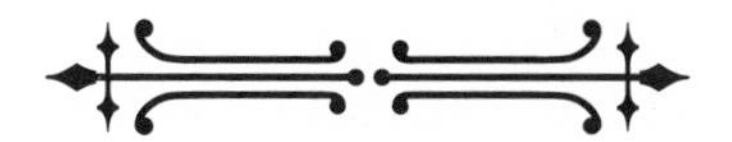

Our plane landed in Little Rock in the early evening, the last splash of sunlight at the far end of the runway, and after we found our bags on the carousel we caught a shuttle to the rental car office, where a man in a tight blue jacket issued us a small red sedan. The hotel room Annie had booked for us was downtown, near the river, and we ate dinner that night at a bar and grill not too far from the Clinton Presidential Center.

The city was very quiet and almost no one was out on the street, which we chalked up to the cool weather. I hadn't brought along a warm enough coat—I was wearing only a suit jacket. Upstairs Annie called her parents to check in on Fisher. Afterward we undressed and, for the sixth time that day, mapped Sally Zinker's address. A small part of me feared that once we reached the address, we'd find the building empty, burned out, an industrial-waste site. It even seemed possible to me that her study was in fact an elaborate test designed to measure a subject's eagerness to believe in something as far-fetched as a mysterious spirit communication machine. Perhaps Sally Zinker was a fabrication, her book written by a team of psychologists, clues about the machine sprinkled all over the Internet to lure people like me—death-obsessed, conspiracy-minded suckers who would believe in almost anything. We would arrive at the building, ring a bell, and a camera would snap our pictures. Psychologists in white coats would rush out, lead us into interview rooms, and map our sad, easily duped brains. Our pictures would ultimately appear in the book these psychologists would publish. *The mug shot of two dupes,* the caption would say. *Three of the fifteen people we told about the device actually paid money and traveled to find it,* they'd write, and *here is what they look like and here is where they live and here are their email addresses.*

Annie encouraged me to think of it as a vacation. If we found Sally and she had a machine, great, but if not, at least we had a few nights in a hotel room together. We threw back the blankets and watched TV for an hour before Annie fell asleep. I wrapped the sheet around me, mummy-like, and stared up at the ceiling, willing myself to fall asleep, but my mind resisted. I was too worked up.

I went into the bathroom and splashed water on my face, watched the water drip off my nose and my eyelashes. Then I flipped open my suitcase and began flinging my clothes back into the compartment, yanking shirts off the hangers in the closet. In the morning we would leave this place. We would drive right back to the airport, return the car, and fly home. We'd be in Shula by morning. We could forget about the Reunion Machine. And Sally Zinker. We could move forward with our lives and await the end like everyone else in the world. Utterly clueless.

Eventually I gave up on giving up and went to bed.

Three hours later I woke to the sound of the weather channel. Annie was dressing at the foot of the bed.

We went downstairs for a quick breakfast before getting back into the rental car.

Annie was wearing tight jeans and a wool blazer over a nice white untucked shirt. She looked very put-together, and I wondered if she'd dressed with Anthony in mind.

The GPS guided us over a bridge, to the north side of the river, to what felt like an industrial part of town—into a neighborhood with long blocks of pharmacies and gas stations and Auto Zones. We passed a Mexican restaurant and a T-Mobile store and then our destination appeared ahead of us on the left, a squat brick building painted white with faded letters across the side that said The Hobby Shoppe.

Shopp*e*—an Old English spelling? A letter variant for the purposes of trademark?

The building appeared to have very little history whatsoever. The front windows were covered with tar paper, and weeds had sprouted up through the cracks in the asphalt. Walking around to the far side, we discovered a green Nissan Xterra, its windows rolled down, a newspaper in the passenger seat, a pair of reading glasses on the dash.

"It's hers," Annie said excitedly. "She's here."

She knocked on the back door, which was heavy and wide. Her knuckles barely made any noise at all against it. A few inches above our heads was a small square window with gridded glass. I reached up and knocked there instead.

About thirty seconds passed—I was on the verge of suggesting we turn away—before we heard a series of dead bolts clicking and turning. Annie looked at me and tried to reassure me with a smile. I stepped back and slipped my hands into my pockets, not wanting to seem too eager. When the door dragged open, there stood the elusive Sally Zinker. She looked very much like her hologram, though her hair was longer and much grayer now. She was wearing khakis and a black fleece. She coughed once, and then again, her face turning red, a balled-up fist like a stone rolled across the open tomb of her mouth.

"Names?" she managed to ask.

"Jim and Annie Byrd," Annie said.

"Very good, you've made it. Please come in. Let's chat."

She stepped aside without a word, creating just enough space for us to enter the building. The door banged shut behind us, and she turned all the dead bolts. We followed her down a short, dark hallway, breathing in a faint mildew smell not quite masked by cleaning chemicals. She directed us into a dingy kitchenette, its Formica counters bubbling, the plastic coating peeling off the cabinets, a set of mustard-yellow chairs that wouldn't have been out of place in a 1970s fast-food chain.

"Coffee's there if you'd like some," she said, disappearing down the hall.

Coffee crystals were scattered across the countertop, which was splotched with dried half-moon coffee stains. In the trash can by the empty watercooler were a dozen food wrappers, a crunched-up white paper bag, plus empty creamer and sugar packets. Once upon a time this kitchen had clearly served as a break room for the Hobby Shoppe's employees. I wondered how many of her meals Sally ate each day in this miserable, overly lit windowless hovel.

I poured us cups of coffee, not because I needed one but because it was a way of distracting myself from what came next, and then sat down in one of the mustard chairs. Annie leaned up against the wall with her arms crossed. When I checked my phone, I realized that the bars were blinking rapidly, and I no longer had service.

Sally returned a few minutes later with thick stacks of paper bound together with oversized metal clips. "So," she said. "Here's how this will work. First you're each going to sign one of these." She dropped the papers on the table and pulled two pens from her pocket. "These," she explained, "are not much different from nondisclosure agreements. The gist of it is, you cannot tell people about this place, and you can't tell people what happens here, and I am not accountable for what happens to you. I can't be held accountable for the nature of your experience. For obvious reasons, I don't want a lot of attention. Not yet anyway. One day I'll publish and the world will know what I've got here, what I've built, but until then it's hush-hush."

"So you have built a machine, then?" I asked.

She grimaced. "I'm not saying either way until you sign these. These agreements also protect you. They guarantee that when I do publish, you'll be referred to by a number, and only I will know your identities. At least for the next fifty years."

"Fifty years?" Annie asked.

Sally nodded. "You'll be dead or a couple of old geezers by then anyway, so what do you care? This"—she pointed to a paragraph halfway down the page, the print small and dense—"is the clause that guarantees your anonymity for the next fifty years."

I took the pen and signed the document. I couldn't imagine telling anyone about this trip, posting about it online, or even telling Fisher or my mother. When I passed the pen to Annie, she hesitated for a moment, as if studying the fine print, before signing her name.

"So, when do we use the machine?" I asked.

Sally smiled. "That would be tomorrow. There are four of you in town right now. I had four here last week, too, and I've got another four on their way next week. If you'd like to meet the others, you're welcome to join us tonight at the Capitol Hotel, about nine p.m. Sort of like a reception, I guess," she said. "But right now I'm going to talk to you both independently and ask you some preliminary questions. These questions will take about twenty minutes apiece. Very painless."

She asked us who wanted to go first. We didn't say anything.

"I'll talk to you first," she said to Annie.

She dragged a chair into the hall and instructed me to sit there until it was my turn. I did as I was told, at least for ten minutes or so. Eventually I stood up and wandered down the hall where I saw another open doorway on the left. I wondered if this was where she kept the machine. I was desperate to have a look at it. We knew nothing at all about how it functioned. Maybe we'd sit at a table together and wait for rippling lights to appear over our heads. Or maybe we'd walk through a giant electric hula hoop and find ourselves floating in the ether with an army of dead souls.

I'd almost reached the doorway when a short man with thick white hair, styled forward like the prow of a ship, stepped out into the hall and nearly collided with me. His deep tan skin, the pompadour, his light blue golf shirt, like something a maintenance man would wear at a resort—he put me in mind of a vacationing televangelist.

"Can I help you, friend?" he asked.

I introduced myself and explained that I was waiting for my interview with Sally.

"I know who you are," he said, in a way that suggested he didn't like me. "My name's Martin Strider." He grinned. His teeth were very white and tightly joined. "I'm the money."

"The money," I said uncertainly.

"I've known Sally for years," he said. "She grew up here, in Little Rock, and I was friends with her daddy, and Sally was always very friendly with my daughter RayAnne, bless her heart. Sally was very good to RayAnne, very good, very kind, didn't treat her any different. We had RayAnne out at the Marcy Free School, for years and years we did, and they helped her quite a bit, but the honest truth is she was never going to be able to live on her own, no matter what, and so she was at home with her momma and me right up until the end. Anyway, I've always kept track of Sally and her many accomplishments. She's like a second daughter. I fronted the money, bought this old Hobby Shoppe for her. It had sat empty for years."

He jingled the change in his pocket and smiled at me again. Then he asked me if I was excited.

"I'm not sure," I said. "Have you ever used it?"

"I don't think I'm supposed to say," he said, shrugging his shoulders. "But yes, I have, I've used it. I won't even try to describe it to you, but believe you me, this thing works. See how far apart we are right now? That's how close I was to RayAnne. I'm telling you, I was right there with her again. We were at the fairgrounds together, and she wanted to go on one of the rides, so we did.

"This machine is going to make a billion dollars, I guarantee you, and you're looking at a man with a thirty percent stake. Never did I ever dream I'd die a billionaire! Never! I'm a successful man, but a billion dollars, that's just incredible, isn't it? I'm pushing for a new name. Reunion Machine, in my personal opinion, is a little lackluster. I keep a list of alternatives.

The Soul Liberator. The Death-Defier. Ghost-Maker. Astralizer. Anyway, I got others. Plenty of others.

"Listen, this machine is going to change the world. It's going to totally transform it. Not only will we get to talk to the dead, we'll know for sure that death isn't the end. And if we do that, what will there be left to fear? Mark my words, this is the beginning of a huge change in our evolution, and it started right here, in this Hobby Shoppe in Little Rock, Arkansas. Mark my words, they're going to build statues of Sally one day. Maybe me, too. Forget about the Bill Clinton Airport. You'll be flying into the Sally Zinker International Airport!"

The kitchenette door squeaked open, and Annie emerged alongside Sally, who seemed surprised to find me talking with Martin.

"I know, I know," he said, nodding his head up and down, "I only came out here in the first place because he was snooping around."

"I wasn't really snooping," I said quickly.

"I'm gone," Martin said, and ducked back into the room at the far end of the hall.

Annie plopped down into the chair in the hallway, as if exhausted, and arched her eyebrows at me as I joined Sally in the kitchenette. Sally closed the door behind us and invited me to sit down at the table.

"So you met Martin," she said. "He's an old

friend. He's been kind enough to let me use this building, and he's provided some of the capital so he comes around every so often. I'm sorry if he bothered you."

"Not at all," I said.

"Just so you know, I'm recording this conversation." She indicated the digital recorder on the table between us. "Like I said, this won't take long."

Consulting her clipboard, she asked me for my age (35), weight (185 lbs), marital status (married), religious affiliation (nondenominational Christian/confused), and number of children (one stepdaughter).

Did I believe in God? (I wanted to.)

Heaven? (No. Or at least not as a place with fluffy white clouds and halos.)

Angels? (Wouldn't that be nice.)

The resurrection of Jesus? (I was more comfortable with a metaphorical interpretation, i.e., the Jesus who lives in our hearts.)

Hell? (As the absence of God, maybe.)

The Devil? (No.)

Evil? (Yes. Evil was us.)

Prophets? (There'd been at least a few over the last fifty thousand years, sure.)

Survival of the soul after death? (I laughed uncomfortably. What was with all these questions?)

Witches? (No.)

Astrology? (In the sense that the planets determine who we are? Doubtful.)

Evolution? (Yes.)

Creationism? (The fossil record was real.)

Aliens? (Were they out there? Probably. Were they here at this very moment? Unlikely.)

Ghosts? (You tell me.)

Reincarnation? (Maybe.)

Did I believe that God controlled events on earth? (God's not a micromanager.)

That he observes what's happening here without getting involved? (Possibly.)

That the Bible is the absolute word of God? (The Bible was written by men about God, not the other way around.)

Did I believe in the existence of parallel universes? (Why not.)

Telekinesis? (Possibly.)

Telepathy? (Did you just ask me that out loud or . . . ?)

"All right," she said. "What about your dreams?"

"My dreams?" I asked.

"Yes, what do you dream about at night? Do you have realistic dreams or cartoonish dreams or—"

"A mix."

"Has anyone close to you ever died?"

"My father, earlier this year."

"Did he appear to you, in any form, in the days just before and after his death?"

"No, he didn't."

"Have you attempted to contact him since his death?"

"I went to a psychic."

"And did you make contact?"

Difficult to know, I said, and explained that my father and I had discussed the possibility of a message that might be transmitted after death but had never formally settled on anything. However, the psychic had provided me with Sally's number, so I was reluctant to call the session an outright failure.

Her face was stoic. "Okay, have you ever woken up to a bright light?"

"A bright light?" I repeated.

"A luminous sphere, for instance."

I imagined a miniature fiery sun floating over my bed, just a few inches above my body, its heat searing my chest red.

"No bright lights," I said. "No luminous spheres."

She asked me if I ever heard voices, inside or outside my head, and if so, if I ever felt compelled to answer these voices. The answer to each of these questions was no.

"What about your sex life?"

"What about it?"

"How is it?"

I wondered how Annie had answered this particular question. If I answered that it was great, and Annie had only said it was okay or decent—or, God forbid, lackluster—what would Sally make of the discrepancy?

"We have a healthy sex life," I said.

"Any unusual medical history I should be aware of?"

"Well, yes, my heart. It stopped a couple of years ago."

"I see," she said, looking up.

"I actually died for a few minutes. Technically. That's partly why I'm here. I don't remember any tunnels or lights or anything else. I was just gone."

She nodded. "I understand. Any pacemakers or—?"

"A HeartNet," I said.

She grimaced and put down her clipboard on the table. Looking me directly in the eyes, she said, "Mr. Byrd, I'm going to be honest with you now. I'm not sure you should use the machine. Not with a device like that in your chest. As I've already told you, there's a lot I still don't know about how this works, and I simply can't say that this would be safe for someone in your condition."

"So you're saying I came for nothing?"

"Not nothing. Your wife can still use the machine, if she wishes."

I wasn't sure what to say. I hadn't anticipated this. My disappointment must have been obvious because she reached across the table for my hand.

"I understand. I really do. You've come here looking for answers, and I'm telling you you won't get them, not personally. It must be a letdown. For the record, I'm not forbidding you from using the machine. I'm simply advising you that it could be dangerous for you to do so."

"It could kill me."

She shrugged. "The Reunion Machine, what it does, is remove you from existence for a tiny, tiny fraction of a second. In a certain sense, it *is* killing you, very, very briefly. I just can't make any guarantees that you would survive the process. It's your decision, of course. Ultimately."

I nodded that I understood. With that, our interview came to an abrupt end. I thanked her and said I'd give it some serious thought before tomorrow morning.

"She wasn't what I expected," Annie said. "She reminded me of those ladies with the water-packs around their waists who are always power walking through our neighborhood at night."

She had one hand on the center console and the other on her knee, and her mood, as far as I could tell, was pleasant. We were on our way back to the hotel. I hadn't told her what I'd learned about my heart device. If I decided to use the machine in spite of Sally's warning, I didn't want Annie to be worried.

We drove back to the hotel and parked the car in the garage. Then we walked downtown toward the river where a crafts fair was under way beneath a giant white tent. I sat down on a bench while Annie shopped. I wasn't sure what I was going to do. To use the machine that might prove life had no end was going to come at a tremendous risk to that same life, which quite possibly would end for having proved it.

I sat there, feeling sorry for myself, while Annie floated through the tents. She returned twenty minutes later with a butterfly broach and a giant clay pot with a silvery glaze that she'd had wrapped in newspaper so that it could make the trip home with us in a carry-on. As she showed me these items, for a brief moment it really did seem like we were simply on vacation together. After the fair we ate lunch at a small sandwich shop down the street.

"If the machine works," I said, "and you really talk to Anthony tomorrow, what will you tell him?"

She chewed and swallowed. "To be honest I don't know." She smiled. "Why, do you think I need some sort of prepared statement?"

"You're joking, but maybe it's not such a bad idea."

She smiled.

"Will you tell him about me?" I asked. "Because he might not take the news well. If I was him, I'm not sure I'd want to know you were married to someone else."

She considered this. "If he's really out there, if this is for real, my bet is he already knows about you. I don't think there will be any use in trying to keep secrets."

"What about his body?" I asked.

"Body?"

"I thought maybe you were hoping Anthony could help you locate his body. Since it never turned up."

She put down her sandwich in its basket. "I don't remember ever telling you about that. In fact, I'm certain that I didn't."

"Your brother," I said.

She dabbed her mouth with her napkin in such a way that indicated she was irritated and that our conversation was over. It was beginning to rain outside now, only we didn't have an umbrella. After I paid the bill, we waited under the awning in front of the restaurant for a few minutes before making a run for it. The hotel was five blocks away, and by the time we reached it, we were both soaking wet, and I could feel blisters forming on my ankles. I yanked off my shoes and socks and followed Annie through the lobby barefoot.

We took a long nap together on the bed upstairs. When I woke up Annie was on the phone near the door. She was in the middle of a new production at Thrill Arts!, and our visit to Little Rock had not come at an ideal time. As a way of raising money for her prison playwriting program, she was staging one of Crazy Ben's plays. All tickets sold would go back to the program. I listened to her politely argue with her set designer for a few minutes before rolling over to face her and let her see that I was awake. She didn't smile at me, and I wondered if she was still irritated about our conversation at lunch.

Once she was off the phone, we decided to walk to the Capitol Hotel restaurant and eat dinner there before we met the other participants in Sally's study. We strolled quietly, arm in arm, through a light misty rain, avoiding puddles. Music blared at a karaoke bar with neon tube lights in the front windows.

I apologized for asking about Anthony's body, explaining that my intention hadn't been to upset or surprise her. I'd simply been curious what she expected of her reunion with Anthony.

"I should have told you, I guess," she said. "It's just not something I like to think about, generally."

"That's more than understandable," I said, taking her hand.

When we reached the restaurant, we were

seated at a table near the front window. We talked about Fisher and her band, which was busy recording an album. Fisher had been pleading with us to help them invest in a new soundboard, and though we'd yet to make our official decision, we were of course going to do it.

After the meal, we paid our bill and walked through the lobby, admiring its vast ornate columns and vaulted ceiling, and wandered upstairs to the balcony, where people were standing near heat lamps with mixed drinks. At the railing, we could stare down at the lazy traffic on the street below. We'd been here for only a few moments, enjoying the view, inhaling all the cigarette smoke, when I saw Sally seated at a faraway patio couch with a woman in a long green dress and a white sweater. I waved over at them, and Sally motioned for us to join them.

"Jim and Annie Byrd," she said, as we approached, "this is Willa Flats."

Willa shot us a look that clearly communicated she wanted us to take our immediate leave, but Sally invited us to sit down in the chairs facing the couch. Without comment, Willa unscrewed the cap from a bottle of water and sipped quietly. She had light brown skin, short dark hair, and a large but attractive face. I guessed her to be roughly our age or perhaps a little younger.

Then Sally waved at someone else at the other end of the bar. A long-faced man came striding toward us. He had gray buzz-cut hair, and his wire-rimmed glasses lent him a vaguely European aspect. He introduced himself as Duke Jones and dragged a chair from another table to sit down by me. We shook hands and made small talk.

Duke, I learned, had once worked for Hewlett-Packard, but now he was employed by a company that made body cams for police. He traveled the country testifying at trials in which a body cam had behaved abnormally or failed. Essentially, he was a professional expert witness. "It's almost always user error," he said. "Nine times out of ten." The cams, apparently, beeped a warning if the footage wasn't being saved properly but half the time the cops would simply click through the warnings so that, when something bad happened, the camera wouldn't be operational. Duke's job was to explain to the jury that the failure was not the camera's fault but the officer's, though he had to explain this in such a way that he didn't piss off the police departments, who were, after all, his customers. This typically meant staying as unemotional as possible, he said, and sticking to vague statements like, "The data in question was never actually captured due to a user malfunction and therefore cannot be retrieved."

I got the sense that Duke was a no-nonsense individual, a person not easily rattled but also a tad robotic. He was twice divorced and lived in Nashville, where his company was based. He wanted to use the machine to talk to his son, who'd died just a few years earlier from cancer. Over the last few years he'd visited a handful of psychics—not highway palm readers or toll-free psychics but people who had demonstrable skills, like Claude—but none of them had been able to connect Duke with his son. Then a friend of his had suggested he call Sally.

I was about to tell him my story when Sally cleared her throat. Now that she had our attention, she crossed her legs and cupped both her hands over the highest knee.

"So," she said, "now that you're all here, a few things you should probably know. First, I can make no promises. If you talk to your dead grandmother or whatever, good for you, but I can't guarantee anything. One gentleman last week said he spent what felt like an entire year talking telepathically to a blob of colored lights. Another woman said she was back in her mother's old house, and it looked exactly the same, and they spent twenty or thirty minutes chatting over tea. So you can understand why I can't tell you how this will go exactly.

"Second, there can be some side effects. Afterward, I mean. Some people get a bad headache, but usually it passes after a few days. Nothing that a little ibuprofen won't help. However, almost everyone who uses the machine—and there've been about forty so far, mind you—gets pretty bad diarrhea immediately afterward. I'd suggest not eating anything morning-of. Third thing you should know—"

"I'm sorry," I said, "but how does it work exactly? What's the design? What does it do to you?"

Everyone looked at me. I'd interrupted.

Sally crossed her arms. "I'll answer your question, Mr. Byrd, but I want to make something very clear. I'm not here to explain myself to you or to explain the machine or to try and convince you of anything. You came to me, did you not? You sought *me* out. You traveled to me. You knocked on my door."

"I don't think my husband is asking you to prove it works," Annie said. "He's just curious."

"I understand," Sally said sharply, "but until I publish, you'll understand if I don't want to say too much about the hows and the whats. The machine is an extension of something I worked on years ago when I was still with the university, I can tell you that much. That's about as much as I'm willing to say about the technology itself. You've all read my book. You're familiar with the daisies. What the machine does, effectively, is grab control of the daisy's flicker state. I've figured out a way to flip the switch, not just for a single daisy but for an entire group of daisies—united into a single system, an object, a body, a brain, whatever."

Sally took a long sip of her drink and then explained that only once she'd begun to wonder about consciousness having an immaterial aspect did it occur to her to test the machine on a living creature: paramecia, earthworms, rats.

"You did this to a rat?" Duke asked with a smile. "You made a rat disappear?"

"It's not disappearance, it's nonexistence. I'm sure you can appreciate the distinction. I haven't been able to achieve total nonexistence, by the way. I can only get to something like twenty-three percent, but that seems to be enough."

"Enough to what?" I asked.

"To dislodge your consciousness from time and space, obviously. To subtract your brain, which wants you to trust only in what you can see and touch, from the overall equation of *you.* It's an out-of-body experience, essentially, because the body no longer exists to contain you. To limit you."

"And this is safe?" Duke asked.

"I'm fairly certain it is," Sally said, nodding. "I've done it a number of times myself, and all signs point to yes. I'm still here. But listen, you're volunteering for this. You don't have to do it. Of course there's a small risk involved.

And anyway, this little zap, it happens very, very fast. A fraction of a second. But it's in this state that consciousness is free to wander. This is bigger than talking with the dead, if you haven't already put that together. It doesn't connect you to any single person. It's a glimpse of the beyond. It bends you toward it. Yes, that's probably a better word, *bend.* What the machine does is bend you away from this life and toward the next."

Falling back into the couch, she took a long sip of her drink, seeming very pleased with herself. We sat quietly for a moment. I looked over at Annie, who was, with a very serious expression, stirring her drink with the tiny plastic straw. Duke scratched behind his ear with his index finger and then examined the tip of his finger. He didn't seem bothered by any of this. Willa was watching Sally very closely. When Sally leaned forward again, she returned to talk of logistics: when to arrive, what to bring, what to expect. Twenty minutes later, Willa was the first to say goodnight, and then Duke stood and stretched and said he looked forward to tomorrow before departing as well. Annie and I were preparing to go, too, when Sally patted my arm and asked if I'd come to a decision.

"Decision about what?" Annie asked me.

"Oh," Sally said, "I'm sorry. I didn't mean

to . . .” She grabbed her purse and stood to go. “I’m off now. I’ll see you both in the morning. Get some sleep. And remember, maybe avoid breakfast tomorrow.”

With that she disappeared through the doors that led back into the hotel. The heat lamps that towered over us sizzled, glowing red. Annie and I sat back down in our chairs. The ice in my second drink had melted, and so I took a sip of that before confessing to Annie that, because of my HeartNet device, using the machine was perhaps not medically advisable. I tried to minimize the risk as much as possible, but Annie’s concern was apparent in her expression: a glassy-eyed sternness.

“Please tell me you’re not actually considering doing it,” she said.

“I haven’t made up my mind yet,” I said.

“Don’t be so stupid,” she said. “Jim, honestly.”

“We’ve come all this way. It’s not that it’s necessarily unsafe for me, it’s just that she hasn’t tested the machine on someone like me yet. Probably it would be fine.”

“But you don’t know that for a fact.”

“Not for a fact, but I think it’s worth the risk, don’t you?”

“I’m not sure that it is.”

“You haven’t been through what I’ve been through,” I said, losing my temper. “You have no idea. I was dead, Annie. I died. And I was gone! Anyway, I don't even need the device. Not all the time. It's only there for emergencies. If it malfunctioned, my heart wouldn't just stop beating."

We'd both been drinking all evening, and my thoughts were a little soupy. I wasn't entirely sure if I had a point to make, but I continued talking until the waiter came over to deliver the bill. I opened it, happy for a reason to avoid eye contact with Annie for a moment. Everyone had left without paying their tabs, I realized—even Sally. I dropped my credit card in the tray and motioned for the waiter to return.

"Listen," Annie said, "I don't have to do this either, Jim. If you'd rather we just go home, we can. To be honest with you, all of this is beginning to feel a little scary. We have Fisher to think about. Maybe we shouldn't be subjecting ourselves unnecessarily to bizarre experiments. I mean, why isn't Sally still at a university, you know? If this is a scientific study, it's extremely unorthodox. Why are we out to drinks like this? Should we really be meeting the other participants? Maybe this, your heart thing, is a sign. It's the universe telling us to stop here. Maybe we should just go home.

"I haven't been through what you've been through, that's true, but you haven't been through what I've been through either. You've never lost the person you love most in the world. You have no idea what that can do to you, Jim, you don't."

Sally opened the door in a pair of jeans and a baggy gray cardigan over a white T-shirt, looking somewhat bedraggled. She led us back into the kitchenette and invited us to make ourselves comfortable while we waited. I was not going to use the machine. Before going to sleep the night before I'd promised Annie that I wouldn't take that risk. I wouldn't put her through that. She would use the machine herself and then we would get on a plane the following day and fly home. When I informed Sally of my decision, she nodded and said that she understood, though I could tell she was disappointed.

A toilet flushed and water rushed through pipes behind the wall. Across the hall from the kitchenette was a bathroom, and its flimsy white door creaked open slowly a few moments later. There was Willa, her eyes squinched, arms loose at her sides. She'd already used the machine. She dried her hands with a crumpled paper towel, a lost expression on her face.

Sally went down the hall and returned with something that looked like an old-fashioned telephone—a wand that was attached via a thin gray cord to a small black box that she carried in the palm of her other hand. She waved the wand across Willa's chest a few times. When I asked her what she was doing, she didn't say anything, only held the little black box up to her face in order to read the tiny numbers that flashed onto a small green screen.

"You'll be fine," she said to Willa. "You're already back up to eighty-nine percent."

"Eighty-nine percent what?" Annie asked.

"Like the universe," Sally said, "most people, on average, exist about ninety-three percent. There's a range. Anything between ninety and ninety-six percent is fairly normal. The machine drops you down to about twenty-three percent for a fraction of a second, but you normalize pretty quickly."

Willa looked at us as if she was going to be sick. Sitting down at the table, she rested her head on her arms.

"Was it worth it?" Annie asked her, daunted.

"It was worth it," Willa reported, and began to delicately massage her temples.

Annie came over to me and took my hands. We were quiet for a moment, just staring into each other's eyes.

"Be careful," I said, as if she had any control over her own safety.

"I'm doing this for both of us. I'll tell you everything that happens."

Would I be able to believe in the afterlife if Annie told me there was one? I wasn't sure. I hoped so.

"If I can talk to your dad, too, I will," she said.

She kissed me on the lips, smiled weakly, and followed Sally out of the kitchen. I peered around the corner to watch them go. At the end of that hallway wasn't just a machine; it was the great beyond, it was Anthony, and he was waiting for her.

"Good luck," I called as she rounded the door.

I sat down beside Willa and reached for a small paper cup at the center of the table. I began to tear the cup into tiny, waxy strips, leaving only its waxy moon bottom. A clock on the wall by the cabinets was dead—or not dead, I realized, but broken. The thin red second hand twitched, trying and failing to keep the time. Willa sat up and blinked her eyes heavily.

"It's like the worst hangover I've ever had," she said.

"What happened in there?" I asked.

She was quiet for a long time and then looked over at me with what seemed to me an expression of pity. "For a long time I was nowhere at all. I just, sort of, was. I was aware of myself, but I was having trouble thinking or focusing. I forgot about the machine. About all of this. Then, very slowly, I began to see things, little snapshots.

Scenes. From my life. I was reliving my life in little bits and pieces. I was a teenager again, going for a run with my sister, and then I was at my house, on the computer, trying to find Sally, and then I was in my sister's apartment." She looked down at her hands. "My sister was a photographer. For the AP. She was shot and killed three years ago in Islamabad."

"God, that's awful. I'm so sorry."

Willa, nodding, stared spacey-eyed at the shredded cup on the table. "It was like I was really there. In her apartment in Beirut. It was so strange. I was standing there, watching her take pictures out her window. This went on for the longest time. I just stood there like an idiot. Then she turned to me and asked if I was ready to go eat."

"Did she know she was dead?"

"I don't know," Willa said. "It wasn't like that. Dead or alive, that didn't really enter into it. We were just together again."

I heard a noise outside in the hallway. It was Annie. She'd already returned! Without acknowledging me at all, she let herself into the bathroom across the hall and slammed the door hard behind her. I was shocked to see her so soon. She couldn't have been gone for more than ten minutes. The lock on the bathroom door clicked before I reached it. Calling to her through it, I asked if she was okay, if I could get her anything, but she didn't answer. I knocked harder and called out again.

"Give her a few minutes," Sally said, behind me. "Be gentle."

"What happened? Did it work?"

Sally shrugged. "You'll have to ask her. Like I said, it's a little different for everyone."

I sat down on the floor outside the bathroom door to wait for Annie.

"Jim," Sally said, "go back in the kitchenette, please. You'll have a chance to talk with Annie, I promise. But I'm going to talk to her first, okay? I find it's best if you try and document the experience as quickly as possible. Before it fades. This might take a little time. But it's important we do this. It's a little bit like a dream. You wake up and as the day goes on, the dream begins to fade. You start to forget."

I stood up. "Are you sure she's okay? Have you waved your little wand thing across her yet?"

"I will. She's fine, Jim. Just go sit down."

Reluctantly I returned to my seat in the kitchenette, where Willa was massaging her temples again. A few minutes later the bathroom door lock clicked, and Annie emerged. Her skin seemed very pale; her eyes, red and swollen. I rushed back out into the hall and put my hand to her back, to let her know that I was here and that I loved her. She looked over at me with the strangest expression. I had the uneasy feeling that she hardly recognized me—or rather, that she was trying to place me.

Ah yes, I could almost see her thinking, *I believe I do know this man.*

"Are you okay?" I asked her.

She nodded. "I'm fine."

"We'll be back soon," Sally said, and led Annie away down the hall.

I sat back down at the table again. Willa smiled weakly at me.

"It'll be okay," she said. "Sally will just ask her to describe what happened, step by step. That's all. She'll even send you a copy of the transcript if you want."

We sat quietly for a long time. I was desperate to think about anything other than Annie's trip in the machine so I asked Willa where she was from.

"Hartford, originally," she said. "But Boston right now. For school."

"Grad school?" I asked.

She nodded. "Divinity school."

"No kidding."

"Why do you say that?"

"No reason, I guess," I said. "So are you planning on being a preacher?"

"Episcopal priest," she said, but seemed distracted now. She turned to face the doorway—in frustration? boredom? I couldn't read her.

Then Willa whipped her head back around, and she was staring at me again.

"You think I'm some kind of hypocrite for coming here," she said. "You think anyone who's training to be a priest shouldn't need to talk to her dead sister using some crazy ghost machine, she should be able to get by on her faith alone."

"I wasn't thinking any of that," I said, though in truth it was exactly what I'd been thinking, or at least considering.

"I mean, just because I want to know for a fact that my sister's out there, just because I want a little proof, does that somehow disqualify me from leading a church? If you say yes to that, you're crazy. Priests get to have their doubts, too. That's their right. Show me a priest who doesn't have any doubts, and I'll show you . . ." Her voice dropped away, and her eyes pattered down to the table. She reached for an empty cup and slapped it down into her lap. I realized now I was not really a true participant in this conversation, that I was a bystander to a debate that had been raging in Willa's head for who knows how long.

"If anything," she continued, "I'll be able to serve better. I mean, I'll really *know*. I'll be able to look people in the eyes, people who come to me with real grief and pain, and I'll be able to tell them with certainty there truly is life after death."

That seemed sensible to me.

Where was Annie? What was taking so long? I couldn't be in that kitchenette any longer. I needed some air. I needed to breathe. I went outside, into the parking lot. An eighteen-wheeler roared by, farting exhaust. Across the street, attached to a gas station, was a car wash, all the stalls currently empty but the concrete dark and wet. I walked along the road for about a quarter mile. The Hobby Shoppe was in an industrial part of town. Weeds were growing up through the cracked lots. To keep from getting hit by any cars, I had to straddle a drainage ditch, one foot on either side of a nasty run-off stream full of beer cans and used condoms and apple cores and shopping bags wrinkled and wet like chunks of pale skin.

Up ahead, an Applebee's beckoned. I went inside and sat down at the bar, ordered a Bud Light with a wedge of lime. Two other men sat at the bar, looking lonely and confused. They stared up at a muted cop procedural on the screen over the bar. The TV detectives were circling a dead body on a golf course in what looked like Miami.

"Do we know who killed him?" I asked one of the men, slipping deep into my Southern accent.

"Do what?" he asked, eyes still locked up on the screen. He seemed irritated to have to make words with his mouth.

The other man, a few seats away, laughed into his beer.

The body was shown on a gurney, sliced open by the medical examiner. Then we, the viewers, were plunged into a sea of blood cells, little red flat balloons bouncing and colliding.

I was grateful to have found this place. Sitting at this bar, with these men, drinking in the middle of the afternoon, it was possible, at least for a moment, to pretend there was no such thing as a Reunion Machine. But ten minutes later I had a text from Annie. She was finished debriefing Sally—and where was I? I settled my tab and walked back to the Hobby Shoppe. Duke had arrived in my absence. He was dressed as if he was about to set out on a long and difficult hike in the mountains, a brown thermal shirt under a fleece jacket. His glasses were strapped to his head with a purple foam band.

"Morning," he said, serious-faced.

"This way," Sally said, and led him back toward the machine.

Annie was in the bathroom again, but this time she admitted me when I tapped on the door. When I entered the room, she was standing at the sink, splashing water across her face. I waited as long as I could, about a minute, before asking if she'd seen him, if she'd contacted Anthony.

"Yes," she said.

"And?"

She turned to me and put her hands on my shoulders. “Jim, listen, if you don’t mind, I’d rather not talk about it right now. I’ll tell you everything, I promise. But I just need a little while to”—she searched for the right word—“figure out what just happened to me. Nothing is wrong, okay? Please don’t think anything is wrong. Sally says what I’m feeling, it’s not unusual. But I just need to sit with this awhile longer. I’m still sort of”—her hands dropped from my shoulders—“processing.”

I told her I understood, though of course I didn’t, not at all. I wanted to know exactly what had happened, and this seemed ominous to me, her wanting to wait. Her wanting to *process.* Never had that word seemed so portentous. Without consulting Sally first, we left the Hobby Shoppe together a few minutes later. I wrapped my arm around her waist as we walked to the car, and though she didn’t pull away from me, she didn’t exactly lean into my embrace either.

Back in the room, Annie said she was wiped out and needed a nap, and so I watched television while she dozed. Soon after waking up again, she called Fisher. School was out, and she was at C-Mac’s house for the afternoon. The call was a quick one. Annie jumped into the shower, and I watched a little television while I waited for her to emerge. Through the door crack I could see her toweling dry, her right foot up on the edge of the tub, steam curling behind her. I stepped into the bathroom and pulled her into a hug. She didn't resist me but neither did I feel any real encouragement or interest. Her towel fell to her feet, and I began to tug off my boxers, but then she kissed me in such a way that I knew meant she didn't want to continue.

"I'm still feeling a little wiped out," she said, touching her stomach. "After dinner maybe?"

"Of course," I said.

"I'm thinking room service, if that's all right."

She began to rub moisturizer into her face.

"So," I said. "Have you processed yet?"

She continued moisturizing, disappearing the white cream into her eyebrows.

"Let's talk about it at dinner," she said.

"I'd like to talk about it now, please." I stepped over to her.

"It's only been three hours, Jim."

"So you won't tell me anything at all then?"

She scooted by me out of the bathroom and sat down on the bed.

"I'm not trying to be evasive, I'm really not. I just don't know how to describe it. It was nothing at all like what I expected. I was all over. Bouncing around. But then, eventually, I found myself back in my old apartment, the one in

Charleston, just sort of lounging around and then in walks Anthony with a couple of his friends, and it was just like it used to be. I mean, I *was* who I used to be, Jim. I was twenty years old, and I was going to be some big movie star actor one day, and I'm so full of, like, hope and excitement, then I see him come through the door . . ." She was crying now. "I just don't know how to put words to it. It was so, so real. It was like time travel or something."

I considered this for a moment. "So you were twenty again? Fisher and me, we didn't exist to you anymore—or yet?"

"I think, vaguely, I was aware of you, yes. You were out there. Or in here." She indicated her heart. "I was overwhelmed, Jim. I don't know what else to say. It was incredible and it was heartbreaking and exhausting."

"What else happened? He just walked in with his friends and that was it or—?"

She shook her head back and forth and closed her eyes. "Jim, I feel like I've been gone for a week. That's what makes this so difficult."

"You spent a whole week with Anthony?"

"Well, I was only gone for a fraction of a second."

"But it felt like a week to you?"

"Maybe," she said. "Yes. Maybe even two weeks."

"So let me get this straight," I said. "Just so I'm

clear. While you were using the machine, you didn't really remember me or Fisher. You were twenty years old again. You were back with your dead husband. And you spent a couple of weeks with him, thinking things were just like they used to be."

She didn't say anything. I could tell I was upsetting her, but I was unable to control myself. While I'd sat in that miserable kitchenette, Annie had spent half a month with Anthony.

"Did you . . ." I couldn't even finish the sentence.

"I can't believe we're having this conversation. He's dead, Jim."

I dressed quickly and grabbed the empty ice bucket off the dresser.

"What are you doing?" she asked.

I wasn't even really sure. I muttered something about a drink and left the room with the bucket in my hand. When I reached the machine halfway down the hall, I stared down into the ice for a minute with the scoop in my hand. Then I tossed the bucket into the mountain of chunky ice and started walking toward the elevator bank, the carpet a blur beneath my feet. I went downstairs to the lobby, poured myself a cup of coffee, and sat down on the couch near the front desk. A flat-screen TV on the wall was showing the news. A group of reporters were discussing a mass shooting at a middle school. The volume was muted, and so I had to read the closed captions. A man with bunched eyebrows and a horsy mouth seemed to be yelling.

>>*This guy, this crazy guy, the shooter, I mean, what do we expect, he had hate in his heart, he was a total villain, he was the worst of us, and so of course it's okay for the government to step in here, don't you think, to work with the manufacturer of this heart device, to do whatever it takes to stop him, to bring him down, blow up his heart and save innocent lives.*

I asked a hotel clerk to please turn up the television, but she couldn't locate the remote. The captions were obviously lagging behind the conversation. A woman on the other side of the anchor desk was talking now and making wild gestures with her hands, and even after it cut away to a commercial break, in which a koala bear was hugging a roll of plush toilet paper, the captions continued to appear:

>>*Let's not make this a political issue, let's not do that, this is bigger than that, we have families who are hurt, we have children that have to be buried and we simply don't know enough yet to say much of anything about the shooter, but you have to admit that it's concerning, when a private company is cooperating with the government to this extent, when you're using a heart device to kill a man remotely. It's an assassination, no matter the target, that's what this is, and you*

have to wonder where this will stop, you have to consider the consequences.

Other hotel guests, passing through the lobby, weren't paying any attention to the television. An elderly gentleman sitting in a nearby chair seemed to be the only other person watching the program. I asked him if he understood what the reporters were saying. Had they mentioned a company called HeartNet? The man shrugged and said he hadn't been paying attention, sorry, he'd been lost in thought. I tossed my coffee in the trash and went out for a walk. The early evening air was a little wet and cold. I had no idea where I was going, only that I wanted to walk.

Where are you? Annie texted.

Are we okay? she asked.

Y, I wrote.

Are you sure?

Y.

Please tell me where you are right now, Jim.

I didn't respond to that one.

Eventually I wound up near the river—it was getting dark—and approaching the river's edge, I could hardly distinguish the water from the shore, except for where the city lights, yellow, orange, and blue, rippled across the surface. If not for the winter and the brown foamy effluvia chumping at the edges of the water, I might have removed my clothes, stepped down into the water, and waded out through the reeds, to squish the mud between my toes and feel the slap of the water against my chest.

Whenever I'm at the beach, I'm always the first one in the ocean. I drop my towel and the chairs and I yank my shirt over my head and I march out briskly, not stopping until I'm out far enough to dive at the first sizable wave. I collapse into this wave, surrender myself to the water, and stay under as long as I can before reemerging to swim a few laps, backstroke, so that I can stare up into the sky and feel the sun's warmth as an opposition to the cold beneath the surface. Here, horizontal, clapped tight between the hands of water and air, I don't feel safe or protected but real, a being in the truest sense of that word.

A hopeful thought occurred to me then, glistening: perhaps Annie had not actually visited with her dead husband but had instead only relived a week that resided in her memory. The machine had simply activated the relevant memories, made them feel fresh again, present, had given them dimensionality. If this was the case, then she hadn't really reconnected with Anthony but with another aspect of herself. This seemed like an important distinction to me. Who didn't live in their own memories from time to time? Possibly the machine had only triggered a very real-seeming hallucination.

What do you bet that right now, somewhere in

the United States, a graduate student with halitosis is devising an experiment in which he will use powerful magnetic fields to create currents of neurons in a human brain that might cause visual hallucinations—bands and balls of light, spectral presences. Somewhere else a neurobiologist is writing a paper that dismisses your dead grandfather's ghost as a communication breakdown between your visual cortex and something called the lateral geniculate nucleus, through which all information passes on its way from the eye. At this very moment, be assured, a schizophrenic man, strapped inside an imaging machine, is being instructed to converse with the voices in his head while his brain is being mapped. On the other side of the country, a woman who claims she is able to leave her body behind is sitting on a cold metal table in a paper gown while two men outside in the hall are quietly discussing her unusually active cerebellum.

All this to say, Annie's reunion with Anthony might not have been real at all. It might have simply been a biological reaction to a powerful wave of radiation—or *whatever.*

Turning away from the river, I climbed up a set of concrete stairs.

Another text buzzed: *Please don't use the machine. YOUR HEART!!!!!!*

I didn't respond to that one either.

Jim? she wrote. *Let's just go home in the morning and go back to normal, please.*

I was almost at the top of the stairs when a dinosaur twice my height came hurtling down the hillside, moving right for me. The creature whipped through the darkness, the white and tan feathers in its head shimmering iridescently. It had a long, muscled neck and its snout was very narrow and sharp. A few feet away from me it stopped to huff loudly through its snout. Two others just like it appeared on top of the hill, bodies hunched forward as if in pursuit of prey.

I hadn't moved an inch. My heart was beating very fast. I was terrified. But then the dinosaurs fell into a chorus line, and the biggest one announced, with a slight Southern twang, the opening of the dinosaur exhibit at the Clinton Presidential Center. For a limited time only, the dinosaur said, kids under five were free. The dinosaurs glowed as if they'd swallowed a light. Before the holograms dispersed and dissolved into the night, they smiled at me.

Not long after that I walked back to the hotel and got in my car.

So where's wifey?" Sally asked.

"I've changed my mind," I said. "I want to use the machine."

“It’s a little late. Are you sure about this?”

“I’m aware of the risks,” I said.

She invited me inside, and I followed her down the hallway, toward the room into which I had yet to be admitted. Chamber number one, she called it, opening the door to a large square room with concrete walls, at the center of which was a massive concrete cylinder. A chamber within a chamber, in other words.

“So who is it you want to contact?” Sally asked. “Your dearly departed dad?”

I nodded. Yes, him. Who else?

“Let me give you some advice. Do you meditate, Jim?”

“I have before, but no, not regularly.”

“It can be a little disorienting, this process, and I think it often helps to hold on to a single image or a mantra. It’s easy to lose yourself in there.”

To the right of the first door was machinery that I never had the chance to properly investigate, then or later: large foam-padded tubes, glossy red panels, computer circuitry, ringed plates, something that looked like a water heater tank. To enter the cylinder, you had to turn left and walk along a narrow passageway lit by naked bulbs in the ceiling. All the walls were made of concrete, and so was the floor, though Sally had laid out small mismatched Oriental rugs, one after the other, a network of oversized swatches that led you to a small ladder that had clearly been taken from an old pool.

She climbed up first and then waited for me at the top. When I reached her, I saw that she was sitting beside an open hatch door that led down into the cylinder.

"I have to go in there?"

"You don't have to do anything," she said.

I peered down into the hole.

"You worried about your heart?" she asked.

"I'm more worried I do this and see nothing at all." Wanting to seem brave, I attempted a smile. "Besides, these HeartNet devices, apparently they're faulty. According to the news, my heart could explode any second anyway."

Sally nodded. "Well, they all do, eventually. Scale back enough, time-wise, and all we are is a quick parade of exploding hearts."

She slid down through the hatch using a small ladder bolted to an inner wall and then stood at the bottom gazing up at me. It was about seven feet deep. I climbed down next. The metal ladder was warm and vibrated gently in my hands. When my feet touched the ground, I turned around and there was Sally, her face hardly visible at all in the darkness. This innermost chamber had no light source of its own. Its diameter was maybe six feet.

I felt as if I'd climbed down into a cave. That's when I noticed the metal strips embedded in the walls, little silvery flaps. She instructed me to stand where she was standing, directly in the middle, and then she climbed back up the ladder. Once she was at the top, she peered down at me again and asked me to toss up my clothes.

"All of them?"

"That's right."

"But . . ."

"This is how it works. Come on."

I did as I was asked, folding everything into a little bundle. I balled up my socks, tucked them in my shoes, and stacked my shoes on top of my clothes. Sally reached down, and I delivered them up into her hands.

"Your watch, too," she said.

I gave her my watch. She wished me luck and shut the hatch, creating a total darkness. I was naked—but not cold. I stuck out my arms and walked forward until my fingertips found the wall. I patted along the rough concrete until I found those little metal strips.

I've never really considered myself claustrophobic, but I admit that I began to panic at the thought of being abandoned down here. It was rather tomb-like, after all. An oversized sarcophagus. I stood very still for a few moments, waiting for something to happen. Then I heard a noise, a motorized gurgling, almost like a sump pump sucking away water. Not just one sump pump but three or four working in concert, the noise growing like an approaching train.

I touched the walls again. The little metal flaps had opened and shuttered toward me, and I burned my fingers on the metal. I backed away, toward the cylinder's center, and waited there with my eyes closed. The noise outside the chamber was growing louder and louder, and now seemed to pulsate. I could feel it traveling as a series of waves, with peaks and valleys, rippling through my body, through my flesh, through my bones. The sensation was nearly pleasant, except then I was reminded of X-ray machines, all those little vibrations, and I began to worry about radiation, about poisoning. It occurred to me I might be sitting in a tremendous microwave oven. What did I really know about the machine, after all? I didn't want to wind up with cancer.

When I opened my mouth, to ask if I was going to be all right, I felt the vibrations in my teeth, felt them travel the short length of my tongue and echo out into the room. I clamped my mouth shut. Then, suddenly, the noise began to shift again, the pulses lunging with the force of ocean waves. I was having trouble breathing, and my fingertips went numb. My toes, too. Head swimming, vision bubbling, my legs fell out from under me, and I collapsed against the concrete. I was dying. Actually dying. This wasn't another panic attack. The machine, somehow, it was disrupting my HeartNet. I was going to die in this stupid hole, in the dark, and what was worse, I'd put myself here. I'd volunteered for this.

I was having trouble focusing. All my thoughts and ideas, they were tiny bits of eggshell lost in the egg white, slippery, impossible to pin down beneath my fingertips. They were confetti before a monstrous floor-to-ceiling fan. I couldn't hold on to a single word or image for more than half a second before it was whipped away, danced away into some outer cavity of darkness, a nothingness that seemed to surround and invade me. The darkness was crowding me out.

I began to panic. My life as Jim Byrd felt remote—even unlikely. It was something that had happened once, thousands of years ago, something I could hardly remember anymore, something that possibly had been a story I'd told myself. I'd made up Jim Byrd. How ludicrous that I'd ever been such a thing as him.

THE TALE OF SUBJECT 44

44: . . . There was no noise at all. Everything was impossibly quiet. A total absence of sound—and light. The darkest dark, all around me. I wasn't me anymore. I was just a little dot. I had no attributes. No personality. I was barely there at all. I felt like a little sea creature tucked way up in the pointy end of the shell. Like I was hiding. This went on for a very long time. Centuries maybe. Aeons.

SZ: But eventually—

44: I began to realize that the darkness wasn't really a nothingness. It was a substance. There was a ripple to it. Like a blanket or a curtain. I was moving through it now. In relation to what, I can't say. But there was definitely movement. More than that, I had a destination. Before now, it hadn't really occurred to me that I was alone, but this hit me all at once, how isolated and alone I'd been until this point. It hurt to be this alone. I felt like maybe I was the only thing that had ever existed. I can't tell you how frightening that was. Slowly I began to remember that, once upon a time, I'd been a man named Jim Byrd. I'd had a life. I'd loved people. I was desperate to find these people. To find anyone—but especially them.

Far off, I began to see shapes.

SZ: Describe them.

44: Blurry bands of light. Thin, chalky. Light beams, I guess. A whole forest of them. The ones at the center of the forest were the strongest. They seemed to have gravity. They were pulling me toward them. I didn't really try to resist. I was one of those beams, too, I realized. Is this normal?

SZ: Bands of light. Discs. Halos. Fiery planets. Flashbulbs. Starry nights. Yes, keep going.

44: There was a . . . crack. A giant crack right down my middle. Reality split in two. Suddenly I was in two places at once. A double-perception or a double-awareness—I'm not sure if there's a technical term for it. I was a beam of light, traveling, but I was also me, Jim Byrd. I had a body again. Hands and feet. I had shape, mass.

I was young, about twenty-three, and I was in my office at the bank. The phone rang, and it was this guy I know, from school, and he was asking me for money, for a loan. Not from the bank but from me, personally. He'd lost a bunch of money on a basketball game, and now he was in trouble, and he needed some quick cash.

SZ: Just so I'm clear, this is an event that actually transpired in your life—or no?

44: Yes. This really happened to me once. But I wasn't just remembering it. I was actually back in my office again. It was incredibly real. I could feel the phone in my hand. The side of my face closest to the window was warm. I told my friend that I didn't have enough money to give him, which was sort of true but not quite, and once we were off the phone, I immediately started to worry about him. What if I'd totally screwed this guy's life, you know? I had the ability to help and I'd turned him down.

Then, just like that, I wasn't in my office anymore. I was in school again. Middle school. In the bathroom. I'd just thrown up my lunch, and I was trying to figure out what to do with my shirt because I had vomit all down the front. I took it off and scrubbed it in the sink but now it was wet. So I used a bunch of paper towels to try and clean it. The bell rang. I was going to be late for class. I put the shirt back on and started running. I was so worried about what the other kids would think. It was this worry, or fear, I think, that had brought me here, that had delivered me to this moment from the last. I'd been worried about my friend, the guy who needed the loan, but now I was worried about my shirt and being late. I'd caught a wave and washed up here, back in school.

My father was standing at the entrance to his classroom when I got there, holding the door open for me. He was my math teacher. He told me to get a move on and hurry it up. I hadn't been to my locker yet so I didn't have my books or my homework. When I tried to explain that to him, he shrugged and said he couldn't help me. Sorry, bub.

He was going to treat me just like every other kid, and I hated him for it. I was so mad and hurt. I felt like he was trying to prove a point to the other kids. But then, as I passed, he noticed my shirt. How wet it was. And gross. Probably he smelled it on me. He told me to go to the nurse and wait there.

But when I turned, to leave the class for the nurse, I found myself in the driveway at my parents' house, and I was shoveling snow. The shovel was in my hands. My hands were numb. I was sweating under my jacket and pants. I was a little older now, a teenager. A hard, icy snowball hit me right in the side of the head, near my ear. It really hurt. Really stung. I turned and saw it was my father who'd thrown it. He came over to me, already apologizing but with this smirk on his face that made it pretty obvious he didn't actually feel bad. He thought it was funny.

Mind you, I was still a light beam, too. I was both things at once. I was in the driveway but I was also in that forest of light beams. I was circling around one of the other light beams, and vaguely I sensed that this was my father, that we were, on some level, sharing this memory. We were engaged in some type of dialogue. We were communicating, but the language was the moment itself.

SZ: Were you aware that he was dead?

44: Not then, no. I wasn't thinking in those terms. This was just something that was happening to both of us. It didn't occur to me that I was making any sort of unusual contact with him. I wasn't thinking about the machine.

SZ: This is also very typical, just so you know. I'm sorry I interrupted. Go on.

44: Well, for a long time, I was just cycling through all these moments, one after the next. I don't know how much detail you want? I was five years old, in my mother's bed, and she was tracing shapes on my back with her finger, but when I rolled over, she was much older, in the recliner at her house, and she wanted me to fix her TV. She wanted me to find the movie channels, but I couldn't seem to work the remote right. The screen went to static, and staring at the static, I thought about the ocean, and just like that, I was at the beach with some friends on a spring break trip. We were tossing the football. I stayed here for a little while. We walked over the dunes to the house we were renting, and I showered, and then we went over to another house, where some girls were throwing a party. One of the girls came over to me, and we started dancing. I spilled some beer on her feet, which she thought was funny, and we wound up in her room.

Everything was so real. So precise. There were these panties and socks spilling out of a red suitcase on the floor, and I couldn't get the button loose on her jeans. One of her press-on nails was loose in the bed, like a piece of plastic in the bedsheets. We got naked. This was my first time having sex. But when I pressed myself against this girl, we were touching but there also seemed to be a huge gap between us. We were both sort of husked out, empty. Life on paper. It was like watching yourself make love in a mirror. You know it's you, but watching yourself, you're not entirely there.

[NOTE: Subject 44 appears visibly uncomfortable.]

SZ: Are you okay? Do you need to use the bathroom again?

44: God, you weren't lying about the stomach thing. No, I'm fine. Let's just get through this.

SZ: You'll be grateful you did this, [SUBJECT

44], trust me. It's useful to get it all out while it's fresh. The experience fades, eventually. Recedes. Your brain prefers there only be one reality, and it will work hard to convince you that your trip in the machine wasn't real.

44: So [SUBJECT 42]'s was like this, too?

SZ: I can't discuss that with you. You'll have to ask her.

44: She said she spent half a month with her first husband.

SZ: As I told you, the experience is slightly different for everyone, though there are clear patterns and trends. There's a logic to it. So, you were cycling through your life . . .

44: Yes. On and on and on. One second I was with Fisher, talking about orangutans, and the next I'm in bed next to [SUBJECT 42] as she's reading through her plays. I'm at church with my mother, and she's crying, in front of everyone, and I'm scooting away from her in the pew, totally embarrassed. Then I'm whipped away, to a car, and I'm with [SUBJECT 42], and we're sixteen again, and she's trying to convince me to go on her church's ski trip. This continued for a long time. I'm tempted to say as long as my life itself. Some scenes I relived two and three times.

How long did you say I was gone—while I was in the machine?

SZ: A fraction of a fraction of a second.

44: Are you sure?

SZ: Time has no bearing in the immaterial world. It doesn't matter how long you were gone from here. It's completely irrelevant. Some people feel like they're gone for a few minutes. Others, an eternity.

44: Well, the more I cycled through all these scenes, the more aware I became that it was happening, that this was a process of some kind. Eventually I was even able to exert a little more control over it. I wound up back on my honeymoon with [SUBJECT 42], and I managed to hold on there for almost two whole days. But the problem was, now that I was more aware, everything felt less alive, less meaningful. Flat, two-dimensional. It was a reflection of my life, not the thing itself. An echo.

SZ: It's often this building awareness that ends the journey, that brings you back into your body. It's sort of like lucid dreaming in that way. Once you realize you're dreaming, it can be harder to remain there. You're pulled back here. I'm not saying that you were dreaming while in the machine, mind you, though I do think there are some interesting similarities between the dream-state and the afterlife. You might be interested to know that, on average, people exist about one-point-two percent less while asleep. I have confirmed this. We travel in dreams. We prepare ourselves for death.

44: Well, I wasn't pulled back into my body. That's not what happened to me—or not exactly. I wasn't whipped back here.

At some point, I found myself back on the stairs at the restaurant in Shula, the one we talked about on the phone where—

SZ: The dog on fire, yes.

44: Right, and I was there with my father. We had our backs pressed flat to the wall and we were standing side by side. Distantly I knew that I'd been here before, that I'd done this. I'd stood here with my father, maybe a thousand times. And not only that, but I began to understand—or remember maybe—that my father had died, that he was dead, that I was here because I was trying to find him.

Anyway, everything was exactly like it had been. Every detail. Except . . .

SZ: What?

44: All around us there was movement. Shapes. Flutters. Other people! We weren't alone. I caught little glimpses of them as they passed me on the stairs, going up and down. Faces, fleeting. Streaming bodies. Like smoke sucked through a fan. Blurs of fleshy light. A man with slick black hair came hurrying by me, an angry look on his face. I saw a woman with a dog in her arms. Clara Lennox. It was Clara Lennox! I couldn't believe it. I stepped down, toward her, and when I did, I sort of—popped loose.

SZ: Popped loose?

44: That's the only way I can think to describe it. I knew something had changed. When I looked back up the stairs, at my father, he was there and so was I.

SZ: You'd stepped outside yourself. You were no longer viewing this from your own perspective, from your own eyes.

44: Right. Exactly.

SZ: Did you snap back into your body or—?

44: No, I tried to talk to him—to my father. Before, when I'd been in my body, I'd only been able to experience these moments as they'd actually happened. It was like we'd been in two different cars on the highway, moving fast, windows up, and neither one of us was actually driving. The route had been predetermined. We'd been stuck in our own lanes. Locked into a script. But I was free now. I could actually say what I wanted to say, do what I wanted to do. So

I called out to him. I asked him if he knew he was dead.

SZ: Did it seem like he could hear you?

44: Maybe. I couldn't tell. He wouldn't look at me. Has this ever happened to anyone else?

SZ: Not exactly like this, no. What did you do next?

44: I just—I raised my hand, reached out, and touched him.

SZ: You touched him.

44: On the arm, yes. Just like this. [*Note: SUBJECT 44 grabs SZ's forearm and squeezes hard.*] It wasn't easy to do. There was a resistance to it. It was like a paper doll reaching off the page. And the weird thing is, I knew I wasn't supposed to even attempt this. I could feel that I was violating some kind of rule. I wasn't supposed to touch him.

SZ: What happened when you did this? Tell me exactly.

44: There was another pop.

SZ: A pop. Describe it.

44: Yeah, like a string. And he was gone. He disappeared. So did everything else. The forest of light beams was gone, too. The restaurant was gone. All that was left was the stairs. The stairs—and me. I was alone again. I felt as if I'd just been ejected from my life.

The stairs were the same but also different. They kept going in either direction, up and down. I wasn't sure what to do. I'd done something wrong, and now there was only this. Stairs, forever.

I'm waiting for you to tell me this is typical.

SZ: Keep going. What did you do next?

44: Well, it was up or down, wasn't it? And I chose up. Because who chooses down, right? I climbed and climbed. Up and up and up. I must have climbed for years. I kept going and going. The stairs in the restaurant, they're winding stairs, if you remember, and without any walls or floors, any points of reference. I couldn't tell where I was on them. They just kept going up forever. I wasn't getting anywhere. That's when I really started to panic. I could remember your machine now, by the way. I knew that's how I'd wound up here. I started calling out for you. I was desperate for help. This might sound dumb, but I thought if you could just hear me, maybe you'd pull the plug on the machine and bring me back. I worried the machine had really killed me, that this was hell and I was doomed to spend the rest of eternity on those stairs. It was terrifying.

SZ: That's incredible. If you don't mind . . . I'd like to . . .

44: What's it say?

SZ: You're still in the sixties. But that's no reason to worry, I assure you.

44: I'm not about to, like, disappear, am I?

SZ: Definitely not. You're here. You're here.

44: I can't believe you have a device that measures how much a person exists.

SZ: Only how much you exist as a physical being. We're only talking about matter. You'll be fine.

44: Do you think—My father always thought it was Clara Lennox who touched him on the stairs, but do you think it's possible that it was me?

SZ: I don't know if I can say one way or the other.

44: If it was me, that would be—what? Time travel? I traveled back in time, as a ghost, grabbed my father, and pulled him into a daisy hole? Or maybe it was me who made the daisy hole to begin with by reaching out for him?

SZ: An interesting theory.

44: Well, I had plenty of time for theories. Sitting and theorizing, that's about all I did. I *was* a theory. A theory busy theorizing about itself. Climbing seemed pointless so I sat. I was tired. Not physically but spiritually. Just drained. You have to understand, I really did feel like I'd been trapped on the stairs for all eternity. Separated from all the people I love. I was being punished. That's how it seemed to me. I'd been so desperate to find proof, and now that I had it, the universe was telling me I wasn't supposed to have been looking for it. That I'd been wrong to want it. Do you ever think we're not supposed to have it? That to a certain extent we're supposed to live in the dark?

SZ: I don't think it's wrong to want answers.

44: Yes, I'm sure you're right. But now that I had an answer—not *the* answer, mind you, but *an* answer—I didn't feel any better for it.

SZ: Tell me, [SUBJECT 44], did you ever escape the stairs or—?

44: No, I didn't, because here's the thing, here's what I eventually came to understand. I didn't *need* to escape. Because there was nowhere else to escape *to*. Because everything—you, me, the world, the afterlife—it's all the same. It's all stairs. Not stairs, but *stairs*. What I mean to say is, everything is everything else. The whole is contained in every single fragment, in every piece. Divide the universe in half and it's still the universe. Divide it a trillion times, and it's still the universe.

I hadn't been removed from existence. Possibly I'd only changed scale. I was a daisy particle! Thinking this made it so. I strobed, sparkled.

Slowly I began to see people again. Those streaming light-shapes. Robert Lennox. Clara. A little dog barking at my feet. My father, too. And [SUBJECT 42]. I saw the lady who used to own the restaurant. People I didn't know, too. I didn't recognize most of them. I saw a woman on her knees with a scrub brush. A fat man with a jowly face staring up at me with sad eyes. I saw you, [SZ]. You were running wires between the spindles with sticky tape. A hundred other people, too. All of you were popping in and out of view, very rapidly, overlapping. You were there together, only you didn't even know it. It was overwhelming.

You know how when you slow down a film enough on the reel you can see the little lines between the frames? Somehow I'd slid between the frames. I was out of sync, and being out of sync, I could see all the other frames, and they were all stacked on top of each other. Somehow, understanding this allowed me to pop back into my life. Into the stream of my life.

SZ: So you were off the stairs?

44: I was and I wasn't. I no longer see the stairs, at this point, let's put it that way. What I see now is a beach. I look up and I'm sitting on a beautiful beach. In a chair. My feet are down in the warm sand. Beer in my hand. The flies are out. The little black ones. I'm swatting at them. I'm a White Hair.

SZ: A what-hair?

44: Older, retired. Nearly bald. Sore-kneed. I'm maybe late sixties. There's a man in a red bathing suit walking toward me with a toddler in his arms. My son. I have a son, and he's calling to me, I can see his mouth moving, but I can't hear him over the noise of the ocean. I look to my left . . .

SZ: What's wrong?

44: It's not [SUBJECT 42]. That's who I expect to find, when I turn, but instead it's someone else, some other woman. [SUBJECT 42]'s gone. She's dead. I remember this. I've outlived her. I can feel her absence tentacling through me. A bubbling emptiness. But the death isn't recent. Enough time has passed that I've settled into this new life. This life without her. What I mean is, it's not an unbearable sadness I feel. I'm not mourning her anymore so much as getting by. The boy—

the man in the red bathing suit—he's ours, [SUBJECT 42]'s and mine, but [SUBJECT 42] has died, and now I'm with this other woman. She's older, too, blond-haired, a dye job, I think, nice-looking. She looks up from her magazine and asks if I've put any lotion on my face. I love this woman! It's different than my love for [SUBJECT 42], but it's real, I can feel it. We're good to each other, me and this woman. We take care of each other. She's good to my son, to Fisher. Fisher, my stepdaughter, she's not here on the beach, but she's still in my life. She's out there somewhere, I know that.

Do you think it's possible that any of this is true, that it's my future and that I somehow saw it? Has anyone else ever seen their future?

SZ: Honestly? No. You're the first.

44: So maybe it wasn't real then.

SZ: You're the first to report something like this, but then again you're also the first to use the machine with a condition such as yours. No other near-death survivors, as far as I'm aware. Maybe you were prepared for this experience, on some level, and didn't even realize it. Maybe you were able to go deeper because of it.

44: The moment on the beach, it was very brief, no more than a couple of seconds, and it was a little fuzzier than everything else I'd seen, a little foggier, very impressionistic. It's also the last thing I remember before waking up in the hole, naked, on the floor, puking my guts out.

SZ: A normal reaction. Nausea. Itchy skin. Swollen ankles. Headaches. Diarrhea. Flu-like symptoms. All very typical. How's your heart?

44: Well, it feels all right. Beating obviously. But my phone still says there's been a connection error. What's your little wand exist-o-meter thingy say—?

SZ: You're up to sixty-four percent now. Your body seems to be taking slightly longer than is typical to recuperate. Again I'm wondering if it has something to do with your particular medical history.

44: Should I be alarmed?

SZ: Not at all. This isn't always very accurate. There's a margin of error. You could very well be in the low seventies. Don't worry. A solid meal and a roll in the hay and you'll be back in the normal range lickety-split.

44: Sex and food help you exist more?

SZ: If you're asking me if I have empirical data to back that up, the answer is no, I don't. But it would make sense, wouldn't it? You'll eventually stabilize.

44: God, if I really saw the future. [SUBJECT 42] . . . Should I tell her what I saw?

SZ: That's your decision, [SUBJECT 44]. That's entirely up to you.

44: But isn't it possible that you don't really understand yet what your machine does? Maybe it just messed with my brain and gave me a really intense hallucination.

SZ: Given the relative consistency of people's experiences, I rather doubt it. Besides, even if I was studying your brain with an MRI machine while you were in the chamber, even if I had these neat little brain scans that showed activation in your—I don't know—your orbital gyri or whatever, even if I had all that, what difference would it make? Would that prove you'd never left your brain behind or would it only mean your brain was, on some level, still connected to your roving consciousness, still registering it the way a seismograph does little far-off vibrations?

Listen, I'll never be able to prove beyond a shadow of a doubt that the machine is doing what I say it can do. I recognize that. But in my heart, I know what it does. I know what it's capable of doing. Maybe you didn't like what you saw, but I suspect deep down you feel the same way. You know where you've been.

44: I don't want to tell her.
SZ: Then don't. Keep it to yourself. She doesn't ever need to know.

I was supremely aware of my body as I left Sally Zinker's. The flex of each follicle in the cool morning breeze, the weight of each step, the rhythm of my breath, the uneven nail on my left thumb, every stomach gurgle. Back at the hotel, riding in the elevator, I examined myself in its three mirrors, turning this way and that. I tugged at my skin and watched it shrug back into its appropriate tautness around my muscles and bones. Where was I in this mess of cells?

Apparently I only sixty-four percent existed—I was a haze, a cloud, halfway to a hologram—but as far as I could tell I was entirely solid. My toes explored the cavities of my shoes, prodding, scrunching. Pushing against the outer world, feeling its shape, its firmness—my shoes, the floor, the mirrors—confirmed that I was here, in this elevator, in this hotel, on this planet, in this life.

My phone rang as the door whooshed open. It was Annie. She'd just woken up. It was almost dawn.

"You used the machine," she said forlornly.

"Hold on," I said. "I'm almost there."

At the door, I fumbled with the key. On the drive here I'd debated what to tell her about what I'd seen, especially my vision of a future in which she was no longer a part of my life. I wondered if any good would come from such an admission. I didn't want to unnecessarily alarm her. What if, by telling her, I'd set a series of events in motion that somehow precipitated her death? I was thinking of Greek tragedies, of kings who tried, vainly, stupidly, to avoid a fate foretold and ended up killing their own fathers and sleeping with their mothers. If ancient literature had taught me anything, it was that to struggle against a predicted future would only guarantee its inevitability.

The door opened, and there she was, in a T-shirt and underwear. I wasn't Oedipus but Odysseus. Seeing her it wasn't fear I felt but an intense longing. I threw my arms around her and kissed her neck and her arms and her mouth. I hadn't planned on doing this. Perhaps sensing my desperation, she pulled me into the room. "Come in at least," she said. We tottered forward, let the door swing shut. She swiveled around and I grabbed her from behind, helping her with her shirt, letting it hit the floor. She leaned back into me, rolling her head to the side, and slowly we waddled over to the bed. I worked loose my shirt. I lay down on top of her, leaving no space at all between our skin.

Distantly I was aware that this moment would end, too soon, that this ache would run away from us, and we would roll over to our separate sides of the bed, to our separate quarters, we would retreat to our separate worlds. But for now, right now, our worlds were, if not the same, at least overlapping. Beneath the blur of her skin, the tiny hairs on her neck, the jut of her shoulder blades, a thought flitted through my brain: an image of our bodies, their boundaries blurred, a confusion of atoms, electrons trading nuclei, our skins merging. Was this why the soul wrapped itself in flesh?

I finished with my face pressed to her chest, her skin glossy where my mouth had been. The world stippled back into view, and we climbed up the bed and under the sheets. I was curled up to her back, my arm around her waist.

"I can't believe you used the machine," she said after a long silence. "I should hate you right now."

"Well, I'm fine," I said, leaving out the fact that my HeartNet had suffered a connection error and was quite possibly offline. "I survived."

She squeezed my hand. "Are you still mad at me? About Anthony?"

"No, not mad."

"Do you want me to tell you what happened? Because I will."

"Please don't."

We were quiet again for a few moments.

"Did you find your father?" she asked.

I nodded. "I think I did, yes."

"It was so real, wasn't it?"

"Real—but, also, somehow, fixed? Pre-determined?"

"I know what you mean. Sort of like reading a book you've already read before. You know where the story's going next, you know how it has to go. The characters can only ever say what they're supposed to say. Still, to be back there again . . ."

"I think I'm still in a state of shock. We followed the script, mostly, but behind each moment, I really did feel like he was there with me, like we were experiencing this together. Like we were talking to each other but the words were the moments themselves."

"Yes, exactly, that's it."

"Would you do it again?" I asked.

"I don't need to."

I couldn't decide if she was being evasive. I kissed her shoulder and rolled away. Our flight left in two hours. I took a long, hot shower while Annie packed our bags. We returned our rental car and then rode a shuttle to the airport, where we ate breakfast in the food court. Stirring her parfait, Annie seemed distracted and vaguely upset. I asked her what was wrong.

"Let's just assume, for a moment, that the

machine worked, that we really reached the afterlife," she said.

"I thought we were already assuming that, but okay."

"When you were there—think back for a second—did you feel like you had the answers to your questions? I mean, did you feel any more certainty about what it means to be alive than you did before?"

Over the loudspeaker, a flight attendant announced a gate change.

"Not really," I admitted. "I was just as confused there as here."

She took a few bites of her parfait and balled up her napkin, dropping it on the tray. I wasn't very hungry either.

"The whole time I was gone," she said, "whether I was with you or Anthony or anyone, I had this feeling that it wasn't over, that I'd only reached another level—I can't think of a better word for it than that, *level*—and there was still more to come. What I mean is, I think there was farther to go. I'd only scratched the surface of it. At the very end, I was on the cusp of it, like if I just reached a little more, I'd get there, to the next place, whatever it was. I was hardly there at all and already I was wondering what came next, you know?" She thought for a moment. "What's that all about?"

We gathered our bags off the floor and started

walking toward our gate. Once we'd boarded the plane, she stuffed her magazine in the seat pocket, and I untied my shoes. Ten minutes later we were in the air, thousands of feet over the earth, shuddering toward home.

"The afterlife had its own afterlife," she said. "That was the feeling I had. One afterlife after the next."

I wasn't at all comforted by that idea, by the possibility of multiple afterlives and a soul hungering through them for eternity. What if we weren't going to lose each other just once—here on earth—but an infinite number of times as we moved through the various levels of consciousness, across the planes of existence? It was an exhausting thought.

She brought her purse into her lap and removed a stack of inmate one-acts. The page on top she'd already marked heavily with red pen. In the top corner, I saw a small check mark. *Killer,* she'd written beneath it. A joke? She looked out the window, into the haze, and then over at me with a pleasant half-smile, which faded away into a serious expression I couldn't quite discern. I thought then of what I'd seen, my glimpse of the future, the beach, the other woman, and I fought the urge to confess every horrible detail to her.

She clicked her red pen, flipped through the papers, and set to work, making little notes in the margins, scrunching her eyes, biting her lower lip, raking her teeth across it absentmindedly. I reclined in my chair and, still watching her, nodded off. The plane was descending when I was jostled awake again, and Annie was putting away her things. The landing gear clunked open beneath us. Annie, knowing me for a nervous flyer, patted the top of my hand and laughed to herself.

"What?"

"It's nothing."

"Tell me."

"You and me," she said.

"What about us?"

"Mr. and Mrs. Lazarus. Back from the dead."

Clara Hopstead Lennox

The dog is on fire! Clara rips the cloth off the dining room table and chases him into the kitchen, but the dog slams into the china cabinet and collapses, all his fur burned away. The smell makes her want to retch. The dog's name is Houdini. He was the runt of the litter, a little cocker spaniel, white and orange. Her sister named him Houdini because he could escape from any chain, any leash, any rope, any situation. She calls up the stairs for Robert, poor Robert, who's been in bed for three days.

She goes to sit in a chair by the window, the sunlight streaming through the glass, so hot across her lap, and she's feeling so tired, but here comes Robert, stomping down the stairs. He jams his arms into his coat. She asks him where he's going, and he says he's off to pay the electric and waves the bill in her face. But she's already paid the electric! It's the gas he needs to pay, not the electric. She's got the notice in an envelope, somewhere. She searches for it in the hutch. He needs to take the notice with him, but he's out the door before she can find it.

• • •

Her father is sitting at her kitchen table with a cup of coffee, his hat in his lap, a baleful look on his face. He's hoping for another loan, and yet he's come round while Robert's at work.

"Do you think Robert'd mind?" he asks.

"I don't know," she says. "I'll see what I can do. We're not exactly in the best shape either, Daddy. We're all doing our best."

"Yes, but we owe the Hausers three months. They've been patient with us but that goodwill won't last long. They've got loans of their own. Plus there's May and her school."

The park. A cool spring day. Little green buds have appeared in all the trees. Birds flit from branch to branch. The streetcar cranks along at the edge of the park, ringing its bell. Clara runs her fingers through her little sister's stringy brown hair as May reads a book.

"What's this one about?" Clara asks.

Irritated to have been roused from her story, May hardly looks up at all. She says it's about a boy who gets into a hot-air balloon and somehow lands in the future. In the future everyone shares everything. The world is ruled by a council of wise elders. There is no war. Machines grow and prepare all the food. Machines transport you from A to B. Machines make you prettier, handsomer.

"Don't you ever wish you'd been born in the future?" May asks her, after a moment.

"Well, you have, sort of," Clara says. "Except it's somebody else's. Not yours."

The future: a fire, a dog, the staircase.

She does her best to avoid the future.

And yet here she is again. Only today there's no fire, thank God. It's the year before the fire. She's on her way down to the sitting room, to join Robert before dinner, when she hears a voice. She lingers for a moment, her hand on the bannister, but can't make out any of the words. Where is it coming from? Not from outside. Not from downstairs.

Robert doesn't believe her.

"You've got a powerful imagination," he says. "You always have."

Robert comes through the front door, shaking his head back and forth.

"I need another trip to Atlanta," he says. "I need to see my cousin."

But she doesn't want to hear any more about Atlanta. Enough about Atlanta! He's been down there twice already this year, and it's not even September. The last time he was gone for a full month, and she was alone in the house with no one but Houdini, the dog, the escape artist, who cannot be contained.

• • •

The dog comes running down the stairs. On fire! How on earth did the dog catch fire? That poor, miserable creature! She runs halfway up the stairs, to the landing, and yells for Robert to please come help, but there's no answer from him. He's useless, in bed again for three whole days. She grabs the dining cloth off the table and goes after the dog to put out the flames. Houdini is already dead, or nearly dead, not moving at all, and all she can do is scream for Robert.

She can't escape him; wherever she goes, he finds her, chases her back to that terrible day, the worst of her life. She throws the dining tablecloth over Houdini but it's too late. He slams into the oven and collapses, dead at her feet, that poor dog, so black and red, still on fire. She goes up the stairs for Robert, shouting, where the smoke is so strong she can't even think straight. Robert's done this. She's sure of it. He's responsible for it. He's set the house on fire. He's killed Houdini. He's done this terrible thing.

Robert—so young, thick-haired—here he comes hustling across the road, dodging traffic. He's out of breath when he reaches her. Never has a smile seemed so out of place on a man's face. He's wearing a new shirt. His pants have been pressed. His shoes are flecked with mud.

"I've been looking all over for you," he says. "Your parents said you were out but didn't know where."

"You've been to see my parents?"

He blushes. "Well, Clara, the thing is . . ."

She has nowhere to go. Already he's pulling out the ring.

Wendell unbuttons the back of her dress and slides his hot hand across her skin. They're in the furniture store, after hours, all the lights off. She scoots away from him. She can't think straight. The store is very hot and stuffy, and he kisses her too hard, his stubble chafing her lips, and his cologne, it's so strong. He smells as if he bathed in a tub of hot bubbling cologne. It's giving her a terrible headache. In fact, she feels ill. She needs some space but isn't sure how to say so without offending him. He's wearing this scent for her, surely. Probably he paid money to smell like that.

"I want you so much," he says.

"I know that," she says, sounding more coy than she intended.

Robert's got the umbrella over her head but it's not raining yet. He's walking her home after a show at the Grand. He keeps looking up at the sky, checking the clouds. It really did seem like it was going to rain only a moment ago, but now the moon is visible again, the clouds scattering.

He can't seem to decide whether to quit with the umbrella.

There are certain things about Robert that are easy to miss if you're not watching out for them.

He can be very gallant, can't he? The way he persists with the umbrella, for instance.

Also he's very steady. Sensible.

Dependable!

He's not always chasing the next best thing.

He doesn't check his hair in the mirror five times an hour.

Films—he doesn't care for them, generally. And yet he took her to one anyway because he knows it's what she enjoys.

At length, the rain begins, and he seems relieved by it.

"Rain," he says to her, as if she hadn't noticed.

Overhead, little drops pat against the umbrella.

Wendell's very first film is playing at the Grand. He's been gone from Shula for over five years. Robert doesn't want to see it, and so Clara goes alone, telling him she's off to visit her parents for a few hours.

Sitting alone in the darkness of the theater, she remembers being here with Wendell, his mouth wet at her neck. She can't believe he's actually done it; he's actually written a movie. It's about an up-and-coming businessman who, shortly after getting engaged to a wealthy heiress, falls in love with a club dancer. Clara can find nothing of Wendell in this story. The plot feels contrived. The characters are humorous, sort of, but also self-serving and vapid.

Here comes Houdini again—on fire! It's Robert's fault. He hasn't been out of bed in three days.

Robert comes down the stairs, looking for his coat, and he waves the electric bill in her face. Someone has to pay the goddamn electric, he screams. But it's not the electric he needs to pay.

"I hate to bother you with this," her father says. "You know I wouldn't ask unless it was absolutely necessary."

"I'll see what I can do. I make no promises."

He asks for more coffee. She tells him there is no more coffee. He's had it all. She wants him gone because Robert will be home soon.

She's sitting in her chair, a band of hot, bright sunlight across her lap, and she's feeling so tired. Robert goes to the fireplace and tosses due notices behind the grate. He says he desperately needs to get away to Atlanta, just for a few days this time, not for a month, and surely she can manage without him for that long?

She can manage, obviously, but she doesn't

want him to leave again. She can't stand the thought of being in this house alone another night. She'll miss his shape in the bed. His weight. His breath. She'll miss the way he mutters in his sleep.

The voice on the stairs follows her to the bottom. It travels as if carried on a dead breeze. She fears she's going crazy. A ghost. It's the only explanation.

"The house is too new to have ghosts," Robert says. "It was only four years old when we bought it. Only one other person lived here, and he didn't die—he moved."

She can't believe Robert's actually bought them a house. An entire house, just for the two of them. Touring the rooms for the first time, she can already imagine it: the curtains, the color schemes, the placement of the furniture.

"Ta-da," Robert says, unveiling a green Dutch sofa in the sitting room.

The sofa is identical to the one at her parents' house. In truth she's always hated that sofa for its particular shade of green, but of course she doesn't say so now. She understands why he's given it to her, even if he's too shy and reserved to ever say so explicitly. It was on that pea-green sofa in her parents' living room that they first made love.

She tells him he's made her incredibly happy.

He wants to show her something else, upstairs—

The dog is on fire! She runs halfway up the stairs and shouts for Robert to come quick and then goes chasing after the dog, screaming for help, but no one comes. No one is there to help the poor dog. All her life she's felt so alone, so separate from everything.

Robert undresses by the bed and slides in alongside her. His legs are so much longer than hers. His feet nearly hang off the end of the bed. They've been together in the darkness for almost ten minutes when he mutters something.

"What did you say?" she asks, pulled away from the edge of sleep, rolling toward him.

"Nothing," he says. "I love you, that's all."

She's feeding Houdini bits of her morning toast under the table.

"We can't afford him," Robert says, his voice rising.

"He won't cost you anything." She brings Houdini into her lap. "He'll eat the scraps."

"Soon enough it might be scraps for us too."

"Don't talk like that. You know I hate it when you talk like that."

He chews his food mournfully for a moment,

then looks up again. "I'm sorry. I shouldn't have said that."

His eyes reveal all: He really is sorry. He hates himself right now. She wishes he wouldn't hate himself so much.

She's on her way to the grocery store for her mother when she spots Wendell across the street with another girl. Sarah Whitney is her name. Clara knows her from school. Wendell has his arm around Sarah's waist. Clara follows at a distance for a few blocks, thinking she might confront him, but when the couple goes into the movie theater, she keeps walking and circles back to the grocery store.

Later that afternoon, when she returns home with the groceries, she realizes she's forgotten the apples. Her mother is upset. Apples were the first item on the list. How on earth could Clara have forgotten to buy the apples?

But Wendell wants to marry her. He says that's what he intends to do. For now he thinks they should keep it a secret, but he wants to be with her forever.

"You don't know what you want," she says.

"I know exactly what I want. I want you, Clara."

They're in the theater, in a back row. Probably this is where he sat with Sarah Whitney, too.

Clara can't bring herself to utter the girl's name aloud. To do so would make it real, whatever is going on between Sarah and Wendell.

After the movie they go for a walk down the street. Wendell keeps his arm around her. He reeks of cologne. Always with that terrible cologne. Her head is pounding. They're almost to her house when she swivels loose from his grip and is sick in the street. When he tries to come near, she shoos him away.

Robert isn't an ugly man. Far from it.

Brooding, yes—but not ugly. Lean and long. Bony.

Distinct—but not ugly.

So why did May say he was ugly?

But Robert dotes on Clara. He really loves her. He's not going to change his mind. Of that she's certain.

He wants to show her something upstairs. He's already bought them a bed for the new house. They're halfway up when—

The dog comes running down the stairs, on fire, and so she grabs the tablecloth, toppling the candles, and chases after him. She doesn't know what else to do. She's too late anyway. The dog is dead. She goes up the stairs for Robert. He's responsible for this. Oh, Robert, why?

• • •

Those stairs. The light is so peculiar there, isn't it? Not to mention the voice. Someone calling out to her. What does Robert have to say about that?

He goes up a few steps and stomps his feet loudly.

"Anyone here?" he shouts. "Hello? Hello?" He pauses, dramatically, with his hand cupped around his ear. After a few moments, he shrugs and stomps the step hard. "If anyone's here we kindly ask you to exit our lovely home. We bought it fair and square. This is the home in which my wife and I intend to raise our children and grow old together. We're not going anywhere. We're here to stay."

Pleased with himself, he descends and takes Clara's hand. Does she feel better now?

He comes down the stairs, looking for his coat, and he waves the electric bill in her face. Someone has to pay the goddamn electric, he screams. He's not himself right now, she tells herself. This isn't Robert.

Here comes Houdini, on fire!

She's sitting in her chair, a band of hot, bright sunlight across her lap, and she's feeling so tired. Robert goes to the fireplace and tosses due notices behind the grate. He says he desperately needs to get away to Atlanta, just for a few days this time, not for a month, and surely she can manage without him for that long? He goes up the stairs to continue packing.

Houdini, the dog, comes running down the stairs, and he's on fire, and no one can save him. She goes halfway up and shouts for Robert to get down here fast. She goes chasing after Houdini with the tablecloth, a gift from her mother two Christmases ago.

Robert strides into the house saying he forgot his coat. He kisses her on the cheek and says he loves her, despite it all. Despite all of what? she wants to know.

Robert comes down the stairs, angry, and when she tries to stop him from going, he glares at her, his face so gaunt, and he tells her she's nothing, that she's as empty as a glass. He says she is incapable of understanding him. He's going back upstairs again, to bed. In bed for three days! It's not natural. She goes to her chair, crying, because she's not empty as a glass. She's only exhausted, and she hates him for saying such horrible things. He wasn't always like this.

Just as she's about to drift off into sleep, he mutters something.

“What was that?” she asks, rolling toward him, throwing her arm over him.

“Nothing,” he says. “I’m sorry. I love you, that’s all.”

The dog is on fire! Her Houdini! That cocker spaniel could escape any room, any cage, any leash, but he’s on fire, he’s burning to death, the poor thing, and there is no one who can save him—no one but her.

V

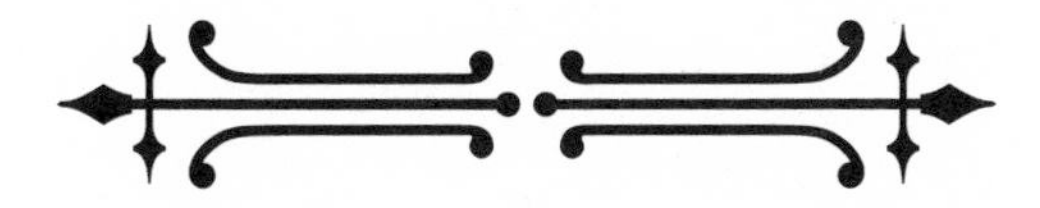

Subject 42

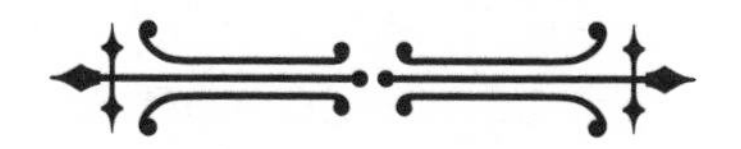

Exit parents and in-laws.
Exit friends.
Childhood heroes.
Hollywood icons.
Lovers and spouses.
Strangers, familiars.

Wes was among the first in our immediate orbit. He was on a long-distance bike ride when he stopped pedaling abruptly, dropped his bike, and hunched down on the shoulder of the road to massage his chest. He thought it was heartburn but an hour later he was on a stretcher in the back of an ambulance.

Annie and I drove over to the hospital that evening to see him. This was only three years after our trip to Little Rock, in the early fall. The weather had already turned cool, the leaves slipping back and forth in the wind, ready to snap loose, a pale half-moon in the sky above the car as we drove. We had the heat going, and Annie pressed her hand to the glass to feel the chill.

"He'll be fine," she said. "You aren't worried, are you?"

"Not terribly," I confessed.

Harriet, his ex, met us in the hallway outside the room when we reached the hospital. She and Wes had never completely reconciled though they were on decidedly better terms. He and Sudeepa had only lasted a few months together, and Harriet was single again, too, working as a filing clerk at a law office in town. She offered us a donut from a nearly empty box. Greasy rings of stalagmite icing were all that was left of the eaten ones. Annie and I politely declined.

"I know what you're thinking," she said. "He's just had a heart attack, and we're handing out donuts. But trust me, he doesn't even know they're out here. I'm not so cruel as that. Someone brought these over earlier. I didn't buy them. I never buy donuts."

It seemed important to her for us to know she hadn't bought the donuts. Harriet was a total hummingbird, never at rest, a very grabby person. Asking you a question she'd latch onto your wrist, squeezing it. She'd kiss both your cheeks when she greeted you. Annie thought her flirty, but to me these gestures seemed more compulsive than overtly sexual. She'd always struck me as somewhat manic.

"How's he doing?" Annie asked.

"Better. Much better. Thank you. He's going

to be fine, just fine. Surgery tomorrow. He's clogged, is what it is."

"Jim had heart surgery a couple of years ago," Annie said. "He's got a HeartNet actually."

It wasn't something we typically told people, but I understood she was simply trying to help Harriet feel less worried.

"Is that right?" she asked. "I had no idea. Wes didn't mention it. Are you doing okay now?"

"No complaints," I said.

She tossed the donuts in the trash.

Eventually I was able to slip into the room and see Wes. He was awake, watching a show about giant fish that lurked at the bottom of rivers. Noticing me, he reached for a remote. The bed motor screeched as it delivered him up to an almost sitting position.

"Hey, buddy," I said. "You look good."

"I'm still here," he said, nodding. "My dad died from a heart attack when he was a few years older than me. I ever tell you that? So did his dad."

"You'll be fine. Medicine's come a long way. This is manageable. Look at me! It's been four years since mine, and I'm still here. The bright side is, you made it, you survived."

"In some ways this is a good thing," he said. "A warning. To get my affairs in order. I was just on the phone with a cryo-brain company, making all the arrangements. They're sending me the paperwork to sign day after tomorrow, so if this ever happens again, I'll be taken care of. My brain will immediately be removed and placed in a deepfreeze. I should have already done it. I've been meaning to for years, but I guess I never really thought this day would come."

I patted him on the feet and told him to get some rest. That was the last time I saw him. He died in surgery the next morning, presumably before he had a chance to make the arrangements for the preservation of his brain.

A complication during surgery, was the doctor's line to Harriet after the surgery, which, it occurs to me now, is true of just about any death—and any life, too. A grand complication.

After that it was my uncle, in Connecticut, in a boating accident.

Lung cancer took Annie's mother about a decade ago.

Her father died two years later when he fell off a ladder in the driveway and concussed his head.

We lost a good friend to a virus she supposedly contracted while traveling through the Amazon.

One of Fisher's ex-girlfriends was killed by a stray bullet one night outside a bar.

Wilson Bizby's car went off a mountain road early one morning, rolled almost a hundred feet, and exploded. The town talked of nothing else for weeks.

Diana, the Fortune Teller, had a seizure and suffocated against a couch cushion.

For Susan, it was a long fight with stomach cancer.

Darryl, as far as I know, is still alive, wherever he is.

My mother's alive, too. She's eighty-one now—and a little dotty. I was over at the house a few days ago. When I got there she was sitting outside in the sunshine talking to Delphine, her live-in Grammer, a larger woman with one of the kindest faces I've ever seen, soft and round. A truly angelic being. When I came through the back gate, Delphine, dressed in a white linen frock, was sitting in the chair opposite my mother, and they were discussing a television show they'd been watching together over the last few weeks. Seeing me, Delphine looked up and informed me that the bird feeders needed seed. My mother has always enjoyed watching the birds from her breakfast table, the wrens and blue jays and cardinals, and so I make it a habit to keep the feeders full.

There I was, up on the rickety stepladder, pouring seeds from a giant bag when my mother said, "God, Bill, you're spilling half the seeds!" I didn't correct her; and neither did Delphine. What would be the point of that? I smiled and nodded: Yes, I was spilling seeds, sorry. This wasn't the first time she'd mistaken me for my father, and I saw no reason to embarrass her for such an innocent error. Better to let her go on thinking he's still around, is my opinion. A pleasant delusion never hurt anyone.

I wish I could report that in her senility my mother has become an easier person to tolerate, softer, more affable, less judgmental—I'm told this can happen as people age—but in truth she is just as unbearable as ever, perhaps even worse. Thank God for Delphine's infinite reserve of patience and kindness. I do wonder if what I'm dealing with now is the true essence of my mother. Aging as a distillation process. The coarse salt bed left behind by the receding ocean.

"There, now you'll have your blue jays," I said to her.

If she has any fears of death, she hasn't revealed them to me. I've never actually told her about the Reunion Machine—about seeing my father again—because I know she wouldn't approve, but I have tried to subtly impart some of what I learned by using it. The soul abides, I tell her. Some aspect of you does. You're like a thought. Or an idea. An echo. An echo in search of other echoes. You do not end here, on this planet, but then again, neither does the questioning. Neither does the doubt. The search for meaning, as unbearable as it sounds, might not end with our death.

I tell her this, I suppose, because I don't want her to expect too much. I don't want her disappointed or confused when she disentangles from her body and finds herself in a place not totally unlike this one.

Two manila envelopes—one addressed to me, one to Annie—arrived in the mail a few months after our return from Little Rock. Annie offered her transcript to me, but I turned down the chance to read it. It was private, I said. It belonged to her. I didn't need to read it.

"Then I won't read yours either," she said.

I was, admittedly, relieved.

I put them both in our safe-deposit box at the bank, and that was that.

For a while, anyway.

A year later Annie was pregnant. She'd been using a diaphragm, and so it was a total surprise. It was only after the birth of our son, William, that I began to doubt my decision to keep my vision from Annie. I'd done my best never to think about that moment on the beach, about a future in which Annie and I were no longer together, in which she was no longer here. But along came William, and with him, a seeming confirmation of what I'd seen and felt in the machine: Annie was going to die; I was going to outlive her. I'd be a White Hair one day, and Annie would not. For a time, even seeing an elderly couple out to dinner or on a walk was enough to drop me into a minor depression. Annie and I were never going to have that, were never going to *be* that. I tried to take solace in the fact that she ate well, she worked out, she exercised. She was fit, healthy.

But my son's every precious breath was a reminder of Annie's fate and of the fact that I'd kept it a secret from her. The guilt was overwhelming, and one afternoon I brought home the transcript and told her she needed to read mine. It was time. I'd kept something from her, I said. Something terrible. She told me not to be dramatic. Still, I stayed downstairs until she was finished reading. Eventually she came and found me, pale, tired, looking like she'd just stumbled out of a bad dream.

"Well, I understand why you didn't tell me," she said.

"I hope you don't hate me."

I was sitting in a chair, and Annie sat down beside me on its fat tan arm.

"You can't control what you saw." She tried to smile but settled instead into a look of quiet frustration. "Any chance you remember the culprit? Is it cancer? Because if it's cancer—"

I shook my head. "I'm sorry, I don't know."

She nodded. "Anyway, what does it matter if the afterlife is real, right?"

"True. That's true."

"I'm not going to obsess over it, if that's what you're wondering."

"We can talk about it as much or as little as you want. We don't have to avoid the topic."

"But you avoided it until now."

"I did—and I apologize."

I looked down into my lap.

"People learn they're going to die every day," she said. "I'm no different. Besides, this isn't next year. This isn't even two years from now."

"More like twenty years, I would think. I'd hardly call twenty years a death sentence."

She grimaced. Probably she hadn't done the math, hadn't put a number to it.

"It's funny though," she said. "When you think about it. You and your heart. I guess I've always assumed it would be you who died first. Not that I wanted it that way, of course, but I'd been preparing myself, I think, for that eventuality."

"I don't blame you. You've been through this before, after all."

"I guess your HeartNet *is* doing its job."

I'd long since had my device repaired and reconnected. What a leap of faith that would have been—to never have had it fixed again.

"But who's this woman?" Annie asked. "Have you ever met her?"

"Never. Maybe she doesn't even exist."

"Somehow I doubt that," she said, looking displeased. "She's out there. Somewhere. Biding her time."

She managed to smile then.

“I never think about her,” I said, which was mostly true. “I’m not, like, keeping an eye out for her, if that worries you.”

“I’d hope not,” she said. “It’s not fun to think about, you being with someone else, but I’m not upset. It’s not wrong to move on. How can I fault you for that, right? Honestly, I’d want you to. I’d want you to be happy.”

I wrapped my hand around her ankle. “Annie, I’m not going to be with someone else.”

“Don’t do that,” she said, suddenly irritable. “Don’t pretend you don’t believe in it. You wouldn’t have given me the transcript unless you did.”

“It’s not that I think it will necessarily come true. I just didn’t want to hide it from you.”

She stared at me. “Jim. Please.”

“I’m sorry,” I said. “I’m really sorry.”

We were both quiet for a few moments. She had William’s baby monitor in her hands. On the screen I could see him thrashing silently in his crib. He’d just woken up from his nap and soon he’d be wailing. Whether she would have handled the pregnancy differently, knowing what she now knew, I didn’t ask. I didn’t want to know.

“The part about you and your father on the stairs,” she said. “It’s incredible. Do you really think it’s possible you were the one who grabbed his arm, that you somehow went back in time and touched him?”

I'd devoted considerable thought to this over the last two years, and though I suspected that it was true, that I'd been responsible for what my father had seen on the stairs, I couldn't prove it. It was just a feeling. When I told her this, Annie's eyes got big.

"Well, feelings matter," she said confidently.

She held up the monitor to look at William and weighed her left breast in the palm of her hand, preparing to go upstairs and nurse him.

"If you do ever see her," she said, "and I'm still on the scene, you'll let me know, right?"

It took me a few seconds to realize she was talking about the woman, my future wife.

"If that's what you want," I said.

"You promise me?"

I nodded.

"Good." She stood up to go; William was crying now. "Because there are probably some things I should tell her. Some things I should warn her about."

I smiled. The sooner this could all become a joke, the better.

And for a long time, it was exactly that. It was something we laughed about.

If you think Wifey Number Two will put up with this, Annie would say after an argument, *you're kidding yourself.*

Out of necessity we had to move forward with

our lives. There were diapers to change, fruits to puree, a baby to rock and get back to sleep in the middle of the night. There were visits to the heart specialist. There was a sump pump in need of constant repair. There were concerts, dinner parties, graduations. Band practices, bass lessons, new theater productions, fund-raisers, an uneasy dinner with a newly paroled convict who leaned across the table and told me, conspiratorially, that I was a lucky man. There were long winter days, black ice on the roads, cold feet under the sheets.

There were beautiful spring mornings, the azalea bushes and pear trees blossoming pink and white up and down the street, the Blue Ridge Mountains hazy and beautiful out beyond the tree line, birds pepping the branches just outside the kitchen window, and the pollen all over everything: the grill lid, the glass table on the deck, the deck itself, the trash cans, the windshields, the mailbox, even our hair and clothes if we lingered too long in the driveway before diving into our cars for work.

Too soon, Fisher left for college. She came home, of course, for long weekends and holidays, but William was only three when she moved out of the house, meaning we essentially raised him as an only child. He's always looked up to Fisher. In some ways, she's been more like an aunt to him than a sister.

William was a contemplative boy, very private, very secretive, but also smart and practical. Truth be told, the older he gets, the more he reminds me of my father. He's studying to be an engineer now at Chapel Hill and dating a girl from Phoenix.

I still work for the bank, though in a different capacity. You won't find too many human loan officers anymore. Most loan applications these days are either handled online by digital assistants or in person by intelligent Grammers, though we do keep a few human loan officers on hand across the state for the larger borrowers who prefer it that way and for those days when the computers are glitchy because of trouble with the servers or because the satellites are un-pingable up there in their geosynchronous orbits.

Everywhere you go, nowadays, there are holograms, on the street, in your office, at the hospital, at your front door with once-in-a-lifetime offers for skin creams and patio furniture, and nobody is much amazed by them anymore. It's easy to forget what it was like in the old days, when looking down the street, you could be sure that everyone you saw was flesh and blood.

I remember when Fisher called home from college that first semester—she wound up at Georgetown—and informed us that she was taking upright bass lessons from an intelligent hologram that looked like Charles Mingus. I was astounded, but of course that's fairly standard now at most universities, isn't it? They are everywhere. They check our heart rates. They analyze our facial expressions and speech. They can read our moods. They call the police if we've been in an accident.

They belong to us, and I suppose we belong to them, too. They *are* us.

Only, no heaven for holograms, as Annie likes to say.

Not as far as we know, goes my line.

My father, Wes, Anthony, my uncle, Annie's parents—will we meet again? I believe we will, in a way, but as for proof of that, I can only offer my story, nothing more. For people like me, however, for those who doubt anything they haven't experienced personally, I suppose my story won't offer much assurance.

Despite the nondisclosure agreements we signed, Annie and I have told plenty of friends about Sally and her machine over the years, and I've always been surprised by how unsurprised people are to learn about it. Kurt and Kitra were visiting us in Shula one Christmas, and out at dinner one night Annie was telling them about the machine when Kurt nodded his head enthusiastically, meaning he wanted to interrupt. "Oh, I totally read about this," he said. "In *The New Yorker*, I think."

"Yeah, I remember that, too," Kitra said. "The Reunion Machine, it's like a giant glass window, right? And you stand in front of it, and there's this fog, and the person you want to talk to sort of appears there in the mist? That's what you're talking about, right?"

"Well, maybe there's a different one," I said, trying to be polite.

Sometimes, when we'd tell our friends about Sally and the Reunion Machine, they'd ask for her contact information, and typically we would oblige, though with a warning that the nature of the experience was unpredictable and physically arduous. *Was it worth it?* was the standard question we'd get, and to this we would answer, unequivocally, that it had been.

For a couple of years we'd hear from Sally on occasion via email. She'd keep us updated on her progress testing and fine-tuning the machine. She was still collecting data, still analyzing, but always she'd mention vague plans for publication. Eventually, she said, the wider world would have to reckon with the machine, whatever it was, but until that time its existence was a not very well-kept secret.

Then one day a friend, to whom we had

provided Sally's contact information, called to tell us that the number had been disconnected. When I tried it, I got the same result. As the weeks passed I began to wonder and went searching online. Very easily I found it, her obituary. She'd died, only sixty-two years old. There was no specific mention of the Reunion Machine, only that she'd retired to her hometown of Little Rock and "pursued her own scientific interests." Curious to learn what was to become of her machine and her research, I thought to call Martin Strider, the man who'd funded the work. I had no trouble tracking him down. As far as I could tell his mind was sound.

"I'm tearing down the Hobby Shoppe," he told me.

"But what about the machine? Will you move it somewhere?"

"That's getting torn down with it. It's the way it needs to be. The machine was just too dangerous, and that's the God honest truth. No way we ever could have marketed that thing."

"Why—did something happen?"

"It killed her is what happened," he said.

"Killed Sally? How?"

"Well, I never understood how it worked to begin with, so I'm not sure I could tell you how exactly, but it did. Maybe she used it too many times. It got to the point she was in there once or twice a week."

"Were you with her when it happened?"

"I was. The doctor called it cardiac arrest, which probably it was, technically speaking, but before the doctor got there, she was sort of phasing in and out."

"Phasing?"

"She was barely there. She was like a ghost."

I didn't know what to say to that. I didn't really believe it. I thought of Sally's device to measure partial existence. I'd often wondered about it. Had I fully recovered? If I didn't look where I was going as I was walking down the hall, would I pass cleanly through a wall? In a moment of mindlessness, would I slip right through the floor at work and land in the basement parking garage? Holding my hand up to the sunlight, I would inspect the outer fringes of my fingers, where the light burns orange through the skin, and wonder if I was any more transparent than the day before that. Not that transparency was necessarily an indication of nonexistence. I wasn't sure what, really, would indicate such a thing. When I gripped my tennis racket, it stayed in my hand. When I swung it and hit the ball, the ball was propelled forward, outward, through the universe. I was capable of causing an effect, and this seemed significant to me.

I was here—wasn't I?

Surely I was.

"But Martin," I said, "please tell me you saved her design? It needs to be studied."

"Her research is in a lockbox. She willed it to a university in Texas, but no one's come to get it."

"Don't throw it away. That was important work she was doing. Even if it wasn't safe, and even if it wasn't going to make you any money, it was important. You have to understand that."

The phone clicked, and he was gone—and so was the machine.

We were out to breakfast recently at a restaurant where a large group of White Hairs had shoved together half the tables and were talking loudly. The mood was jubilant, excited. They were there to celebrate the fortieth wedding anniversary of one of the couples with an old country breakfast. Scrambled eggs and bacon and canned peaches and grits and copious amounts of coffee were spread across the maze of tabletops. The honored husband and wife—a man in a pink polo shirt and blazer and a woman with gray close-cropped hair in a white linen tunic dress—sat at the head of the table, smiling pleasantly at all their friends.

When the woman stood up to deliver a toast in honor of her husband and her speech slipped to the floor, he was the first one out of his chair, dropping to his hands and knees to retrieve it for her. He delivered it up into her reach and then held up his hands for the group to see. Covered in syrup, he said, smiling. His wife dunked her napkin in her ice water and began to wipe his palms clean.

Annie and I, seated as we were in a nearby booth, watched all of this. Neither one of us commented on this display of affection, though I'm certain we were both thinking the same thing, that we were never going to be that couple. No fortieth for us. I tried to catch Annie's eye, but she quickly returned her focus to the menu. She asked me what I was having. I slid my hand across the table, patted hers, and told her I was leaning toward the French toast with a side of cheese grits. She nodded. That sounded lovely to her.

It's not so much the afterlife that concerns me these days, but the next few years. We're in our late fifties now, pushing sixty, and I can feel our time here together running out. I can't be sure when it will happen, or how, but one day I will wake up in a world without Annie.

It's not something we often talk about anymore.

I haven't even told her about something that happened a couple of weeks ago, when, during my lunch hour, I was waiting for an oil change down the street from the bank and a tall woman with short blond hair came into the waiting room and sat down in a chair across from me with a magazine. I recognized her immediately. One of the mechanics entered the room to pour himself some coffee and scratch his ass in plain view, and the woman glanced over at me, widened her eyes, and smiled furtively. I didn't dare return her smile. Even to make eye contact with this woman seemed to me like a deep transgression.

I tried not to stare. I didn't want to know her name or where she was from. I didn't want to know anything about her, but then the mechanic, the ass-scratcher, turned to her and said, "We almost got your Mazda ready, Mrs. Trout, just a few more minutes." Trout—did I know any Trouts in town? I tried to erase the name from my memory. Pretending to take a phone call, I went outside to stand alone in the parking lot. To engage with this woman at all, to learn anything more about her, I feared, might have dire consequences. Maybe even just learning her last name had already set off a series of events that I couldn't control.

I'd promised to tell Annie if I ever saw this woman, but I will admit now that it is a promise I have not kept. I haven't mentioned this woman to her. I can't bear to bring it up.

I do take some solace in the knowledge that Annie and I will probably meet again one day, of course I do, but at the same time, I often worry that our ability to interact and love each other on the other side will be limited in crucial ways. There is a certain gulf between souls, I think, that can only be bridged with cells, with blood—with matter. I think of Annie, in the doorway of our hotel room in Little Rock, wrapping me up in her arms, receiving me.

Two hands, clapped.

Moments like these, I suspect, are why we give up being echoes, give up being ideas, why we dare to assume a physical form and brave a world such as ours, so full of tragedy and fear and pain, murders and rapes, war, ceaseless brutality and conflict. We wouldn't subject ourselves to this unless it was worth it, on some level.

We are here for the heat. For the friction. For the difficult mess. Easy for me to say, I suppose, since I've lived a life of relative comfort. I understand and appreciate this fact, I really do.

Yesterday, a Saturday, I went on a long walk through Shula. I passed the dog park, where people sat quietly on picnic tables in sweatpants and yoga tights, staring at their phones while their dogs became better acquainted. Near the corner an older gentleman with a large gray beard played songs on his guitar. Bob Dylan, I realized as I approached. A Grammer. He was here, on this street corner, and undoubtedly on a dozen others at that very moment, all over town, to promote an upcoming concert tour.

I walked by my bank, past the parking garage where once upon a time I'd almost died, along the streets I've known all my life. I'm not sure I understood where I was going until I was nearly downtown. By this point, I'd walked almost three miles. Two kids on skateboards zoomed by me and nearly knocked me sideways—both real, I think. Three joggers singing the theme song for some new television show ran into me, vaporous, and continued on their way. A frog-like woman with a sandwich board swiped her hand through my chest as she tried to lure me into a restaurant. It's often difficult to suss out the Grammers from the Actuals. People don't like to leave their homes anymore, and some cities, I'm told, have taken to beaming in Grammers to maintain the illusion of activity and commerce. Go for a walk downtown and probably a third of the people you see on the streets really aren't there.

Sweaty and exhausted, I texted Annie and asked her to please come pick me up.

I was at the edge of Shula's historic district now, among the older houses. Every year, it seemed, the city was reinventing itself for a new future. On the next block a major construction project was under way, and half the homes on one side of the street had been torn down to make room for a development. Annie and I had been watching this project unfold for some time with interest.

The Lennox home had been razed, along with four adjacent houses, to make way—this, according to a billboard—for a multi-use building of shops and high-end apartments. On the other side of the perimeter fence that kept pedestrians from tumbling down into the site was a deep orange hole that the bulldozers had ripped open in the earth.

It is the nature of my job to sometimes visit construction sites such as this one, and so I know well how easy it is to demolish a house, and I'm aware how silly it is to mourn wood, concrete, and plaster. And yet I'd been sad to learn that the city had approved this project, had approved the plan to obliterate this piece of Shula's history. No one had consulted me, of course. I had no voice in such matters. The future no longer belonged to me or Annie.

It was late afternoon now, almost evening, and the construction crew had called it quits for the day. I walked the fence line until I came to a small gap, where I managed to squeeze through, snagging my shirt, ripping a small hole. I was wearing khakis and a dress shirt, so I did my best to look official, like I was supposed to be here. I walked down a long dirt ramp, and soon I was at the squishy bottom, surrounded by long lengths of bundled rebar and unburied drainage tubes, the mud squelching up over the ramparts of my shoes.

I tried to approximate where the staircase had been, and once I was on the spot, stood there and gazed up to the street where pedestrians—White Hairs, Grammers, children—were strolling by on the sidewalk. Nobody was paying me any attention. I was probably twelve feet below them, looking up at a sheer wall of caked red earth. Behind me lurked the heavy machinery, Bobcats and cranes, idle at the bottom of the pit that they had helped to create. A few feet away, I saw that a small porcelain shard had been loosed from the earth. A blue-and-white triangle—from a plate perhaps. Clara's wedding china? It seemed possible. Soon it would be shoveled under with everything else, covered with foundation concrete. Large rocks protruded from the mud in places. Scraped stones. Bedrock.

I closed my eyes. I could feel my heartbeat confusing itself, whirling in my chest. My breath was uneven. It had been years since my last anxiety attack, and I'd forgotten the overwhelming sense of helplessness that shrilled up through you, that wimbling dread that, whatever this was, you'd have to face it alone, that you were on your own.

Then, warm and firm, her hand at my neck: I could feel the contact of each finger, the bulb of her thumb, a nail's hard edge. Next, the heat of her voice in my ear: What was I doing down here? Wasn't I ready to go home? Already my heart was sliding back into an even beat. I was going to be all right. I opened my eyes, and, thank God, there she was.

Acknowledgments

Thank you to my early readers, Leslie Cayce, Reed Johnson, John Lane; to my editor, Laura Perciasepe, for every single note and question and conversation; to Katie Freeman, Jynne Martin, Geoffrey Kloske, and all the other amazing folks at Riverhead; to my agent, Jin Auh, for keeping the faith through all 72,000 iterations of this book; to her assistant, Jessica Friedman, and everyone else at the Wylie Agency; to my friends, my parents, my family; to Catherine, Eleanor, and Juniper.

Center Point Large Print
600 Brooks Road / PO Box 1
Thorndike, ME 04986-0001 USA

(207) 568-3717

US & Canada:
1 800 929-9108
www.centerpointlargeprint.com

Center Point
6/12/18
37.95